X IS FOR XMAS

10 TALES OF HOLIDAY CRIMES BY . . .

John Gregory Betancourt

William G. Bogart

Lillian Stewart Carl

Wilkie Collins

Ron Goulart

Sue Ann Jaffarian

Johnston McCulley

Meredith Nicholson

and

Elizabeth Zelvin

X IS FOR XMAS

10 CHRISTMAS MYSTERIES

EDITED BY CARLA COUPE

WILDSIDE PRESS

X IS FOR XMAS

Published by Wildside Press LLC.
www.wildsidebooks.com

CONTENTS

INTRODUCTION

Carla Coupe

Christmas is a time for giving, for receiving...and for mysteries, murder, and mayhem. We've collected ten Christmas stories, old and new, that will spike your eggnog, trim your tree, and hopefully add a dash of spice to your Christmas cheer.

In John Gregory Betancourt's "A Christmas Pit," Peter "Pit Bull" Geller not only saves the life of his old college friend Davy Hunt, he manages to find the perfect Christmas gift for the man who has everything.

A bust of Shakespeare, young love, and Christmas are featured in Wilkie Collins' little-known classic, "Mr. Wray's Cash Box."

An unexpected encounter with a dying Santa lands Sue Ann Jaffarian's amateur sleuth Odelia Grey in hot water, both with the police and a group of killers. Can Odelia save her skin in "Ho Ho Homicide?"

There's a war on and blackouts are the rule, even in Hollywood. Rookie cop Johnny Regan foils the crooks and solves a murder in William G. Bogart's "Murder on Santa Claus Lane."

Pickpocket Thubway Tham has a code of conduct, even if it's not one shared by his nemesis, Detective Craddock. In Johnston McCulley's "Thubway Tham's Chrithtmath," Tham metes out justice and brings Christmas cheer.

Holidays are hell for alcoholics, but being a member of Alcoholics Anonymous helps Bruce stay sober *and* solve a murder in Liz Zelvin's "Death Will Trim Your Tree."

In Johnston McCulley's classic "Death Plays Santa Claus," Detective Mike O'Hara just wants to be with his family on Christmas, but instead, he's called out to investigate Santa Claus' murder.

Lillian Stewart Carl channels Charles Dickens in "A Stake of Holly." Tim Cratchit turns detective in Victorian London at the deathbed behest of his mentor and patron, Ebenezer Scrooge. With the help of the spirits, he solves an old case—and finds new love.

Thief Billy 'The Hopper' Aikens must overcome a host of obstacles to return an unwanted gift in "A Reversible Santa Claus," by Meredith Nicholson. His persistence pays off and restores amity between two bitter enemies, not to mention an honest bit of cash for Billy and his wife.

Oscar Sayles contemplates a Christmas murder in Ron Goulart's "Believing in Santa." He can't make a triumphant comeback without his dummy, Screwy Santa, now in the clutches of his vindictive ex-wife. Can he rescue Screwy Santa, take out his ex, and return to his former glory as children's entertainer?

So sit back, grab a mug of hot chocolate or eggnog, and prepare yourself for events most sinister. These ten great holiday tales are sure to send a chill down your spine!

A CHRISTMAS PIT

John Gregory Betancourt

When my doorbell rang, the sound jolted through me like an electric shock. I accidentally sloshed Jack Daniels across my lap and began cursing all unexpected visitors.

Carefully, so I wouldn't spill another drop, I set the bottle on my night table, grabbed my walking stick, and swung my ruined legs over the side of the bed. Standing usually hurt, but I'd already drunk enough to feel a comfortable numbness instead.

The doorbell rang a second time, an annoying *brzzz* that set my teeth on edge.

"Stop that racket! I'm coming!" I yelled. I shrugged a robe over my underwear, knotting the belt halfheartedly, and limped out into my rather Spartan family room.

By the time I turned the deadbolt and yanked open the front door, I half expected to find the hallway deserted. The brats upstairs enjoyed playing jokes like that—"bait the cripple," I called it.

Tonight, however, I found a soggy young man in an Atlanta Braves baseball cap and a cheap brown coat. Water pooled around him and the duffel bag he'd set down. Rain—that explained why my legs had been aching worse than usual.

"What do you want?" I demanded. "Don't you know what time it is?"

Involuntarily, he covered his mouth and nose and took a half step back. I had to reek like a distillery.

"Uh...six o'clock?" he said. His voice had a slight southern twang.

"Oh." Only six o'clock? My sense of time was shot; I would have sworn it was past midnight. "I thought it was later than that. It gets dark early now."

"Are you...Peter Geller?" he asked hesitantly.

"Yes. You're here to see *me*?"

"Sir...David Hunt sent me."

I had gone to college with Davy. We had been in the same fraternity. Since Davy came from old money, he got in because his family had always belonged to Alpha Kappa. I got in because I was smart: all the jocks and rich kids needed help to keep up their GPAs. Sometimes I had resented it, being used, but it got me into all the parties, and I still graduated at the top of our class.

My life had been a downward spiral after college. I had landed a plum job at an investment bank, but overwork and my always-racing mind led to a nervous breakdown. Six months later, a taxi ran me over and left me permanently crippled. I lost touch with everyone I'd ever known and began trying to drink myself to death, until Davy called me out of the blue to help him out when he was being blackmailed. That had been five months ago. We'd had dinner and drinks a dozen times since then, rekindling our old friendship. In fact, earlier this afternoon I had been wondering what to give Davy for Christmas. He already had everything money could buy.

"Are you some sort of social worker?" I asked warily.

"No, sir! I'm Bob Charles." At my puzzled look, he added, "Cree's brother."

"Got any I.D.?"

"Uh…sure." He dug around his coat's inside pocket. "Driver's license? Passport?"

"Either."

He handed me a military passport. Marine Corps issue, and the name under his picture read "PFC Robert E. Charles."

I nodded, my mental wheels starting to turn. Cree was the actress-slash-model Davy had been talking about marrying. Like Cher and Madonna, she only used one name.

"I guess you'd better come in," I said.

"Thanks." He scooped up his duffel bag and entered my apartment, looking around curiously. I didn't own much these days: a worn yellow sofa, a pair of white-and-yellow wingback chairs, a battered coffee table, and thanks to the miracle of Ikea, two tall wooden bookcases mostly devoted to bric-a-brac. No clocks, no calendar, no TV—nothing to remind me of the outside world. Nothing to stimulate my mind and set it racing again.

"How is Davy?" I asked.

"Good. He and Cree just left for Cancún."

"Oh? I thought he had business in New York tomorrow." At least, that's what he'd told me over the weekend.

Bob shrugged. "Cree's doing a photo shoot for *Sports Illustrated*—filling in at the last minute—so they decided to turn it into a vacation. They're flying out tonight. Probably already in the air."

He pulled off his coat, revealing an off-the-bargain-rack suit. I waved vaguely at the sofa.

"Sit down. Let me clean up. I wasn't expecting visitors. If you want a drink, help yourself—there's beer in the fridge."

* * * *

Twenty minutes later, I'd washed my face, run a razor over a three-day growth of beard, combed my hair, and put on nearly-clean slacks and a sweater. I almost felt human again, and I'd gotten rid of the worst of the whiskey smell.

Unfortunately, I had also begun to sober up, and with returning mental sharpness came all-too-familiar pains in both legs. Alcohol blunted my senses better than drugs; that's why I drank as much and as often as possible. I only stopped when I had to.

Finally I limped back out to the family room. Bob leaped up when he saw me, running one hand quickly across his nearly-shaved head and pulling his suit jacket straight.

"Let me guess," I said, really studying him for the first time. His too-short hair and well-developed muscles screamed military. "You just got out of the service and decided to pay your sister a visit. She suggested Davy might be able to find you a job."

He gaped. "Did you talk to Cree?"

Slowly I settled into one of the wingback chairs, folded my hands across my belly, and stretched out both legs. They hurt less that way.

I said: "Why else would an ex Marine come to Philadelphia, if not to see your sister and her fiancé? You're dressed up—I assume for a job interview—though I'd lose the baseball cap next time. But the *real* question," I said, warming to the subject, "is why Davy Hunt sent you here."

Bob frowned, brow furrowing. "He said he trusted your opinion. If you think I'm good enough, he'll take me on."

"In what capacity?"

"Bodyguard."

I raised my eyebrows slightly. "Davy needs a bodyguard?"

"My sister thinks so."

After their problem with blackmailers, I understood Cree's concern. Davy's net worth ran somewhere upwards of fifty million dollars—more than enough to make him a target for opportunists.

I opened my mouth, but before I could say anything, the doorbell rang again. From outside came faint childish giggles.

"You can start by taking care of those kids," I said to Bob. "Ask them not to bother me again."

"Sir!" Like a panther, he sprang to the door and threw it open. Ten-year-old boys scattered, screaming, as he gave chase. I heard Bob shouting something about "whooping hides" if they bothered me again, then several doors slammed shut.

When he returned, he was grinning. "I love kids," he said. "I don't think they'll bother you again, sir. At least, not for a few days."

"Thanks." Maybe bodyguards had their uses.

"Then you'll give me a try?"

I stared at him blankly. "I don't follow you."

"Sir, I'm supposed to be your bodyguard for the next few days. You can kick the tires. Try me out. Make sure I'm everything I ought to be to keep David safe."

"I don't *need* a bodyguard. I don't *want* a bodyguard. I leave my apartment once or twice a month at most!"

"David knew you'd say that." His brow furrowed. "He told me to tell you—beg your pardon, sir—to shut up and pitch in."

Just like Davy to be blunt with me. Maybe I *did* object too much. Maybe it *did* take a kick in the pants to get me moving. But did I really need a bodyguard?

It wasn't for me, though. It was for Davy. If he valued my opinion this much…well, I needed to get him a Christmas present anyway. This would be it, as I would let him know the next time I saw him!

"Very well." I motioned unhappily with one hand. I'd need rent money soon, anyway. "You can start bodyguarding in the morning. It's time I ran some errands, anyway."

Rent money meant a trip to Atlantic City and the casinos. Sometimes having a trick memory helped, like when I needed to know the number of face cards played from an eight-deck blackjack shoe.

"It'll be over sooner if I start tonight, sir."

"'Over sooner'?" I chuckled. "Bob, you sound like you don't want to baby-sit a seedy drunken cripple!"

"Sir!" He looked alarmed. "I never said that!"

"Then you *do* want to baby-sit a seedy drunken cripple?"

"That's a fool's argument, sir." He shrugged with wry humor. "You know I can't win. I just thought you'd want me out by Christmas day."

"I don't care. Start when you want. End when you want. It's all the same."

"Thank you, sir."

"Do you have a place to sleep?"

"Uh…not yet. I was hoping to bunk here."

It figured. Why did I suddenly feel like Oscar Madison from *The Odd Couple*, with an eager-beaver Felix about to move in?

"There's only one bed," I said, "and I'm usually passed out in it."

"The sofa is fine—after sleeping in a Humvee for six months, pretty much anything will do. Just give me a blanket and I'll be out like a log."

"There's one in the linen closet." I jerked my head toward the back of the apartment. "And an extra pillow on the top shelf."

Using my walking stick, I levered myself unsteadily to my feet. My legs ached again. Slowly I limped toward my bedroom, thoughts of Jack Daniels and sweet oblivion dancing in my head.

* * * *

Sometime later—it could have been hours, it could have been days—a loud humming filled my ears. It took a few minutes, but I finally realized the noise came from outside my skull. It shrilled on and on, incessant and very annoying.

When I couldn't stand it any longer, I rolled over and opened my eyes. Daylight leaked in around the blinds, casting a pallid gray light over my bedroom. Groaning, I got my feet to the floor and sat up.

The world swung and tilted. My head throbbed and my eyes burned. It had been a long while since I'd felt this sick. Usually when pain and nausea and headaches hit, I can lie still and wait for them to pass. This humming grated on my nerves so much, though, that I rose and stumbled toward the door.

When I entered the kitchen, the noise grew louder. But what brought me up short was the brilliant, blinding light.

Every surface gleamed. Steel and chrome and glass shone and glistened. The burnt-out bulbs in the ceiling fixture had been replaced, the dishes in the sink had been washed, and my months-old collection of pizza boxes had disappeared from the counter. Underfoot, the white-with-gold-specks linoleum had a new glossy sheen. Even the trashcan had a fresh white plastic liner.

The humming came from the family room. Bob Charles slowly moved into view, pulling a little canister vacuum around the floor, sucking up dirt and dust bunnies. He wore a clean white shirt and tie, but had on the same brown pants as yesterday.

"Good morning," he called cheerfully, switching off the vacuum. "Ready for breakfast?"

"What do you think you're doing?" I demanded. My voice came out as a croak.

"Tidying up."

"Don't you know the difference between a maid and a bodyguard? I was still in bed!"

"It's ten-thirty in the morning. You've been asleep for more than sixteen hours, Pit. Half the day is gone!"

"Not asleep. Unconscious. Delightfully, *painlessly* unconscious. And how do you know my nickname?"

"Nickname?"

"Pit. Short for Pit-Bull. Got it in college."

"Didn't you mention it yesterday?"

I shrugged. "Maybe."

But I hadn't. I could remember every word we had exchanged from the second I opened my front door to the second I'd gone to bed. Names, faces, facts, figures—I never forgot anything.

Maybe Davy had called me Pit, and Bob picked up on it subconsciously. I could only think of one other person besides Davy who still called me by my old nickname, and it seemed unlikely that Bob had ever met an organized crime figure like "Mr. Smith," as he called himself.

Bob was staring at my legs. I realized I hadn't put on a robe. Gray Jockey shorts didn't do much to hide the hideously scarred flesh running from my ankles to my hips.

Swallowing, Bob looked away. Pity—that was always the worst. It showed in his eyes.

"In case you're wondering," I said bitterly, "I got run over by a taxi." Everyone always wanted to know what had happened, even if they were too embarrassed to ask.

"David didn't say anything about that." Bob forced his gaze back to my face. "He did tell me to take you out for breakfast today, though—on him."

"I don't like going out. But maybe I'll make an exception this morning." Time to pay Davy back for sticking me with Cree's brother. I used to read *Gourmet* magazine; I knew some *very* expensive places to eat in Philadelphia.

* * * *

An hour later we left my apartment. Bob wanted to drive downtown in his battered old VW Rabbit, but I refused. Folding my legs into that tiny box of a car would have been torture.

Instead, we ambled up the sidewalk toward the Frankford El, our breaths pluming in the cold December air. The sun played hide-and-seek through holes in the clouds while an icy wind stirred leaves in the gutter. Far off, I heard an elevated train rumble past.

As we walked, Bob kept alert. Northwood is a small blue-collar section of Philadelphia, and it had definitely seen better years. But it was safe enough by daylight, and in the years I'd lived here, I had never had a problem beyond kids playing "bait the cripple" with my doorbell.

"This neighborhood is a dump," Bob said. "You should find a better place to live."

"I don't like change."

"Those kids over there—" He nodded toward a boarded-up row house across the street where three teenagers in stocking caps watched us with predatory eyes. "They'd be happy to roll you for your cash."

"I think they're about to try it," I said. All three had gotten up and begun to cross the street toward us.

"Keep walking," Bob said. He turned to face the three. "I'll catch up in a minute."

"Do you need help?"

"I can take care of a couple of kids."

"Be careful." My mind started racing, taking in every detail. "The one on the left has a weapon in his pocket."

"How do you know?" Bob demanded.

"He keeps touching it through his pants. I don't think the others are armed."

"Get going."

"But—"

"Move!"

Spoken like a true bodyguard. I wasn't about to argue.

Turning, I limped quickly up the street. Motion caught my eye as I reached the corner. I half turned as a dark-skinned man in a gray silk suit seized my arm and propelled me toward the street.

"Relax, Mr. Geller," he said softly. "Mr. Smith wants to see you."

A white Lincoln Town Car roared up. Before it came to a stop, the back door popped open. My escort put his hand on the back of my head, pressing gently but firmly, and half guided, half pushed me into the lavender-scented back seat. Then he slid in next to me and slammed the door. We accelerated.

My abduction had taken less than five seconds. That had to be a record.

Twisting around, I gazed over my shoulder at the rapidly-receding figure of my bodyguard. Those three kids skirted my bodyguard and continued up the block. When Bob turned to check on me, a priceless look of shock appeared on his face. I had vanished. He began to run toward the Frankford El.

Turning back, I made myself comfortable, wincing a little as I uncrimped my legs.

"Hello, Pit," said a smooth voice beside me.

"Mr. Smith." I nodded to him. With his salt-and-pepper hair swept back and his neatly-manicured hands, he cut the perfect picture of a crime lord. As always, he wore an expensive Italian suit, blue this time with a white carnation at the lapel. "If you wanted to talk to me," I said, "a simple invitation would have sufficed."

"Not with your new, ah, *friend* looking on." Smith smiled a predator's smile. Since our paths first crossed, he had developed quite an interest in me—due no doubt to my trick memory, which had dredged up his real name from a chance meeting many years before. Since then, I knew he had been researching my life—even going so far as bugging my phone.

"What brings you to my neighborhood?" I asked.

"I would like you to meet my associate, Mr. Jones."

"Jones?" I raised my eyebrows and turned to the dark-skinned man next to me. "You've got to be kidding." Of African descent, with a diamond stud earring in his left ear, Mr. Jones seemed as fashionably well-groomed as Mr. Smith.

"Jones *is* my birth name," said Mr. Jones gravely. "Though I've been thinking of changing it to Tortelli to fit in better with the rest of the boys."

Mr. Smith gave a snort, then added, "Mr. Jones would not kid you about his name, Mr. Geller."

"Of course not." I sighed. Why did things like this always happen to me?

Then Smith lifted his left hand to my eye level. He held a miniature tape recorder. With his thumb, he pressed PLAY. Eleven beeps sounded—a phone being dialed. A moment later, I heard a woman answer:

"Hello?"

"Janice?" asked the voice of my bodyguard.

"Yeah."

"This is Bob. He went for it."

She laughed. "How fast can you get him to sign off on you?"

"A few days. God, he's depressing."

"Put a bullet in his head when you're done. Put him out of his misery. Can't have him talking to Hunt, anyway."

A chill went through me. Smith pressed the STOP button and returned the recorder to his pocket. It felt like I'd been struck in the stomach by a sledgehammer. Thank God I hadn't bothered to remove the bug in my telephone. Bob Charles had completely taken me in.

"Mr. Jones is in charge of your neighborhood," Smith said. "If you'd like your guest removed quietly, he will handle the extraction. As a personal favor to me, of course."

"Removed?" I said. "Extraction?"

"It is a specialty of mine." Mr. Jones smiled, showing beautiful white teeth.

"Uh...that won't be necessary," I said with a slight shudder. "I'd prefer to handle him myself."

Smith nodded. Mr. Jones passed me an ivory-colored business card with gold-embossed type. It said simply, JONES & ASSOCIATES and gave a phone number with a local exchange.

"If you need help, call me day or night," Jones said. "Any friend of Mr. Smith's is a friend of mine."

"Thank you." I pocketed his card. Not that I ever intended to call—but it would have been rude to refuse, and I thought it prudent to be very polite and very respectful to Mr. Jones.

Our Town Car glided to a stop in front of my apartment building. Mr. Jones got out, and awkwardly I did the same.

"Thank you," I said to Mr. Smith. "I owe you one."

"Yes, you do," he said.

Mr. Jones slipped back into the car, and they drove off together. I watched until they disappeared around the corner.

Suddenly, my life had gotten a lot more complicated.

* * * *

Bob returned to my apartment half an hour later, looking cold and annoyed. I let him in and dead-bolted the door. Then I looked him over. Hard to believe he planned to kill me. I had always considered myself a pretty good judge of character, and he had fooled me completely. Damn it, I had actually begun to *like* him, with his goofy gung-ho act.

"No black eyes," I said, "and no bullet wounds, punctures, scuffs, or scrapes. Those boys must not have been much trouble after all."

"They knew enough to steer clear of me."

"See why I don't leave my apartment?" I limped back toward the kitchen. "It's an unpleasant world. And it's much too tiring."

"What happened to *you*?" Bob demanded, following. "I couldn't find you anywhere!"

"Oh, a friend gave me a lift home. I ordered a pizza. I hope you like pepperoni. It's the only topping that goes well with scotch."

I sagged into a well-padded kitchen chair and took a slice from the takeout box. Sal's Pizza & Hoagies had dropped it off five minutes ago. I had already poured myself a large drink—mostly soda-water, with just a splash of booze to give it the right smell, mostly for Bob's benefit. I couldn't appear to change my alcoholic behavior lest it tip him off that I knew too much.

"Pepperoni is fine." He got a beer from the fridge.

"Better stick with water," I told him, wagging a finger. "Bodyguards *never* drink on duty. Hazard of the trade."

Silently he put it back. I could tell it annoyed him, though. One point for me.

* * * *

After lunch, I announced my plans to visit the Free Library of Phila-delphia...not our local branch, which specialized more in popular fiction than world-class research materials, but the large one on Vine Street in Center City. A plan had begun to form in the back of my mind...layers of deception, baited with promises of fast and easy money.

"The library? Can't you use the internet?" Bob asked. "Everything's online now."

"Not the material I'm looking for. And anyway, I'd still have to go to the library. I don't own a computer."

I didn't add that I blamed computers in part for the information-overload that had led to my nervous breakdown.

* * * *

On our second try, we reached the Frankford El without difficulty. I bought tokens; slowly we climbed up to the platform. Fortunately the train came quickly.

We sat in a nearly-empty car, and I focused my attention on the floor, analyzing stains and scuff-marks, trying not to look out the windows. Too much scenery, too much color and motion, tended to bring on anxi-ety attacks. I felt a rising sense of panic from Mr. Smith's warning. What would my fake-bodyguard do if I suddenly curled into a fetal ball on the floor?

"If we get separated," Bob said suddenly, "we need a plan. A place to regroup."

I looked at his face. "My apartment?"

"That will do if we're in this area. I meant someplace downtown, while we're out today."

"There's a House of Coffee at 20th and Vine. That's half a block from the library."

He nodded. "Good."

I went back to studying the floor. We rode in silence until we reached Race Street, and there we got out.

Shoppers bustled on the sidewalk, carrying bags and boxes, hurrying on holiday errands. Street vendors hawked caps and scarves and bric-a-brac. Brakes squealed and horns blared from the street. A bus rumbled past, spewing exhaust and carbon dioxide.

I felt a crawling sensation all over. Nervous jitters, just nervous jit-ters. Too many people and too much noise—

"Are you all right?" Bob asked.

I blinked rapidly, trying to stay focused. "I feel overwhelmed—"

"Come on." He grabbed my arm and propelled me forward. With his help, I managed to cross the street, and we headed toward Vine. I kept my gaze fixed on the sidewalk.

"Clear the way!" Bob bellowed. "Sick man coming through!"

To my surprise, people actually moved for him—shoppers, business-men, kids, even a pair of nuns—and we made rapid progress. Finally we passed through the double doors and into the sanctuary of the Free Library. A soothing silence washed over me. Better, better, so much better here. I closed my eyes, just breathing, and felt muscles starting to uncoil.

Bob said softly, "If you need to go home—"

"I'll be fine. The outside world is…difficult sometimes. I shouldn't go into crowds on holidays." I swallowed. "I'm feeling better now. Really."

The card catalog of my youth had been replaced by computer terminals. I eased into a hard wooden chair, stretched my legs out as far as I could, and began my search for books on New York City banks.

Bob, with the occasional bored yawn, kept watch over my shoulder. I began jotting down titles and Dewey Decimal System numbers. When I had ten books selected, Bob took the list.

"I'll find them," he said.

Within twenty minutes, he returned with eight of the ten volumes. Not a bad average—he made a fair research assistant.

The Manhattan Federal Trust sounded like a good choice. After suffering a series of financial losses in the late 1960s, it merged with Third Continental Loan, forming the Manhattan Third Federal Loan and Trust. It suffered a huge loss in 1973, when one of its armored cars had been hijacked. A half-dozen name-changes, mergers, and acquisitions later, I lost the trail in a 1991 Savings and Loan collapse. There didn't seem to be a surviving corporate entity.

I sat back. Yes, it would do nicely.

"Why do you care about this particular bank?" Bob asked suddenly.

"My father did some work there a long time ago," I said. "Can you find microfilm of back issues of the *New York Times*? I need to see July, 1973."

"The whole month?"

"Yes. And maybe part of August."

"You're the boss." Shrugging, he went to find a librarian.

Meanwhile, I returned to the computerized card catalog and began looking up volumes on the U.S. legal system—choosing more for titles than content. I had no intention of reading them if I could avoid it.

"You're in luck," Bob announced when he finally returned. "They have the *New York Times* going back over a hundred years on microfiche.

A lady is setting up the viewer now. They have a private room you can use, too."

"Excellent!" I beamed as I handed over my new list. "When I'm done, I'll need these books. Can you find them?"

"Sure."

When he glanced at the titles, his eyes widened. Volumes like *Circumventing the American Tax System*, *Overseas Tax Havens*, and *Criminal Statutes of Limitations: A State by State Guide* must have caught him by surprise.

"What are you planning?" he asked.

"Bodyguards aren't supposed to ask questions," I said with a wink. "I'm doing some research."

"If this is illegal, I want to know. I might be held responsible as an accomplice—"

I laughed. "Since when is research a criminal act? I'm thinking of writing a book."

He frowned, clearly unsatisfied. But I offered no more explanations.

"Where do I go for the *Times*?" I asked.

"Over here." Turning, he led the way to a small room at the back of the library. An elderly woman had a machine set up for me, and while Bob went off to find my legal books, I began to skim newspaper headlines. Minutes ticked by. My bodyguard returned with a stack of hardbacks, then settled into the chair next to mine.

Finally I found what I wanted: an article dated July 19, 1973. Five men made off with an estimated half million dollars in cash by hijacking an armored truck on the Brooklyn Bridge in broad daylight. It had been a daring robbery, ably executed.

"Way to go, Dad!" I muttered just loud enough for Bob to hear. Never mind that I hadn't been born yet when the robbery took place—thanks to my accident, I looked thirty years older than my actual age.

I printed out the article, folded it up, and stuck it in my shirt pocket. *Bait*. The library charged thirty cents for the printout, and I paid the lady happily.

"That's all I needed from the *Times*," I said as I limped out of the room. I found an empty reading table and pretended to study tax evasion and statutes of limitations for the next half hour. The volumes seemed interminable.

At last, just when I couldn't take it any more, my stomach growled, announcing dinnertime. Another chance to gouge my assassin-bodyguard? I'd see how far I could run up his credit cards before letting him off the hook.

"I don't think Davy would mind springing for dinner instead of breakfast," I told Bob, closing *Offshore Flight: Where and How to Take Your Money*.

"Probably not," he said.

"There's a little seafood house around the corner called Charley's Red. Supposed to be pretty good, too."

He perked up. "I could go for some surf and turf."

"You won't be disappointed."

How could he be? It was a four-star restaurant with a wine list to die for.

* * * *

Dinner was sublime. I ordered a bottle of Dom Perignon Rose 1988 with my caviar-and-truffle-stuffed lobster *à la* Charley. As I kept telling Bob throughout the meal, "Don't worry, it's on Davy."

Bob could only grin and nod. Finally, after a delightful chocolate soufflé followed by a glass of aged port, I could eat no more. I leaned back and patted my too-full belly.

Bob received the check and blanched. Dinner for the two of us came to almost $750, I saw. Not including tip.

"They expect a 25% gratuity," I told him, feeling generous: service *had* been exceptional.

"I…I'm afraid I can't, sir." He gulped. "There's only a couple hundred left on my credit card. David was going to reimburse me!"

"Oh." So much for running up Bob's credit cards. The possibility that my bodyguard might be broke had never occurred to me. "I'll handle it, then."

I pulled out my AmEx. At least I knew Bob's finances now. Could I somehow use that to my advantage? I would have to think on it.

After I signed the credit card receipt, I found I could barely stand. So much for keeping my head clear. I had no choice but to agree to a taxi—which Bob said he would pay for, to make up for dinner. We rode in warmth and comfort back to my apartment.

There, I set my trap. I accidentally "forgot" to remove the robbery article when I tossed my shirt into the bathroom hamper. I carefully left the lid up and the article in plain sight. Neat-freak that he was, I knew Bob would rush to close the hamper's lid, and when he did, he would spot the printout.

If he didn't conclude that my father had been in on the armored car heist, he was dumber than he looked. That, plus the research on offshore tax havens, painted me as a criminal at work…something he could try to turn to his advantage.

"Good night!" I said as I headed to my bedroom with a fresh bottle of whiskey. I carried it mostly for show; I had no intention of clouding my mind further tonight. "Oh, I'll be up early—we have to go to Atlantic City tomorrow."

"Want me to drive?" he offered.

"No need. Casinos return your bus fare in quarters when you get there, plus they sometimes throw in coupons for lunch and other freebies." I had a drawer full of Golden Nugget tee-shirts to prove it.

* * * *

As I lay in bed, thoughts racing, I mentally reviewed the recording Mr. Smith had played for me—and realized I had made a huge mistake.

Every button on a telephone keypad has a different sound. Since I remembered each tone on Mr. Smith's recording perfectly, it was a simple matter to match them up to numbers. Two seconds later, I had Janice's phone number. If I'd thought of it in time, I could have used a reverse directory at the library to look up her name and address.

Calling myself a drunken idiot, I picked up my phone's receiver, punched number 4 so the dial tone went away, and said in a low voice: "Please tell Mr. Smith I'm going to the Azteca Casino on the nine o'clock bus tomorrow morning. When I get there, I'd like my bodyguard's complimentary drink spiked—something that will tie him up in the bathroom for an hour or so. I'm going to win a million dollars at the blackjack tables. Don't worry, I'll give it back. If Mr. Smith is willing to help, I'll owe him another favor. If not—well, I'll manage on my own."

I hung up. Then I opened my night table's drawer and removed four pens from the neat row inside, along with an unused pocket notebook. In tiny, cribbed lettering, I began making lists of fictional transactions using several different colors of ink and alternating between sloppy and neat handwriting. First came dates, then names of various casinos, and amounts I had won. At the bottom of each page, I noted the anonymous Swiss or Brazilian bank account into which the money had been wired. My fictional net worth climbed rapidly into the millions.

Of course, I included all the secret pass codes anyone might need to get the money out. I emphasized that part on the inside front cover: *Funds not accessible without account numbers and pass codes.* Bob would read those words first when he opened the notebook.

* * * *

My legs and back ached fiercely the next morning. When I couldn't take the pain any more, I rose and stumbled into the bathroom. I gulped four aspirins with a glass of tepid tap-water. God, I needed a real drink.

Someone had lowered the hamper's lid. I peeked inside. The print-out in my shirt pocket had been removed, then put back—but not quite folded properly. Sloppy, sloppy work.

Returning to my room, chuckling to myself, I dressed in black Dockers and a navy blue shirt—more leftovers from my Wall Street days—then took a small suitcase from my closet and began to pack... underwear, socks, shirts, pants. Everything I'd need for an extended trip. I needed to convince Bob I planned on fleeing the country.

My bodyguard appeared in the doorway. "Going somewhere?"

"In case I decide to spend the night."

He nodded. "I'll bring my bag, too."

* * * *

An hour later we were on the bus. The drone of wheels on pavement, the murmur of little old ladies on their weekly gambling junket, the soft hiss of recycled air from the blowers overhead—I found it all curiously soothing. As I let myself relax, I began to open up and chat confidentially with Bob...part two of my plan.

"My father used to be involved with organized crime," I confessed in a low voice. Never mind that he had been a plumber. "He hijacked that armored car on the Brooklyn Bridge. The one I read about yesterday."

"What happened?" Bob asked. "Was he caught?"

"Not caught," I said. "Killed. His body turned up in the New Jersey wetlands near where Giants Stadium stands today. He had a bullet in his head, mob execution-style. I don't know what happened to the money, but I found out who did the hit a few years ago."

"Who?"

"Well...let's just say he's come a long way in the last thirty years. He runs the Azteca Casino. That's why I gamble there a lot—every dollar I take away is a little piece of my revenge."

He looked puzzled. "I thought odds favored the house."

"For most games." I chuckled. "You'd never guess I'm worth nearly as much as Davy Hunt, would you?"

He gaped at me. "Then why are you stuck in that shabby little apartment? You should live like a king!"

I lowered my voice confidentially. "Because," I said, "I don't want to attract the IRS's attention. If I started spending hundreds of thousands of dollars, they'd want to know where I got it."

"The tax havens," he said slowly. "That's why you were researching them!"

"Bingo."

He frowned. "Why are you telling *me*?"

"Because," I said grandly, "this is it. Today is my final day. I'm going to make one last big score and retire to Brazil while I wait for the statute of limitations on income tax evasion to pass. I want you to come with me as my bodyguard and assistant. I'll need help, and I think you're the man for the job."

He chewed his lip thoughtfully. This was a lot for him to consider. Would he go for it?

"If you're worried about salary," I added, "I'll pay you a lot better than Davy—starting with a $20,000 signing bonus as soon as our plane lands. That buys a lot in South America. When we come back, we'll both be set for life. What do you say?"

"It's a deal!" He offered his hand, and we shook on it.

Bait taken—hook, line, and sinker.

* * * *

Our bus rolled into Atlantic City on schedule and stopped at Bally's. We filed off with the old people, collecting vouchers for $20 in quarters, redeemable inside at the information booth. I shivered in the brisk wind while Bob collected our luggage. I should have worn a heavier coat.

"What next?" he asked, setting the bags down on the sideway.

"Go in and get our quarters, then we'll walk over to the Azteca."

He then ran inside with our vouchers. A few minutes later he came back carrying two rolls of quarters. Then, carrying our bags, we ambled toward the Azteca.

Shaped like a South American pyramid, the hotel-casino offered three hundred and thirty luxury hotel rooms, most with views of the Boardwalk and the Atlantic Ocean. The entire ground floor consisted of slot machines, gaming tables, bars, restaurants, shops, and two theaters for concerts and stage shows.

I surveyed the elbow-to-elbow holiday crowds. Too loud, too bright, too busy…your typical Atlantic City gambling hall. From experience, I knew I would need several stiff drinks to make it through the day. Adrenaline would keep me going for now, though.

"Where do we start?" Bob asked.

"Check our coats and bags," I said, "then take the quarters and play the slots slowly. Pretend you don't know me, but watch my back. Things will get crazy when I start winning big."

"How did you deal with it in the past?"

"I always kept my winnings under ten thousand per casino so they wouldn't catch on and blacklist me. Today, though, I'm going for broke. A million or more, all from the Azteca."

He whistled. "You can do that?"

"Trick brain, remember?" I tapped my forehead with an index finger. "Don't worry, I'll win. Just keep your eyes open and watch my back."

Without another word, I limped to the line of blackjack tables. I kept going until I found one where a cute Asian lady was shuffling fresh decks, and I took the chair farthest to the left. I'd see everyone else's cards before mine. With 416 cards in play, knowing how many of each denomination remained in the shoe gave me a decided advantage, especially as we got toward the end.

I removed two hundred dollars from my billfold—gambling seed money, normally kept under my mattress—and bought a stack of chips. A man slid into the empty seat next to mine. I recognized Mr. Smith from the faint lavender scent.

"Good morning," I said without looking in his direction.

"That was quite a boast you made," he said. "A million dollars at blackjack?"

"I can do it, as you know."

He said, "That's why I'm here. I have to protect the casino's interests. You are a very dangerous man, Mr. Geller."

He set a tray of chips on the table before him—all bright pink and all stamped $100. He anted one. I risked $5. The three others at our table bet between $5 and $20.

The dealer began to draw cards from the shoe. A smattering of face cards and numbers for the others, a pair of jacks for Mr. Smith, a king and a four for me. Smith split his jacks, then hit for a twenty and a nineteen. I hit and drew an eight—busted. The house held at seventeen.

Nineteen cards gone. Four percent of the deck. A couple more hands and the odds would tilt in my favor.

Mr. Smith collected $200. The dealer swept away my $5 chip. We repeated. Mr. Smith won another $100, and I lost another $5. Repeat. I had a push, Smith lost. Repeat, and we both won.

A blonde in a skimpy mock-Aztec costume and too much eye-shadow approached. She had drinks on a tray.

"Compliments of the house," she said, setting them in the blackjack table's built-in cup holders. Ginger ale for Mr. Smith, watery scotch-and-soda for me.

"Thanks." I gulped mine in three swallows. "Bring me two more," I said before she disappeared.

Three more hands, sixty-seven cards burned. I increased my bet to $25. I split aces, then doubled down—easy wins. Three hands later, I increased my bets to $50. By that point, my initial investment had swelled to eight hundred dollars. Then twelve hundred. Then sixteen hundred.

Our dealer trashed the cards and began shuffling fresh decks together. My drinks arrived.

"You're good," said Mr. Smith, nodding.

"Yes," I agreed. I swallowed scotch-and-soda and felt myself relaxing, falling into the groove.

Suddenly Smith asked, "Would you like to play at a high-stakes table with the house's money? Management uses shills to keep the action hopping. There's nothing like a big spender on a winning streak to stir up the crowd."

"What about my bodyguard?"

"He's having that special drink you ordered right now."

Casually, I glanced over at the slots. Bob was chatting with a different waitress in a mock-Aztec outfit. She held out a little plastic glass of what looked like cola, and he took it. As he sipped, he casually glanced in my direction, but showed no sign of recognizing me. Good boy.

"Ten minutes," said Mr. Smith, "and you'll be on your own."

Ten minutes. Eight to ten hands.

"I can wait that long."

* * * *

It took almost fifteen minutes for Bob's drink to take effect. But when it hit, he hightailed it for the men's room at warp speed, leaving me alone.

I finished my hand—a $240 win—and tossed the dealer a $20 chip. Mr. Smith gathered up his winnings. By my count, I now had $7,600 in front of me.

"Follow me," Smith said.

He threaded his way through the blackjack and craps and roulette tables to a small door marked PRIVATE: EMPLOYEES ONLY. Inside, the noise and bustle of the casino gave way to fluorescent lights, cheap blue carpeting, and stark white walls broken only by glass doors showing tiny offices.

At the office marked CASINO MANAGER, Smith went in. I followed.

"Harvey," he said to the pudgy-faced man at the desk, "this is Mr. Geller, the guest I told you about."

"Hiya, Mr. Geller." Harvey wiped a sweaty hand on his pants before offering it to me. We shook. He went on, "I have your paperwork ready."

"Paperwork?" I asked.

"Legal forms you have to sign."

"Lawyers run everything now," said Mr. Smith half apologetically. "In the old days, Harvey would have broken your legs if you tried to skip with the casino's money. Now he'll have you arrested."

"What a kidder!" Harvey said, laughing. "Can you imagine *me* breaking anyone's legs?"

Actually, I couldn't. But since Mr. Smith seemed serious, I gave a shrug and a smile.

Harvey held out a clipboard. I skimmed the one-page form—*I, Peter Geller, acknowledge that I am playing with the Azteca Casino Corporation's money*, yada yada yada. *I hereby warrant that all monies won or lost remain the sole and exclusive property of the Azteca Casino Corporation and will be surrendered before I leave the premises.*

Harmless enough. I signed, pressing hard for three carbonless copies.

As soon as I finished, Harvey handed me the yellow copy from the bottom. Then he pushed a chip caddy loaded with gold chips stamped $1,000 across his desk. Ten stacks of ten chips each—one hundred thousand dollars. My hands began to tremble, and it wasn't from alcohol this time. I had never had this much money before…even if it wasn't mine to keep.

"What about my earlier winnings?" I asked.

"Give me your chips," said Harvey.

I did so. Harvey counted them quickly, took a lockbox from his drawer, opened it, and peeled seven crisp thousand-dollar bills and six hundreds from a roll. Without comment, he passed them to me.

"Thanks." I tucked them into my billfold.

"Come, Pit," said Mr. Smith with a smile. "A fortune awaits!"

* * * *

My bodyguard still hadn't returned. Uneasy and suddenly self-conscious, I settled down in the well-padded leather highboy seat at the left side of a high-stakes table in the center of the casino. Velvet ropes cordoned the players off from the general public, and floodlights bathed our seats in a warm yellow glow. Overhead, a blue neon sign blinked HIGH STAKES PLAYERS ONLY—$100,000 MINIMUM. I was the only player.

A young guy with his blond hair in a crew cut nodded to me, then began unsealing fresh packs of cards. As he shuffled, an elderly man with a string tie and cowboy hat settled into the highboy next to me. A girl brought him a tray with a quarter million dollars in chips. A few seconds later, an Arab—complete with robes and bodyguards—took the seat farthest right. I noted how the casino staff called him "your highness" and brought him drinks and bowls of green and red Christmas M&Ms without being asked. He had to be a regular.

I definitely felt out of my league.

Cowboy-hat seemed to sense my uneasiness. He jabbed me in the ribs with an elbow and said, "First time here in the spotlight, huh, son?" He had a slight drawl. I noticed the heavy silver ring on his left index finger said A&M—probably Texas A&M University.

"Yes, sir," I said.

"Internet money?" he asked.

"Mob money."

Cowboy-hat got real quiet after that. I shifted uneasily in my chair. Then Smith returned and patted me on the shoulder.

"Good luck," he said.

"Thanks. You're not playing?"

"I'll check back later. I have other duties."

"Of course."

Our dealer cleared his throat. "Ready, gentlemen?"

I threw out a $1,000 chip. Time to get the ball rolling.

* * * *

If only it had been my money. Never had I seen such a lucky streak.

I won my first six opening hands as I began to count cards. I won most of the middle hands where I knew enough to guess what might turn up. I won all the late hands, where the odds had shifted in my favor. Weird, wacky, wonderful luck—where were you when I needed you, when that taxi ran me down?

My winning streak continued throughout the first hour. Shoe after shoe, I beat the house consistently. The dealer began paying me in $10,000 chips. I hadn't even known that denomination existed. My money grew…half a million, then nearly a million. Mr. Smith would never doubt me again.

And Smith had been right about the buzz a big winner created. Behind the velvet rope, a crowd gathered to cheer me on. I started to sweat; the whispers and bursts of applause pushed my senses toward overload. Those three watery scotch-and-sodas helped, but not nearly enough.

Suddenly I noticed Bob Charles at the front of the gawkers. He looked pale and shaky. He must have recovered from his sudden "stomach ailment."

"Mr. Smith says you need a drink," a voice said at my elbow. It was the same girl who had drugged Bob. She held out a tray. "Compliments of the house, sir."

"Thanks." Since everything in front of me belonged to the casino, I had no worries about being drugged.

It was another scotch-and-soda; I gulped it down. Strong this time, the way I liked.

"Bring me another?" I asked.

"Of course, sir." She vanished.

Tex leaned in close and said, "Better watch that stuff, if you expect to keep winning. Gotta stay sharp, son!"

"Drink or die," I said unhappily. "I can't function sober."

He laughed. "Then maybe I should take up drinking, the way my luck's running!"

His stack of chips had been cut in half over the last two hours. Further down the table, the prince barely held his own.

I bet $50,000—and got a blackjack. Cowboy-hat drew to a 12 and busted. Too many face-cards still in play...with the dealer showing a five, I would have stayed.

My new drink came, and I downed it fast. The rising tide of voices began to grow muted; my hands stopped shaking. My world narrowed down to the cards.

But first, I reminded myself, I had to take care of Bob.

"I have to take a bathroom break," I said to the dealer. "May I leave my chips here?"

"Of course, sir."

"Don't worry, son," said Cowboy-hat. "I'll keep an eye on 'em for ya!"

"Thanks." I smiled wanly at him.

I rose, leaning heavily on my walking stick, and gave Bob a glance and a subtle follow-me jerk of my head. Then I limped to the men's room.

It was moderately busy inside. We stood side by side at the urinals, waiting until we were alone. Then I handed him my billfold with the $7,600 still inside.

"I have my million," I said. "There's a travel agency across the street. Buy two one-way tickets to Rio de Janeiro. I doubt if there's a direct flight from Atlantic City, but we should be able to make it with a couple of connections. Cut it as close as possible. When it's time to go, signal me. I'll cash out and we'll run for the plane. As fast as a cripple like me can run, anyway."

"Got it," he said.

* * * *

I returned to the high-stakes table and found Mr. Smith had replaced Cowboy-hat. My chips had not been touched. Fortunately for me, most of the watchers had dispersed.

Our dealer began shuffling new decks of cards.

"Is everything going as planned?" Smith asked.

"I think so."

"I saw your friend leave. You should have let Mr. Jones remove him for you, you know."

"Human life has value," I said.

"You should watch out for yourself, not someone who's trying to kill you."

I shrugged. "Perhaps I made a mistake. But I like him, and I think he's basically a decent guy. He just took a wrong step somewhere."

"Are you sure you won't change your mind?"

"I'm more stubborn than sensible. Besides, it's almost Christmas. 'Tis the season of brotherly love, and all that mushy holiday stuff. I couldn't have his 'removal' on my conscience."

"What's next?" Smith asked.

"Bob is out buying tickets to Rio de Janeiro. He'll be on the afternoon plane. That's where you come in."

"I suppose he needs a lift to the airport?"

"I'm going to cash out when he returns. I'll give instructions at the cashier's booth for the winnings to be wired into a nonexistent Brazilian bank account. Then, on my way out the door, someone can grab me, force me into a car, and drive off with me. Bob will think I'm being kidnapped and take off for Brazil alone."

"Why would he?"

"Because," I said smugly, "he's going to have my little black notebook with all the pass codes and bank account numbers. He'll think he's struck it rich."

"Until he gets there and finds out there's no money."

"Right."

"Then he'll come back, hunt you down, and kill you for making a fool out of him."

"He'll stay there. I'm sure he'll call once he gets to Rio and finds out he's been duped. I'll simply tell him he'll be arrested for conspiracy to commit murder if he returns to the United States. I imagine you still have that recording."

"Of course."

"I'll borrow it and play it back for him. He won't dare return. End of problem!"

Smith shook his head. "You overly complicate things, Pit. Remove him and move on with your life."

"That's not an option."

"Your plan is ridiculous."

"But you'll help me," I said.

He shrugged. "I find it fairly amusing. But once it's done, I have a real job for you in Las Vegas. One for which you are uniquely qualified."

"As long as I don't have to break the law," I said, "I'll go. I always keep my word."

The dealer asked, "Ready, gentlemen?" He had finished stacking the cards in the shoe.

Smith excused himself. The prince and I both anted, and our game began anew.

* * * *

By the time Bob returned, I had won another hundred and forty thousand. A new crowd gathered beyond the velvet ropes. Bob eased his way to the front and signaled me by tapping his wristwatch. Time to catch our plane.

"That's it for me," I said, rising. I tossed the dealer a $1,000 chip. "Thanks for everything."

"Thank *you*, sir!" he said, beaming.

I gathered my winnings onto a tray, then limped to the cashier's station. Mr. Smith sat comfortably ensconced behind the brass grill.

"How much did you win?" he asked in a low voice as I passed him my chips.

"One-point-two million," I whispered smugly, "plus change."

"It's a good thing you *were* playing with the house's money. How soon do you want to be abducted?"

"As we leave. We'll go through the doors onto Atlantic Avenue. Do you have a pen and paper?"

"Here." He slid them over to me.

I jotted down wiring instructions for the money and passed it back.

"Might as well go through the motions," I said. "May I have a receipt for the wire?"

Chuckling, he made one up. I tucked it into my little notebook, which I kept in hand as I limped off for the Atlantic Avenue doors. There Bob Charles waited impatiently, pretending to study a marquee. I paused beside him. From the corner of my eyes, I saw men in black suits starting to converge on us.

"I already wired the money to my Brazilian account from the courtesy counter. But I don't think they're going to let me leave here safely."

Casually I dropped the notebook. "Cover that with your foot. Pick it up when I'm out the door—they can't find it on me. It has the pass codes for my anonymous bank accounts. If I can, I'll catch up at the airport."

Without bothering to retrieve my coat or bag from the checkroom, I headed for the door. The bellman opened it for me, and shivering at the sudden cold, I stepped outside.

Smith's men followed on my heels—goons built like refrigerators. I had seen both of them before at Smith's illegal casino outside of Philadelphia.

A white Town Car sat idling in front, and they grabbed my elbows and hustled me inside. I didn't struggle.

As I twisted around, we accelerated into traffic. I glimpsed Bob running out the front door. He stood there, staring after me, a look of anger on his face.

He cared what happened to me. I saw it, and in that moment I knew I had made the right decision. Better to handle him myself than let Smith and Jones do it. He *was* basically a decent guy.

"Thanks, fellows," I said to the goons.

Mr. Smith sat in the front passenger seat. He opened a small window in the bulletproof partition separating our seats.

"Where next?" he asked. "The airport?"

"Take a ten minute drive, then back to the casino. I have to pick up my coat and bag. Then I'll catch the bus home."

"You heard the man," Smith said to our chauffeur.

"Yes, sir!" he said.

The goons and I settled back.

* * * *

We didn't even make it five blocks—police cars with blinking lights cut us off, front and back. Our driver slammed on the brakes; we fishtailed, then came to a screeching halt.

As uniformed officers leaped from their cars with drawn weapons, Smith's goons reached for their guns.

"Don't do that," I said in a low voice. "This has to be a mistake."

A bullhorn blared: "Get out of the car with your hands up!"

"I'm not happy, Pit," said Mr. Smith. He got out of the car and raised his hands. The chauffeur and goons did the same.

Slowly, painfully, I followed.

"You are in big trouble," Smith told the policemen who advanced. "Do you know who I am?"

None replied. They forced his hands onto the roof of his Town Car and began frisking him. Another officer began reading us all our Miranda rights.

That's when I spotted Bob Charles sitting in one of the patrol cars. He must have gone running to the cops instead of taking off for Brazil with my money. I nodded to him, and he grinned back.

"That's him—that's Peter Geller!" he said, climbing out and pointing at me. "They were kidnapping him!"

A police lieutenant took my elbow and drew me to one side. "Mr. Charles flagged down a patrol car," he said, "and reported your abduction. He said you won big at the casino and they weren't going to let you keep it. Is that true?"

"No," I said emphatically. I gestured at the Town Car and Mr. Smith. "This is some kind of misunderstanding. I work for the casino. These men are all friends of mine. We were taking an early supper."

The lieutenant frowned. "What about the money he said you won? More than a million dollars, wasn't it?"

"Nonsense. I was playing with the casino's money. Here—see for yourself!"

I pulled out the yellow copy of the form I'd signed. The lieutenant scanned it, snorted, then said to the other cops:

"Let them go. We've made a mistake."

"Thank you," said Mr. Smith. He straightened his tie and jacket.

The lieutenant stalked back to Bob, and they exchanged heated words. Bob read the yellow form, then stared at me in disbelief. When the lieutenant made Bob get out and lean up against the hood of the police car, I watched with amusement.

Of course, the officer turned up two wallets—one of them mine—plus the notebook of bank account numbers and plane tickets. He studied them, then stalked back to me.

"Is this yours?" He held out my wallet.

"Yes. Bob was holding onto it for me."

He frowned. "And two tickets to Rio?"

"Also mine."

"Notebook?"

"Yep. Mine."

His eyes narrowed. He knew something odd had gone down, but for the life of him he couldn't figure it out.

"I think you all had better come with me to the station," he said.

I shrugged. "As you wish." To Mr. Smith, I said, "Perhaps you can recommend a good lawyer?"

"He'll meet us there," Smith said grumpily, reaching for his cell phone.

* * * *

I rode in the back of the police car with Bob. The cops hadn't bothered to handcuff either one of us. Mr. Smith and his goons were following in their Town Car.

"Are you insane?" Bob demanded. "I just saved your life! Why are you doing this to me?"

"Maybe I'm a little bit cranky, but I'm hardly insane." I chuckled. "You asked me to kick your tires, Bob. Congrats. You passed the test."

His breath caught in his throat. "A…test. This whole thing…."

"That's right. And I can *almost* recommend you to Davy Hunt."

"Almost?"

"There's one matter you still have to take care of."

He looked puzzled. "I don't understand…."

"Janice."

He paled. "How—how do you know—"

"Trick brain, remember?" I grinned. "Tell the police how Janice tried to set up Davy using the two of us, and I'll get you cleared of all charges by morning."

* * * *

Once Bob started talking to the police, he had quite a story to tell. When he got out of the Marines, an old girlfriend contacted him, got him to come to Philadelphia, and told him she worked as the private secretary for a billionaire sleazebag named David Chatham Hunt.

A year ago, Janice had a romantic fling with her boss. Presents were given, promises were made…apparently, she expected the relationship to go farther than Davy did. When he broke things off and started dating a supermodel named Cree, she took it very hard.

Janice planned her revenge with meticulous care. As his private secretary, she knew Davy's position on the Board of Directors at Hunt Industries was provisional. Any hint of a scandal, and he'd get the boot. Davy couldn't allow that to happen.

And that's where Bob came in. Janice knew about my friendship with Davy, and she thought my personal recommendation would get Bob hired as bodyguard, cutting through a lot of red tape. Apparently she believed she could lure Davy into a final romantic tryst…one where Bob would be present to take blackmail photos.

It could have worked. Davy might well have fallen into her trap. I could easily envision my old friend having one last fling with his secretary, just to get her off his back.

Once Janice was arrested, she collapsed into hysterics at the police station, confessed everything, and ultimately pleaded guilty to conspiracy charges. Her case would never go to trial, saving Davy a lot of embarrassment.

Thanks to Mr. Smith's lawyer, Bob Charles ended up with probation and stern warnings from a judge. He never spent a single night in jail. Best of all, on my recommendation, Davy hired him as his personal bodyguard. I thought they would go well together. Bob had certainly proved himself to my satisfaction.

* * * *

"And that's the whole story," I said to Davy and Cree over Christmas dinner. Cree had cooked it herself—a beautiful roast goose with cranberry sauce, mashed sweet potatoes, green bean casserole, and a delightful selection of home-baked pies.

"Incredible," Davy said, shaking his head. "You know what the worst part of this whole mess is?"

"What?" I asked.

"Janice was the best secretary I ever had."

Cree punched him on the arm—hard.

"But my new secretary seems just as good," he added quickly.

"Better," said Cree. She turned to me. "I picked him out myself. No more office romances, right, Davy?"

"Right!" he agreed. But he seemed a little wistful.

I chuckled. "It took a long time and cost a small fortune, but what do you think of *my* present?" I asked.

"Present?" Davy scratched his head and looked at Cree, who shrugged. "Did I miss something?"

I raised my wineglass in salute. "For the man who has everything—a new secretary and a new bodyguard. Merry Christmas, Davy!"

John Gregory Betancourt is a best-selling science fiction and fantasy author, as well as a mystery writer. His Peter "Pit Bull" Geller series is his most popular creation, and one story, "Horse Pit," won the Black Orchid award from the Nero Wolfe Society and *Alfred Hitchcock's Mystery Magazine*.

MR WRAY'S CASH BOX

OR, THE MASK AND THE MYSTERY

A Christmas Sketch

Wilkie Collins

I

I should be insulting the intelligence of readers generally, if I thought it at all necessary to describe to them that widely-celebrated town, Tidbury-on-the-Marsh. As a genteel provincial residence, who is unacquainted with it? The magnificent new hotel that has grown on to the side of the old inn; the extensive library, to which, not satisfied with only adding new books, they are now adding a new entrance as well; the projected crescent of palatial abodes in the Grecian style, on the top of the hill, to rival the completed crescent of castellated abodes, in the Gothic style, at the bottom of the hill—are not such local objects as these perfectly well known to any intelligent Englishman? Of course they are! The question is superfluous. Let us get on at once, without wasting more time, from Tidbury in general to the High Street in particular, and to our present destination there—the commercial establishment of Messrs Dunball and Dark.

Looking merely at the coloured liquids, the miniature statue of a horse, the corn plasters, the oil-skin bags, the pots of cosmetics, and the cut-glass saucers full of lozenges in the shop window, you might at first imagine that Dunball and Dark were only chemists. Looking carefully through the entrance, towards an inner apartment, an inscription; a large, upright, mahogany receptacle, or box, with a hole in it; brass rails protecting the hole; a green curtain ready to draw over the hole; and a man with a copper money shovel in his hand, partially visible behind the hole; would be sufficient to inform you that Dunball and Dark were not chemists only, but "Branch Bankers" as well.

It is a rough squally morning at the end of November. Mr Dunball (in the absence of Mr Dark, who has gone to make a speech at the vestry meeting) has got into the mahogany box, and has assumed the whole business and direction of the branch bank. He is a very fat man, and looks absurdly over-large for his sphere of action. Not a single customer has, as yet, applied for money—nobody has come even to gossip with the branch banker through the brass rails of his commercial prison house. There he sits, staring calmly through the chemical part of the shop into the street—his gold in one drawer, his notes in another, his elbows on his ledgers, his copper shovel under his thumb; the picture of monied loneliness; the hermit of British finance.

In the outer shop is the young assistant, ready to drug the public at a moment's notice. But Tidbury-on-the-Marsh is an unprofitably healthy place; and no public appears. By the time the young assistant has ascertained from the shop clock that it is a quarter past ten, and from the weather-cock opposite that the wind is "sou'-sou'-west," he has exhausted all external sources of amusement, and is reduced to occupying himself by first sharpening his penknife, and then cutting his nails. He has completed his left hand, and has just begun on the right hand thumb, when a customer actually darkens the shop door at last!

Mr Dunball starts, and grasps the copper shovel: the young assistant shuts up his penknife in a hurry, and makes a bow. The customer is a young girl, and she has come for a pot of lip salve.

She is very neatly and quietly dressed; looks about eighteen or nineteen years of age; and has something in her face which I can only characterize by the epithet—lovable. There is a beauty of innocence and purity about her forehead, brow, and eyes—a calm, kind, happy expression as she looks as you—and a curious home-sound in her clear utterance when she speaks, which, altogether, make you fancy, stranger as you are, that you must have known her and loved her long ago, and somehow or other ungratefully forgotten her in the lapse of time. Mixed up, however, with the girlish gentleness and innocence which form her more prominent charm, there is a look of firmness—especially noticeable about the expression of her lips—that gives a certain character and originality to her face. Her figure—

I stop at her figure. Not by any means for want of phrases to describe it; but from a disheartening conviction of the powerlessness of any description of her at all to produce the right effect on the minds of others. If I were asked in what particular efforts of literature the poverty of literary material most remarkably appears, I should answer, in personal descriptions of heroines. We have all read these by the hundred—some of them so carefully and finely finished, that we are not only informed about the lady's eyes, eyebrows, nose, cheeks, complexion, mouth, teeth, neck, ears, head, hair, and the way it was dressed; but are also made acquainted with the particular manner in which the sentiments below made the bosom above heave or swell; besides the exact position of head in which her eyelashes were just long enough to cast a shadow on her cheeks. We have read all this attentively and admiringly, as it deserves; and have yet risen from the reading, without the remotest approach to a realization in our own minds of what sort of a woman the heroine really was. We vaguely knew she was beautiful, at the beginning of the description; and we know just as much—just as vaguely—at the end.

Penetrated with the conviction above-mentioned, I prefer leaving the reader to form his own realization of the personal appearance of the customer at Messrs Dunball and Dark's. Eschewing the magnificent beauties of his acquaintance, let him imagine her to be like any pretty intelligent girl whom he knows—any of those pleasant little fire-side angels, who can charm us even in a merino morning gown, darning an old pair of socks. Let this be the sort of female reality in the reader's mind; and neither author, nor heroine, need have any reason to complain.

Well; our young lady came to the counter, and asked for lip salve. The assistant, vanquished at once by the potent charm of her presence, paid her the first little tribute of politeness in his power, by asking permission to send the gallipot home for her.

"I beg your pardon, miss," said he; "but I think you live lower down, at No. 12. I was passing; and I think I saw you going in there, yesterday, with an old gentleman, and another gentleman—I think I did, miss?"

"Yes: we lodge at No. 12," said the young girl; "but I will take the lip salve home with me, if you please. I have a favour, however, to ask of you before I go," she continued very modestly, but without the slightest appearance of embarrassment; "if you have room to hang this up in your window, my grandfather, Mr Wray, would feel much obliged by your kindness."

And here, to the utter astonishment of the young assistant, she handed him a piece of cardboard, with a string to hang it up by, on which appeared the following inscription, neatly written:—

Mr Reuben Wray, pupil of the late celebrated John Kemble, Esquire, begs respectfully to inform his friends and the public that he gives lessons in elocution, delivery, and reading aloud, price two-and-sixpence the lesson of an hour. Pupils prepared for the stage, or private theatricals, on a principle combining intelligent interpretation of the text, with the action of the arms and legs adopted by the late illustrious Roscius of the English stage, J. Kemble, Esquire; and attentively studied from close observation of Mr J.K. by Mr R.W. Orators and clergymen improved (with the strictest secrecy), at three-and-sixpence the lesson of an hour. Impediments and hesitation of utterance combated and removed. Young ladies taught the graces of delivery, and young gentlemen the proprieties of diction. A discount allowed to schools and large classes.

Please to address, Mr Reuben Wray (late of the Theatre Royal, Drury Lane), 12, High Street, Tidbury-on-the-Marsh.

No Babylonian inscription that ever was cut, no manuscript on papyrus that ever was penned, could possibly have puzzled the young assistant more than this remarkable advertisement. He read it all through in a state of stupefaction; and then observed, with a bewildered look at the young girl on the other side of the counter:—

"Very nicely written, miss; and very nicely composed indeed! I suppose—in fact, I'm sure Mr Dunball"—Here a creaking was heard, as of some strong wooden construction being gradually rent asunder. It was Mr Dunball himself, squeezing his way out of the branch bank box, and coming to examine the advertisement.

He read it all through very attentively, following each line with his forefinger; and then cautiously and gently laid the cardboard down on the counter. When I state that neither Mr Dunball nor his assistant were quite certain what a "Roscius of the English stage" meant, or what precise branch of human attainment Mr Wray designed to teach in teaching "Elocution," I do no injustice either to master or man.

"So you want this hung up in the window, my—in the window, miss?" asked Mr Dunball. He was about to say, "my dear"; but something in the girl's look and manner stopped him.

"If you could hang it up without inconvenience, sir."

"May I ask what's your name? and where you come from?"

"My name is Annie Wray; and the last place we came from was Stratford-upon-Avon."

"Ah! indeed—and Mr Wray teaches, does he?—elocution for half-a-crown—eh?"

"My grandfather only desires to let the inhabitants of this place know that he can teach those who wish it, to speak or read with a good delivery and a proper pronunciation."

Mr Dunball felt rather puzzled by the straightforward, self-possessed manner in which he—a branch banker, a chemist, and a municipal authority—was answered by little Annie Wray. He took up the advertisement again; and walked away to read it a second time in the solemn monetary seclusion of the back shop.

The young assistant followed. "I think they're respectable people, sir," said he, in a whisper; "I was passing when the old gentleman went into No. 12, yesterday. The wind blew his cloak on one side, and I saw him carrying a large cash box under it—I did indeed, sir; and it seemed a heavy one."

"Cash box!" cried Mr Dunball. "What does a man with a cash box want with elocution, and two-and-sixpence an hour? Suppose he should be a swindler!"

"He can't be, sir: look at the young lady! Besides, the people at No. 12 told me he gave a reference, and paid a week's rent in advance."

"He did—did he? I say, are you sure it was a cash box?"

"Certain, sir. I suppose it had money in it, of course?"

"What's the use of a cash box, without cash?" said the branch banker, contemptuously. "It looks rather odd, though! Stop! maybe it's a wager. I've heard of gentlemen doing queer things for wagers. Or, maybe, he's cracked! Well, she's a nice girl; and hanging up this thing can't do any harm. I'll make enquiries about them, though, for all that."

Frowning portentously as he uttered this last cautious resolve, Mr Dunball leisurely returned into the chemist's shop. He was, however, nothing like so ill-natured a man as he imagined himself to be; and, in spite of his dignity and his suspicions, he smiled far more cordially than he at all intended, as he now addressed little Annie Wray.

"It's out of our line, miss," said he; "but we'll hang the thing up to oblige you. Of course, if I want a reference, you can give it? Yes, yes! of course. There! there's the card in the window for you—a nice prominent place (look at it as you go out)—just between the string of corn plasters and the dried poppy-heads! I wish Mr Wray success; though I rather think Tidbury is not quite the sort of place to come to for what you call elocution—eh?"

"Thank you, sir; and good morning," said little Annie. And she left the shop just as composedly as she had entered it.

"Cool little girl, that!" said Mr Dunball, watching her progress down the street to No. 12.

"Pretty little girl, too!" thought the assistant, trying to watch, like his master, from the window.

"I should like to know who Mr Wray is," said Mr Dunball, turning back into the shop, as Annie disappeared. "And I'd give something to find out what Mr Wray keeps in his cash box," continued the banker-chemist, as he thoughtfully re-entered the mahogany money chest in the back premises.

You are a wise man, Mr Dunball; but you won't solve those two mysteries in a hurry, sitting alone in that branch bank sentry-box of yours!—Can anybody solve them? I can.

Who is Mr Wray? and what has he got in his cash box?—Come to No. 12, and see!

II

Before we go boldly into Mr Wray's lodgings, I must first speak a word or two about him, behind his back—but by no means slanderously. I will take his advertisement, now hanging up in the shop window of Messrs Dunball and Dark, as the text of my discourse.

Mr Reuben Wray became, as he phrased it, a "pupil of the late celebrated John Kemble, Esquire" in this manner. He began life by being apprenticed for three years to a statuary. Whether the occupation of taking casts and clipping stones proved of too sedentary a nature to suit his temperament, or whether an evil counsellor within him, whose name was *Vanity*, whispered:—"Seek public admiration, and be certain of public applause,"—I know not; but the fact is, that, as soon as his time was out, he left his master and his native place to join a company of strolling players; or, as he himself more magniloquently expressed it, he went on the stage.

Nature had gifted him with good lungs, large eyes, and a hook nose; his success before barn audiences was consequently brilliant. His professional exertions, it must be owned, barely sufficed to feed and clothe him; but then he had a triumph on the London stage, always present in the far perspective to console him. While waiting this desirable event, he indulged himself in a little intermediate luxury, much in favour as a profitable resource for young men in extreme difficulties—he married; married at the age of nineteen, or thereabouts, the charming Columbine of the company.

And he got a good wife. Many people, I know, will refuse to believe this,—it is a truth, nevertheless. The one redeeming success of the vast social failure which his whole existence was doomed to represent, was this very marriage of his with a strolling Columbine. She, poor girl, toiled as hard and as cheerfully to get her own bread after marriage, as before; trudged many a weary mile by his side from town to town, and never uttered a complaint; praised his acting; partook his hopes; patched his clothes; pardoned his ill-humour; paid court for him to his manager; made up his squabbles;—in a word, and in the best and highest sense of that word, loved him. May I be allowed to add, that she only brought him one child—a girl? And, considering the state of his pecuniary resources, am I justified in ranking this circumstance as a strong additional proof of her excellent qualities as a married woman?

After much perseverance and many disappointments, Reuben at last succeeded in attaching himself to a regular provincial company—Tate Wilkinson's at York. He had to descend low enough from his original dramatic pedestal before he succeeded in subduing the manager. From the leading business in Tragedy and Melodrama, he sank at once, in the established provincial company, to a "minor utility"—words of theatrical slang signifying an actor who is put to the smaller dramatic uses which the necessities of the stage require. Still, in spite of this, he persisted in hoping for the chance that was never to come; and still poor Columbine faithfully hoped with him to the last.

Time passed—years of it; and this chance never arrived; and he and Columbine found themselves one day in London, forlorn and starving. Their life at this period would make a romance of itself, if I had time and space to write it; but I must get on, as fast as may be, to later dates; and the reader must be contented merely to know that, at the last gasp—the last of hope; almost the last of life—Reuben got employment, as an actor of the lower degree, at Drury Lane.

Behold him, then, now—still a young man, but crushed in his young man's ambition for ever—receiving the lowest theatrical wages for the lowest theatrical work; appearing on the stage as soldier, waiter, footman, and so on; with not a line in the play to speak; just showing his poverty-shrunken carcase to the audience, clothed in the frowsiest habiliments of the old Drury Lane wardrobe, for a minute or two at a time, at something like a shilling a night—a miserable being, in a miserable world; the World behind the Scenes!

John Philip Kemble is now acting at the theatre: and his fame is rising to its climax. How the roar of applause follows him almost every time he leaves the scene! How majestically he stalks away into the Green Room, abstractedly inhaling his huge pinches of snuff as he goes! How the poor inferior brethren of the buskin, as they stand at the wing and stare upon him reverently, long for his notice; and how few of them can possibly get it! There is, nevertheless, one among this tribe of unfortunates whom he has really remarked, though he has not yet spoken to him. He has detected this man, shabby and solitary, constantly studying his acting from any vantage-ground the poor wretch could get amid the dust, dirt, draughts, and confusion behind the scenes. Mr Kemble also observes, that whenever a play of Shakespeare's is being acted, this stranger has a tattered old book in his hands; and appears to be following the performance closely from the text, instead of huddling into warm corners over a pint of small beer, with the rest of his supernumerary brethren. Remarking these things, Mr Kemble over and over again intends to speak to the man, and find out who he is; and over and over again utterly forgets it. But, at last, a day comes when the long-deferred personal communication really takes place; and it happens thus:—

A new Tragedy is to be produced—a pre-eminently bad one, by-the-by, even in those days of pre-eminently bad Tragedy-writing. The scene is laid in Scotland; and Mr Kemble is determined to play his part in a

Highland dress. The idea of acting a drama in the appropriate costume of the period which that drama illustrates, is considered so dangerous an innovation, that no one else dare follow his example; and he, of all the characters, is actually about to wear the only Highland dress in a Highland play. This does not at all daunt him. He has acted Othello, a night or two before, in the uniform of a British General Officer, and is so conscious of the enormous absurdity of the thing, that he is determined to persevere, and start the reform in stage costume, which he was afterwards destined so thoroughly to carry out.

The night comes; the play begins. Just as the stage waits for Mr Kemble, Mr Kemble discovers that his goatskin purse—one of the most striking peculiarities of the Highland dress—is not on him. There is no time to seek it—all is lost for the cause of costume!—he must go on the stage exposed to public view as only half a Highlander! No! Not yet! While everybody else hurries frantically hither and thither in vain, one man quickly straps something about Mr Kemble's waist, just in the nick of time. It is the lost purse! and Roscius after all steps on the stage, a Highlander complete from top to toe!

On his first exit, Mr Kemble inquires for the man who found the purse. It is that very poor player whom he has already remarked. The great actor had actually been carrying the purse about in his own hands before the performance; and, in a moment of abstraction, had put it down on a chair, in a dark place behind the prompter's box. The humble admirer, noticing everything he did, noticed this; and so found the missing goatskin in time, when nobody else could.

"Sir, I am infinitely obliged to you," says Mr Kemble, courteously, to the confused, blushing man before him—"You have saved me from appearing incomplete, and therefore ridiculous, before a Drury Lane audience. I have marked you, sir, before; reading, while waiting for your call, our divine Shakespeare—the poetic bond that unites all men, however professional distances may separate them. Accept, sir, this offered pinch—this pinch of snuff."

When the penniless player went home that night, what wonderful news he had for his wife! And how proud and happy poor Columbine was, when she heard that Reuben Wray had been offered a pinch of snuff out of Mr Kemble's own box!

But the kind-hearted tragedian did not stop merely at a fine speech and a social condescension. Reuben read Shakespeare, when none of his comrades would have cared to look into the book at all; and that of itself was enough to make him interesting to Mr Kemble. Besides, he was a young man; and might have capacities which only wanted encouragement.

"I beg you to recite to me, sir," said the great John Philip, one night; desirous of seeing what his humble admirer really could do. The result of the recitation was unequivocal: poor Wray could do nothing that hundreds of his brethren could not have equalled. In him, the yearning to become a great actor was only the ambition without the power.

Still, Reuben gained something by the goatskin purse. A timely word from his new protector raised him two or three degrees higher in the company, and increased his salary in proportion. He got parts now with some lines to speak in them; and—condescension on condescension!—Mr Kemble actually declaimed them for his instruction at rehearsal, and solemnly showed him (oftener, I am afraid, in jest than earnest) how a patriotic Roman soldier, or a bereaved father's faithful footman, should tread the stage.

These instructions were always received by the grateful Wray in the most perfect good faith; and it was precisely in virtue of his lessons thus derived—numbering about half-a-dozen, and lasting about two minutes each—that he afterwards advertised himself, as teacher of elocution and pupil of John Kemble. Many a great man has blazed away famously before the public eye, as pupil of some other great man, from no larger a supply of original educational fuel than belonged to Mr Reuben Wray.

Having fairly traced our friend to his connection with Mr Kemble, I may dismiss the rest of his advertisement more briefly. All, I suppose, that you now want further explained, is:—How he came to teach elocution, and how he got on by teaching it.

Well: Reuben stuck fast to Drury Lane theatre through rivalries, and quarrels, and disasters, and fluctuations in public taste, which overthrew more important interests than his own. The theatre was rebuilt, and burnt, and rebuilt again; and still Old Wray (as he now began to be called) was part and parcel of the establishment, however others might desert it. During this long lapse of monotonous years, affliction and death preyed cruelly on the poor actor's home. First, his kind, patient Columbine died; then, after a long interval, Columbine's only child married early;—and woe is me!—married a sad rascal, who first ill-treated and then deserted her. She soon followed her mother to the grave, leaving one girl—the little Annie of this story—to Reuben's care. One of the first things her grandfather taught the child was to call herself Annie Wray. He never could endure hearing her dissolute father's name pronounced by anybody; and was resolved that she should always bear his own.

Ah! what woeful times were those for the poor player! How many a night he sat in the darkest corner behind the scenes, with his tattered Shakespeare—the only thing about him he had never pawned—in his hand, and the tears rolling down his hollow, painted cheeks, as he thought on the dear lost Columbine, and Columbine's child! How often those tears still stood thick in his eyes when he marched across the stage at the head of a mock army, or hobbled up to deliver the one eternal letter to the one eternal dandy hero of high Comedy!—Comedy, indeed! If the people before the lamps, who were roaring with laughter at the fun of the mercurial fine gentleman of the play, had only seen what was tugging at the heart of the miserable old stage footman who brought him his chocolate and newspapers, all the wit in the world would not have saved the comedy from being wept over as the most affecting tragedy that was ever written.

But the time was to come—long after this, however—when Reuben's connection with the theatre was to cease. As if fate had ironically bound up together the stage destinies of the great actor and the small, the year of Mr Kemble's retirement from the boards, was the year of Mr Wray's dismissal from them.

He had been, for some time past, getting too old to be useful—then, the theatrical world in which he had been bred was altering, and he could not alter with it. A little man with fiery black eyes, whose name was Edmund Kean, had come up from the country and blazed like a comet through the thick old conventional mists of the English stage. From that time, the new school began to rise, and the old school to sink; and Reuben went down, with other insignificant atoms, in the vortex. At the end of the season, he was informed that his services were no longer required.

It was then, when he found himself once more forlorn in the world—almost as forlorn as when he had first come to London with poor Columbine—that the notion of trying elocution struck him. He had a little sum of money to begin with, subscribed for him by his richer brethren when he left the theatre. Why might he not get on as a teacher of elocution in the country, just as some of his superior fellow-players got on in the same vocation in London? Necessity whispered, Doubt not, but try. He had a grandchild to support—so he did try.

His method of teaching was exceedingly simple. He had one remedy for the deficiencies of every class whom he addressed—the Kemble remedy: he had watched Mr Kemble year by year, till he knew every inch of him; and, so to speak, had learnt him by heart. Did a pupil want to walk the stage properly?—teach him Mr Kemble's walk. Did a rising politician want to become impressive as an orator?—teach him Mr Kemble's gesticulations in Brutus. So again, with regard to strictly vocal necessities. Did gentleman number one, wish to learn the art of reading aloud?—let him learn the Kemble cadences. Did gentleman number two, feel weak in his pronunciation?—let him sound vowels, consonants, and crack-jaw syllables, just as Mr Kemble sounded them on the stage. And, out of what book were they to be taught?—from what manual were the clergymen and orators, the aspirants for dramatic fame, the young ladies whose delivery was ungraceful, and the young gentlemen whose diction was improper, to be all alike improved! From Shakespeare—every one of them from Shakespeare! He had no idea of anything else: literature meant Shakespeare to him. It was his great glory and triumph, that he had Shakespeare by heart. All that he knew, every tender and lovable recollection, every small honour he had gained in his own poor blank sphere, was somehow sure to be associated with William Shakespeare!

And why not? What is Shakespeare but a great sun that shines upon humanity—the large heads and the little, alike? Have not the rays of that mighty light penetrated into many poor and lowly places for good? What marvel then that they should fall, pleasant and invigorating, even upon Reuben Wray?

So—right or wrong—with Shakespeare for his textbook, and Mr Kemble for his model, our friend in his old age bravely invaded provincial England as a teacher of elocution, with all its supplementary accomplishments. And, wonderful to relate, though occasionally enduring dreadful privations, he just managed to make elocution—or what passed instead of it with his patrons—keep his grandchild and himself!

I cannot say that any orators or clergymen anxiously demanded secret improvement from him (see advertisement) at three-and-sixpence an hour; or that young ladies sought the graces of delivery, and young gentlemen the proprieties of diction (see advertisement again) from his experienced tongue. But he got on in other ways, nevertheless. Sometimes he was hired to drill the boys on a speech day at a country school. Sometimes he was engaged to prevent provincial amateur actors from murdering the dialogue outright, and incessantly jostling each other on the stage. In this last capacity, he occasionally got good employment, especially with regular amateur societies, who found his terms cheap enough, and his knowledge of theatrical discipline inestimably useful.

But chances like these were as nothing to the chances he got when he was occasionally employed to superintend all the toilsome part of the business in arranging private theatricals at country houses. Here, he met with greater generosity than he had ever dared to expect: here, the letter from Mr Kemble, vouching for his honesty and general stage-knowledge—the great actor's legacy of kindness to him, which he carried about everywhere—was sure to produce prodigious effect. He and little Annie, and a third member of the family whom I shall hereafter introduce, lived for months together on the proceeds of such a windfall as a private theatrical party—for the young people, in the midst of their amusement, found leisure to pity the poor old ex-player, and to admire his pretty granddaughter; and liberally paid him for his services full five times as much as he would ever have ventured to ask.

Thus, wandering about from town to town, sometimes miserably unsuccessful, sometimes re-animated by a little prosperity, he had come from Stratford-upon-Avon, while the present century was some twenty-five years younger than it is now, to try his luck at elocution with the people of Tidbury-on-the-Marsh—to teach the graces of delivery at seventy years of age, with half his teeth gone! Will he succeed? I, for one, hope so. There is something in the spectacle of this poor old man, sorely battered by the world, yet still struggling for life and for the grandchild whom he loves better than life—struggling hard, himself a remnant of a bygone age, to keep up with a new age which has already got past him, and will hardly hear his feeble voice of other times, except to laugh at it—there is surely something in this which forbids all thought of ridicule, and bids fair with everybody for compassion and goodwill.

But we have had talk enough, by this time, about Mr Reuben Wray. Let us now go at once and make acquaintance with him—not forgetting his mysterious cash box—at No. 12.

III

The breakfast things are laid in the little drawing-room at Reuben's lodgings. This drawing-room, observe, has not been hired by our friend; he never possessed such a domestic luxury in his life. The apartment, not being taken, has only been lent to him by his landlady, who is hugely impressed by the tragic suavity of her new tenant's manner and "delivery". The breakfast things, I say again, are laid. Three cups, a loaf, half-a-pound of salt butter, some moist sugar in a saucer, and a black earthenware tea-pot, with a broken spout; such are the sumptuous preparations which tempt Mr Wray and his family to come down at nine o'clock in the morning, and yet nobody appears!

Hark! there is a sound of creaking boots, descending, apparently, from some loft at the top of the house, so distant is the noise they make at first. This sound, coming heavily nearer and nearer, only stops at the drawing-room door, and heralds the entry of—

Mr Wray, of course? No!—no such luck: my belief is, that we shall never succeed in getting to Mr Wray personally. The individual in question is not even any relation of his; but he is a member of the family, for all that; and as the first to come downstairs, he certainly merits the reward of immediate notice.

He is nearly six feet high, proportionately strong and stout, and looks about thirty years of age. His gait is as awkward as it well can be; his features are large and ill-proportioned, his face is pitted with the small-pox, and what hair he has on his head—not much—seems to be growing in all sorts of contrary directions at once. I know nothing about him, personally, that I can praise, but his expression; and that is so thoroughly good-humoured, so candid, so innocent even, that it really makes amends for everything else. Honesty and kindliness look out so brightly from his eyes, as to dazzle your observation of his clumsy nose, and lumpy mouth and chin, until you hardly know whether they are ugly or not. Some men, in a certain sense, are ugly with the lineaments of the Apollo Belvedere; and others handsome, with features that might sit for a caricature. Our new acquaintance was of the latter order.

Allow me to introduce him to you:—*the gentle reader—Julius Caesar*. Stop! start not at those classic syllables; I will explain all.

The history of Mr Martin Blunt, alias "Julius Caesar," is a good deal like the history of Mr Reuben Wray. Like him, Blunt began life with strolling players—not, however, as an actor, but as stage-carpenter, candle-snuffer, door-keeper, and general errand-boy. On one occasion, when the company were ambitiously bent on the horrible profanation of performing Shakespeare's Julius Caesar, the actor who was to personate the emperor fell ill. Nobody was left to supply his place—every other available member of the company was engaged in the play; so, in despair, they resorted to Martin Blunt. He was big enough for a Roman hero; and that was all they looked to.

They first cut out as much of his part as they could, and then half crammed the rest into his reluctant brains; they clapped a white sheet about the poor lad's body for a toga, stuck a truncheon into his hand, and a short beard on his chin; and remorselessly pushed him on the stage. His performance was received with shouts of laughter; but he went through it; was duly assassinated; and fell with a thump that shook the surrounding scenery to its centre, and got him a complete round of applause all to himself.

He never forgot this. It was his first and last appearance; and, in the innocence of his heart, he boasted of it on every occasion, as the great distinction of his life. When he found his way to London; and as a really skilful carpenter, procured employment at Drury Lane, his fellow-workmen managed to get the story of his first performance out of him directly, and made a standing joke of it. He was elected a general butt, and nicknamed "Julius Caesar," by universal acclamation. Everybody conferred on him that classic title; and I only follow the general fashion in these pages. If you don't like the name, call him any other you please: he is too good-humoured to be offended with you, do what you will.

He was thus introduced to old Wray:—

At the time when Reuben was closing his career at Drury Lane, our stout young carpenter had just begun to work there. One night, about a week before the performance of a new Pantomime, some of the heavy machinery tottered just as Wray was passing by it; and would have fallen on him, but for "Julius Caesar" (I really can't call him Blunt!), who, at the risk of his own limbs, caught the tumbling mass; and by a tremendous exertion of main strength arrested it in its fall, till the old man had hobbled out of harm's way. This led to gratitude, friendship, intimacy. Wray and his preserver, in spite of the difference in their characters and ages, seemed to suit each other, somehow. In fine, when Reuben started to teach elocution in the country, the carpenter followed him, as protector, assistant, servant, or whatever you please.

"Julius Caesar" had one special motive for attaching himself to old Wray's fortunes, which will speedily appear, when little Annie enters the drawing-room. Awkward as he might be, he was certainly no encumbrance. He made himself useful and profitable in fifty different ways. He took round handbills soliciting patronage; constructed the scenery when Mr Wray got private theatrical engagements; worked as journeyman-carpenter when other resources failed; and was, in fact, ready for anything, from dunning for a bad debt, to cleaning a pair of boots. His master might at times be as fretful as he pleased, and treat him like an infant during occasional fits of crossness—he never replied, and never looked sulky. The only things he could not be got to do, were to abstain from inadvertently knocking everything down that came in his reach, and to improve the action of his arms and legs on the principle of the late Mr Kemble.

Let us return to the drawing-room, and the breakfast-things. "Julius Caesar," of the creaking boots, came into the room with a small work-box (which he had been secretly engaged in making for some time past) in one hand, and a new muslin cravat in the other. It was Annie's birthday. The box was a present; the cravat, what the French would call, a homage to the occasion.

His first proceeding was to drop the work-box, and pick it up again in a great hurry; his second, to go to the looking glass (no such piece of furniture ornamented his loft bedroom), and try to put on the new cravat. He had only half tied it, and was hesitating, utterly helpless, over the bow, when a light step sounded on the floor-cloth outside. Annie came in.

"Julius Caesar at the looking-glass! Oh, good gracious, what can have come to him!" exclaimed the little girl with a merry laugh.

How fresh, and blooming, and pretty she looked, as she ran up the next moment; and telling him to stoop, tied his cravat directly—standing on tiptoe. "There," she cried, "now that's done, what have you got to say to me, sir, on my birthday!"

"I've got a box; and I'm so glad it's your birthday," says Julius Caesar, too confused by the suddenness of the cravat-tying to know exactly what he is talking about.

"Oh, what a splendid work-box! how kind of you, to be sure! what care I shall take of it! Come, sir, I suppose I must tell you to give me a kiss after that," and, standing on tiptoe again, she held up her fresh rosy cheek to be kissed, with such a pretty mixture of bashfulness, gratitude, and arch enjoyment in her look, that "Julius Caesar," I regret to say, felt inclined then and there to go down upon both his knees and worship her outright.

Before the decorous reader has time to consider all this very improper, I had better, perhaps, interpose a word, and explain that Annie Wray had promised Martin Blunt, (I give his real name again here, because this is serious business,) yes; had actually promised him that one day she would be his wife. She kept all her promises; but I can tell you she was especially determined to keep this.

Impossible! exclaims the lady reader. With her good looks she might aspire many degrees above a poor carpenter; besides, how could she possibly care about a great lumpish, awkward fellow, who is ugly, say what you will about his expression?

I might reply, madam, that our little Annie had looked rather deeper than the skin in choosing her husband; and had found out certain qualities of heart and disposition about this poor carpenter, which made her love—aye, and respect and admire him too. But I prefer asking you a question, by way of answer. Did you never meet with any individuals of your own sex, lovely, romantic, magnificent young women, who have fairly stupefied the whole circle of their relatives and friends by marrying particularly short, scrubby, matter-of-fact, middle-aged men, showing, too, every symptom of fondness for them into the bargain? I fancy you must have seen such cases as I have mentioned; and, when you can explain them to my satisfaction, I shall be happy to explain the anomalous engagement of little Annie to yours.

In the meantime it may be well to relate, that this odd love affair was only once hinted at to Mr Wray. The old man flew into a frantic passion directly; and threatened dire extremities if the thing was ever thought of more. Lonely, and bereaved of all other ties, as he was, he had, in regard to his granddaughter, that jealousy of other people loving her, which is of all weaknesses, in such cases as his, the most pardonable and the most pure. If a duke had asked for Annie in marriage, I doubt very much whether Mr Wray would have let him have her, except upon the understanding that they were all to live together.

Under these circumstances, the engagement was never hinted at again. Annie told her lover they must wait, and be patient, and remain as brother and sister to one another, till better chances and better times came. And "Julius Caesar" listened, and strictly obeyed. He was a good deal like a large, faithful dog to his little betrothed: he loved her, watched over her, guarded her, with his whole heart and strength; only asking in return, the privilege of fulfilling her slightest wish.

Well; this kiss, about which I have been digressing so long, was fortunately just over, when another footstep sounded outside; the door opened; and—yes! we have got him at last, in his own proper person! Enter Mr Reuben Wray!

Age has given him a stoop, which he tries to conceal, but cannot. His cheeks are hollow; his face is seamed with wrinkles, the work not only of time, but of trial, too. Still, there is vitality of mind, courage of heart about the old man, even yet. His look has not lost all its animation, nor his smile its warmth. There is the true Kemble walk, and the true Kemble carriage of the head for you, if you like!—there is the second-hand tragic grandeur and propriety, which the unfortunate "Julius Caesar" daily contemplates, yet cannot even faintly copy! Look at his dress, again. Threadbare as it is (patched, I am afraid, in some places), there is not a speck of dust on it, and what little hair is left on his bald head is as carefully brushed as if he rejoiced in the love-locks of Absalom himself. No! though misfortune, and disappointment, and grief, and heavy-handed penury have all been assailing him ruthlessly enough for more than half a century, they have not got the brave old fellow down yet! At seventy years of age he is still on his legs in the prize-ring of Life; badly punished all over (as the pugilists say), but determined to win the fight to the last!

"Many happy returns of the day, my love," says old Reuben, going up to Annie, and kissing her. "This is the twentieth birthday of yours I've lived to see. Thank God for that!"

"Look at my present, grandfather," cries the little girl, proudly showing her work-box. "Can you guess who made it?"

"You are a good fellow, Julius Caesar!" exclaims Mr Wray, guessing directly. "Good morning; shake hands."—(Then, in a lower voice to Annie)—"Has he broken anything in particular, since he's been up?" "No!" "I'm very glad to hear it. Julius Caesar, let me offer you a pinch of snuff," and here he pulled out his box quite in the Kemble style. He had his natural manner, and his Kemble manner. The first only appeared when anything greatly pleased or affected him—the second was for those ordinary occasions when he had time to remember that he was a teacher of elocution, and a pupil of the English Roscius.

"Thank ye, kindly, sir," said the gratified carpenter, cautiously advancing his huge finger and thumb towards the offered box.

"Stop!" cried old Wray, suddenly withdrawing it. He always lectured to Julius Caesar on elocution when he had nobody else to teach, just to keep his hand in. "Stop! that won't do. In the first place, "Thank ye, kindly, sir," though good-humoured, is grossly inelegant. "Sir, I am obliged to you," is the proper phrase—mind you sound the i in obliged—never say obleeged, as some people do; and remember, what I am now telling you, Mr Kemble once said to the Prince Regent! The next hint I have to give is this—never take your pinch of snuff with your right hand finger and thumb; it should be always the left. Perhaps you would like to know why?"

"Yes, please, sir," says the admiring disciple, very humbly.

" 'Yes, if you please, sir,' would have been better; but let that pass as a small error.—And now, I will tell you why, in an anecdote. Matthews was one day mimicking Mr Kemble to his face, in Penruddock—the great scene where he stops to take a pinch of snuff. 'Very good, Matthews; very like me,' says Mr Kemble complacently, when Matthews had done; 'but you have made one great mistake.' 'What's that?' cries Matthews sharply. 'My friend, you have not represented me taking snuff like a gentleman: now, I always do. You took your pinch, in imitating my Penruddock, with your right hand: I use my left—a gentleman invariably does, because then he has his right hand always clean from tobacco to give to his friend!'—There! remember that: and now you may take your pinch."

Mr Wray next turned round to speak to Annie; but his voice was instantly drowned in a perfect explosion of sneezes, absolutely screamed out by the unhappy "Julius Caesar," whose nasal nerves were convulsed by the snuff. Mentally determining never to offer his box to his faithful follower again, old Reuben gave up making his proposed remark, until they were all quietly seated round the breakfast table: then, he returned to the charge with renewed determination.

"Annie, my dear," said he, "you and I have read a great deal together of our divine Shakespeare, as Mr Kemble always called him. You are my regular pupil, you know, and ought to be able to quote by this time almost as much as I can. I am going to try you with something quite new—suppose I had offered you the pinch of snuff (Mr Julius Caesar shall never have another, I can promise him); what would you have said from Shakespeare applicable to that? Just think now!"

"But, grandfather, snuff wasn't invented in Shakespeare's time—was it?" said Annie.

"That's of no consequence," retorted the old man: "Shakespeare was for all time: you can quote him for everything in the world, as long as the world lasts. Can't you quote him for snuff? I can. Now, listen. You say to me, "I offer you a pinch of snuff?" I answer from Cymbeline (Act iv, scene 2): "Pisanio! I'll now taste of thy drug." There! won't that do? What's snuff but a drug for the nose? It just fits—everything of the divine Shakespeare's does, when you know him by heart, as I do—eh, little Annie? And now give me some more sugar; I wish it was lump for your sake, dear; but I'm afraid we can only afford moist. Anybody called about the advertisement? A new pupil this morning—eh?"

No! no pupils at all: not a man, woman, or child in the town, to teach elocution to yet! Mr Wray was not at all despondent about this; he had made up his mind that a pupil must come in the course of the day; and that was enough for him. His little quibbling from Shakespeare about the snuff had put him in the best of good humours. He went on making quotations, talking elocution, and eating bread and butter, as brisk and happy, as if all Tidbury had combined to form one mighty class for him, and resolved to pay ready money for every lesson.

But after breakfast, when the things were taken away, the old man seemed suddenly to recollect something which changed his manner altogether. He grew first embarrassed; then silent; then pulled out his Shakespeare, and began to read with ostentatious assiduity, as if he were especially desirous that nobody should speak to him.

At the same time, a close observer might have detected Mr "Julius Caesar" making various uncouth signs and grimaces to Annie, which the little girl apparently understood, but did not know how to answer. At last, with an effort, as if she were summoning extraordinary resolution, she said:—

"Grandfather—you have not forgotten your promise?"

No answer from Mr Wray. Probably, he was too much absorbed over Shakespeare to hear.

"Grandfather," repeated Annie, in a louder tone; "you promised to explain a certain mystery to us, on my birthday."

Mr Wray was obliged to hear this time. He looked up with a very perplexed face.

"Yes, dear," said he; "I did promise; but I almost wish I had not. It's rather a dangerous mystery to explain, little Annie, I can tell you! Why should you be so very curious to know about it?"

"I'm sure, grandfather," pleaded Annie, "you can't say I am over-curious, or Julius Caesar either, in wanting to know it. Just recollect—we had been only three days at Stratford-upon-Avon, when you came in, looking so dreadfully frightened, and said we must go away directly. And you made us pack up; and we all went off in a hurry, more like prisoners escaping, than honest people."

"We did!" groaned old Reuben, beginning to look like a culprit already.

"Well," continued Annie; "and you wouldn't tell us a word of what it was all for, beg as hard as we might. And then, when we asked why you never let that old cash box (which I used to keep my odds and ends in) out of your own hands, after we left Stratford—you wouldn't tell us that, either, and ordered us never to mention the thing again. It was only in one of your particular good humours, that I just got you to promise you would tell us all about it on my next birthday—to celebrate the day, you said. I'm sure we are to be trusted with any secrets; and I don't think it's being very curious to want to know this."

"Very well," said Mr Wray, rising, with a sort of desperate calmness; "I've promised, and, come what may, I'll keep my promise. Wait here; I'll be back directly." And he left the room, in a great hurry.

He returned immediately, with the cash box. A very battered, shabby affair, to make such a mystery about! thought Annie, as he put the box on the table, and solemnly laid his hands across it.

"Now, then," said old Wray, in his deepest tragedy tones, and with very serious looks; "Promise me, on your word of honour—both of you—that you'll never say a word of what I'm going to tell, to anybody, on any account whatever—I don't care what happens—on any account whatever!"

Annie and her lover gave their promises directly, and very seriously. They were getting a little agitated by all these elaborate preparations for the coming disclosure.

"Shut the door!" said Mr Wray, in a stage whisper. "Now sit close and listen; I'm ready to explain the mystery."

IV

"I suppose," said old Reuben, "you have neither of you forgotten that, on the second day of our visit to Stratford, I went out in the afternoon to dine with an intimate friend of mine, whom I'd known from a boy, and who lived at some little distance from the town—"

"Forget that!" cried Annie! "I don't think we ever shall—I was frightened about you, all the time you were gone."

"Frightened about what?" asked Mr Wray sharply. "Do you mean to tell me, Annie, you suspected—"

"I don't know what I suspected, grandfather; but I thought your going away by yourself, to sleep at your friend's house (as you told us), and not to come back till the next morning, something very extraordinary. It was the first time we had ever slept under different roofs—only think of that!"

"I'm ashamed to say, my dear"—rejoined Mr Wray, suddenly beginning to look and speak very uneasily—"that I turned hypocrite, and something worse, too, on that occasion. I deceived you. I had no friend to go and dine with; and I didn't pass that night in any house at all."

"Grandfather!"—cried Annie, jumping up in a fright—"What can you mean!"

"Beg pardon, sir," added "Julius Caesar," turning very red, and slowly clenching both his enormous fists as he spoke—"Beg pardon; but if you was put upon, or made fun of by any chaps that night, I wish you'd just please tell me where I could find 'em."

"Nobody ill-used me," said the old man, in steady, and even solemn tones. "I passed that night by the grave of William Shakespeare, in Stratford-upon-Avon Church!"

Annie sank back into her seat, and lost all her pretty complexion in a moment. The worthy carpenter gave such a start, that he broke the back rail of his chair. It was a variation on his usual performances of this sort, which were generally confined to cups, saucers, and wine-glasses.

Mr Wray took no notice of the accident. This was of itself enough to show that he was strongly agitated by something. After a momentary silence, he spoke again, completely forgetting the Kemble manner and the Kemble elocution, as he went on.

"I say again, I passed all that night in Stratford Church; and you shall know for what. You went with me, Annie, in the morning—it was Tuesday: yes, Tuesday morning—to see Shakespeare's bust in the church. You looked at it, like other people, just as a curiosity—I looked at it, as the greatest treasure in the world; the only true likeness of Shakespeare! It's been done from a mask, taken from his own face, after death—I know it: I don't care what people say, I know it. Well, when we went home, I felt as if I'd seen Shakespeare himself, risen from the dead! Strangers would laugh if I told them so; but it's true—I did feel it. And this thought came across me, quick, like the shooting of a sudden pain:— I must make that face of Shakespeare mine; my possession, my companion, my great treasure that no money can pay for! And I've got it!—Here!—the only cast in the world from the Stratford bust is locked up in this old cash box!"

He paused a moment. Astonishment kept both his auditors silent.

"You both know," he continued, "that I was bred apprentice to a statuary. Among other things, he taught me to take casts: it was part of our business—the easiest part. I knew I could take a mould off the Stratford bust, if I had the courage; and the courage came to me: on the Tuesday, it came. I went and bought some plaster, some soft soap, and a quart basin—those were my materials—and tied them up together in an old canvas bag. Water was all I wanted besides; and that I saw in the church vestry, in the morning—a jug of it, left I suppose since Sunday, where it had been put for the clergyman's use. I could carry my bag under my cloak quite comfortably, you understand. The only thing that troubled me now was how to get into the church again, without being suspected. While I was thinking, I passed the inn door. Some people were on the steps, talking to some other people in the street: they were making an appointment to go all together, and see Shakespeare's bust and grave that very afternoon. This was enough for me: I determined to go into the church with them."

"What! and stop there all night, grandfather?"

"And stop there all night, Annie. Taking a mould, you know, is not a very long business; but I wanted to take mine unobserved; and the early morning, before anybody was up, was the only time to do that safely in the church. Besides, I wanted plenty of leisure, because I wasn't sure I should succeed at first, after being out of practice so long in making casts. But you shall hear how I did it, when the time comes. Well, I made up the story about dining and sleeping at my friend's, because I didn't know what might happen, and because—because, in short, I didn't like to tell you what I was going to do. So I went out secretly, near the church; and waited for the party coming. They were late—late in the afternoon, before they came. We all went in together; I with my bag, you know, hid under my cloak. The man who showed us over the church in the morning, luckily for me, wasn't there: an old woman took his duty for him in the afternoon. I waited till the visitors were all congregated round Shakespeare's grave, bothering the poor woman with foolish questions about him. I knew that was my time, and slipped off into the vestry, and opened the cupboard, and hid myself among the surplices, as quiet as a mouse. After a while, I heard one of the strangers in the church (they were very rude, boisterous people) asking the other, what had become of the 'old fogey with the cloak?' and the other answered that he must have gone out, like a wise man, and that they had all better go after him, for it was precious cold and dull in the church. They went away: I heard the doors shut, and knew I was locked in for the night."

"All night in a church! Oh, grandfather, how frightened you must have been!"

"Well, Annie, I was a little frightened; but more at what I was going to do, than at being alone in the church. Let me get on with my story though. Being autumn weather, it grew too dark after the people went, for me to do anything then; so I screwed my courage up to wait for the morning. The first thing I did was to go and look quietly, all by myself, at the bust; and I made up my mind that I could take the mould in about three or four pieces. All I wanted was what they call a mask: that means just a forehead and face, without the head. It's an easy thing to take a mask off a bust—I knew I could do it; but, somehow, I didn't feel quite comfortable just then. The bust began to look very awful to me, in the fading light, all alone in the church. It was almost like looking at the ghost of Shakespeare, in that place, and at that time. If the door hadn't been locked, I think I should have run out of the church; but I couldn't do that; so I knelt down and kissed the grave-stone—a curious fancy coming over me as I did so, that it was like wishing Shakespeare good night—and then I groped my way back to the vestry. When I got in, and had shut the door between me and the grave, I grew bolder, I can tell you; and thought to myself—I'm doing no harm; I'm not going to hurt the bust; I only want what an Englishman and an old actor may fairly covet, a copy of Shakespeare's face; why shouldn't I eat my bit of supper here, and say my prayers as usual, and get my nap into the bargain, if I can? Just as I thought that—*bang* went the clock, striking the hour! It almost knocked me down, bold as I felt the moment before. I was obliged to wait till it was all still again, before I could pull the bit of bread and cheese I had got with me out of my pocket. And when I did, I couldn't eat: I was too impatient for the morning; so I sat down in the parson's armchair; and tried, next, whether I could sleep at all."

"And could you, grandfather?"

"No—I couldn't sleep either; at least, not at first. It was quite dark now; and I began to feel cold and awe-struck again. The only thing I could think of to keep up my spirits at all, was first saying my prayers, and then quoting Shakespeare. I went at it, Annie, like a dragon; play after play—except the tragedies; I was afraid of them, in a church at night, all by myself. Well: I think I had got half through the Midsummer Night's Dream, whispering over bit after bit of it; when I whispered myself into a doze. Then I fell into a queer sleep; and then I had such a dream! I dreamt that the church was full of moonlight—brighter moonlight than ever I saw awake. I walked out of the vestry; and there were the fairies of the Midsummer Night's Dream—all creatures like sparks of silver light—dancing round the Shakespeare bust! The moment they caught sight of me, they all called out in their sweet nightingale voices:—'Come along, Reuben! sly old Reuben! we know what you're here for, and we don't mind you a bit! You love Shakespeare, and so do we—dance, Reuben, and be happy! Shakespeare likes an old actor; he was an actor himself—nobody sees us! we're out for the night! foot it, old Reuben—foot it away!' And we all danced like mad: now, up in the air; now, down on the pavement; and now, all round the bust five hundred thousand times at least without stopping, till—*bang* went the clock! and I woke up in the dark, in a cold perspiration."

"I'm in one too!" gasped "Julius Caesar," dabbing his brow vehemently with a ragged cotton pocket handkerchief.

"Well, after that dream I fell to reciting again; and got another doze; and had another dream—a terrible one, about ghosts and witches, that I don't recollect so well as the other. I woke up once more, cold, and in a great fright that I'd slept away all the precious morning daylight. No! all dark still! I went into the church again, and then back to the vestry, not being able to stay there. I suppose I did this a dozen times without knowing why. At last, never going to sleep again, I got somehow through the night—the night that seemed never to be done. Soon after daybreak, I began to walk up and down the church briskly, to get myself warm, keeping at it for a long time. Then, just as I saw through the windows that the sun was rising, I opened my bag at last, and got ready for work. I can tell you my hand trembled and my sight grew dim—I think the tears were in my eyes; but I don't know why—as I first soaped the bust all over to prevent the plaster I was going to put on it from sticking. Then I mixed up the plaster and water in my quart basin, taking care to leave no lumps, and finding it come as natural to me as if I had only left the statuary's shop yesterday; then—but it's no use telling you, little Annie, about what you don't understand; I'd better say shortly I made the mould, in four pieces, as I thought I should—two for the upper part of the face, and two for the lower. Then, having put on the outer plaster case to hold the mould, I pulled all off clean together, and looked, and knew that I had got a mask of Shakespeare from the Stratford bust!"

"Oh, grandfather, how glad you must have been then!"

"No, that was the odd part of it. At first, I felt as if I had robbed the bank, or the King's jewels, or had set fire to a train of gunpowder to blow up all London; it seemed such a thing to have done! Such a tremendously daring, desperate thing! But, a little while after, a frantic sort of joy came over me: I could hardly prevent myself from shouting and singing at the top of my voice. Then I felt a perfect fever of impatience to cast the mould directly; and see whether the mask would come out without a flaw. The keeping down that impatience was the hardest thing I had had to do since I first got into the church."

"But, please, sir, whenever did you get out at last? Do pray tell us that!" asked "Julius Caesar".

"Not till after the clock had struck twelve, and I'd eaten all my bread and cheese," said Mr Wray, rather piteously. "I was glad enough when I heard the church door open at last, from the vestry where I had popped in but a moment before. It was the same woman came in who had shown the bust in the afternoon. I waited my time; and then slipped into the church; but she turned round sharply, just as I'd got half way out, and came up to me. I never was frightened by an old woman before; but I can tell you, she frightened me. 'Oh! there are you again!' says she: 'Come, I say! this won't do. You sneaked out yesterday afternoon without paying anything; and you sneak in again after me, as soon as I open the door this morning—ain't you ashamed of being so shabby as that, at your age?—ain't you?' I never paid money in my life, Annie, with pleasure, till I gave that old woman some to stop her mouth! And I don't recollect either that I'd ever tried to run since leaving the stage (where we had a good deal of running, first and last, in the battle scenes); but I ran as soon as I got well away from the church, I can promise you—ran almost the whole way home."

"That's what made you look so tired when you came in, grandfather," said Annie; "we couldn't think what was the matter with you at the time."

"Well," continued the old man, "as soon as I could possibly get away from you, after coming back, I went and locked myself into my bedroom, pulled the mould in a great hurry out of the canvas bag, and took the cast at once—a beautiful cast! a perfect cast! I never produced a better when I was in good practice, Annie! When I sat down on the side of the bed, and looked at Shakespeare—my Shakespeare—got with so much danger, and made with my own hands—so white and pure and beautiful, just out of the mould! Old as I am, it was all I could do to keep myself from dancing for joy!"

"And yet, grandfather," said Annie reproachfully, "you could keep all that joy to yourself: you could keep it from me!"

"It was wrong my love, wrong on my part not to trust you—I'm sorry for it now. But the joy, after all, lasted a very little while—only from the afternoon to the evening. In the evening, if you remember, I went out to the butcher's to buy something for my own supper; something I could fancy, to make me comfortable before I went to bed (you little thought how I wanted my bed that night!). Well, when I got into the shop, several people were there; and what do you think they were all talking about? It makes me shudder even to remember it now! They were talking about a cast having been taken—feloniously taken, just fancy that, from the Stratford bust!"

Annie looked pale again instantly at this part of the story. As for "Julius Caesar," though he said nothing, he was evidently suffering from a second attack of the sympathetic cold perspiration which had already troubled him. He used the cotton handkerchief more copiously than ever just at this moment.

"The butcher was speaking when I came in," pursued Mr Wray. "'Who's been and took it,' says the fellow, (his grammar and elocution were awful, Annie!) 'nobody don't know yet; but the Town Council will know by to-morrow, and then he'll be took himself.' 'Ah," says a dirty little man in black, 'he'll be cast into prison, for taking a cast—eh?' They laughed, actually laughed at this vile pun. Then another man asked how it had been found out. 'Some says,' answered the butcher, 'he was seen a doin' of it, through the window, by some chap looking in accidental like: some says, nobody don't know but the churchwardens, and they won't tell till they've got him.' 'Well," says a woman, waiting with a basket to be served, 'but how will they get him?—(two chops, please, when you're quite ready)—that's the thing: how will they get him?' 'Quite easy; take my word for it;' says the man who made the bad pun. 'In the first place, they've posted up handbills, offering a reward for him; in the second place, they're going to examine the people who show the church; in the third place—' 'Bother your places!' cried the woman, 'I wish I could get my chops.' 'There you are Mum,' says the butcher, cutting off the chops, 'and if you want my opinion about this business, it's this here: they'll transport him right away, in no time.' 'They can't,' cries the dirty man, 'they can only imprison him.' 'For life—eh?' says the woman, going off with the chops. 'Be so kind as to let me have a couple of kidneys,' said I; for my knees knocked together, and I could stand it no longer."

"Then you thought, grandfather, that they suspected you?"

"I thought everything that was horrible, Annie. However, I got my kidneys, and went out unhindered, leaving them still talking about it. On my way home I saw the handbill—the handbill itself! Ten pounds reward for apprehending the man who had taken the cast! I read it twice through, in a sort of trance of terror. My mask taken away, and myself put in prison, if not transported—that was the prospect I had to give me an appetite for the kidneys. There was only one thing to be done: to get away from Stratford while I had the chance. The night-coach went that very evening, straight through to this place, which was far enough off for safety. We had some money, you know, left, after that last private-theatrical party, where they treated us so generously. In short, I made you pack up, Annie, as you said just now, and got you both off by the coach, in time, not daring to speak a word about my secret, and as miserable as I could be the whole journey. But let us say no more about that—here we are, safe and sound! and here's my face of Shakespeare—my diamond above all price—safe and sound, too! You shall see it; you shall look at the mask, both of you, and then, I hope, you'll acknowledge that you know as much as I do about the mystery!"

"But the mould," cried Annie; "haven't you got the mould with you, too?"

"Lord bless my soul!" exclaimed Mr Wray, slapping both hands, in desperation, on the lid of the cash box. "Between the fright and the hurry of getting away, I quite forgot it—it's left at Stratford!"

"Left at Stratford!" echoed Annie, with a vague feeling of dismay, that she could not account for.

"Yes: rolled up in the canvas bag, and poked behind the landlord's volumes of the Annual Register, on the top shelf of the cupboard, in my bedroom. Between thinking of how to take care of the mask, and how to take care of myself, I quite forgot it. Don't look so frightened, Annie! The people at the lodgings are not likely to find it; and if they did, they wouldn't know what it was, and would throw it away. I've got the mask; and that's all I want—the mould is of no consequence to me, now—it's the mask that's everything—everything in the world!"

"I can't help feeling frightened, grandfather; and I can't help wishing you had brought away the mould, though I don't know why."

"You're frightened, Annie, about the Stratford people coming after me here—that's what you're frightened about. But, if you and Julius Caesar keep the secret from everybody—and I know you will—there is no fear at all. They won't catch me back at Stratford again, or you either; and if the churchwardens themselves found the mould, that wouldn't tell them where I was gone, would it? Look up, you silly little Annie! We're quite safe here. Look up, and see the great sight I'm going to show you—a sight that nobody in England can show, but me;—the mask! the mask of Shakespeare!"

His cheeks flushed, his fingers trembled, as he took the key out of his pocket and put it into the lock of the old cash box. "Julius Caesar," breathless with wonder and suspense, clapped both his hands behind him, to make sure of breaking nothing this time. Even Annie caught the infection of the old man's triumph and delight, and breathed quicker than usual when she heard the click of the opening lock.

"There!" cried Mr Wray, throwing back the lid; "there is the face of William Shakespeare! there is the treasure which the greatest lord in this land doesn't possess—a copy of the Stratford bust! Look at the forehead! Who's got such a forehead now? Look at his eyes; look at his nose. He was not only the greatest man that ever lived, but the handsomest, too! Who says this isn't just what his face was; his face taken after death? Who's bold enough to say so? Just look at the mouth, dropped and open—that's one proof? Look at the cheek, under the right eye; don't you see a little paralytic gathering up of the muscle, not visible on the other side?—that's another proof! Oh, Annie, Annie! there's the very face that once looked out, alive and beaming, on this poor old world of ours! There's the man who's comforted me, informed me, made me what I am! There's the 'counterfeit presentment,' the precious earthly relic of that great spirit who is now with the angels in Heaven, and singing among the sweetest of them!"

His voice grew faint, and his eyes moistened. He stood looking at the mask, with a rapture and a triumph which no speech could express. At such moments as those, even through that poor, meagre face, the immortal spirit within could still shine out in the beauty which never dies!— even in that frail old earthly tenement, could still vindicate outwardly the divine destiny of all mankind!

They were yet gathered silently round the Shakespeare cast, when a loud knock sounded at the room door. Instantly, old Reuben banged down the lid of the cash box, and locked it; and as instantly, without waiting for permission to enter, a stranger walked in.

He was dressed in a long greatcoat, wore a red comforter round his neck, and carried a very old and ill-looking cat-skin cap in his hand. His face was uncommonly dirty; his eyes uncommonly inquisitive; his whiskers uncommonly plentiful; and his voice most uncommonly and determinately gruff, in spite of his efforts to dulcify it for the occasion.

"Miss, and gentlemen both, beggin' all your pardons," said this new arrival, "vich is Mr Wray?" As he spoke, his eyes travelled all round the room, seeing everything and everybody in it; and then glancing sharply at the cash box.

"I am Mr Wray, sir," exclaimed our old friend, considerably startled, but recovering the Kemble manner and the Kemble elocution as if by magic.

"Wery good," said the stranger. "Then beggin' your pardon again, sir, in pertickler, could you be so kind as to 'blige me with a card o' terms? It's for a young gentleman as wants you, Mr Wray," he continued in a whisper, approaching the old man, and quite abstractedly leaning one hand on the cash box.

"Take your hand off that box, sir," cried Mr Wray, in a very fierce manner, but with a very trembling voice. At the same moment "Julius Caesar" advanced a step or two, partially doubling his fist. The man with the cat-skin cap had probably never before been so nearly knocked down in his life. Perhaps he suspected as much; for he took his hand off the box in great hurry.

"It was inadwertent, sir," he remarked in explanation—"a little inadwertency of mine, that's all. But could you 'blige me vith that card o' terms? The young gentleman as wants it has heerd of your advertisement; and, bein' d'awful shaky in his pronounciashun, as vell as 'scruciatin' bad at readin' aloud, he's 'ard up for improvement—the sort o' secret thing you gives, you know, to the oraytors and the clujjymen, at three-and-six an hour. You'll heer from him in secret, Mr Wray, sir; and precious vork you'll 'ave to git him to rights; but do just 'blige me 'vith the card o' terms and the number of the 'ouse; 'cos I promised to git 'em for him today."

"There is a card, sir, and I will engage to improve his delivery be it ever so bad," said Mr Wray, considerably relieved at hearing the real nature of the stranger's errand.

"Miss, and gentlemen both, good mornin'," said the man, putting on his cat-skin cap, "you'll heer from the young gentleman today; and wotever you do, sir, mind you keep the h'applicashun a secret—mind that!" He winked; and went out.

"I declare," muttered Mr Wray, as the door closed, "I thought he was a thief-taker from Stratford. Think of his being only a messenger from a new pupil! I told you we should have a pupil today. I told you so."

"A very strange-looking messenger, grandfather, for a young gentleman to choose!" said Annie.

"He can't help his looks, my dear; and I'm sure we shan't mind them, if he brings us money. Have you seen enough of the mask? if you hav'nt I'll open the box again."

"Enough for today, I think, grandfather. But, tell me, why do you keep the mask in that old cash box?"

"Because I've nothing else, Annie, that will hold it, and lock up too. I was sorry, my dear, to disturb your "odds and ends," as you call them; but really there was nothing else to take. Stop! I've a thought! Julius Caesar shall make me a new box for the mask, and then you shall have your old one back again."

"I don't want it, grandfather! I'd rather we none of us had it. Carrying a cash box like that about with us, might make some people think we had money in it."

"Money! People think I have any money! Come, come, Annie! that really won't do! That's much too good a joke, you sly little puss, you!" And the old man laughed heartily, as he hurried off, to deposit the precious mask in his bedroom.

"You'll make that new box, Julius Caesar, won't you?" said Annie earnestly, as soon as her grandfather left the room.

"I'll get some wood, this very day," answered the carpenter, "and turn out such a box, by tomorrow, as—as—" He was weak at comparisons; so he stopped at the second "as".

"Make it quick, dear, make it quick," said the little girl, anxiously; "and then we'll give away the old cash box. If grandfather had only told us what he was going to do, at first, he need never have used it; for you could have made him a new box beforehand. But, never mind! make it quick, now!"

Oh, "Julius Caesar!" strictly obey your little betrothed in this, as in all other injunctions! You know not how soon that new box may be needed, or how much evil it may yet prevent!

V

Perhaps, by this time, you are getting tired of three such simple, homely characters as Mr and Miss Wray, and Mr "Julius Caesar," the carpenter. I strongly suspect you, indeed, of being downright anxious to have a little literary stimulant provided in the shape of a villain. You shall taste this stimulant—double distilled; for I have two villains all ready for you in the present chapter.

But, take my word for it, when you know your new company, you will be only too glad to get back again to Mr Wray and his family.

About three miles from Tidbury-on-the-Marsh, there is a village called Little London; sometimes, popularly entitled, in allusion to the characters frequenting it, "Hell-End." It is a dirty, ruinous-looking collection of some dozen cottages, and an ale-house. Ruffianly men, squalid women, filthy children, are its inhabitants. The chief support of this pleasant population is currently supposed to be derived from their connection with the poaching and petty larcenous interests of their native soil. In a word, Little London looks bad, smells bad, and is bad; a fouler blot of a village, in the midst of a prettier surrounding landscape, is not to be found in all England.

Our principal business is with the ale-house. The "Jolly Ploughboys" is the sign; and Judith Grimes, widow, is the proprietor. The less said about Mrs Grimes's character, the better; it is not quite adapted to bear discussion in these pages. Mrs Grimes's mother (who is now bordering on eighty) may be also dismissed to merciful oblivion; for, at her daughter's age, she was—if possible—rather the worse of the two. Towards her son, Mr Benjamin Grimes (as one of the rougher sex), I feel less inclined to be compassionate. When I assert that he was in every respect a complete specimen of a provincial scoundrel, I am guilty, according to a profound and reasonable maxim of our law, of uttering a great libel, because I am repeating a great truth.

You know the sort of man well. You have seen the great, hulking, heavy-browed, sallow-complexioned fellow often enough, lounging at village corners, with a straw in his mouth and a bludgeon in his hand. Perhaps you have asked your way of him; and have been answered by a growl and a petition for money; or, you have heard of him in connection with a cowardly assault on your rural policeman; or a murderous fight with your friend's gamekeeper; or a bad case for your other friend, the magistrate, at petty sessions. Anybody who has ever been in the country, knows the man—the ineradicable plague-spot of his whole neighbour-hood—as well as I do.

About eight o'clock in the evening, and on the same day which had been signalized by Mr Wray's disclosures, Mrs Grimes, senior—or, as she was generally called, "mother Grimes"—sat in her armchair in the private parlour of The Jolly Ploughboys, just making up her mind to go to bed. Her ideas on this subject rather wanted acceleration; and they got it from her dutiful son, Mr Benjamin Grimes.

"Coom, old 'ooman, why doesn't thee trot up stairs?" demanded this provincial worthy.

"I'm a-going, Ben,—gently, Judith!—I'm a-going!" mumbled the old woman, as Mrs Grimes, junior, entered the room, and very unceremoniously led her mother off.

"Mind thee doesn't let nobody in here tonight," bawled Benjamin, as his sister went out. "Chummy Dick's going to coom," he added, in a mysterious whisper.

Left to himself to await the arrival of Chummy Dick, Mr Grimes found time hung rather heavy on his hands. He first looked out of the window. The view commanded a few cottages and fields, with a wood beyond on the rising ground,—a homely scene enough in itself; but the heavenly purity of the shining moonlight gave it, just now, a beauty not its own. This beauty was not apparently to the taste of Mr Grimes, for he quickly looked away from the window back into the room. Staring dreamily, his sunken sinister grey eyes fixed upon the opposite wall, encountering there nothing but four coloured prints, representing the career of the prodigal son. He had seen them hundreds of times before; but he looked at them again from mere habit.

In the first of the series, the prodigal son was clothed in a bright red dress coat, and was just getting on horseback (the wrong side); while his father, in a bright blue coat, helped him on with one hand, and pointed disconsolately with the other to a cheese-coloured road, leading straight from the horse's fore-feet to a distant city in the horizon, entirely composed of towers. In the second plate, master prodigal was feasting between two genteel ladies, holding gold wine glasses in their hands; while a debauched companion sprawled on the ground by his side, in a state of cataleptic drunkenness. In the third, he lay on his back; his red coat torn, and showing his purple skin; one of his stockings off; a thunderstorm raging over his head, and two white sows standing on either side of him—one of them apparently feeding off the calf of his leg. In the fourth—

Just as Mr Grimes had got to the fourth print he heard somebody whistling a tune outside, and turned to the window. It was Chummy Dick; or, in other words, the man with the cat-skin cap, who had honoured Mr Wray with a morning call.

Chummy Dick's conduct on entering the parlour had the merit of originality as an exhibition of manners. He took no more notice of Mr Grimes than if he had not been in the room; drew his chair to the fireplace; put one foot on each of the hobs; pulled a little card out of his greatcoat pocket; read it; and then indulged himself in a long, steady, unctuous fit of laughter, cautiously pitched in what musicians would call the "minor key".

"What dost thee laugh about like that?" asked Grimes.

"Git us a glass of 'ot grog fust—two lumps o' sugar, mind!—and then, Benjamin, you'll know in no time!" said Chummy Dick, maintaining an undercurrent of laughter all the while he spoke.

While Benjamin is gone for the grog, there is time enough for a word or two of explanation.

Possibly you may remember that the young assistant at Messrs Dunball and Dark's happened to see Mr Wray carrying his cash box into No. 12. The same gust of wind which, by blowing aside old Reuben's cloak, betrayed what he had got under it to this assistant, exposed the same thing, at the same time, to the observation of Mr Grimes, who happened to be lounging about the High Street on the occasion in question. Knowing nothing about either the mask or the mystery connected with it, it was only natural that Benjamin should consider the cash box to be a receptacle for cash; and it was, furthermore, not at all out of character that he should ardently long to be possessed of that same cash, and should communicate his desire to Chummy Dick.

And for this reason. With all the ambition to be a rascal of first-rate ability, Mr Grimes did not possess the necessary cunning and capacity, and had not received the early London education requisite to fit him for so exalted a position. Stealing poultry out of a farmyard, for instance, was quite in Benjamin's line; but stealing a cash box out of a barred and bolted-up house, standing in the middle of a large town, was an achievement above his powers—an achievement that but one man in his circle of acquaintance was mighty enough to compass—and that man was Chummy Dick, the great London housebreaker. Certain recent passages in the life of this illustrious personage had rendered London and its neighbourhood very insecure, in his case, for purposes of residence, so he had retired to a safe distance in the provinces; and had selected Tidbury and the adjacent country as a suitable field for action, and a very pretty refuge from the Bow Street Runners into the bargain.

"Wery good, Benjamin; and not too sveet," remarked Chummy Dick, tasting the grog which Grimes had brought him. He was not, by any means, one of your ferocious housebreakers, except under strong provocation. There was more of oil than of aqua fortis in the mixture of his temperament. His robberies were marvels of skill, cunning, and cool determination. In short, he stole plate or money out of dwelling houses, as cats steal cream off breakfast tables—by biding his time, and never making a noise.

"Hast thee seen the cash box?" asked Grimes, in an eager whisper.

"Look at my 'and, Benjamin," was the serenely triumphant answer. "It's bin on the cash box! You're all right: the swag's ready for us."

"Swag! Wot be that?"

"That's swag!" said Chummy Dick, pulling half-a-crown out of his pocket, and solemnly holding it up for Benjamin's inspection. "I haven't got a fi' pun' note, or a christenin' mug about me; but notes and silver's swag, too. Now, young Grimes, you knows swag; and you'll have your swag before long, if you looks out sharp. If it ain't quite so fine a night tomorrer—if there ain't quite so much of that moonshine as there is now to let gratis for nothin'—why, we'll 'ave the cash box!"

"Half on it for me! Thee knows't that, Chummy Dick!"

"Check that 'ere talky-talky tongue of your'n; and you'll 'ave your 'alf. I've bin to see the old man; and he's gived me his wisitin' card, with the number of the 'ouse. Ho! ho! ho! think of his givin' his card to me! It's as good as inwitin' one to break into the 'ouse—it is, every bit!" And, with another explosion of laughter, Chummy Dick triumphantly threw Mr Wray's card into the fire.

"But that ain't the pint," he resumed, when he had recovered his breath. "We'll stick to the pint—the pint's the cash box." And, to do him justice, he did stick to the point, never straying away from it, by so much as a hair's breadth, for a full half-hour.

The upshot of the long harangue to which he now treated Mr Benjamin Grimes, was briefly this: he had invented a plan, after reading the old man's advertisement first, for getting into Mr Wray's lodgings unsuspected; he had seen the cash box with his own eyes, and was satisfied, from certain indications, that there was money in it—he held the owner of this property to be a miser, whose gains were all hoarded up in his cash box, stray shillings and stray sovereigns together—he had next found out who were the inmates of the house; and had discovered that the only formidable person sleeping at No. 12 was our friend the carpenter—he had then examined the premises; and had seen that they were easily accessible by the back drawing-room window, which looked out on the wash-house roof—finally, he had ascertained that the two watchmen appointed to guard the town, performed that duty by going to bed regularly at eleven o'clock, and leaving the town to guard itself; the whole affair was perfectly easy—too easy in fact for anybody but a young beginner.

"Now, Benjamin," said Chummy Dick, in conclusion—"mind this: no wiolence! Take your swag quiet, and you takes it safe. Wiolence is sometimes as bad as knockin' up a whole street—wiolence is the downy cracksman's last kick-out when he's caught in a fix. Fust and foremost, you've got your mask," (here he pulled out a shabby domino mask,) "wery good; nobody can't swear to you in that. Then, you've got your barker," (he produced a pistol,) "just to keep 'em quiet with the look of it, and if that won't do, there's your gag and bit o' rope" (he drew them forth,) "for their mouths and 'ands. Never pull your trigger, till you see another man ready to pull his. Then you must make your row; and then you make it to some purpose. The nobs in our business—remember this, young Grimes!—always takes the swag easy; and when they can't take it easy, they takes it as easy as they can. That's visdom—the visdom of life!"

"Why thee bean't a-going, man?" asked Benjamin in astonishment, as the philosophical housebreaker abruptly moved towards the door.

"Me and you must'nt be seen together, tomorrer," said Chummy Dick, in a whisper. "You let me alone: I've got business to do tonight—never mind wot! At eleven tomorrer night, you be at the cross roads that meets on the top of the common. Look out sharp; and you'll see me."

"But if so be it do keep moonshiny," suggested Grimes.

"On second thoughts, Benjamin," said the housebreaker, after a moment's reflection, "we'll risk all the moonshine as ever shone—High Street, Tidbury, ain't Bow Street, London!—we may risk it safe. Moon, or no moon, young Grimes! tomorrer night's our night!"

By this time he had walked out of the house. They separated at the door. The radiant moonlight falling lovely on all things, fell lovely even on them. How pure it was! how doubly pure, to shine on Benjamin Grimes and Chummy Dick, and not be soiled by the contact!

VI

During the whole remainder of Annie's birthday, Mr Wray sat at home, anxiously expecting the promised communication from the mysterious new pupil whose elocution wanted so much setting to rights. Though he never came, and never wrote, old Reuben still persisted in expecting him forthwith; and still waited for him as patiently the next morning, as he had waited the day before.

Annie sat in the room with her grandfather, occupied in making lace. She had learnt this art, so as to render herself, if possible, of some little use in contributing to the general support; and, sometimes, her manufacture actually poured a few extra shillings into the scantily filled family coffer. Her lace was not at all the sort of thing that your fine people would care to look at twice—it was just simple and pretty, like herself; and only sold (when it did sell, and that alas! was not often!) among ladies whose purses were very little better furnished than her own.

"Julius Caesar" was downstairs, in the back kitchen, making the all-important box—or, as the landlady irritably phrased it, "making a mess about the house." She was not partial to sawdust and shavings, and almost lost her temper when the glue pot invaded the kitchen fire. But work away, honest carpenter! Work away, and never mind her! Get the mask of Shakespeare out of the old box, and into the new, before night comes; and you will have done the best day's work you ever completed in your life!

Annie and her grandfather had a great deal of talk about the Shakespeare cast, while they were sitting together in the drawing-room. If I were to report all old Reuben's rhapsodies and quotations during that period, I might fill the whole remaining space accorded to me in this little book. It was only once that the conversation varied at all. Annie just asked, by way of changing the subject a little, how a plaster cast was taken from the mould; and Mr Wray instantly went off at a tangent, in the midst of a new quotation, to tell her. He was still describing, for the second time, how the plaster and water were to be mixed, how the mixture was to be left to "set," and how the mould was to be pulled off it, when the landlady, looking very hot and important, bustled into the room, exclaiming:—

"Mr Wray, sir! Mr Wray! Here's Squire Colebatch, of Cropley Court, coming upstairs to see you!" She then added, in a whisper: "He's very hot-tempered and odd, sir, but the best gentleman in the world—"

"That will do, ma'am! that will do!" interrupted a hearty voice, outside the door. "I can introduce myself; an old playwriter and an old play-actor don't want much introduction, I fancy! How are you, Mr Wray? I've come to make your acquaintance: how do you do, sir!"

Before the Squire came in, Mr Wray's first idea was that the young gentleman pupil had arrived at last—but when the Squire appeared, he discovered that he was mistaken. Mr Colebatch was an old gentleman with a very rosy face, with bright black eyes that twinkled incessantly, and with perfectly white hair, growing straight up from his head in a complete forest of venerable bristles. Moreover, his elocution wanted no improvement at all; and his "delivery" proclaimed itself at once, as the delivery of a gentleman—a very eccentric one, but a gentleman still.

"Now, Mr Wray," said the Squire, sitting down, and throwing open his greatcoat, with the air of an old friend; "I've a habit of speaking to the point, because I hate ceremony and botheration. My name's Matthew Colebatch; I live at Cropley Court, just outside the town; and I come to see you, because I've had an argument about your character with the Reverend Daubeny Daker, the Rector here!"

Astonishment bereft Mr Wray of all power of speech, while he listened to this introductory address.

"I'll tell you how it was, sir," continued the Squire. "In the first place, Daubeny Daker's a canting sneak—a sort of fellow who goes into poor people's cottages, asking what they've got for dinner, and when they tell him, he takes the cover off the saucepan and sniffs at it, to make sure that they've spoken the truth. That's what he calls doing his duty to the poor, and what I call being a canting sneak! Well, Daubeny Daker saw your advertisement in Dunball's shop window. I must tell you, by-the-by, that he calls theatres the devil's houses, and actors the devil's missionaries; I heard him say that in a sermon, and have never been into his church since! Well, sir, he read your advertisement; and when he came to that part about improving clergymen at three-and-sixpence an hour (it would be damned cheap to improve Daubeny Daker at that price!) he falls into one of his nasty, cold-blooded, sneering rages, goes into the shop, and insists on having the thing taken down, as an insult offered by a vagabond actor to the clerical character—don't lose your temper, Mr Wray, don't, for God's sake—I trounced him about it handsomely, I can promise you! And now, what do you think that fat jackass Dunball did, when he heard what the parson said? Took your card down!—took it out of the window directly, as if Daubeny Daker was King of Tidbury, and it was death to disobey him!"

"My character, sir!" interposed Mr Wray.

"Stop, Mr Wray! I beg your pardon; but I must tell you how I trounced him. Half an hour after the thing had been taken down, I dropped into the shop. Dunball, smiling like a fool, tells me about the business. 'Put it up again, directly!' said I; 'I won't have any man's character bowled down like that by people who don't know him!' Dunball makes a wry face and hesitates. I pull out my watch, and say to him, 'I give you a minute to decide between my custom and interest, and Daubeny Daker's.' I happen to be what's called a rich man, Mr Wray; so Dunball decided in about two seconds, and up went your advertisement again, just where it was before!"

"I have no words, sir, to thank you for your kindness," said poor old Reuben.

"Hear how I trounced Daubeny Daker, sir—hear that! I met him out at dinner, the same night. He was talking about you, and what he'd done— as proud as a peacock! @#In fact,@# says he, at the end of his speech, @#I considered it my duty, as a clergyman, to have the advertisement taken down.@# @#And I considered it my duty, as a gentleman,@# said I, @#to have it put up again.@# Then, we began the argument (he hates me, because I once wrote a play—I know he does). I won't tell you what he said, because it would distress you. But it ended, after we'd been at it, hammer and tongs, for about an hour, by my saying that his conduct in setting you down as a disreputable character, without making a single enquiry about you, showed a want of Christianity, justice, and common sense. @#I can bear with your infirmities of temper, Mr Colebatch,@# says he, in his nasty, sneering way; @#but allow me to ask, do you, who defend Mr Wray so warmly, know any more of him than I do?@# He thought this was a settler; but I was at him again, quick as lightning. @#No, sir; but I'll set you a proper example, by going tomorrow morning, and judging of the man from the man himself!@# That was a settler for him: and now, here I am this morning, to do what I said."

"I will show you, Mr Colebatch, that I have deserved the honour of being defended by you," said Mr Wray, with a mixture of artless dignity and manly gratitude in his manner, which became him wonderfully; "I have a letter, sir, from the late Mr Kemble—"

"What, my old friend, John Philip!" cried the Squire; "let's see it instantly! He, Mr Wray, was @#the noblest Roman of them all,@# as Shakespeare says."

Here was an inestimable friend indeed! He knew Mr Kemble and quoted Shakespeare. Old Reuben could actually have embraced the Squire at that moment; but he contented himself with producing the great Kemble letter.

Mr Colebatch read it, and instantly declared that, as a certificate of character, it beat all other certificates that ever were written completely out of the field; and established Mr Wray's reputation as above the reach of all calumny. "It's the most tremendous crusher for Daubeny Daker that ever was composed, sir!" Just as the old gentleman said this, his eyes encountered little Annie, who had been sitting quietly in the corner of the room, going on with her lace. He had hardly allowed himself leisure enough to look at her, in the first heat of his introductory address, but he made up for lost time now, with characteristic celerity.

"Who's that pretty little girl?" said he; and his bright eyes twinkled more than ever as he spoke.

"My granddaughter, Annie," answered Mr Wray, proudly.

"Nice little thing! how pretty and quiet she sits making her lace!" cried Mr Colebatch, enthusiastically. "Don't move, Annie; don't go away! I like to look at you! You won't mind a queer old bachelor, like me—will you? You'll let me look at you—won't you? Go on with your lace, my dear, and Mr Wray and I will go on with our chat."

This "chat" completed what the Kemble letter had begun. Encouraged by the Squire, old Reuben artlessly told the little story of his life, as if to an intimate friend; and told it with all the matchless pathos of simplicity and truth. What time Mr Colebatch could spare from looking at Annie—and that was not much—he devoted to anathematising his implacable enemy, Daubeny Daker, in a series of violent expletives; and anticipating, with immense glee, the sort of consummate "trouncing" he should now be able to inflict on that reverend gentleman, the next time he met with him. Mr Wray only wanted to take one step more after this in the Squire's estimation, to be considered the phoenix of all professors of elocution, past, present, and future: and he took it. He actually recollected the production of Mr Colebatch's play—a tragedy all bombast and bloodshed—at Drury Lane Theatre; and, more than that, he had himself performed one of the minor characters in it!

The Squire seized his hand immediately. This play (in virtue of which he considered himself a dramatic author,) was his weak point. It had enjoyed a very interrupted "run" of one night; and had never been heard of after. Mr Colebatch attributed this circumstance entirely to public misappreciation; and, in his old age, boasted of his tragedy wherever he went, utterly regardless of the reception it had met with. It has often been asserted that the parents of sickly children are the parents who love their children best. This remark is sometimes, and only sometimes, true. Transfer it, however, to the sickly children of literature, and it directly becomes a rule which the experience of the whole world is powerless to confute by a single exception!

"My dear sir!" cried Mr Colebatch, "your remembrance of my play is a new bond between us! It was entitled—of course you recollect—*The Mysterious Murderess*. Gad, sir, do you happen to call to mind the last four lines of the guilty Lindamira's death scene? It ran thus, Mr Wray:—"

Murder and midnight hail! Come all ye horrors!

My soul's congenial darkness quite defies ye!

I'm sick with guilt!—What is to cure me?—This! (Stabs herself)

Ha! ha! I'm better now—(smiles faintly)—I'm comfortable! (Dies)

"If that's not pretty strong writing, sir, my name's not Matthew Colebatch! and yet the besotted audience failed to appreciate it! Bless my soul!" (pulling out his watch) "one o'clock, already! I ought to be at home! I must go directly. Goodbye, Mr Wray. I'm so glad to have seen you, that I could almost thank Daubeny Daker for putting me in the towering passion that sent me here. You remind me of my young days, when I used to go behind the scenes, and sup with Kemble and Matthews. Goodbye, little Annie! I'm a wicked old fellow, and I mean to kiss you some day! Not a step further, Mr Wray; not a step, by George, sir; or I'll never come again. I mean to make the Tidbury people employ your talents; they're the most infernal set of asses under the canopy of heaven; but they shall employ them! I engage you to read my play, if nothing else will do, at the Mechanics' Institution. We'll make their flesh creep, sir; and their hair stand on end, with a little tragedy of the good old school. Goodbye, till I see you again, and God bless you!" And away the talkative old Squire went, in a mighty hurry, just as he had come in.

"Oh, grandfather! what a nice old gentleman!" exclaimed Annie, looking up for the first time from her lace cushion.

"What unexampled kindness to me! What perfect taste in everything! Did you hear him quote Shakespeare?" cried old Reuben, in an ecstasy. They went on alternately, in this way, with raptures about Mr Colebatch, for something like an hour. After that time, Annie left her work, and walked to the window.

"It's raining—raining fast," she said. "Oh, dear me! We can't have our walk today!"

"Hark! there's the wind moaning," said the old man. "It's getting colder, too. Annie! we are going to have a stormy night."

Four o'clock! And the carpenter still at his work in the back kitchen. Faster, "Julius Caesar"; faster. Let us have that mask of Shakespeare out of Mr Wray's cash box, and snugly ensconced in your neat wooden casket, before anybody goes to bed tonight. Faster, man!—Faster!

VII

For some household reason not worth mentioning, they dined later that day than usual at No. 12. It was five o'clock before they sat down to table. The conversation all turned on the visitor of the morning; no terms in Mr Wray's own vocabulary being anything like choice enough to characterize the eccentric old squire, he helped himself to Shakespeare, even more largely than usual, every time he spoke of Mr Colebatch. He managed to discover some striking resemblance to that excellent gentleman (now in one particular, and now in another), in every noble and venerable character, throughout the whole series of the plays—not forgetting either, on one or two occasions, to trace the corresponding likeness between the more disreputable and intriguing personages, and that vindictive enemy to all plays, players, and playhouses, the Reverend Daubeny Daker. Never did any professed commentator on Shakespeare (and the assertion is a bold one) wrest the poet's mighty meaning more dexterously into harmony with his own microscopic ideas, than Mr Wray now wrested it, to furnish him with eulogies on the goodness and generosity of Mr Matthew Colebatch, of Cropley Court.

Meanwhile, the weather got worse and worse, as the evening advanced. The wind freshened almost to a gale; and dashed the fast-falling rain against the window, from time to time, with startling violence. It promised to be one of the wildest, wettest, darkest nights they had had at Tidbury since the winter began.

Shortly after the table was cleared, having pretty well exhausted himself on the subject of Mr Colebatch, for the present, old Reuben fell asleep in his chair. This was rather an unusual indulgence for him, and was probably produced by the especial lateness of the dinner. Mr Wray generally took that meal at two o'clock, and set off for his walk afterwards, reckless of all the ceremonial observances of digestion. He was a poor man, and could not afford the luxurious distinction of being dyspeptic.

The behaviour of Mr "Julius Caesar," the carpenter, when he appeared from the back kitchen to take his place at dinner, was rather perplexing. He knocked down a salt-cellar; spurted some gravy over his shirt; and spilt a potato, in trying to transport it a distance of about four inches, from the dish to Annie's plate. This, to begin with, was rather above the general average of his number of table accidents at one meal. Then, when dinner was over, he announced his intention of returning to the back kitchen for the rest of the evening, in tones of such unwonted mystery, that Annie's curiosity was aroused, and she began to question him. Had he not done the new box yet? No! Why, he might have made such a box in an hour, surely? Yes, he might. And why had he not? "Wait a bit, Annie, and you'll see!" And having said that, he laid his large finger mysteriously against the side of his large nose, and walked out of the room forthwith.

In half-an-hour afterwards he came in again, looking very sheepish and discomposed, and trying, unsuccessfully, to hide an enormous poultice—a perfect loaf of warm bread and water—which decorated the palm of his right hand. This time, Annie insisted on an explanation.

It appeared that he had conceived the idea of ornamenting the lid of the new box with some uncouth carvings of his own, in compliment to Mr Wray and the mask of Shakespeare. Being utterly unpractised in the difficult handiwork he proposed to perform, he had run a splinter into the palm of his hand. And there the box was now in the back kitchen, waiting for lock and hinges, while the only person in the house who could put them on, was not likely to handle a hammer again for days to come. Miserable "Julius Caesar!" Never was well-meant attention more fatally misdirected than this attention of yours! Of all the multifarious accidents of your essentially accidental life, this special casualty, which has hindered you from finishing the new box tonight, is the most ill-timed and the most irreparable!

When the tea came in Mr Wray woke up; and as it usually happens with people who seldom indulge in the innocent sensuality of an after-dinner nap, changed at once, from a state of extreme somnolence to a state of extreme wakefulness. By this time the night was at its blackest; the rain fell fierce and thick, and the wild wind walked abroad in the darkness, in all its might and glory. The storm began to affect Annie's spirits a little, and she hinted as much to her grandfather, when he awoke. Old Reuben's extraordinary vivacity immediately suggested a remedy for this. He proposed to read a play of Shakespeare's as the surest mode of diverting attention from the weather; and, without allowing a moment for the consideration of his offer, he threw open the book, and began Macbeth.

As he not only treated his hearers to every one of the Kemble pauses, and every infinitesimal inflection of the Kemble elocution, throughout the reading; but also exhibited a serious parody of Mrs Siddons' effects in Lady Macbeth's sleep-walking scene, with the aid of a white pocket-handkerchief, tied under his chin, and a japanned bedroom candlestick in his hand—and as, in addition to these special and strictly dramatic delays, he further hindered the progress of his occupation by vigilantly keeping his eye on "Julius Caesar," and unmercifully waking up that ill-starred carpenter every time he went to sleep, (which, by the way, was once in every ten minutes,) nobody can be surprised to hear that Macbeth was not finished before eleven o'clock. The hour was striking from Tidbury Church, as Mr Wray solemnly declaimed the last lines of the tragedy, and shut up the book.

"There!" said old Reuben, "I think I've put the weather out of your head, Annie, by this time! You look sleepy, my dear; go to bed. I had a few remarks to make, about the right reading of Macbeth's dagger-scene, but I can make them tomorrow morning, just as well. I won't keep you up any longer. Good night, love!"

Was Mr Wray not going to bed, too? No: he never felt more awake in his life; he would sit up a little, and have a good "warm" over the fire. Should Annie bear him company? By no means! he would not keep poor Annie from her bed, on any account. Should "Julius Caesar"?—Certainly not! He was sure to go to sleep immediately; and to hear him snore, Mr Wray said, was worse than hearing him sneeze. So the two young people wished the old man goodnight, and left him to have his "warm," as he desired. This was the way in which he prepared himself to undergo that luxurious process:—

He drew his armchair in front of the fire, then put a chair on either side of it, then unlocked the cupboard, and took out the cash box that contained the mask of Shakespeare. This he deposited upon one of the side chairs; and upon the other he put his copy of the Plays, and the candle. Finally, he sat down in the middle—cosy beyond all description—and slowly inhaled a copious pinch of snuff.

"How it blows, outside!" said old Reuben, "and how snug I am, in here!"

He unlocked the cash box, and taking it on his knee, looked down on the mask that lay inside. Gradually, the pride and pleasure at first appearing in his eyes, gave place to a dreamy fixed expression. He gently closed the lid, and reclined back in his chair; but he did not shut up the cash box for the night, for he never turned the key in the lock.

Old recollections were crowding on him, revived by his conversation of the morning with Mr Colebatch; and now evoked by many a Shakespeare association of his own, always connected with the treasured, the inestimable mask. Tender remembrances spoke piteously and solemnly within him. Poor Columbine—lost, but never forgotten—moved loveliest and holiest of all those memory shadows, through the dim world of his waking visions. How little the grave can hide of us! The love that began before it, lasts after it. The sunlight to which our eyes looked, while it shone on earth, changes but to the star that guides our memories when it passes to heaven!

Hark! The church clock chimes the quarters; each stroke sounds with the ghostly wildness of all bell-tones, when heard amid the tumult of a storm, but fails to startle old Reuben now. He is far away in other scenes; living again in other times. Twelve strikes; and then, when the clock bell rings its long midnight peal, he rouses—he hears that.

The fire has died down to one, dull, red spot: he feels chilled; and sitting up in his chair, yawning, tries to summon resolution enough to rise and go upstairs to bed. His expression is just beginning to grow utterly listless and weary, when it suddenly alters. His eyes look eager again; his lips close firmly; his cheeks get pale all at once—he is listening.

He fancies that, when the wind blows in the loudest gusts, or when the rain dashes heaviest against the window, he hears a very faint, curious sound—sometimes like a scraping noise, sometimes like a tapping noise. But in what part of the house—or even whether outside or in—he cannot tell. In the calmer moments of the storm, he listens with especial attention to find this out; but it is always at that very time that he hears nothing.

It must be imagination. And yet, that imagination is so like a reality that it has made him shudder all over twice in the last minute.

Surely he hears that strange noise now! Why not get up, and go to the window, and listen if the faint tapping comes by any chance from outside, in front of the house? Something seems to keep him in his chair, perfectly motionless—something makes him afraid to turn his head, for fear of seeing a sight of horror close at his side—

Hush! it sounds again, plainer and plainer. And now it changes to a cracking noise—close by—at the shutter of the back drawing-room window.

What is that, sliding along the crack between the folding doors and the floor?—a light!—a light in that empty room which nobody uses. And now, a whisper—footsteps—the handle on the lock of the door moves—

"Help! Help! for God's sake!—Murder! Mur—"

Just as that cry for help passed the old man's lips, the two robbers, masked and armed, appeared in the room; and the next instant, Chummy Dick's gag was fast over his mouth.

He had the cash box clasped tight to his breast. Mad with terror, his eyes glared like a dead man's, while he struggled in the powerful arms that held him.

Grimes, unused to such scenes, was so petrified by astonishment at finding the old man out of bed, and the room lit up, that he stood with his pistol extended, staring helplessly through the eyeholes of his mask. Not so with his experienced leader. Chummy Dick's ears and eyes were as quick as his hands—the first informed him that Reuben's cry for help (skilfully as he had stifled it with the gag) had aroused some one in the house: the second instantly detected the cash box, as Mr Wray clasped it to his breast.

"Put up your pop-gun, you precious yokel, you!" whispered the housebreaker fiercely. "Look alive; and pull it out of his arms. Damn you! Do it quick! They're awake, up stairs!"

It was not easy to "do it quick." Weak as he was, Reuben actually held his treasure with the convulsive strength of despair, against the athletic ruffian who was struggling to get it away. Furious at the resistance, Grimes exerted his whole force, and tore the box so savagely from the old man's grasp, that the mask of Shakespeare flew several feet away, through the open lid, before it fell, shattered into fragments on the floor.

For an instant, Grimes stood aghast at the sight of what the contents of the cash box really were. Then, frantic with the savage passions produced by the discovery, he rushed up to the fragments, and, with a horrible oath, stamped his heavy boot upon them, as if the very plaster could feel his vengeance. "I'll kill him, if I swing for it!" cried the villain, turning on Mr Wray the next moment, and raising his horse-pistol by the barrel over the old man's head.

But, exactly at the same time, brave as his heroic namesake, "Julius Caesar" burst into the room. In the heat of the moment, he struck at Grimes with his wounded hand. Dealt even under that disadvantage, the blow was heavy enough to hurl the fellow right across the room, till he dropped down against the opposite wall. But the triumph of the stout carpenter was a short one. Hardly a second after his adversary had fallen, he himself lay stunned on the floor by the pistol-butt of Chummy Dick.

Even the nerve of the London housebreaker deserted him, at the first discovery of the astounding self-deception of which he and his companion had been the victims. He only recovered his characteristic coolness and self-possession when the carpenter attacked Grimes. Then, true to his system of never making unnecessary noise, or wasting unnecessary powder, he hit "Julius Caesar" just behind the ear, with unerring dexterity. The blow made no sound, and seemed to be inflicted by a mere turn of the wrist; but it was decisive—he had thoroughly stunned his man.

And now, the piercing screams of the landlady, from the bedroom floor poured quicker and quicker into the street, through the opened window. They were mingled with the fainter cries of Annie, whom the good woman forcibly detained from going into danger down stairs. The female servant (the only other inmate of the house) rivalled her mistress in shrieking madly and incessantly for help, from the window of the garret above.

"The whole street will be up in a crack!" cried Chummy Dick, swearing at every third word he uttered, and hauling the partially-recovered Grimes into an erect position again, "there's no swag to be got here! Step out quick, young yokel, or you'll be nabbed!"

He pushed Grimes into the back drawing-room; hustled him over the window-sill on to the wash-house roof, leaving him to find his own way, how he could, to the ground; and then followed, with Mr Wray's watch and purse, and a brooch of Annie's that had been left on the chimney-piece, all gathered into his capacious greatcoat pocket in a moment. They were not worth much as spoils; but the dexterity with which they were taken instantly with one hand, while he had Grimes to hold with the other; and the strength, coolness, and skill he displayed in managing the retreat, were worthy even of the reputation of Chummy Dick. Long before the two Tidbury watchmen had begun to think of a pursuit, the housebreaker and his companion were out of reach—even though the Bow Street Runners themselves had been on the spot to give chase. How long the old man has kept in that one position!—crouching down there in the corner of the room, without stirring a limb or uttering a word. He dropped on his knees at that place, when the robbers left him; and nothing has moved him from it since.

When Annie broke away from the landlady, and ran down stairs—he never stirred. When the long wail of agony burst from her lips, as she saw the dead look of the brave man lying stunned on the floor—he never spoke. When the street door was opened; and the crowd of terrified, half-dressed neighbours all rushed together into the house, shouting and trampling about, half panic-stricken at the news they heard—he never noticed a single soul. When the doctor was sent for; and, amid an awful hush of expectation, proceeded to restore the carpenter to his senses—even at that enthralling moment, he never looked up. It was only when the room was cleared again—when his granddaughter came to his side, and, putting her arm round his neck, laid her cold cheek close to his—that he seemed to live at all. Then, he just heaved a heavy sigh; his head dropped down lower on his breast; and he shivered throughout his whole frame, as if some icy influence was freezing him to the heart.

All that long, long time he had been looking on one sight—the fragments of the mask of Shakespeare lying beneath him. And there he kept now—when they tried in their various methods to coax him away—still crouching over them; just in the same position; just with the same hard, frightful look about his face that they had seen from the first.

Annie went and fetched the cash box; and tremblingly put it down before him. The instant he saw it, his eyes began to flash. He pounced in a fury of haste upon the fragments of the mask, and huddled them all together into the box, with shaking hands, and quick panting breath. He picked up the least chip of plaster that the robber had ground under his boot; and strained his eyes to look for more, when not an atom more was left. At last, he locked the box, and caught it up tight to his breast; and then he let them raise him up, and lead him gently away from the place.

He never quitted hold of his box, while they got him into bed. Annie, and her lover, and the landlady, all sat up together in his room; and all, in different degrees, felt the same horrible foreboding about him, and shrank from communicating it to one another. Occasionally, they heard him beating his hands strangely on the lid of the box; but he never spoke; and, as far as they could discover, never slept.

The doctor had said he would be better when the daylight came.— Did the doctor really know what was the matter with him?—And had the doctor any suspicion that something precious had been badly injured that night, besides the mask of Shakespeare?

VIII

By the next morning the news of the burglary had not only spread all through Tidbury, but all through the adjacent villages as well. The very first person who called at No. 12, to see how they did after the fright of the night before, was Mr Colebatch. The old gentleman's voice was heard louder than ever, as he ascended the stairs with the landlady. He declared he would have both the Tidbury watchmen turned off, as totally unfit to take care of the town. He swore that, if it cost him a hundred pounds, he would fetch the Bow Street Runners down from London, and procure the catching, trying, convicting, and hanging of "those two infernal housebreakers" before Christmas came. Invoking vengeance and retribution in this way, at every fresh stair, the Squire's temperament was up at "bloodheat," by the time he got into the drawing-room. It fell directly, however, to "temperate" again, when he found nobody there; and it sank twenty degrees lower still, at the sight of little Annie's face, when she came down to see him.

"Cheer up, Annie!" said the old gentleman with a last faint attempt at joviality. "It's all over now, you know: how's grandfather? Very much frightened still—eh?"

"Oh, sir! frightened, I'm afraid out of his mind!" and unable to control herself any longer, poor Annie fairly burst into tears.

"Don't cry, Annie! no crying! I can't stand it—you mustn't really!" said the Squire in anything but steady tones, "I'll talk him back into his mind; I will, as sure as my name's Matthew Colebatch—Stop!" (here he pulled out his voluminous India pocket handkerchief, and began very gently and caressingly to wipe away her tears, as if she had been a little child, and his own daughter). "There, now we've dried them up—no we haven't! there's one left—And now that's gone, let's have a little talk about this business, my dear, and see what's to be done. In the first place, what's all this I hear about a plaster cast being broken?"

Annie would have given the world to open her heart about the mask of Shakespeare, to Mr Colebatch; but she thought of her promise, and she thought, also, of the Town Council of Stratford, who might hear of the secret somehow, if it was once disclosed to anybody; and might pursue her grandfather with all the powers of the law, miserable and shattered though he now was, even to his hiding-place, at Tidbury-on-the-Marsh.

"I've promised, sir, not to say anything about the plaster cast to anybody," she began, looking very embarrassed and unhappy.

"And you'll keep your promise," interposed the Squire; "that's right—good, honest little girl! I like you all the better for it; we won't say a word more about the cast; but what have they taken? what have the infernal scoundrels taken?"

"Grandfather's old silver watch, sir, and his purse with seventeen and sixpence in it, and my brooch—but that's nothing."

"Nothing— Annie's brooch nothing!" cried the Squire, recovering his constitutional testiness. "But, never mind, I'm determined to have the rascals caught and hung, if it's only for stealing that brooch! And now, look here, my dear; if you don't want to put me into one of my passions, take that, and say nothing about it!"

"Take" what? Gracious powers! "Take" Golconda! He had crumpled a ten pound note into her hand!

"I say, again, you obstinate little thing, don't put me in one of my passions!" exclaimed the old gentleman, as poor Annie made some faint show of difficulty in taking the gift. "God forbid I should think of hurting your feelings, my dear, for such a paltry reason as having a few more pounds in my pocket, than you have in yours!" he continued, in such serious, kind tones, that Annie's eyes began to fill again. "We'll call that bank note, if you like, payment beforehand, for a large order for lace, from me. I saw you making lace, you know, yesterday; and I mean to consider you my lace manufacturer in ordinary, for the rest of your life. By George!"—he went on, resuming his odd abrupt manner,— "it's unknown the quantity of lace I shall want to buy! There's my old housekeeper, Mrs Buddle—hang me, Annie, if I don't dress her in nothing but lace, from top to toe, inside and out, all over! Only mind this, you don't set to work at the order till I tell you! We must wait till Mrs Buddle has worn out her old stock of petticoats, before we begin— eh? There! there! there! Don't go crying again! Can I see Mr Wray? No?— Quite right! Better not disturb him so soon. Give him my compliments, and say I'll call tomorrow. Put up the note! Put up the note! And don't be low-spirited—and don't do another thing, little Annie; don't forget you've got a queer old friend, who lives at Cropley Court!"

Running on in this way, the good Squire fairly talked himself out of the room, without letting Annie get in a word edgewise. Once on the stairs, he fell foul of the housebreakers again, with undiminished fury. The last thing the landlady heard him say, as she closed the street-door after him, was, that he was off now, to "trounce" the two Tidbury watch-men, for not stopping the robbery—to "trounce them handsomely," as sure as his name was Matthew Colebatch!

Carefully putting away the kind old gentleman's gift, (they were penniless before she received it), Annie returned to her grandfather's room. He had altered a little, as the morning advanced, and was now occupied over an employment which it wrung her heart to see—he was trying to restore the mask of Shakespeare.

The first words he had spoken since the burglary, were addressed to Annie. He seemed not to know that the robbers had effected their retreat, before she got down stairs; and asked whether they had hurt her. Calmed on this point, he next beckoned the carpenter to him, and entreated, in an eager whisper, to have some glue made directly. They could not imagine, at first, what he wanted it for; but they humoured him gladly.

When the glue was brought, he opened his cash box, with a look of faint pining hope in his face, that it was very mournful to see, and began to arrange the fragments of the mask, on the bed before him. They were shattered past all mending; but still he moved them about here and there, with his trembling hands, murmuring sadly, all the while, that he knew it was very difficult, but felt sure he should succeed at last. Sometimes he selected the pieces wrongly; stuck, perhaps, two or three together with the glue; and then had to pull them apart again. Even when he chose the fragments properly, he could not find enough that would join sufficiently well to reproduce only one poor quarter of the mask in its former shape. Still he went on, turning over piece after piece of the broken plaster, down to the very smallest, patiently and laboriously, with the same false hope of success, and the same vain perseverance under the most dishearten-ing failure, animating him for hours together. He had begun early in the morning—he had not given up, when Annie returned from her interview with Mr Colebatch. To know how utterly fruitless all his efforts must be, and still to see him so anxiously continuing them in spite of failure, was a sight to despair over, and to tremble at, indeed.

At last, Annie entreated him to put the fragments away in the box, and take a little rest. He would listen to nobody else; but he listened to her, and did what she asked; saying that his head was not clear enough for the work of repairing, today; but that he felt certain he should succeed tomorrow. When he had locked the box, and put it under his pillow, he laid back, and fell into a sleep directly.

Such was his condition! Every idea was now out of his mind, but the idea of restoring the mask of Shakespeare. Divert him from that; and he either fell asleep, or sat up vacant and speechless. It was suspension, not loss of the faculties, with him. The fibre of his mind relaxed with the breaking of the beloved possession to which it had been attached. Those still, cold, plaster features had been his thought by day, his dream by night; in them, his deep and beautiful devotion to Shakespeare— beautiful as an innate poetic faith that had lived through every poetic privation of life—had found its dearest outward manifestation. All about that mask, he had unconsciously hung fresh votive offerings of pride and pleasure, and humble happiness, almost with every fresh hour. It had been the one great achievement of his life, to get it; and the one great determination of his life, to keep it. And now it was broken! The dearest household god, next to his grandchild, that the poor actor had ever had to worship, his own eyes had seen lying shattered on the floor!

It was this—far more than the fright produced by the burglary,—that had altered him, as he was altered now.

There was no rousing him. Everybody tried, and everybody failed. He went on patiently, day after day, at his miserably hopeless task of joining the fragments of the plaster; and always had some excuse for failure, always some reason for beginning the attempt anew. Annie could influence him in everything else,—for his heart, which was all hers, had escaped the blow that had stunned his mind,—but, on any subject connected with the mask, her interference was powerless.

The good Squire came to try what he could do—came every day; and joked, entreated, lectured, and advised, in his own hearty, eccentric manner; but the old man only smiled faintly; and forgot what had been said to him, as soon as the words were out of the sayer's mouth. Mr Colebatch, reduced to his last resources, hit on what he considered a first-rate stratagem. He privately informed Annie, that he would insist on his whole establishment of servants, with Mrs Buddle, the housekeeper, at their head, learning elocution; so as to employ Mr Wray again, in a duty he was used to perform. "None of those infernal Tidbury people will learn," said the kind old Squire; "so my servants shall make a class for him, with Mrs Buddle at the top, to keep them in order. Set him teaching in his own way; and he must come round—he must from force of habit!" But he did not. They told him a class of new pupils was waiting for him; he just answered he was very glad to hear it; and forgot all about the matter the moment afterwards.

The doctor endeavoured to help them. He tried stimulants, and tried sedatives; he tried keeping his patient in bed, and tried keeping him up; he tried blistering, and tried cupping; and then he gave over; saying that Mr Wray must certainly have something on his mind, and that physic and regimen were of no use. One word of comfort, however, the doctor still had to speak. The physical strength of the old man had failed him very little, as yet. He was always ready to be got out of bed, and dressed; and seemed glad when he was seated in his chair. This was a good sign; but there was no telling how long it might last.

It had lasted a whole week—a long, blank melancholy winter's week! And now, Christmas Day was fast coming; coming for the first time as a day of mourning, to the little family who, in spite of poverty and all poverty's hardening disasters, had hitherto enjoyed it happily and lovingly together, as the blessed holiday of the whole year! Ah! how doubly heavy-hearted poor Annie felt, as she entered her bedroom for the night, and remembered that that day fortnight would be Christmas Day!

She was beginning to look wan and thin already. It is not joy only, that shows soonest and plainest in the young: grief—alas that it should be so—shares, in this world, the same privilege: and Annie now looked, as she felt, sick at heart. That day had brought no change: she had left the old man for the night, and left him no better. He had passed hours again, in trying to restore the mask; still instinctively exhibiting from time to time some fondness and attention towards his grandchild—but just as hopelessly vacant to every other influence as ever.

Annie listlessly sat down on the one chair in her small bedroom, thinking (it was her only thought now,) of what new plan could be adopted to rouse her grandfather on the morrow; and still mourning over the broken mask, as the one fatal obstacle to every effort she could try. Thus she sat for some minutes, languid and dreamy—when, suddenly, a startling and a wonderful change came over her, worked from within. She bounded up from her chair, as dead-pale and as dead-still as if she had been struck to stone. Then, a moment after, her face flushed crimson, she clasped her hands violently together, and drew her breath quick. And then, the paleness came once more—she trembled all over—and knelt down by the bedside, hiding her face in her hands.

When she rose again, the tears were rolling fast over her cheeks. She poured out some water, and washed them away. A strange expression of firmness—a glow of enthusiasm, beautiful in its brightness and purity—overspread her face, as she took up her candle, and left the room.

She went to the very top of the house, where the carpenter slept; and knocked at his door.

"Are you not gone to bed yet, Martin?"—she whispered—(the old joke of calling him "Julius Caesar" was all over now!)

He opened the door in astonishment, saying he had only that moment got upstairs.

"Come down to the drawing-room, Martin," she said; looking brightly at him—almost wildly, as he thought. "Come quick! I must speak to you at once."

He followed her downstairs. When they got into the drawing-room, she carefully closed the door; and then said:—

"A thought has come to me, Martin, that I must tell you. It came to me just now, when I was alone in my room; and I believe God sent it!"

She beckoned to him to sit by her side; and then began to whisper in his ear—quickly, eagerly, without pause.

His face began to turn pale at first, as hers had done, while he listened. Then it flushed, then grew firm like hers, but in a far stronger degree. When she had finished speaking, he only said, it was a terrible risk every way—repeating "every way" with strong emphasis; but that she wished it; and therefore it should be done.

As they rose to separate, she said tenderly and gravely:—

"You have always been very good to me, Martin: be good, and be a brother to me more than ever now—for now I am trusting you with all I have to trust."

Years afterwards when they were married, and when their children were growing up around them, he remembered Annie's last look, and Annie's last words, as they parted that night.

IX

The next morning, when the old man was ready to get out of bed and be dressed, it was not the honest carpenter who came to help him as usual, but a stranger—the landlady's brother. He never noticed this change. What thoughts he had left, were all preoccupied. The evening before, from an affectionate wish to humour him in the caprice which had become the one leading idea of his life, Annie had bought for him a bottle of cement. And now, he went on murmuring to himself, all the while he was being dressed, about the certainty of his succeeding at last in piecing together the broken fragments of the mask, with the aid of this cement. It was only the glue, he said, that had made him fail hitherto; with cement to aid him, he was quite certain of success.

The landlady and her brother helped him down into the drawing-room. Nobody was there; but on the table, where the breakfast things were laid, was placed a small note. He looked round inquisitively when he first saw that the apartment was empty. Then, the only voice within him that was not silenced—the voice of his heart—spoke, and told him that Annie ought to have been in the room to meet him as usual.

"Where is she?" he asked eagerly.

"Don't leave me alone with him, James," whispered the landlady to her brother, "there's bad news to tell him."

"Where is she?" he reiterated; and his eye got a wild look, as he asked the question for the second time.

"Pray, compose yourself, sir; and read that letter," said the landlady, in soothing tones; "Miss Annie's quite safe, and wants you to read this." She handed him the letter.

He struck it away; so fiercely that she started back in terror. Then he cried out violently for the third time:

"Where is she?"

"Tell him," whispered the landlady's brother, "tell him at once, or you'll make him worse."

"Gone, sir," said the woman—"gone away; but only for three days. The last words she said were, tell my grandfather I shall be back in three days; and give him that letter with my dearest love. Oh, don't look so, sir—don't look so! She's sure to be back."

He was muttering "gone" several times to himself, with a fearful expression of vacancy in his eyes. Suddenly, he signed to have the letter picked up from the ground; tore it open the moment it was given to him; and began to try to read the contents.

The letter was short, and written in very blotted unsteady characters. It ran thus:—

Dearest Grandfather,

I never left you before in my life; and I only go now to try and serve you, and do you good. In three days, or sooner, if God pleases, I will come back, bringing something with me that will gladden your heart, and make you love me even better than ever. I dare not tell you where I am going, or what I am going for—you would be so frightened, and would perhaps send after me to fetch me back; but believe there is no danger! And oh, dear dear grandfather, don't doubt your little Annie; and don't doubt I will be back as I say, bringing something to make you forgive me for going away without your leave. We shall be so happy again, if you will only wait the three days! He—you know who—goes with me, to take care of me. Think, dear grandfather, of the blessed Christmas time that will bring us all together

again, happier than ever! I can't write any more, but that I pray
God to bless and keep you, till we meet again!
ANNIE WRAY.

He had not read the letter more than half through, when he dropped
it, uttering the one word, "gone," in a shrill scream, that it made them
shudder to hear. Then, it seemed as if a shadow, an awful, indescribable
shadow, were stealing over his face. His fingers worked and fidgeted
with an end of the tablecloth close by him; and he began to speak in faint
whispering tones.

"I'm afraid I'm going mad; I'm afraid something's frightened me
out of my wits," he murmured, under his breath. "Stop! let me try if
I know anything. There now! there! That's the breakfast table: I know
that. There's her cup and saucer; and there's mine. Yes! and that third
place, on the other side, whose is that?—whose, whose, whose? Ah! my
God! my God! I am mad! I've forgotten that third place!" He stopped,
shivering all over. Then, the moment after, he shrieked out—"Gone! who
says she's gone? It's a lie; no, no, it's a cruel joke put upon me. Annie! I
won't be joked with. Come down, Annie! Call her, some of you! Annie!
they've broken it all to pieces—the plaster won't stick together again!
You can't leave me, now they've broken it all to pieces! Annie! Annie!
Come and mend it! Annie! little Annie!"

He called on her name for the last time, in tones of entreaty un-
utterably plaintive; then sank down on a chair, moaning; then became
silent—doggedly silent—and fiercely suspicious of everything. In that
mood he remained, till his strength began to fail him; and then he let
them lead him to the sofa. When he lay down, he fell off quickly into a
heavy, feverish slumber.

Ah, Annie! Annie! Carefully as you watched him, you knew but little
of his illness; you never foreboded such a result of your absence as this;
or, brave and loving as your purpose was in leaving him, you would have
shrunk from the fatal necessity of quitting his bedside for three days
together!

Mr Colebatch came in shortly after the old man had fallen asleep,
accompanied by a new doctor—a medical man of great renown, who had
stolen a little time from his London practice, partly to visit some rela-
tions who lived at Tidbury, and partly to recruit his own health, which
had suffered in repairing other people's. The good Squire, the moment he
heard that such assistance as this was accidentally available in the town,
secured it for poor old Reuben, without a moment's delay.

"Oh, sir!" said the landlady, meeting them down stairs; "he's been
going on in such a dreadful way! What we are to do, I really don't know."

"It's lucky somebody else does," interrupted the Squire, peevishly.

"But you don't know, sir, that Miss Annie's gone—gone without saying where!"

"Yes, I happen to know that too!" said Mr Colebatch; "I've got a letter from her, asking me to take care of her grandfather, while she's away; and here I am to do what she tells me. First of all, ma'am, let us get into some room, where this gentleman and I can have five minutes' talk in private."

"Now, sir"—said the Squire, when he and the doctor were closeted together in the back parlour—"the long and the short of the case is this:— A week ago, two infernal housebreakers broke into this house, and found old Mr Wray sitting up alone in the drawing-room. Of course, they frightened him out of his wits; and they stole some trifles too—but that's nothing. They managed somehow to break a plaster cast of his. There's a mystery about this cast, that the family won't explain, and that nobody can find out; but the fact appears to be, that the old man was as fond of his cast as if it was one of his children—a queer thing, you'll say; but true, sir; true as my name's Colebatch! Well: ever since, he's been weak in his mind; always striving to mend this wretched cast, and taking no notice of anything else. This sort of thing has lasted for six or seven days.—And now, another mystery! I get a letter from his granddaughter—the kindest, dearest little thing!—begging me to look after him— you never saw such a lovely, tender-hearted letter!—to look after him, I say, while she's gone for three days, to come back with a surprise for him that she says will work miracles. She don't say what surprise—or, where she's going—but she promises to come back in three days; and she'll do it! I'd stake my existence on little Annie sticking to her word! Now the question is—till we see her again, and all this precious mystery's cleared up—what are we to do for the poor old man?—what?—eh?"

"Perhaps"—said the doctor, smiling at the conclusion of this characteristic harangue—"perhaps, I had better see the patient, before we say any more."

"By George! what a fool I am!"—cried the Squire—"Of course!— see him directly—this way, doctor: this way!"

They went into the drawing-room. The sufferer was still on the sofa, moving and talking in his sleep. The doctor signed to Mr Colebatch to keep silence; and they sat down and listened.

The old man's dreams seemed to be connected with some of the later scenes in his life, which had been passed at country towns, in teaching country actors. He was laughing just at this moment.

"Ho! Ho! young gentlemen"—they heard him say—"do you call that acting? Ah, dear! dear! We professional people don't bump against each other on the stage, in that way—it's lucky you called me in, before your friends came to see you!—Stop, sir! that won't do! You mustn't die in that way—fall on your knee first; then sink down—then—Oh, dear! How hard it is to get people to have a proper delivery, and not go dropping their voices, at the end of every sentence. I shall never—never—"

Here the wild words stopped; then altered, and grew sad.

"Hush! Hush!"—he murmured, in husky, wandering tones—"Silence there, behind the scenes! Don't you hear Mr Kemble speaking now? Listen, and get a lesson, as I do. Ah! Laugh away, fools, who don't know good acting when you see it!—Let me alone! What are you pushing me for? I'm doing you no harm! I'm only looking at Mr Kemble—Don't touch that book!—it's my Shakespeare—yes! mine. I suppose I may read Shakespeare if I like, though I am only an actor at a shilling a night!—A shilling a night;—starving wages—Ha! Ha! Ha!—starving wages!"

Again the sad strain altered to a still wilder and more plaintive key.

"Ah!" he cried now, "don't be hard with me! Don't for God's sake! My wife, my poor dear wife, died only a week ago! Oh, I'm cold! starved with cold here, in this draughty place. I can't help crying, sir; she was so good to me! But I'll take care and go on the stage when I'm called to go, if you'll please not take any notice of me now; and not let them laugh at me. Oh, Mary! Mary! Why has God taken you from me? Ah! Why! why! why!"

Here, the murmurs died away; then began again, but more confusedly. Sometimes his wandering speech was all about Annie; sometimes it changed to lamentations over the broken mask; sometimes it went back again to the old days behind the scenes at Drury Lane.

"Oh, Annie! Annie!" cried the Squire, with his eyes full of tears; "why did you ever go away?"

"I am not sure," said the doctor, "that her going may not do good in the end. It has evidently brought matters to a climax with him; I can see that. Her coming back will be a shock to his mind—it's a risk, sir; but that shock may act in the right way. When a man's faculties struggle to recover themselves, as his are doing, those faculties are not altogether gone. The young lady will come back, you say, the day after tomorrow?"

"Yes, yes!" answered the Squire, "with a @#surprise,@# she says. What surprise? Good Heavens! Why couldn't she say what!"

"We need not mind that," rejoined the other. "Any surprise will do, if his physical strength will bear it. We'll keep him quiet—as much sleep as possible—till she comes back. I've seen some very curious cases of this kind, Mr Colebatch; cases that were cured by the merest accidents, in the most unaccountable manner. I shall watch this particular case with interest."

"Cure it, doctor! cure it; and, by Jupiter! I'll—"

"Hush! you'll wake him. We had better go now. I shall come back in an hour, and will tell the landlady where she can let me know, if anything happens before that."

They went out softly; and left him as they had found him, muttering and murmuring in his sleep.

On the third day, late in the afternoon, Mr Colebatch and the doctor were again in the drawing-room at No. 12; and again intently occupied in studying the condition of poor old Reuben Wray.

This time, he was wide awake; and was restlessly and feebly moving up and down the room, talking to himself, now mournfully about the broken mask, now fiercely and angrily about Annie's absence. Nothing attracted his notice in the smallest degree; he seemed to be perfectly unaware that anybody was in the room with him.

"Why can't you keep him quiet?" whispered the Squire; "why don't you give him an opiate, or whatever you call it, as you did yesterday?"

"His grandchild comes back today," answered the doctor. "Today must be left to the great physician—Nature. At this crisis, it is not for me to meddle, but to watch and learn."

They waited again in silence. Lights were brought in; for it grew dark while they kept their anxious watch. Still no arrival!

Five o'clock struck; and, about ten minutes after, a knock sounded on the street door.

"She has come back!" exclaimed the doctor.

"How do you know that already?" asked Mr Colebatch, eagerly.

"Look there, sir!" and the doctor pointed to Mr Wray.

He had been moving about with increased restlessness, and talking with increased vehemence, just before the knock. The moment it sounded he stopped; and there he stood now, perfectly speechless and perfectly still. There was no expression on his face. His very breathing seemed suspended. What secret influences were moving within him now? What dread command went forth over the dark waters in which his spirit toiled, saying to them, "Peace! be still!" That, no man—not even the man of science—could tell.

As the door opened, and the landlady's joyful exclamation of recognition, sounded cheerily from below, the doctor rose from his seat, and gently placed himself close behind the old man.

Footsteps hurried up the stairs. Then, Annie's voice was heard, breathless and eager, before she came in. "Grandfather, I've got the mould! Grandfather, I've brought a new cast! The mask—thank God!—the mask of Shakespeare!"

She flew into his arms, without even a look at anybody else in the room. When her head was on his bosom, the spirit of the brave little girl deserted her for the first time since her absence, and she burst into an hysterical passion of weeping before she could utter another word.

He gave a great cry the moment she touched him—an inarticulate voice of recognition from the spirit within. Then his arms closed tight over her; so tight, that the doctor advanced a step or two towards them, showing in his face the first look of alarm it had yet betrayed.

But, at that instant, the old man's arms dropped again, powerless and heavy, by his side. What does he see now, in that open box in the carpenter's hand? The Mask!—his Mask, whole as ever! White, and smooth, and beautiful, as when he first drew it from the mould, in his own bedroom at Stratford!

The struggle of the vital principle at that sight—the straining and writhing of every nerve—was awful to look on. His eyes rolled, distended, in their orbits; a dark red flush of blood heaved up and overspread his face; he drew his breath in heavy, hoarse gasps of agony. This lasted for a moment—one dread moment; then he fell forward, to all appearance death-struck, in the doctor's arms.

He was borne to the sofa, amid the silence of that suspense which is too terrible for words. The doctor laid his finger on his wrist, waited an instant, then looked up, and slightly nodded his head. The pulse was feebly beating again, already!

Long and delicate was the process of restoring him to animation. It was like aiding the faint new life to develop itself in a child just born. But the doctor was as patient as he was skilful; and they heard the old man draw his breath again, gently and naturally, at last.

His weakness was so great, that his eyelids closed at his first effort to look round him. When they opened again, his eyes seemed strangely liquid and soft—almost like the eyes of a young girl. Perhaps this was partly because they turned on Annie the moment they could see.

Soon, his lips moved; but his voice was so faint, that the doctor was obliged to listen close at his mouth to hear him. He said, in fluttering accents, that he had had a dreadful dream, which had made him very ill, he was afraid; but that it was all over, and he was better now, though not quite strong enough to receive so many visitors yet. Here his strength for speaking failed, and he looked round on Annie again in silence. In a minute more he whispered to her. She went to the table and fetched the new mask; and, kneeling down, held it before him to look at.

The doctor beckoned Mr Colebatch, the landlady, and the carpenter, to follow him into the back-room.

"Now," said he, "I've one, and only one, important direction to give you all; and you must communicate it to Miss Wray when she is a little less agitated. On no account let the patient imagine he's wrong in thinking that all his troubles have been the troubles of a dream. That will be the weak point in his intellectual consciousness for the rest of his life. When he gets stronger, he is sure to question you curiously about his dream; keep him in his self-deceit, as you value his sanity! He's only got his reason back by getting it out of the very jaws of death, I can tell you—give it full time to strengthen! You know, I dare say, that a joint which is dislocated by a jerk, is also replaced by a jerk. Consider his mind, in the same way, to have been dislocated by one shock, and now replaced by another; and treat his intellect as you would treat a limb that had only just been slipped back into its proper place—treat it tenderly. By the bye," added the doctor, after a moment's consideration, "if you can't get the key of his box, without suspicion, pick the lock; and throw away the fragments of the old cast (which he was always talking about in his delirium)—destroy them altogether. If he ever sees them again, they may do him dreadful mischief. He must always imagine what he imagines at present, that the new cast is the same cast that he has had all along. It's a very remarkable case, Mr Colebatch, very remarkable: I really feel indebted to you for enabling me to study it. Compose yourself, sir, you're a little shaken and startled by this, I see; but there's no danger for him now. Look there: that man, except on one point, is as sane as ever he was in his life!"

They looked, as the doctor spoke. Mr Wray was still on the sofa, gazing at the mask of Shakespeare, which Annie supported before him, as she knelt by his side. His arm was round her neck; and, from time to time, he whispered to her, smiling faintly, but very happily, as she replied in whispers also. The sight was simple enough; but the landlady, thinking on all that had passed, began to weep as she beheld it. The honest carpenter looked very ready to follow her example; and Mr Colebatch probably shared the same weakness at that moment, though he was less candid in betraying it. "Come," said the Squire, very huskily and hastily, "we are only in the way here; let us leave them together!"

"Quite right, sir," observed the doctor; "that pretty little girl is the only medical attendant fit to be with him now! I wait for you, Mr Colebatch!"

"I say, young fellow," said the Squire to the carpenter, as they went down stairs, "be in the way tomorrow morning: I've a good deal to ask you in private when I'm not all over in a twitter, as I am at present. Now our good old friend's getting round, my curiosity's getting round too. Be in the way tomorrow, at ten, when I come here. Quite ready, doctor! No!

after you, if you please. Ah, thank God! We came into this house mourners, and we go out of it to rejoice. It will be a happy Christmas, doctor, and a merry New Year, after all!"

X

When ten o'clock came, the Squire came—punctual to a minute. Instead of going up stairs, he mysteriously sent for the carpenter into the back parlour.

"Now, in the first place, how is Mr Wray?"—said the old gentleman, as anxiously as if he had not already sent three times the night before, and twice earlier in the morning, to ask that very question.

"Lord bless you, sir!"—answered the carpenter with a grin, and a very expressive rubbing of the hands—"He's coming to again, after his nice sleep last night, as brave as ever. He's dreadful weak still, to be sure; but he's got like himself again, already. He's been down on me twice in the last half hour, sir, about my elocution; he's making Annie read Shakespeare to him; and he's asking whether any new pupils are coming—all just in the old way again. Oh, sir, it is so jolly to see him like that once more—if you'll only come up stairs—"

"Stop, till we've had our talk"—said the Squire—"sit down. By the bye! has he said anything yet about that infernal cash box?"

"I picked the lock of the box this morning, sir, as the gentleman told me; and buried every bit of plaster out of it, deep in the kitchen garden. He saw the box afterwards, and gave a tremble, like. @#Take it away,@# says he, @#never let me see it again: it reminds me of that dreadful dream.@# And then, sir, he told us about what had happened, just as if he really had dreamt it; saying he couldn't get the subject quite out of his head, the whole thing was so much as if it had truly taken place. Afterwards, sir, he thanked me for making the new box for the cast—he remembered my promising to do that, though it was only just before all our trouble!"

"And of course, you humour him in everything, and let him think he's right?"—said the Squire—"He must never know that he hasn't been dreaming, to his dying day."

And he never did know it—never, in this world, had even a suspicion of what he owed to Annie! It was but little matter; they could not have loved each other better, if he had discovered everything.

"Now, master carpenter," pursued the Squire, "you've answered very nicely hitherto. Just answer as nicely the next question I ask. What's the whole history of this mysterious plaster cast? It's no use fidgeting! I've seen the cast; I know it's a portrait of Shakespeare! And I've made up my mind to find out all about it. Do you mean to say you think I'm not a friend fit to be trusted? Eh, you sir?"

"I never could think so, after all your goodness, sir. But, if you please, I really did promise to keep the thing a secret," said the carpenter, looking very much as if he were watching his opportunity to open the door, and run out of the room; "I promised, sir; I did, indeed!"

"Promised a fiddlestick!" exclaimed the Squire, in a passion. "What's the use of keeping a secret that's half let out already? I'll tell you what, you Mr—, what's your name? There's some joke about calling you Julius Caesar. What's your real name, if you really have one?"

"Martin Blunt, sir. But don't, pray don't ask me to tell the secret! I don't say you would blab it, sir; but if it did leak out, like; and get to Stratford-upon-Avon,"—here he suddenly became silent, feeling he was beginning to commit himself already.

"Stop! I've got it!" cried Mr Colebatch. "Hang me, if I haven't got it at last!"

"Don't tell me, sir! Pray don't tell me, if you have!"

"Stick to your chair, Mr Martin Blunt! No shirking with me! I was a fool not to suspect the thing, the moment I saw it was a portrait of Shakespeare. I've seen the Stratford bust, Master Blunt! You're afraid of Stratford, are you?—Why? I know! Some of you have been taking that cast from the Stratford bust, without leave—it's as like it, as two peas! Now, young fellow, I'll tell you what! if you don't make a clean breast to me at once, I'm off to the office of the *Tidbury Mercury*, to put in my version of the whole thing, as a good local anecdote! Will you tell me? or will you not?—I'm asking this in Mr Wray's interests, or I'd die before I asked you at all!"

Confused, threatened, bullied, bawled at, and out-manoeuvred, the unfortunate carpenter fairly gave way. "If it's wrong in me to tell you, sir, it's your fault what I do," said the simple fellow; and he forthwith retailed, in a very roundabout, stammering manner, the whole of the disclosure he had heard from old Reuben—the Squire occasionally throwing in an explosive interjection of astonishment, or admiration; but, otherwise, receiving the narrative with remarkable calmness and attention.

"What the deuce is all this nonsense about the Stratford Town Council, and the penalties of the law?"—cried Mr Colebatch, when the carpenter had done—"But never mind; we can come to that afterwards. Now tell me about going back to get the mould out of the cupboard, and making the new cast. I know who did it! It's that dear, darling, incomparable little girl!—but tell me all about it—come! quick, quick!— don't keep me waiting!"

"Julius Caesar" got on with his second narrative much more glibly than with the first. How Annie had suddenly remembered, one night, in her bedroom, about the mould having been left behind—how she was determined to try and restore her grandfather's health and faculties, by going to seek it; and how he (the carpenter), had gone also, to protect her—how they got to Stratford, by the coach (outside places, in the cold, to save money)—how Annie appealed to the mercy of their former landlord; and instead of inventing some falsehood to deceive him, fairly told her whole story in all its truth—how the landlord pitied them, and promised to keep their secret—how they went up into the bed-room, and found the mould in the old canvas bag, behind the volumes of the Annual Register, just where Mr Wray had left it—how Annie, remembering what her grandfather had told her, about the process of making a cast, bought plaster, and followed out her instructions; failing in the first attempt, but admirably succeeding in the second—how they were obliged, in fright-ful suspense, to wait till the third day for the return coach; and how they finally got back, safe and sound, not only with the new cast, but with the mould as well.—All these particulars flowed from the carpenter's lips, in a strain of homely eloquence, which no elocutionary aid could have furnished with one atom of additional effect, that would have done it any good whatever.

"We'd no notion, sir," said "Julius Caesar," in conclusion, "that poor Mr Wray was so bad as he really was, when we went away. It was a dreadful trial to Annie, sir, to go. She went down on her knees to the landlady—I saw her do it, half wild, like; she was in such a state—she went down on her knees, sir, to ask the woman to be as a daughter to the old man, till she came back. Well, sir, even after that, it was a toss-up whether she went away, when the morning came. But she was obliged to do it. She durstn't trust me to go alone, for fear I should let the mould tumble down, when I got it (which I'm afraid, sir, was very likely!)—or get into some scrape, by telling what I oughtn't, where I oughtn't; and so be taken up, mould and all, before the Town Council, who were going to put Mr Wray in prison, only we ran off to Tidbury; and so—"

"Nonsense! stuff! they could no more put him in prison for taking the cast than I can," cried the Squire. "Stop! I've got a thought! I've got a thought at least, that's worth—Is the mould here?—Yes or No?"

"Yes, sir! Bless us and save us, what's the matter!"

"Run!" cried Mr Colebatch, pacing up and down the room like mad. "No. 15 in the street! Dabbs and Clutton, the lawyers! Fetch one of them in a second! Damn it, run! or I shall burst a blood vessel!"

The carpenter ran to No. 15; and Mr Dabbs, who happened to be in, ran from No. 15. Mr Colebatch met him at the street door, dragged him into the back parlour, pushed him on to a chair, and instantly stated the case between Mr Wray and the authorities at Stratford, in the fewest possible words and the hastiest possible tones. "Now," said the old gentleman at the end, "can they, or can they not, hurt him for what he's done?"

"It's a very nice point," said Mr Dabbs, "a very nice point indeed, sir."

"Hang it, man!" cried the Squire, "don't talk to me about @#nice points,@# as if a point was something good to eat! Can they, or can they not, hurt him? Answer that in three words!"

"They can't," said Dabbs, answering it triumphantly in two.

"Why?" asked the Squire, beating him by a rejoinder in one.

"For this reason," said Dabbs. "What does Mr Wray take with him into the church? Plaster of his own, in powder. What does he bring out with him? The same plaster, in another form. Does any right of copyright reside in a bust two hundred years old? Impossible. Has Mr Wray hurt the bust? No; or they would have found him out here, and prosecuted directly—for they know where he is. I heard of the thing from a Stratford man, yesterday, who said they knew he was at Tidbury. Under all these circumstances, where's there a shadow of a case against Mr Wray? Nowhere!"

"Capital, Dabbs! Capital! You'll be Lord Chancellor some day: never heard a better opinion in my life! Now, Mr Julius Caesar Blunt, do you see what my thought is? No! Look here. Take casts from that mould till your arms ache again; clap them upon slabs of black marble to show off the white face; sell them, at a guinea each, to the loads of people who would give anything to have a portrait of Shakespeare; and then open your breeches' pockets fast enough to let the gold tumble in, if you can! Tell Mr Wray that; and you tell him he's a rich man, or—no don't, you're no more fit to do it properly than I am! Tell every syllable you've heard here to Annie, directly; she'll know how to break it to him; go! Be off!"

"But what are we to say about how we got the mould here, sir? We can't tell Mr Wray the truth."

"Tell him a flam, of course! Say it's been found in the cupboard, by the landlord, at Stratford, and sent on here. Dabbs will bear witness that the Stratford people know he's at Tidbury, and know they can't touch him: he's sure to think that a pretty good proof that we are right. Say I bullied you out of the secret, when I saw the mould come here—say anything—but only go, and settle matters at once! I'm off to take my walk, and see about the black slabs at the stone masons. I'll be back in an hour, and see Mr Wray."

The next moment, the impetuous old Squire was out of the house; and before the hour was up, he was in it again, rather more impetuous than ever.

When he entered the drawing-room, the first sight that greeted him was the carpenter, hanging up a box containing the mask (with the lid taken off) boldly and publicly over the fireplace.

"I'm glad to see that, sir," said Mr Colebatch, shaking hands with Mr Wray. "Annie has told you my good news—eh?"

"Yes, sir," answered the old man; "the best news I've heard for some time: I can hang up my treasure there, now, where I can see it all day. It was rather too bad, sir, of those Stratford people to go frightening me, by threatening what they couldn't do. The best man among them is the man who was my landlord; he's an honest, careful fellow, to send me back my old canvas bag, and the mould (which must have seemed worthless to him), just because they were belonging to me, and left in my bedroom. I'm rather proud, sir, of making that mask. I can never repay you for your kindness in defending my character, and taking me up as you've done— but if you would accept a copy of the cast, now we have the mould to take it from, as Annie says—"

"That I will, and thankfully," said the Squire, "and I order five more copies, as presents to my friends, when you begin to sell to the public."

"I really don't know, sir, about that," said Mr Wray, rather uneasily. "Selling the cast is like making my great treasure very common; it's like giving up my particular possession to everybody."

Mr Colebatch parried this objection instantly. Could Mr Wray, he asked, seriously mean to be so selfish as to deny to other lovers of Shakespeare the privilege he prized so much himself, of possessing Shakespeare's portrait?—to say nothing of as good as plumply refusing a pretty round sum of money at the same time. Could he be selfish enough, and inconsiderate enough to do that? No: Mr Wray, on consideration, allowed he could not. He saw the subject in a new light now; and begging Mr Colebatch's pardon, if he had seemed selfish or unthankful, he would take the Squire's advice.

"That's right!" said the old gentleman. "Now I'm happy. You'll soon be strong enough, my good friend, to take the cast yourself."

"I hope so," said Mr Wray. "It's very odd that a mere dream should make me feel so weak as I do—I suppose they told you, sir, what a horrible dream it was. If I didn't see the mask hanging up there now, as whole as ever, I should really believe it had been broken to pieces, just as I dreamt it. It must have been a dream, you know, sir of course; for I dreamt that Annie had gone away and left me; and I found her at home as usual, when I woke up. It seems, too, that I'm a week or more behindhand, in my notion about the day of the month. In short, sir, I should almost think myself bewitched," he added, pressing his trembling hand over his forehead, "if I didn't know it was near Christmas time, and didn't believe what sweet Will Shakespeare says in Hamlet—a passage, by-the-by, sir, which Mr Kemble always regretted to see struck out of the acting copy."

Here he began to declaim—faintly, but still with all the old Kemble cadences—the exquisite lines to which he referred; the Squire beating time to each modulation, with his forefinger:—

> *Some say, that ever 'gainst that season comes,*
> *Wherein our Saviour's birth is celebrated,*
> *This bird of dawning singeth all night long:*
> *And then they say no spirit dares stir abroad;*
> *The nights are wholesome; then no planets strike,*
> *No fairy takes, nor witch hath power to charm,*
> *So hallow'd and so gracious is the time.*

"There's poetry!" exclaimed Mr Colebatch, looking up at the mask. "That's a cut above my tragedy of the Mysterious Murderess, I'm afraid. Eh, sir? And how you recite,—splendid! Hang it! we havn't had half our talk, yet, about Shakespeare and John Kemble. A chat with an old stager like you, is new life to me, in such a barbarous place as this! Ah, Mr Wray!" (and here the Squire's voice lowered, and grew strangely tender for such a rough old gentleman), "you are a happy man, to have a grand-child to keep you company at all times, but especially at Christmas time. I'm a lonely old bachelor, and must eat my Christmas dinner without wife or child to sweeten the taste to me of a single morsel!"

As little Annie heard this, she rose, and stole up to the Squire's side. Her pale face was covered with blushes (all her pretty natural colour had not come back yet); she looked softly at Mr Colebatch, for a moment—then looked down—then said—

"Don't say you're lonely sir! If you would let me be like a grandchild to you, I should be so glad. I—I always make the plum pudding, sir, on Christmas Day, for grandfather—if he would allow,—and if—if you—"

"If that little love isn't trying to screw her courage up to ask me to taste her plum pudding, I'm a Dutchman"—cried the Squire, catch-ing Annie in his arms, and fairly kissing her—"Without ceremony, Mr Wray, I invite myself here, to a Christmas dinner. We would have had it at Cropley Court; but you're not strong enough yet, to go out these cold nights. Never mind! All the dinner, except Annie's pudding, shall be done by my cook; Mrs Buddle, the housekeeper, shall come and help;

and we'll have such a feast, please God, as no king ever sat down to! No apologies, my good friend, on either side: I'm determined to spend the happiest Christmas Day I ever did in my life; and so shall you!"

And the good Squire kept his word. It was, of course, noised abroad over the whole town, that Matthew Colebatch, Esquire, Lord of the Manor of Tidbury-on-the-Marsh, was going to dine on Christmas Day with an old player, in a lodging house. The genteel population were universally scandalized and indignant. The Squire had exhibited his levelling tendencies pretty often before, they said. He had, for instance, been seen cutting jokes in the High Street with a travelling tinker, to whom he had applied in broad daylight to put a new ferrule on his walking stick; he had been detected coolly eating bacon and greens in one of his tenant farmer's cottages; he had been heard singing, "Begone, dull care," in a cracked tenor, to amuse another tenant farmer's child. These actions were disreputable enough; but to go publicly, and dine with an obscure stage-player, put the climax on everything! The Reverend Daubeny Daker said the Squire's proper sphere of action, after that, was a lunatic asylum; and the Reverend Daubeny Daker's friends echoed the sentiment.

Perfectly reckless of this expression of genteel popular opinion, Mr Colebatch arrived to dinner at No. 12, on Christmas Day; and, what is more, wore his black tights and silk stockings, as if he had been going to a grand party. His dinner had arrived before him; and fat Mrs Buddle, in her lavender silk gown, with a cambric handkerchief pinned in front to keep splashes off, appeared auspiciously with the banquet. Never did Annie feel the responsibility of having a plum-pudding to make, so acutely as she felt it, on seeing the savoury feast which Mr Colebatch had ordered, to accompany her one little item of saccharine cookery.

They sat down to dinner, with the Squire at the top of the table (Mr Wray insisted on that); and Mrs Buddle at the bottom (he insisted on that also); old Reuben and Annie, at one side; and "Julius Caesar" all by himself (they knew his habits, and gave him elbow room), at the other. Things were comparatively genteel and quiet, till Annie's pudding came in. At sight of that, Mr Colebatch set up a cheer, as if he had been behind a pack of fox-hounds. The carpenter, thrown quite off his balance by noise and excitement, knocked down a spoon, a wine glass, and a pepperbox, one after the other, in such quick succession, that Mrs Buddle thought him mad; and Annie—for the first time, poor little thing, since all her troubles—actually began to laugh again, as prettily as ever. Mr Colebatch did ample justice, it must be added, to her pudding. Twice did his plate travel up to the dish—a third time it would have gone; but the faithful housekeeper raised her warning voice, and reminded the old gentleman that he had a stomach.

When the tables were cleared, and the glasses filled with the Squire's rare old port, that excellent man rose slowly and solemnly from his chair, announcing that he had three toasts to propose, and one speech to make; the latter, he said, being contingent on the chance of his getting properly at his voice, through two helpings of plum-pudding; a chance which he thought rather remote, principally in consequence of Annie's having rather overdone the proportion of suet in mixing her ingredients.

"The first toast," said the old gentleman, "is the health of Mr Reuben Wray; and God bless him!" When this had been drunk with immense fervour, Mr Colebatch went on at once to his second toast, without pausing to sit down—a custom which other after-dinner orators would do well to imitate.

"The second toast," said he, taking Mr Wray's hand, and looking at the mask, which hung opposite, prettily decorated with holly,—"the second toast, is a wide circulation and a hearty welcome all through England, for the Mask of Shakespeare!" This was duly honoured; and immediately Mr Colebatch went on like lightning to the third toast.

"The third," said he, "is the speech toast." Here he endeavoured, unsuccessfully, to cough up his voice out of the plum pudding. "I say, ladies and gentlemen, this is the speech toast." He stopped again, and desired the carpenter to pour him out a small glass of brandy; having swallowed which, he went on fluently.

"Mr Wray, sir," pursued the old gentleman, "I address you in particular, because you are particularly concerned in what I am going to say. Three days ago, I had a little talk in private with those two young people. Young people, sir, are never wholly free from some imprudent tendencies; and falling in love's one of them." (At this point, Annie slunk behind her grandfather; the carpenter, having nobody to slink behind, put himself quite at his ease, by knocking down an orange.) "Now, sir," continued the Squire, "the private talk that I was speaking of, leads me to suppose that those two particular young people mean to marry each other. You, I understand, objected at first to their engagement; and like good and obedient children, they respected your objection. I think it's time to reward them for that, now. Let them marry, if they will, sir, while you can live happily to see it! I say nothing about our little darling there, but this:—the vital question for her, and for all girls, is not how high, but how good, she, and they, marry. And I must confess, I don't think she's altogether chosen so badly." (The Squire hesitated a moment. He had in his mind, what he could not venture to speak—that the carpenter had saved old Reuben's life when the burglars were in the house; and that he had shown himself well worthy of Annie's confidence, when she asked him to accompany her, in going to recover the mould from Stratford.) "In short, sir," Mr Colebatch resumed, "to cut short this speechifying, I don't think you can object to let them marry, provided they can find means of support. This, I think, they can do. First there are the profits sure to come from the mask, which you are sure to share with them, I know." (This prophecy about the profits was fulfilled: fifty copies of the cast were ordered by the new year; and they sold better still, after that.) "This will do to begin on, I think, Mr Wray. Next, I intend to get our friend there a good berth as master-carpenter for the new crescent they're going to build on my land, at the top of the hill—and that won't be a bad thing, I can tell you! Lastly, I mean you all to leave Tidbury, and live in a cottage of mine that's empty now, and going to rack and ruin for want of a tenant. I'll charge rent, mind, Mr Wray, and come for it every quarter myself, as regular as a tax-gatherer. I don't insult an independent man by the offer of an asylum. Heaven forbid! but till you can do better, I want you to keep my cottage warm for me. I can't give up seeing my new grandchild sometimes! And I want my chat with an old stager, about the British Drama and glorious John Kemble! To cut the thing short, sir: with such a prospect before them as this, do you object to my giving the healths of Mr and Mrs Martin Blunt that are to be!"

Conquered by the Squire's kind looks and words, as much as by his reasons, Old Reuben murmured approval of the toast, adding tenderly, as he looked round on Annie, "If she'll only promise always to let me live with her!"

"There, there!" cried Mr Colebatch, "don't go kissing your grandfather before company like that you little jade; making other people envious of him on Christmas Day! Listen to this! Mr and Mrs Martin Blunt that are to be—married in a week!" added the old gentleman peremptorily.

"Lord, sir!" said Mrs Buddle, "she can't get her dresses ready in that time!"

"She shall, ma'am, if every mantua-making wench in Tidbury stitches her fingers off for it! and there's an end of my speech-making!" Having said this, the Squire dropped back into his chair with a gasp of satisfaction.

"Now we are all happy!" he exclaimed, filling his glass; "and now we'll set in to enjoy our port in earnest—eh, my good friend?"

"Yes; all happy!" echoed old Reuben, patting Annie's hand, which lay in his; "but I think I should be still happier, though, if I could only manage not to remember that horrible dream!"

"Not remember it!" cried Mr Colebatch, "we'll all remember it—all remember it together, from this time forth, in the same pleasant way!"

"How? How?" exclaimed Mr Wray, eagerly.

"Why, my good friend!" answered the Squire, tapping him briskly on the shoulder, "we'll all remember it gaily, as nothing but a *story for a Christmas fireside!*"

A popular mid-Victorian author, William Wilkie Collins wrote several of the earliest recognized detective and suspense novels, including *The Moonstone* and *The Woman in White*. His works were also known for their commentary on current social injustices. "Mr Wray's Cash Box" was first published in 1851.

HO HO HOMICIDE

AN ODELIA GREY SHORT STORY

Sue Ann Jaffarian

Suddenly, my life had become a John le Carré novel.

Directly behind me was a woman with a gun. Ahead of me, near the end of the mall service corridor, was a man wearing a long dark trench coat and a fedora tilted slightly over one eye. He had a thick black beard and leaned against the wall next to a *No Smoking* sign. Clenched between his teeth was a lit cigarette.

"Bring her here," he ordered for the second time in a voice heavy with an Eastern European accent.

The woman poked the gun harder and deeper into my plus size flesh. I remained still, frozen to the floor as if wearing cement overshoes. Dangling from each of my hands were several large and very heavy shopping bags. My mind raced with only two issues: 1) how did I get into this jam? and 2) how do I get out of it without getting my Christmas goose cooked?

The answer to my first question was easy. It's all Santa's fault. That's right, I'm laying this whole mess at the black-booted feet of Santa Claus. None of this would have happened if Santa hadn't sat his big fat red velvet behind next to my big fat denim-clad behind.

With only five shopping days left till Christmas, I, Odelia Patience Grey, found myself at Friendship Mall, the state of the art mall in Las Piernas, California. The place was mobbed with people, most with eyes of glazed frenzy, as they tried to finish their shopping on this last weekend before the big day. Having finished my Christmas shopping weeks ago, there was no good reason for my being here except that I was being held hostage by a peace-on-earth, goodwill toward men mentality that had outlived its usefulness by one day. Meaning yesterday, when my father called and begged me to take my crazy stepmother shopping as a favor to him, I should have said bah humbug and hung up.

But I love my Dad and it was Christmas. Even when he announced that Gigi wanted me to drive all the way to their house, pick her up and drive her all the way to Las Piernas to go to Friendship Mall, I didn't waiver in my commitment to holiday good cheer.

That was yesterday.

Today I'd had to listen to Gigi's endless prattle. She had talked non-stop the entire forty-five minute drive to the mall, the entire twenty minutes it had taken us to find a parking spot, and the entire time I escorted her from one packed store to another. Even stopping for lunch had not slowed down her mouth or her criticism of me one iota. The highlight of lunch was when Gigi tipped her bowl of soup. It splashed across the table and into my lap like a fast-moving lava flow. After lunch, I'd had to make a quick emergency stop at Lane Bryant to purchase a new pair of jeans and panties. As I left the store, a small child pushing a stroller plowed into the back of my legs and about severed the Achilles tendon on my right foot. Well, okay, not really sever it, but the assault was enough to make me yelp in pain and to draw blood.

The Ghost of Christmas Miserable had obviously decided to pay me a visit.

After telling Gigi she'd have to continue shopping without me, I hobbled to a bench and sat down. Injured foot aside, I considered the stroller incident a blessing. It bought me time alone and a chance to sit down for a while. At least until Santa plopped his big butt down next to me with all the grace of an elephant dancing the Nutcracker.

I glanced over at my new bench buddy, trying hard not to scowl as his shoulder knocked into mine. It was then that I noted that his Santa suit was grimy and tattered. Spying an empty bench a few yards away, I decided to move before he asked me to sit on his knee. I was in the midst of picking up my purse and shopping bag with my soiled clothing when the grubby Santa grabbed my arm.

Whipping my head around, I found myself face to face with him. His dirty beard had slipped, uncovering thin pale lips. He blinked slowly but said nothing. He blinked again and tightened his grip on me. Without a sound, his lips squeezed together until all the blood drained from them. I thought at first he was drunk, but there was no smell of alcohol.

I tried to pry his fingers from my arm while he continued to blink and stare. Just as I was about to call out for help, he spoke.

"Help me." The two words were barely audible, but filled with fear.

I stopped trying to get away from him. "Are you ill?"

With his other arm, he reached around in front like he was making a grab at me but only succeeded in banging into my shopping bag as he slumped against me. I tried to disentangle his hand from the bag while supporting him, but didn't have much luck. Finally, his body shuddered a few times and went still.

"Are you ill?" I asked again.

I couldn't reach my cell phone so I shouted out to people walking nearby. "Call 9-1-1." Most ignored me and kept walking. Others stared but kept walking. A few stood frozen to the floor and stared slack-jawed.

I made eye contact with a man carrying a Gap bag. "You," I barked. "Call 9-1-1." My order surprised him but he did as I asked. "This man is ill," I continued, keeping the shopper locked in my sight as he punched numbers on his cell phone. "Get an ambulance."

A young woman in jeans and a sweatshirt pushed her way through the small crowd that had formed. "I'm a doctor," she announced.

The doctor squatted in front of Santa while I held him with one arm around him from behind and the other held against his chest. She checked his pulse then began working her hands quickly around his torso.

"Shouldn't we remove his coat?" I asked her.

She ignored me as her hands traveled up and down his legs, including between them. It looked more like a frisk job than an examination.

I was about to question her doctoring methods when the crowd stepped closer. I freed one of my hands and held it up. "Stay back. Give him some room."

Just then a woman in the group let out a little scream. Another followed. Everyone stared at me as if I were insane. Some scuttled away. The doctor disappeared as another woman screamed. This one louder than all the rest. I turned toward the scream and saw Gigi standing on the far right of the crowd, her hands slapped against both sides of her face in horror.

"Odelia, what have you done now?"

It was then I noticed the hand I was holding out to the crowd was covered with blood.

* * * *

"How do you know Leon Weinberg?"

The man questioning me was a detective with the Las Piernas police who'd been called by mall security. He had introduced himself as Detective Aidan Wong. Standing alert but silent in a corner was a city cop. Seated at the far end of the table fidgeting with an unlit cigarette was Gigi. We were in a small conference room in the mall security office. The questioning had been going on for nearly an hour. It had been almost two hours since Santa expired in my arms.

"Who's Leon Weinberg?" I asked in return.

"The dead Santa."

"Santa's Jewish?"

The detective studied me over the top of his wire framed glasses. "Why not? At least he wouldn't mind working on Christmas."

"He's not the usual mall Santa, is he?"

"I'm supposed to be asking the questions here, Ms. Grey."

"Well," I continued, ignoring his comment, "seems to me that mall Santas are a bit more photogenic. This one was dirty and had a ragged beard. He was also on the second floor, not on the first floor where Santa usually sits in these places."

I was about to say more when Gigi interrupted. "How much longer you gonna be?" she demanded, looking from me to Wong. "It's getting late and I have more shopping to do. I still don't have a thing for Dee Dee's girls." As she spoke, her beehive hairdo, dyed remarkably like Pepto Bismol, nodded in time to her words.

Detective Wong started to say something, but I stopped him. "I'll handle this," I told him. "Believe me, you don't want to get involved."

Gigi looked hard at the detective. "I'm just her stepmother, ya know? She's no blood of mine." As she ranted, she shook the unlit cigarette like a conductor's baton. "Takes after her no-good run-off mother, this one does. My kids would never do such a thing."

Detective Wong and I exchanged looks, then he said to me, "Be my guest."

I turned to Gigi. "Did you bring your cell phone?"

She pursed her lips in disapproval, but nodded.

"Please turn it on and go shopping. When you're done, just call me and I'll find you and we'll go home." I paused. "In fact, why don't you leave your packages and I'll take them to the car when I'm done here. That way you won't have to lug them around."

"Don't know why you can't stay out of trouble like normal people." Gigi was still mumbling about my shortcomings as she was led by a woman with mall security back to the shopping area.

I heard a throat clear and turned my attention back to Detective Wong.

"So, how do you know Leon Weinberg?" he asked again.

"I don't know Leon Weinberg," I insisted. "The man sat down next to me on the bench and two minutes later he was dead."

"Just like that?" He snapped his fingers.

"Yes, just like that." I resisted the urge to snap my fingers back at him. Instead, I turned one of my legs so he could see the gouge in my ankle. "I was the victim of hit-and-run stroller rage. See? Then I sat down on the bench to rest and along came Santa…um…Mr. Wienberg."

"You didn't know he'd been shot?"

"As I told you before, I knew nothing until I saw blood on my hands. Just before he collapsed, he asked me to help him. He never said how or why."

"And this woman, this doctor, you said she examined him and left."

"She claimed she was a doctor. But she more or less frisked him then took off." I paused. "Should I be calling my lawyer?"

Detective Wong knitted his brows in my direction. "I don't know, Ms. Grey, should you?"

I had done nothing wrong except sit my butt down on a bench to rest, but still, maybe having someone here to help me through the questions would help. But who? Seth Washington, lawyer and hubby of my best friend, Zee, was out of town, as was my husband, Greg Stevens. That left two people who could advise me: my boss, Michael Steele, a crackerjack corporate attorney and royal pain in my butt, and Detective Devon Frye of the Newport Beach police. Dev had already bailed me out of more pickles than I care to say. The choice was between enduring Steele's obnoxious remarks and Dev's stern admonitions to keep out of trouble. It was a tough call.

I looked up at Detective Wong. "May I have my cell phone? I'd like to call Detective Devon Frye of the Newport Beach police. He's a friend." Upon arrival, the police had confiscated my tote bag and the bag containing my soiled clothing. They had searched both, including Gigi's bags, which had set her off like a Fourth of July rocket.

"Dev Frye is a friend of yours?" There was disbelief in the detective's voice.

I nodded.

"Then why don't I call him for you?" Detective Wong produced his own phone.

"The number is 949-555-8297," I said, trying to being helpful. "That's his direct line."

Detective Wong shot me a stern look as he punched in the numbers. He didn't have to wait long before his call was answered. "Hey, Dev. Aidan Wong in Las Piernas here." A pause. "Doing fine, thanks. Same ole', same ole. You know how it is." Another pause. "The reason I'm calling is I have someone here who says she's a friend of yours. An Odella Grey."

"That's Odelia," I corrected.

Detective Wong's look changed from stern to a mild scowl before he turned his back to me and lowered his voice. I strained to hear his end of the conversation, not doubting for a minute Dev was giving him an earful of my colorful past with corpses.

"That was her?" Detective Wong turned around and openly stared at me while he listened to Dev. "Uh huh. I see." He held the phone out to me. There was an odd look on his face, like a smirk that was too pooped to complete the task. "He wants to speak with you."

My first inclination was to refuse the call, but I knew that would be a stupid thing to do. After all, I wanted Dev to help me, not to tell Wong to lock me up and throw away the key. I took the phone.

"Hi. Dev? I know this looks a tad odd, but I could really use your help." I was gripped by the babble gods, powerless to stop. "You see, all I did was sit down on a bench and Santa, well not the real Santa, sat next to me and died. I swear I had nothing, absolutely nothing to do with it and I have no idea who this person is…was. And I promise I—" Dev stopped me mid-sentence. I listened to him a few minutes, smart enough now to keep my mouth shut. When he was through, I handed the phone back to Detective Wong. "Your turn again."

Shortly after the call to Dev, I found myself back out in the mall loaded down with shopping bags. Detective Wong had told me to collect Gigi and to go home. Pronto. Under no circumstances was I to play detective in his city. His warning was also word-for-word what Dev had ordered me to do. They could have saved their breath. A pack of angry elves riding rabid reindeer could not have gotten me involved with Santa's murder. All I wanted was to find Gigi, drop her off at her house and head home to a hot bath and Chinese takeout.

I made my way through the throngs of crazed shoppers and holiday decorations toward the exit nearest my car. My plan was to drop off the shopping bags then head back in to find Gigi. I'd called her cell phone but got no answer. She probably couldn't hear it with it stuffed in her handbag.

I was almost to the exit when someone bumped into me hard. I stumbled a bit but didn't fall, but I did lose my grip on the large shopping bags. They dropped to the ground in piles around me. Before I could dust myself off and gather up the bags, I was shoved again. This time I went down to my knees. Two people asked if I was alright. Someone else hooked a hand under one of my arms to help me to my feet.

I turned to thank my Good Samaritan only to find myself face to face with the woman who'd claimed to be a doctor. At the same time, I noticed that she had my arm in a death grip and was sticking something hard into my ribs with her other hand. I couldn't see what it was, but past experience told me it wasn't an umbrella.

She leaned in close. "Pick up the bags and get moving. Back that way."

The direction she was indicating wasn't out the door but back into the stream of shoppers. In a way, I was relieved. In spite of the gun, I felt safer inside. At least if she shot me, there would be witnesses. Then I remembered, no witnesses had come forward when Santa was shot.

"Did you kill Mr. Weinberg?"

She gave me a little shove. "Get moving, I said. And don't try anything funny. Just act normal."

I almost took the time to explain to her that having a gun jabbed into your ribs was in no way, shape or form normal. But then again, neither is a Jewish Santa being shot at the mall the weekend before Christmas. So I buttoned my lip, picked up my shopping bags, and moved in the direction she'd indicated.

We were walking as fast as the crowd would allow. The woman stayed to my left just a footstep behind me and directed me by poking the gun to the left or right as if I were a horse guided by kicks. Soon we were near where the real mall Santa held court and the woman directed me to the right towards the service corridor which housed the restrooms and maintenance area. Fear settled in the pit of my stomach like bad sushi. I should be home decorating my Christmas tree, getting drunk on spiked eggnog, and putting antlers on Wainwright, our dog. Not being led to possible slaughter.

As we entered the long empty corridor, I spotted the man in the trench coat and fedora.

I took a tiny step, then another. It was a hesitant two-step that just might land me alongside Santa in the County Morgue, or it might buy me time to think through a plan of escape. We were close to him now. My nose tingled as it took in the smell of his smoke.

"There's no smoking," I told him.

He removed the cigarette from his lips and studied it with a slow half smile. "You Americans are so intolerant when it comes to tobacco." He leaned closer. "So what did you tell the police?"

"About what?" I asked.

"Do not play games. I do not like such things. Did Weinberg give you the merchandise?"

"You mean the dead Santa?"

The spy who came in from the mall held the lit cigarette under my nose. I could feel the heat close to my nostrils and began to worry he was going to shove it up one.

"Like I told the police, I didn't know Mr. Weinberg."

"You expect me to believe Weinberg simply sat down next to you, a complete stranger, and died?" He snapped his fingers as Detective Wong had. "Just like that?" For the second time that day, I found snapping fingers to be annoying. Had I not been carrying shopping bags, this time I would have snapped back, gun or no gun, cigarette or no cigarette.

"Just like that," I replied without the desired snap. I locked eyes with the man. "I guess he didn't want to die alone."

He held the cigarette a bit closer. I braced myself for the burn I was sure was coming. After a few seconds, the creep withdrew it. Taking a few steps back, he flicked ash to the floor, stuck it back between his lips and took a long drag. As he exhaled, he stubbed the butt out on the *No Smoking* sign.

Keeping my eyes on the man in front of me, I strained my ears for sounds of other people, hoping someone would be either going in or out of one of the nearby restrooms. But all was silent. Didn't people in Las Piernas need to pee? Then I had second thoughts. There was a gun in my back. Dollars to donuts the thug in front of me had one also. Suddenly, the last thing I wanted was some unsuspecting holiday shopper stumbling upon this little gathering.

"One more time," the man said. "Where is the merchandise from Weinberg?"

He jerked his chin and the woman behind me pressed the gun deeper into my back, pushing me to move closer to him. My knees threatened to buckle. I could feel perspiration pooling under my arms, but forced myself to stand still and continue the eye contact.

"The merchandise?" he prompted again.

In silence, I held out the Lane Bryant bag to him. He took it and rummaged through my dirty clothing until he extracted something of interest. He smiled at me. Maybe he got off on dirty granny panties.

"Excellent," he said as he held up a small velvet pouch in triumphant.

Opening it, he dumped the contents into the palm of his hand. Out poured three huge diamonds; bigger than any I'd ever seen in my life. The fluorescent light in the corridor danced merrily on their facets as the creep displayed them. Geez, why hadn't the cops found those?

"Did you and Weinberg really think you would get away with this?" He held the diamonds out for my inspection.

Wide-eyed, I shook my head. "I had no idea those were in there. Truly."

He laughed and jerked his chin again to the woman behind me. "Take care of her."

The gun left my back. I had no idea where it was and I didn't want to know.

"Not here, you fool," he snapped. "Take her into one of the toilets."

Quickly, I analyzed the situation. Even though the woman was much younger and probably stronger, she was half my size. If I could disarm her in the bathroom, I might be able to strong arm her enough to save my neck. But the minute I tried to leave, the guy would easily take me down. He might even come in after me.

The gun was back in its place, prodding me to move towards the ladies room. The man had forgotten me, focused instead on admiring his treasure. If I was to have half a chance, I would have to make a move right here. Right now.

Without warning, the door leading from the mall banged open and a custodian wheeling a maintenance cart of cleaning supplies entered the corridor. In the split second of surprise, I grabbed the remaining shopping bags with both hands and swung them with all my might in a wide circle. I struck the woman first, knocking the gun from her hand, and followed up and through into the head of the man as he reached for his own gun. The second impact caused the handles on the heavy bags to break, launching them out of my grip. I didn't know what Gigi had purchased, but I was thankful it wasn't bags of socks.

I took off down the corridor in the direction of the custodian. Much to my surprise, he pulled a gun of his own and aimed it at me.

"Police, freeze!"

I froze.

* * * *

Once again, I found myself seated in the conference room of the Friendship Mall Security Office. But this time I was a guest, not a detainee. Apparently, Detective Wong and his men had found the diamonds when they searched my bags earlier and left them there, hoping I would lead them to the real murderers.

Leon Weinberg, it turned out, wasn't Santa after all, but had been a career jewel thief. He had stolen the three spectacular diamonds from a master diamond cutter, who had Russian mob connections. The two goons who killed him and grabbed me had been part of the retrieval team.

"You used Odelia as bait?" The question was directed at Detective Wong by Dev Frye. Sure I wouldn't be able to keep out of trouble, Dev had driven to Las Piernas as soon as he had hung up from our earlier call. Good man.

"It worked, didn't it?" Detective Wong smirked at his colleague from Newport Beach.

A moment later, Dev escorted me to the door. Looking back over my shoulder, I saw that Aidan Wong was still sprawled on the floor, blood running from his mouth.

Something told me all he'd want for Christmas would be his two front teeth.

Sue Ann Jaffarian is the critically acclaimed author of three mystery series: the Odelia Grey mystery series, the Ghost of Granny Apples mystery series, and the Madison Rose Vampire Mysteries. She is also the author of the Holidays From Hell short story series available through e-books only. In addition to being a writer, Sue Ann is a full-time paralegal for a Los Angeles law firm and a sought-after motivational speaker.

MURDER ON SANTA CLAUS LANE

William G. Bogart

"Big Ben" Slattery was at the wheel of the police cruiser, and he steered the car deftly through the heavy traffic along Hollywood Boulevard. Johnny Regan, young and lean-looking, sat slumped in the seat beside him.

For six months now, ever since getting on the force, Regan had been riding the bus with Big Ben. Slattery was a big truck-horse of a guy, jovial and easy-going. He was well established on the Force, and he had shown Regan the ropes. They got along.

But tonight was different. For the past half hour Big Ben had been whistling "Holy Night" in an off key. Suddenly Johnny Regan blurted out:

"It was the night before Christmas, and all through the house... Aw, nuts!"

Big Ben looked across at him, his Irish blue eyes crinkling.

"What's the matter, kid?" he demanded. "Ain't you got that old Christmas spirit at all?"

"A fine thing it is," Regan grunted.

"Tomorrow night Christmas Eve, and what do we have to do? Spend it riding around in this crate! They ought to give every cop in L. A. a night off."

"Sure," said Slattery. "And have every punk crook in town having the time of his life. I had off last year. You'll probably get off next—"

He broke off, cocked an ear as he heard the small group of young people singing on the next corner.

Slattery slowed the car, pulled toward the curb. Girls' voices were raised sweetly in a carol, and Big Ben's heavy face beamed. "Now, ain't that just swell—" he started.

"Aw," grunted Johnny Regan. "Come on." He waved his arm impatiently. "Look at things. No lights. Dimouts! Maybe even a blackout tomorrow night. And they used to call this Santa Claus Lane!"

But nothing Regan said could dim Ben Slattery's cheerfulness. Lights or no lights, he had the spirit, and he kept on humming:

Hark, the herald angels sing...

Their loud-speaker crackled and the voice of the dispatcher came crisply over the air:

"Car Two-nineteen, attention. An emergency call. A woman in distress. Car Two-nineteen . . ."

Johnny Regan's gray eyes brightened a trifle.

"Maybe she's a blond and needs help. Anything to relieve the monotony! Let's roll!"

* * * *

Two-nineteen was their car and their call. The address given by the dispatcher was not far. Ben Slattery tramped his brogan down on the gas and they were off.

Moments later they cut down the side street of small movie studios and rooming houses—Poverty Row, as it was known in the trade.

Ben Slattery flicked on the adjustable spotlight and searched house numbers. He slowed before a house half-way down the block, stopped, and pulled on the brake.

"All right, kid," he said. "Run in and see what the dame wants."

He leaned back, pushed his cap to the back of his shaggy head, and started to whistle "Holy Night" again.

Johnny Regan gave his partner a pained frown and slid out of the car. He hard-heeled up the walk, was just feeling around for the bell button when the outside door was jerked open.

"Oh, I'm so glad you're here!" a woman's voice said with relief.

She must have been waiting for him just inside the vestibule. A dim light glowed far back in the hallway, so that Regan could not get a good look at her features. But she appeared to be young, slim-built. Probably pretty.

He grinned in the half darkness.

"What's up, lady? We got a call—"

"My baby," she started, voice worried:

"He's ill. I've got to get down to the corner drugstore for something and I haven't a phone."

"I guess we could run down there for you," Regan said.

"Oh, no," the woman said swiftly. "I'll have to go myself. It's a special prescription and I want to make certain that the druggist compounds it correctly. If you could just stay with Cecil a moment— "

She looked up at him, hopefully, then motioned to the open doorway behind her. Another light glowed dimly in there, a small night light of some sort. The woman turned and led the way.

"He's just fallen asleep again," she said. "If you'll just be very quiet. It will only take me a moment."

* * * *

Johnny Regan saw the plainly furnished room, and the open doorway to the room beyond. The woman looked up at him again appealingly, and she wasn't bad to look at. Not bad at all.

"Just a moment, lady, until I tell my partner," Regan said, "then I'll be right back."

"Hurry," she pleaded.

He moved outside, went back to the car, was grinning when he met Ben Slattery's inquisitive eyes.

"She was," he announced.

"She was what?" Big Ben demanded.

"A blonde! Nice, too. Look, I got to mind her kid while she runs down to the corner a moment. The baby's sick, and she's got no one to leave it with."

"What *is* this," Slattery growled. "A diaper service?"

"Now, listen," said Regan. "Only a moment, see? We've got to help her out."

A limping footstep sounded behind Johnny Regan, and he turned to recognize old Peter Kelsey, watchman at Acme Features, hobbling down the sidewalk. Pete was a nice old guy. Many a night in the quiet hours before dawn they stopped by to have a cup of coffee with him in his watchman's shack just inside the small studio grounds. Acme Features was one of the smaller Poverty Row outfits, and was located around the corner.'

* * * *

"The leg bothering you again, Pete?" Regan asked with feeling, as the elderly man came limping up.

The watchman nodded. "I guess we're going to have rain for Christmas, looks like." He rubbed his thigh, smiling. "I can always tell."

From the open coupe window, Big Ben said:

"Come on, Pete. I'll give you a lift the rest of the way." He jerked his big thumb at Regan. "My partner's got to play nursemaid for a bit."

As Ben Slattery opened the door, Regan hurried back to the house. The police coupe was moving down the street as the blonde opened the front door again.

"Okay, lady," he said. "I'll wait here for you."

She nodded toward the car disappearing down the block. Regan noted that she had slipped on a light sports coat and beret.

"Isn't your partner waiting for you?" she asked.

"He's got to run an errand," Regan said truthfully. He hoped Ben would take his time, and that the blonde would be back before him. He thought it might be kind of nice talking to her for a while. She was the kind who could take your mind off Christmas, and the fact that tomorrow night you had to work.

"Be quiet now," she whispered. "Don't frighten Cecil." She hurried out then.

Johnny Regan tiptoed into the drably furnished living room, gingerly sat down on the edge of a chair. He took off his cap, then put it on again, feeling foolish. What the blazes did you do if a baby started bawling?

He started listening for the slightest sound that would indicate the baby was waking up.

He found himself holding his breath, waiting. It occurred to him that it must be an awful strain to be a father. After a while he relaxed a little bit. No sound had come from the adjoining bedroom. Long quiet moments passed. Certainly the woman ought to be back.

He must have waited fifteen minutes, and was remembering that they had a box to pull shortly on another part of their beat when, disturbed now, Regan got up and tiptoed toward the bedroom. Maybe there was something wrong with the kid. Maybe it had—died!

The thought jerked him into swift action. Using his flashlight, Regan stepped to the doorway of the adjoining room, snapped the light briefly, stared around for the crib.

And he continued to stare.

The room contained a battered washstand, a portable clothes-closet, two straight-back chairs and a single metal bed. The bed was made up and covered with a cheap imitation chenille spread.

There was no crib and no baby.

"Well, I'll be a son!" Regan muttered and slammed toward the hall door.

What kind of a gag was this? Why had the blonde phoned?

In the vestibule he remembered. Phoned? What a dope he was! She had said she must run down to the druggist's because she *had* no phone. Then how in blazes had she phoned the police?

Reagan reached the sidewalk, was staring around looking for either the blonde or his partner, when he heard the shots. Two of them, flat and hard in the stillness of the long side street.

And they came from down there around the corner where Big Ben had headed with old Pete Kelsey!

* * * *

Johnny Regan was running. It seemed he would never reach the end of the long block. He swung the corner, unloosening the flap of his holster as he ran. He saw his big partner's police coupe parked near the entrance drive of Acme Features. The door was hanging open.

Another shot sounded then, from inside the grounds of the movie company. Regan slammed through the open gates, caught the vaguest glimpse of a big form just swinging around the corner of one of the buildings. He started to raise his gun.

"It's me, kid!" his partner yelled at him. "Look out!" He waved an arm. "Over there! That back fence!"

Just as he called the warning, Big Ben jerked around in a peculiar manner. There was the crack of a shot. Regan thought, "The guy's hit!" He dashed forward, keeping close to the building wall in a low crouch.

Slattery was hit. His left arm dangled uselessly. But his big blocky features were grim as he jerked his chin toward the rear, gloomy lot.

"Fence back there," he explained tersely. "Two guys hiding. Watch it!"

"You wait here!" Regan said, and pushed past his big partner and slithered along the wall, covered by shadows of the night. He was thinking that it was his fault that Slattery was hurt. If he hadn't been such a sucker for a dame's attractive figure—

Grimly, with the .38 raised in his fist, he neared the end of the studio building, got the swift blur of a dodging form. A man was leaping toward the wire fence that enclosed the rear of the studio lot. Regan leaped out into the open and leveled the heavy weapon in his first.

A slug screamed inches from his head!

Regan threw himself down to the ground, whipped around, tried to locate source of that shot. He saw the second man going up over another section of the fence. He snapped a quick shot, looked back to see what had happened to the first fellow.

He was over the fence and gone.

Johnny Regan jerked to his feet and took out after the second man. Big Ben was running up behind him.

"I think you winged that second one, kid!" he was calling softly.

Then both of them heard the second man's feet slap the sidewalk beyond the wire fence and start running. Before Regan could even get a bead on the man, he had disappeared down a narrow alley that cut between two buildings beyond the studio lot.

Even as Johnny Regan raced toward the fence there was the sound of a car motor roaring into life. Then the motor sound was quickly fading in the distance.

Slattery drew up, swore vehemently. "Lost them!" he said.

Johnny Regan saw his friend's limply hanging arm.

"You need attention," he said. He started toward the studio building.

"Where's old Pete?" he asked abruptly. He had just remembered the watchman.

"He's all right," Ben Slattery said. His voice sounded suddenly tired. "Those two guys jumped us as we headed toward Pete's office. I shoved Pete on ahead of me inside the doorway. I might have banged his head or something. I was pretty rough about it."

* * * *

Just then, in the doorway of a small building just inside the gates, old Pete himself appeared. He seemed to limp more than usual, and he was rubbing his forehead.

"You all right, old-timer?" Slattery asked, more worried about the elderly watchman than he was about himself.

Pete nodded. "I've called the police. I guess I got a little dizzy. I banged my head on the wall when you pushed me inside the doorway." He looked at Big Ben Slattery and smiled, though he was still trembling. "Thank you for saving my life."

He reached out, touched the officer's arm gratefully, not noticing that the arm dangled strangely. Slattery involuntarily winced.

"Ben needs some attention," Regan said swiftly, and urged his friend toward the small office. At the same time, within the long block beyond the gates, police sirens were already sounding shrilly in the night.

Regan was thinking that this was a fine thing indeed. Old Pete had had to call the police, and here he, Johnny Regan, was the police! He had certainly bungled things in a fine way!

All because of a baby—a blond baby!

It was almost dawn when they were finally back at Headquarters and tall, alert-looking Lieutenant Anderson had checked out the men on his division. Johnny Regan and his partner, Ben Slattery, were the last ones there, remaining behind, and now the Lieutenant was saying:

"And so those crooks were apparently after some Christmas bonus money that Acme was holding on hand for various employees. It's too bad they got away."

That's the way he said it, quietly, but Regan knew what Lieutenant Anderson was thinking. A couple of patrol cops on the job and crooks had slipped right through their fingers. And all because he, Johnny Regan, had been taken in by a blonde.

Only by the slightest margin had his partner missed death. And Slattery had even risked that in order to warn Regan as he had run into the Acme grounds.

"You better take a few days leave, Slattery, until that arm is in shape," the lieutenant was saying.

The way he said it, Regan thought, was even including Slattery in a silent reprimand for letting the potential killers get away. And just recently around Headquarters they had been talking about how Slattery was in line for promotion. He deserved it. He had been some time on the force.

Lieutenant Anderson looked at Johnny Regan.

"We've checked with that rooming house," he said. "A woman rented a room there for a few days. She and her husband, the landlady said. They just moved out tonight. No forwarding address. They must have been spotting that Acme job, and the woman probably knew about that empty apartment right inside the ground floor, and worked that gag to get you and Slattery off the beat while the men pulled the job."

"Slattery's not to be blamed for this, sir," Regan blurted suddenly. "It was all my fault. I fell for that woman's story. I should have checked more closely."

"Regan probably saved my life, Lieutenant," Slattery said quickly. "If it hadn't been for him—"

* * * *

That was like Slattery, Regan thought. Taking the blame equally. He wanted to protest, to explain that if it hadn't been for his own carelessness—

But Lieutenant Anderson finished:

"So you'll have to handle that beat alone, tomorrow night, Regan. I'm too short of men to put anyone on with you, and I've promised these others that they could have Christmas Eve off."

"Yes sir," said Johnny Regan, and he and Slattery went out.

Regan had his own car parked down the street.

"I'll run you home, Ben," he said.

Both of them were pretty quiet on the ride through the early dawn, and both of them were thinking, especially Regan. This was the heck of a Christmas present to give his friend—a slug through the arm.

When Slattery climbed out, he said, grinning:

"Keep away from blondes, kid." But his face was pale. He had lost some blood.

"I'm sorry for what happen—" Regan began.

"Forget it," Slattery said.

And because there was nothing else to say, Johnny Regan drove off. He kept thinking about that blond woman, and the fact that she must be tied in with the crooks, and he was wondering how he could get a lead to the gang....

He stopped around at the boarding house later that same morning. He talked to the landlady, but all she could tell was what she had told the police last night. The blond woman and her husband—"Goodness sakes, he might not even be her husband!"—had moved last night, leaving in a hurry, never even giving her a forwarding address for mail.

She took Regan in and showed him the small flat where the baby was supposed to have been sleeping last night.

"Of course I didn't have the door locked," she explained. "So many people are always coming in and out to look at rooms. Why, that hussy even kept the key to my front door, and she must have known I was going out last night!"

"Yes," Regan said. "You sure can't trust some people."

He looked briefly but sharply around the small flat. He was wondering if there could be something that the blond might have left behind— some little thing that would give him a lead to the gang.

He found nothing.

Later, when he came on duty that night, his eyes burned from lack of sleep and he found himself in a tense, thoughtful mood. In the Department six months, and what a showing he had made! If he could only get a line on those crooks!

About eleven o'clock it started to rain. He recalled old Pete Kelsey's prediction last evening. He guessed he ought to stop around and see Pete a moment.

It was a dreary night. Lights were dimmed in shops. Last night he had been growling because they would have to work tonight—Christmas Eve. But it wouldn't have been so bad with jovial Ben Slattery in the car. Now it was like a hearse!

Regan steered the police coupe down the long block leading to the Acme Studio. The rain kept coming down. He was midway in the block when the blackout sirens sounded. The weird, banshee wails shivered through the dismal night.

* * * *

Regan watched to see if there were any cars moving in the block. All traffic except police and fire department cars was supposed to pull to the curb and park during an air raid warning. There had been several to date, here on the Coast.

But Regan saw no traffic moving within the block. It was deserted. Or was it?

He was nearing the corner, driving slowly because of the suddenly blacked-out street lights, when he noted the sedan parked in gloom at the curb. He thought he detected the movement of someone behind the wheel. A girl!

Johnny Regan slowed as he passed, tried to get a closer look at the woman. Reflection of his own lighted headlamps gave him a partial glimpse of a face that was swiftly turned away from him.

Funny! He thought of that blond dame last night. He could have sworn—

A hunch told him to keep on driving, not stopping, not letting on that he had seen anyone in the car. Because he was suddenly thinking of old Pete Kelsey, and that Pete would be on duty at the Acme Studio just around the next corner. Could that woman parked there in the darkened sedan be a lookout for the gang?

Regan didn't turn at the corner. Instead, he rolled down another block, gathering speed in the darkness, cut around the square and headed back to the movie lot. Leaving the car parked in blackness in a nearby alley, he hurried toward the studio gates.

He saw an air-raid warden just disappearing down the block in the darkness. He was tempted to hail the man, then decided against it. He had pulled a boner last night. Perhaps his uneasiness now was just imagination.

He noted that old Pete had the studio entrance gates locked, as they should be. Regan moved along the fence in the utter blackout darkness, located a spot alongside one of the buildings just inside the high fence, then started climbing over. He dropped lightly to the ground inside.

Pete's office was in darkness. But that was as it should be, too. The watchman had naturally closed the blackout curtains.

Regan hurried up to the door, started to reach for the knob, then gave a start as he saw the door partway open. And no light came from inside at all!

He hurried across the threshold, had taken two or three steps when he almost stumbled headlong over the limp form lying on the floor. He dropped to his knees as he heard the man's groan in the darkness.

"Pete!"

The old man mumbled something. Regan bent close.

"It's Regan, the cop," he said. "Tell me, Pete!"

The old man's words were faint.

"They shot me—chest," he said. He coughed, and Regan didn't like the sound of that cough. "I'm done for, Regan. There's nothing you can do. But try—get them—three men—guns—"

Johnny Regan tried to prod the information out of the old man. He caught the words:

"Office—there—"

The main office, that would be it.

The watchman was trying to tell him that the gunmen were in the main office of the studio, just across the lot!

"Pete!" Regan urged. "You're going to be all right. I'll be right back."

* * * *

The old fellow was trying to say something. He held to Johnny Regan's arms, and Regan heard the faint words:

"I bought lights—other Christmas tree. Thought they might let me—"

Then, suddenly, his aged body went limp in Regan's arms. The officer felt for a pulse. There was none. Old Pete was dead!

Grimly, Johnny Regan whipped to his feet, unholstered his gun and spun toward the doorway. In a way, the blackout aided him. He moved swiftly across the dark area between the buildings, positive that no one watching from the main office could spot him.

He realized that the gunmen had tried a daring scheme. Almost trapped last night, they would hardly return tonight. That's the way the police would figure. That's the way they figured the police would figure. And so they had come back!

Pay-day was the day after Christmas here at Acme. That bonus money was probably still in the company safe.

Regan thought these things as he moved soundlessly toward the building. In the darkness, another dark blot of darkness took form between his eyes. The main office door—open! He approached it.

And just as he was two feet away, a man's figure appeared in that doorway. The fellow spotted the cop, dived back, kicked the door shut as he called a warning to someone within.

Johnny Regan hit the door and crashed it open before it could be locked. He fired instantly and saw a man drop, knew he was dead even before he dropped on his knees beside him.

He caught the barest glimpse of another man leaping toward him, then something slammed down on his head, the gun in the man's hand. He pitched forward, hit the floor, slid, gained his feet and whirled. His gun had fallen and someone was hurtling toward him in the gloom, now that there was no flashlight. Two forms, because he could hear the men's forced breathing.

Regan crashed into one man, and with a blur of movement knocked the fellow's gun hand aside, grasped the man's wrist, twisted until there was a gasp of pain. The weapon clattered to the floor.

The second man seized him from behind.

Regan hunched forward, tried to fling the man over his shoulders. But the fellow hung on. The patrolman twisted, slammed a fist into the man's face. He broke free, dived aside and crashed into a wall. His hand slid along the wall and touched a row of light switches. He flicked one on.

Light flooded the room. One man was leaping toward him. The other was down on the floor, searching around for his gun. Johnny Regan saw his own gun, flung himself down in a dive and clawed out for the weapon.

But the one crook had reached his own gun first.

"Don't move!" he rapped out at Regan.

The gun in the man's fist covered him steadily. Regan climbed slowly to his feet, watching the dark-haired man's heavy, menacing features.

"Get his flashlight," the man covering the cop said.

The second man behind Regan moved close, frisked the officer, and stood back.

"All right," the man with the gun snapped. "Turn off that light. Move!"

Regan edged backward toward the light switches located on the wall.

"Use that flashlight and keep it shielded!" the gunman said to his partner. "These other lights on here might bring a raft of cops!"

* * * *

Johnny Regan's hand went up to the wall switches. He turned slightly to look at them. Something old Pete had said as he was dying flashed through his mind. There was a little lettered metal plate on the wall that made him remember.

He flicked the switch, found himself caught in the beam of the flashlight. The man with the gun came close to him and prodded him across the room. They moved through a doorway.

Regan saw that they had opened another door so that it shielded the office safe, which was open. The door was opened in such a way that, Johnny Regan realized, not even the light of the flashlight could ever be seen from outside.

"Aren't you going to give this guy a slug?" the man holding the flashlight demanded.

"Wait, you chump!" snapped the man who was moving toward the safe. He handed the gun over to his partner. "Wait until we're finished here," he said. "Then."

He bent down, continued rifling the drawers of the open safe. He dumped things into a sack that he had rested on the office floor. Regan was held covered by the light and the gun in the second man's hand.

He knew what was coming. The instant they were finished, and ready to scram, he got a slug. They had already murdered the watchman. A cop killing would make the rap no worse.

Regan's eyes glittered. There was nothing he could do. Nothing to do but die! If only someone—

He heard it then, the shrill whine of a police siren. The two men heard it, too, and the man bent down in front of the open safe came to his feet with a snarl.

"Douse that light!" he yelled automatically, obviously forgetting their captive.

As the light flicked out, Johnny Regan dived. He dived into the man who had been holding the gun, twisted it free of the man's frantic grasp, reversed it in his fist and fired. It was all done in a breathless instant of time.

The man screamed, swayed against Regan.

The officer shoved him aside, heard him crash down to the floor. But Johnny Regan was leaping after the other fellow, trailing the sounds of the man's thudding feet toward the front office door.

The man dived through, straight into the glare of the flashlights and the guns held by police converging on the doorway.

"He's a killer!" Regan yelled, as he saw a heavy gun barrel rap down across the escaping man's head.

That's all Regan waited to see, and then he kept running. He saw the sedan that was moving slowly past in the street outside. He fired a shot overhead and the girl at the wheel drew up in sheer horror, probably figuring the shot was fired directly at her.

Regan pulled her from behind the wheel, held her arm. She was the blonde from the rooming house.

"You and I, lady, are going to have a little talk about Cecil," Regan said grimly. "Remember?"

And as they passed through the entrance gates, rejoining the police who were gathered there, Johnny Regan looked at the two small treelike shrubs that were brightly illuminated with colored Christmas tree lights.

* * * *

The air raid warden was there too. "So I saw these lights," he was saying excitedly, "and hurried over here to complain to the night watchman, and found him in there—dead!"

"Old Pete tried to tell me as he was dying," Johnny Regan added quietly. "He said something about buying lights for his trees. Each year he used to light them up here, but this year he was worried because the dimout rules might not allow it. He was telling Slattery and me about it one night."

"You mean you managed to turn on these tree lights?" someone asked.

Regan nodded. "When they ordered me to turn off the lights inside the office, I saw the lettered plate for the switch that controlled the gate entrance lights. I took a chance that old Pete had hooked his Christmas tree lights up on that circuit. I snapped it on as I shut the other lights off."

The block warden was saying they had better get the lights off. The police were loading a wounded killer and two dead ones into a car. Regan was still holding the woman.

He pushed her toward one of the officers.

"Take care of her a moment, will you?" he said. "I want to call up Slattery and tell him I've got it all straightened out."

"You got what straightened out?"

"Blond trouble," said Johnny Regan grimly.

––––––––––––––

William G. Bogart was a prolific pulp writer whose work appeared in numerous detective fiction magazines in the 1940s and early 1950s. He also wrote several Doc Savage novels.

THUBWAY THAM'S CHRITHTMATH

Johnston McCulley

There was a flurry of fine snow in the stinging air as Thubway Tham came to a stop at a corner of Madison Square, the collar of his overcoat turned up and his gloved hands thrust deep down into the pockets.

It was a little after seven o'clock on Christmas Eve, and Thubway Tham had been purchasing presents. He had them in his pockets now—a new pipe for "Nosey" Moore, who conducted the lodging house where Tham had a room he called home, and a duplicate of it for Detective Craddock.

Thubway Tham chuckled at the thought of a pickpocket of the professional variety giving a Christmas present to the detective assigned to watch him and capture him if he could. But the relationship between himself and Detective Craddock was peculiar in many ways. Each considered the other a foe-man worthy of his steel. For almost two years Detective Craddock had been trying to catch Thubway Tham "with the goods," that being the only way in which he could land the little dip in the big gray prison up the river, but the detective's efforts had availed him nothing.

And now Thubway Tham stood back against a building and watched the happy, jostling crowd. Men rushed here and there, their arms filled with bundles of odd shapes and sizes. Women chatted gayly as they hurried toward the nearest subway entrances. The people seemed happy, and the weather was just right. Tham felt that it was going to be a good Christmas.

He watched the throng for a time, and then lighted a cigarette, took half a dozen puffs at it to get it going properly, bent his head against the force of the stinging wind, and crossed the street to enter Madison Square.

Though it was far too cold to sit on a bench, Thubway Tham wandered from force of habit to the corner where he did sit on pleasant afternoons. He was hoping that he might run across Detective Craddock—and he did.

Just then the big officer came slowly along the walk, chewing at a cigar and watching those who passed. As they met, Craddock grinned.

"Tho I thee your ugly fathe again, do I?" Thubway Tham said by way of greeting.

"Even so, Tham! This is indeed an unexpected pleasure," Detective Craddock told him. "I little expected to run across you in this part of our fair city at this hour of the evening. I had a lurking suspicion that you traveled toward the south when dusk came and remained in that section about which the least said the better."

"Ith that tho?" Tham wanted to know. "And what ith the matter with the part of town in which I live?"

"There is nothing the matter with that part of town, Tham, but some of the people there are under suspicion."

"Uh-huh! Everybody ith under thuthpithion if we leave it to thome of you withe copperth," Tham said. "I wath jutht thtandin' here watchin' the crowd."

"It'll bear watching—in spots," Detective Craddock retorted, grinning again.

"Tho?"

"So! It certainly gratifies me, Tham, to find you out in the open like this. Were you in the subway, now, I'd have to keep an eye on you continually, and I have other things to do this evening. Men of your ilk, Tham, are especially active in the happy Christmas throngs."

"Ith that tho? My goodneth!" Thubway Tham gasped out. "Any crook who would thteal from a perthon on Chrithtmath Eve ought to be thot at thunrithe."

"Tham, that sentiment, coming from you, rather surprises me," the detective admitted.

"You thay, Craddock, that I am a dip and—"

"I'll say again that you are!"

"Maybe tho! But, if I do happen to be a dip—and I ain't thayin' that I am—take it from me that I would not work on a night like thith!"

"No?"

"No!" Thubway Tham declared earnestly. "There are dayth and dayth on which a dip can work. And if one thtealth from a man or woman what might be money for Chrithtmath prethentth, it would be bad luck."

"Oh, I see! I'm getting a new angle on crook superstition!" Craddock said.

"It ith not thuperththition—it ith jutht common dethenthy!" Thubway Tham declared. "I would go hungry before I would thteal on Chrithtmath Eve!"

"And I believe that you actually mean it!" Detective Craddock exclaimed. "I feel greatly relieved, Tham. I won't have to shadow you tonight."

"You couldn't thadow an elephant," Tham told him. "Craddock, you are a copper, but you're dethent and have thome thenthe. I'll thay that much."

"Thank you kindly!" said Craddock, bowing.

"And tho," Thubway Tham added, pulling a little package from one of his big overcoat pockets, "I have gone and bought you a Chrithtmath prethent."

"Tham, you overwhelm me!" the detective declared. "This is not offered in—er—in the nature of a bribe?"

"Craddock, don't be an ath!"

"I humbly beg your pardon, Tham. Thanks! A pipe!"

"You thmoke, don't you?"

"I do, and I happen to need a new pipe. I'll have a little present for you tomorrow, Tham, if I happen to run across you. But understand me, old-timer, I'd take you in this minute if I had the goods on you."

"That ith underthtood," Tham replied. "When you get the goodth on me, Craddock, I'd ought to be taken in and given twithe the limit. I'll thay I had!"

"Nevertheless, old boy, one of these days—"

"I know that old thpeech!" Thubway Tham interrupted. "One of thethe dayth you are goin' to catch me dead to rightth and thend me up the river for about fifteen or twenty yearth. Uh-huh! It theemth to me that I have been hearin' that thtory for quite thome little time now. But I'll thay thith much, Craddock—if I ever am taken in, I hope you'll be the copper to do it and get all the credit."

"Thank you kindly, again!"

"Even if you are a thort of thimp at timeth," Tham added. "Merry Chrithtmath!"

Detective Craddock grinned as Thubway Tham continued along the walk, looked at the pipe and put it into his pocket, and then walked briskly in the opposite direction, toward a corner where he believed that he had important business. Some pickpocket, it had been reported, was working there.

Thubway Tham meant what he had said. He never lifted a leather on Christmas Eve, or on the Fourth of July. He felt sure that it would prove to be ill luck. Of course, if there were extenuating circumstances, he might feel called upon to do so—but he never had met such extenuating circumstances.

He crossed over to Broadway and walked slowly in the direction of Times Square. There, he had decided, he would take a subway express for downtown, go to the lodging house of Nosey Moore, give Mr. Moore his pipe, and then retire.

Though he had few real friends in the world, Thubway Tham felt happy. The spirit of Christmas was upon him. It was as though the folks of the world were all in one big family, and he belonged. He purchased newspapers he did not want and gave them back to the newsboys. He bought a sprig of holly and put it in the buttonhole of his lapel. When men and women jostled him and almost knocked him off the walk and into the street, Thubway Tham did not glare, as he would have glared on any other day.

Descending into the subway, Thubway Tham waited on the crowded platform until a downtown express roared in and boarded one of the crowded cars. As the train started its dash through the big tube, Tham could not help wishing that it was not Christmas Eve. Here were so many "business" chances!

Tham saw half a dozen men near him, any one of whom would have been a prospective victim had he been at "work." But he did not contemplate breaking his rule. There were no extenuating circumstances, as far as he could see.

He glanced around at the happy faces, listened to meaningless chatter, yawned once or twice. He pulled off his gloves and dropped them into an overcoat pocket. It was hot in the crowded car.

And then his eyes bulged suddenly!

Within six feet of him he saw a small-sized man deliberately "lift a leather."

Thubway Tham experienced mingled emotions. In the first place it was unpardonable to lift a leather on Christmas Eve, and the man who did it deserved bad luck for a year. In the next place the subway was sacred to Thubway Tham. All recognized crooks realized that fact and left the subway strictly to Tham. And here was some man Tham did not know lifting a leather on a forbidden day, and doing it in the subway.

"Why, the dirty thneak!" Thubway Tham growled to himself. "It would therve him right if—"

A sudden idea came to Tham. He glanced at the pickpocket and then at the man standing to the right of the pickpocket. Yes, that was the victim, Tham felt sure; the man's overcoat was dark gray, and it was through the flap of a dark gray overcoat that the pickpocket had reached to lift the wearer's wallet. Well, the crook had nerve to continue to stand beside his victim.

"I'll bet that poor fellow needth the money," Tham told himself. "Maybe it ith Chrithtmath money! And that dirty thneak touched him for hith purthe right before my eyeth. Hith work wath coarthe at that!"

Tham's idea was completed by this time. He would touch the dip in turn, he decided, and restore the purse to its owner. That would be a kind act, and Christmas was the time for kind acts, the way Tham saw things.

He swayed forward as the train dashed around a curve and got nearer the pickpocket. He awaited his chance, when the train was coming into the station. His hand darted forward, the purse was taken, and slipped down into Tham's overcoat pocket.

The train stopped, the doors went open, and the owner of the purse got out. Tham stepped out of the car behind him and tried to catch him before he got up to the street. He managed it as the street was reached and touched the other man on the arm.

"Well?" the other said snappily as he turned.

Tham had not expected such a surly tone, but he told himself that perhaps this man had troubles. He grinned and extended the pocketbook.

"You dropped your purthe, thir," Thubway Tham said. "Here it ith!"

The other man looked at him blankly for an instant.

"My—oh, yes, my purse!" he exclaimed. "And you picked it up, I suppose?"

"Thomething like that," Tham admitted.

"Um! And how does it happen that you didn't keep it?" the other asked snapping the purse open.

"That would be a dirty trick on Chrithtmath Eve," Thubway Tham told him. "That ith right—open it and count the money. Think that I thtole thome of it?"

"Certainly not, my man," the other responded. "Had you been wanting to steal, I suppose you would have retained the whole thing. Let me see! A hundred and five—that is correct! Here!"

He extended a five-dollar bill toward Thubway Tham.

"I wath not thinkin' of getting any reward for returnin' the purthe," Tham said.

"Yes, I appreciate that fact, my man, but you are going to take this five just the same," the other replied. "Buy yourself something for Christmas—anything you like. And—thanks! I thank you very much! I—er—appreciate this!"

Thubway Tham accepted the bill. "That ith all right, thir," he said.

And then the other man smiled and turned away. Thubway Tham looked after him and grinned. It struck Tham as funny that he should return a purse stolen by somebody else, and one that still held a hundred dollars, and get a reward for doing it.

Tham was several blocks from the establishment of Nosey Moore, but it was not so cold now, and Thubway Tham decided that he would walk the remainder of the distance rather than descend into the subway again and wait for a train. So he went off down the busy street less than half a block behind the man to whom he had returned the stolen purse.

He had lifted a leather on Christmas Eve, but there had been extenuating circumstances, Tham told himself. He had stolen from a thief and returned the loot to its owner. Tham felt a sudden glow that came from what he considered a kind deed well done. He promised himself that he would spend that five dollars for something that he could keep as a memento of the occasion.

Three blocks down the street he went, and then he came to a sudden stop where some children were singing in the street. Tham waited at the edge of the crowd, already feeling in a pocket for a coin to give when the collection was gathered. He heard two men talking to one side, and when he turned, thinking that he recognized one of the voices, he saw that it was the man to whom he had returned the purse.

"I call it rich!" the man was saying. "The fellow made a mistake, naturally. He saw somebody drop a purse and ran after me and handed it back, thinking that it was mine. A hundred and five in it, too. I gave the boob a five for his honesty, and he broke his tongue thanking me!"

At that his companion laughed.

"Ha, ha!" laughed the man to whom Tham had returned the purse. "A cool hundred to the good! Here it is—see? I'll put it with this other hundred of mine, roll it all together. Some little celebration we'll have tomorrow!" At that he discarded the leather, and a few moments later Thubway Tham picked it up, opened it and found that it contained a card bearing the owner's name and address; then tucked it safely away in an inside pocket.

Thubway Tham felt his blood boiling. So! He had believed that he was doing a kind act, and this man—this crook—had taken advantage of it! And now he was boasting, and calling Thubway Tham a boob! That was the worst of it!

It seemed to Tham that he saw red for a moment. He wanted an instant revenge! He wanted to get back that money, since it did not belong to the man to whom he had given it.

Here, Tham told himself, were extenuating circumstances. If he committed a robbery on this man it would be a just affair. But here was no leather to lift. The scoundrel had wrapped the bills around his own hundred dollars and had put the roll into his coat pocket. Getting it would be more difficult than lifting a leather after the established fashion.

Yet Tham was determined. He forgot all thought of Christmas. He forgot superstition and the season and remembered only that he must get that roll of bills.

When the two men started down the street, Thubway Tham followed them through the crowd. He did not even see the little girl who held out a hat for a coin now that the singing was at an end. He saw nothing except the scoundrel who had duped him.

And Tham felt ill at ease, too, because this was not in the subway, where he generally worked. He did not want to make the attempt until he was reasonably sure of success. Thubway Tham did not wish to spend Christmas Day in prison, waiting for trial on a serious charge. And the true story, if told, would not be believed and would not help him if it was believed.

He remained just far enough behind to avoid being seen and recognized by the man to whom he had given the purse. On down the street they went through the joyous, jostling throng. They approached another corner where young street singers were at work, and Tham thought that possibly he might make the attempt there, if his prospective victim stopped to listen to the singing.

They stopped. Thubway Tham glanced around quickly, searching for the best getaway in case ill luck befell him. He glanced back—and was in time to witness a scene.

Detective Craddock was plowing his way through the crowd. Tham thought at first that the detective was coming straight to him to engage him in conversation and spoil his chances for getting the money back. Craddock had journeyed downtown on police business, he supposed, and it was bad fortune that he should appear at this corner at this particular time.

But Craddock, it was evident, had not seen Thubway Tham. He went around the edge of the crowd. Three quick steps forward the detective took—and touched on the shoulder the man to whom Thubway Tham had given the purse!

"I want you, Canderon!" Craddock said.

There was a curse and a short scuffle. Tham shuddered.

"Now, take it easy!" he heard Detective Craddock saying. "We've been looking for you for five or six months. You were foolish to come back to town so soon, Canderon. We'll take a little trip to headquarters now. As for your friend—"

But Canderon's companion had darted into the crowd and disappeared.

"Probably somebody else that's wanted badly," Craddock said. "Come along, Canderon!"

The detective scattered the immediate crowd with a few growls and led his prisoner away. Thubway Tham slipped after them. Confound it! Craddock had spoiled things now! What fate was it that had brought

Craddock there just at the wrong minute? Was Thubway Tham to lose his chance for revenge?

Craddock, he knew, was bound for a patrol box on the next corner, there to flash a message for the wagon. There seemed little chance for Thubway Tham to do anything.

Tham remembered that roll of bills in the man's pocket. He wanted the roll. He wanted the hundred dollars, and he wanted Conderon's hundred also, by way of profit and revenge. And the presence of Craddock spoiled things!

"Yeth, the thimp!" Tham said growlingly to himself. "Why couldn't he have found hith man a few minuteth later? Thith ith what I get for givin' him a Chrithtmath prethent!"

Detective Craddock went directly to the patrol box, paying no attention to the low mouthings of the prisoner. Tham followed a few feet behind. Curious ones stopped to turn and stare. They came to the patrol box, and Craddock sent in his call and waited.

Thubway Tham was desperate now. His chance to get that roll of bills was lost, he told himself. Craddock, even as he thought this, turned and saw him and grinned.

"Why, hello, Tham," he said.

"Hello, yourthelf!" Tham replied, stepping nearer, "Made a catch, did you?"

"I certainly have, Tham. Mr. Canderon, here, is badly wanted for swindling women and children. Better take a lesson from this, Tham, and lead a straight and honest life. If you don't, I'll be taking you in like this one of these days."

"Yeth?" Tham said. "Maybe tho and maybe not. Tho thith bird hath been swindlin' women, hath he? He lookth like that thort of a cuth. I hope he getth twenty yearth!"

"Tham, wishing bad luck to a brother in crime?"

"He ith no brother of crime of mine," Tham declared stoutly. "I don't care if you hang him!"

"Yes, he'll get a few years to think it over," Craddock replied, chuckling. "He'll eat his Christmas dinner in jail, Tham. You be careful that you don't."

The prisoner had regarded Thubway Tham with amazement at first, and now he turned his face away from the curious throng and looked down the street. Tham stepped a little closer.

"Craddock, lay off that thtuff!" he said in low tones. "Callin' me a crook in front of all thethe folkth? Wonder you wouldn't make them go on about their buthineth!"

Detective Craddock turned quickly to see that the crowd was growing denser and pressing closer. A patrolman came charging through it.

"Need any help, Craddock?" he asked.

"Just send these people about their business," Craddock said.

The patrolman whirled toward the crowd and brandished an arm, meaning that he expected an instant dispersal of the mob. Craddock watched him at the work.

But Mr. Canderon at that moment decided that he did not wish to eat his Christmas dinner in jail if it could be avoided. While Craddock's back was turned, Canderon gave a quick spring forward, knocked Craddock to his knees, and jerked himself free.

Craddock's yell as he struggled to get to his feet caused the patrolman to turn and rush to the rescue. But Thubway Tham had acted already.

Tham saw his chance. He hurled himself forward and thrust out a leg. Mr. Canderon crashed to the pavement, and Tham, with a flying leap, was a-straddle him. There was a sharp, fierce tussle. And then Craddock and the patrolman were at the scene, a blackjack descended, and Mr. Canderon passed out momentarily.

And then Tham got to his feet and started brushing his clothes. The "wagon" arrived, and the prisoner was turned over. Detective Craddock stepped up to Thubway Tham and slapped him on the shoulder.

"Thanks, Tham!" he said. "Good work! I must be growing careless. But I am rather surprised that you'd help an officer against a crook."

"But there are crookth and crookth," Thubway Tham recited.

"He might have escaped in the crowd. You certainly bowled him over."

"I tripped him," Tham explained.

"A good job, too! Tham, I appreciate it! And that reminds me—I won't be able to see you tomorrow, because when I reported an hour ago I got orders to go to Philadelphia tomorrow and bring back a prisoner. Hot way to spend Christmas."

"Tough luck," Tham commented.

"But you're going to have a Christmas present from me, old-timer! Here is a five-dollar bill. You buy yourself something you really want and tell me about it later."

"Yeth, but—" Tham began.

"Go on and take it, or you'll make me feel mean. And I want to be square with you so, in case I get the chance to land you, I can do it with an easy conscience."

Tham accepted the bill. "Thanks, Craddock!" he said. "Buthineth ith exthellent thith evenin'."

Craddock waved his hand and went down the street. Thubway Tham, chuckling, walked rapidly in the other direction. He had the five Craddock had given him, and the five Canderon had given him for returning the purse—and the two hundred he had lifted from the latter's pocket as they had wrestled across the walk.

Before Thubway Tham went to his room that night he made a little journey to the home of the man whose wallet he was carrying. Tham returned the wallet and with it the one hundred and five dollars it had contained when its owner entered the subway. Joy was in Tham's heart, for he had made glad the heart of another.

"Merry Chrithtmath!" Thubway Tham said with a happy smile as he hurried toward the lodging house of Nosey Moore. "Merry Chrithtmath! I'll thay that it ith!"

Johnston McCulley is best known as the creator of Zorro, although he wrote more than fifty novels, numerous short stories, and screenplays for both television and movies. He wrote more than 110 stories about Thubway Tham over a 50-year period. Tham's adventures have been collected in two volumes by Wildside Press, *Adventures of Thubway Tham* and *Tales of Thubway Tham*.

DEATH WILL TRIM YOUR TREE

Elizabeth Zelvin

I sat on the floor in Jimmy and Barbara's living room with a pile of blinking electrical spaghetti in my lap and ground my teeth. For this I'd stayed sober for 357 days and changed my whole life? Cursing the malevolence of circuitry, I began to disentangle the single strand of tiny bulbs that I'd finally gotten to light up all at the same time from the rest.

"Think of it as a meditation," Barbara said, perky as one of Santa's elves.

"You wanna take over?"

"I can't. I'm making latkes." Barbara does Chanukah along with Christmas. She showed me puppy eyes soft with regret. Her feminism flies south at this time of year. Women cook. Men wrestle with the frigging lights.

"Why don't you run over to Broadway and pick up some that work?" Jimmy suggested. Computer geniuses supervise.

I growled low in my throat, sounding more like a pit bull than I expected. Jimmy took it in stride.

"These lights are obsolete, anyhow," he said. "With the new ones, if one bulb goes out, the rest stay on. Replace the one, and you're back in business."

"Thank you for sharing."

I didn't bother asking so how come we were still using the old ones. I knew the answer: Barbara never throws anything out. I picked bits of last year's tinsel off my sweater, grabbed my down vest off the back of a chair, and headed for the door.

"Bruce!" Barbara called after me. "While you're at it, pick up a pint of sour cream."

I could pretend I hadn't heard. But I'd probably get the sour cream. As people were always telling me, AA interferes not only with your drinking but also with such cherished traits as surliness and willingness to disappoint people.

I headed for Manny's Hardware over on Broadway. Manny was long gone, but the hole in the wall he'd founded in 1923 still carried everything you could possibly need, from the oddball size of screw to a giant silver samovar that had been sitting there for years. Or maybe they kept selling and replacing it, one samovar at a time.

In spite of its eight million people, New York is a small town. In the old days, I knew someone in every bar I stumbled into. Now, wherever I went, I saw someone from the program. AA meetings are better lit than bars, so the faces stayed with me.

At Manny's, I recognized the clerk.

"Hi, Tim." I read the name off his shirt, greeting him as I would have at a meeting.

He nodded, giving me a half-smile to acknowledge that he knew me too but wasn't about to break my anonymity by saying so. We said, "What's happening?" and "Not much," and then we were ready to talk hardware. I described the kind of lights I needed. He said they'd been flying off the shelves, but he still had a few boxes in stock. They *never* don't have what you need at Manny's.

"Give me a minute," he said. "I'll go in the back and get them."

Tim opened a door in the wall behind the counter. I could see a stockroom bigger than the shop. A half-open door in the rear offered a glimpse of one of those hidden New York back yards that visitors don't even know exist. The tall, narrow space was lined with ceiling-high gray metal shelves crammed with merchandise and towers of giant brown boxes. He'd have a job finding one carton.

"I may be a while. I know we've got 'em, though."

"No problem."

Tim sketched a salute and dove into the storeroom, closing the door behind him.

I browsed the shelves for a while, decided I didn't need a set of Phillips head screwdrivers or a non-stick pizza stone, and went out front for a smoke. The faint jingle of Salvation Army Santa Claus bells served as background music. The even fainter scent of pine trees from Maine and Canada stacked three deep on wooden scaffolding down the street provided ambience. I drifted off, thinking about nothing in particular. I was far away when a female voice broke into my reverie.

"They're not closed, are they? If I don't find red and gold tinsel, I'll have a panic attack."

New Yorkers.

I dropped the butt I held pinched between my fingers. Grinding it out with the toe of my shoe, I realized I'd stood there long enough to suck up and crush out four cigarettes.

"No, it's open. The clerk went out back to find something for me."

I held the door, which clanged the way shop doors do, and let her precede me into the store. She was a tall, thin woman with a white streak bisecting jet black hair like Cruella de Vil, bundled up in a faux fur coat with matching trim on her faux leather gloves. She lugged a bulging Zabar's shopping bag in each hand.

"Yoohoo!" She bumped her way through the narrow aisle to the counter. "Can I get some service here?"

Tim did not appear.

"He's been gone for a while," I said. "Maybe I should go back there and take a look."

"Don't mind me," she said. "I love Manny's. I could browse in here forever."

Her eyes lit up as she spotted a cut-glass punch bowl on the highest shelf. I'd better get Tim back out here, or she'd be asking me to get it down for her.

I ducked under a hinged flap in the counter top, then opened the stockroom door.

"Tim?" I called. "You've got a customer."

No answer. I marched down the narrow aisle toward the rear door. An open carton blocked the way. Christmas lights. I straddled it and proceeded to the door. It wasn't ajar any more, though a strip of thin winter light still filtered in. I pushed it open with my shoulder and stepped out into the yard.

Tim lay sprawled face down on the concrete, to one side and a few yards beyond the back door. If he was dead, I didn't want to touch the body. I'd rather keep my DNA to myself. But if he wasn't dead, and I failed to help, I'd feel guilty. No more Jack Daniel's to help me blow it off, either. I took a cautious stroll around him, hands in my pockets. The far side of his head, crumpled like a ball of paper, lay in an ooze of blood and brains. Too late for CPR, then.

I closed my eyes and took a few deep breaths until the desire to throw up subsided. I'd better call 911. To tell the truth, I would rather have walked away. But for the new me, that was not an option. As I drew my cell phone from my pocket, I looked around the yard. No handy two-by-four coated with blood and gray matter in sight. Tim had fallen onto concrete. The area wasn't exactly a garbage dump. But recent litterers had left six cigarette butts, seven pop tops, and three candy wrappers within a foot of his outstretched hand.

I would have picked the litter up, out of respect for the abandoned body. But I didn't think the police would appreciate it. I'd better make my call from out front, with the lady customer as witness. While I was at it, I could scoop up my own butts, hopefully before the cops got there. Taking one last look at the body, I saw a familiar-looking bronze coin half hidden by the sprawl of his hip. He'd gone outside wearing only a white T shirt and faded jeans. They'd pulled apart when he fell. I could see a bit of pale skin in between. It looked smooth and vulnerable.

I squatted and fished the coin out with my thumb and forefinger: a medallion with the AA triangle and "3 months" on one side, the Serenity Prayer engraved so small that I had to squint to read it on the other. The bronze was antiqued, so it wasn't shiny. But it didn't look worn, not as if it had been hanging out in somebody's pocket for years. These "chips" were cherished in the fellowship. The only way you could get one was by staying sober for ninety days. Or stealing it off a corpse. I tucked the chip into the pocket of my jeans.

I went back into the store and out the front. Cruella was still there. I broke the news and said I'd call 911.

"I live right around the corner," she said. She looked longingly at the pile of shiny housewares and appliances she'd selected from Manny's shelves and piled on the counter by the cash register. "Do you think it would be okay if I pop back home and get my holiday goodies into the fridge before they spoil? I could come back."

"Please don't go," I said. "The cops might take a dim view of your leaving. And I would really appreciate it if you'd tell them you saw me go behind the counter only a few minutes before I found—before I called the police."

"When you put it that way—oh, why not?" She put the Zabar's bags gently down on the sidewalk and flexed her fingers. "I'll stay. It's Christmas."

Shortly after that, the uniformed cops arrived, then two detectives, crime scene folks, and a parade of snoopy Upper West Siders who didn't want to miss the excitement. It knocked the warm fuzzies from Cruella being nice right out of me. When the detectives asked if I'd known Tim outside the store, I lied. They took my address and told me where to report to be fingerprinted. Then they shooed me off the scene along with the nosy neighbors.

When I got back to Jimmy and Barbara's, I told them what had happened and showed them the ninety-day chip.

"It's evidence, Bruce!" Barbara's voice soared into a shocked squeak. She kind of lost the moral high ground when she added, "Couldn't you have picked up those lights while you were at it?"

"Don't get your panties in a twist, peanut," Jimmy said. "I'll order some online."

"Why did you take it, Bruce?" Barbara said. "Here, have some latkes."

"I'm not sure," I said. "I had some kind of goofy idea of protecting AA. I didn't want cops busting into every meeting in the city to ask questions."

"They'll figure out he was in AA sooner or later," Jimmy said. "The guy had a job and an apartment. At the very least, they'll find a meeting list."

"Okay, so AA was part of his life. But a chip on the scene makes it part of his death. I didn't want them getting the wrong idea."

"Maybe it's the right idea," Barbara said. "Maybe somebody in the program killed him."

"Oh, come on," I said. "Lots of people carry their anniversary coins on them all the time."

"It wasn't his coin," Jimmy said.

"How do you know?" Barbara asked.

"You knew Tim?" I asked. Why was I surprised? Jimmy knew everyone.

"I go to the hardware store now and then," he said. "I knew Tim from meetings. If he was alone in the store, we'd talk."

"Still, how do you know it wasn't his chip?"

"He didn't have ninety days," Jimmy said. "Last week, I went into Manny's to get the new Christmas tree stand."

"Bruce didn't even notice the stand," Barbara said.

"Yes, I did. I noticed the tree didn't fall down this year. Yet. Go on, Jimmy."

"I asked Tim if he wanted to qualify at the Thursday step meeting. He said, and I quote, 'I don't have the clean time. I'm only seventy-two days back from a slip.'"

"Then the chip must have belonged to the murderer," Barbara said. "Bruce, you should have left it there."

Oops.

In the next couple of weeks, with some reluctant help from Jimmy and overenthusiastic help from Barbara, I trolled the twelve-step programs for gossip that might suggest a motive for Tim's death. Tim was a well-known chronic relapser. He'd get a few months together and then pick up. So far, he'd managed not to lose the job at Manny's. But the slips meant that he was perennially on Step One, admitting he was powerless over alcohol. He could put dealing with all his other shortcomings on hold. Like cheating on his girlfriend, Suzanne, whose tearful share I heard one night at a meeting.

"What was I supposed to do?" she wailed to the group of thirty or so alcoholics. "Break up with him every time he had a slip?""

I heard a few quiet mutters of "Yes!" and "Go to Al-Anon!" The woman next to me said, "Stop going to the hardware store for oranges." It's what people trying to recover from addictive relationships tell each other.

"I told him I'd move in with him," Suzanne said, "when he got a year together. I thought it would motivate him to stay sober."

More mutters and a sigh or two from the folks who had mentioned Al-Anon.

"But he didn't want me to move in. He said he wanted to leave his options open. Ha!" For a moment, the rage broke through. "He was seeing someone else, I know he was. And now he's dead!" She broke down sobbing.

Afterward, Suzanne came over to the woman next to me. I eavesdropped, pretending to take part in the conversation of a group of guys I didn't know, as they rattled on.

"In Al-Anon they talk about the three Cs," her friend said. "You didn't cause it, you can't cure it, and you can't control it"—"it" in this case being Tim's drinking.

"I don't get it," Suzanne said. "I loved him. How could I not try to help him stay sober?"

They also talked about Tim's infidelity. Her friend tried to give her some tough love about jealousy, possessiveness, and paranoia being shortcomings that could only hurt her in the end. That went right over Suzanne's head as she obsessed about who the woman Tim was seeing on the side could be. She thought it might be somebody Tim had met at Manny's, if not a program person. Her friend didn't think it could have been a program person, but she got flustered in the middle of telling Suzanne why not. I understood. No alcoholic with good long-term sobriety would have thirteenth-stepped—the polite term for hitting on a newcomer—someone whose recovery was as shaky as Tim's. And of course Suzanne had done just that.

She might have killed him. She was plenty messed up herself. And messed-up alcoholics have some predictable symptoms, including poor judgment, impulsive behavior, denial, and simmering rage that could blow any time. All it would have taken was an angry confrontation, a moment when she lost control, and a blunt instrument.

We also found Tim's sponsor, Malcolm. He'd been in the program for ten years or so, and Jimmy knew him. Jimmy reported back to us that Malcolm had talked mostly about his own moral dilemma. Did he owe it to society to tell the police what he knew? Or did he still owe it to Tim to protect his anonymity?

"What did he know?" I asked.

"He wouldn't tell me," Jimmy said. "And no, I didn't try to pry it out of him. I told him that if his conscience was bothering him, he should go to the police."

Barbara and I had a good time speculating about what Tim might have told Malcolm and nobody else. Sponsees are supposed to be completely honest with their sponsors. Maybe Tim had turned over a resentment list. The idea is that you're supposed to let go all your grudges with the help of a Higher Power. But Tim, with his periodic relapses, could have made the list of resentments without being ready to let them go.

I uncovered one of Tim's secrets when I ran into a guy I knew, Gary, in a church basement that hosted a lot of meetings. I was on my way to AA; he had just come out of a Debtors Anonymous meeting.

"Did you hear about the program guy who got murdered?" he asked.

Gary had never been Mr. Anonymity. If I told him I'd not only found the body, but also been the last person to see him alive, it would be all over the city in a week.

"Yes," I said. "Did you know him?" Hey, if my Higher Power hadn't wanted me to hear Gary's gossip, I wouldn't have run into him.

"I owed him money," Gary said. "He got me a couple of power tools I wanted at a discount. I just started DA, and if I want to be solvent, I have to make a plan to repay all my debts and not incur any new ones. I cut up all my credit cards, but to tell the truth, I'm not so sure I can get by without them. Say, do you think now that he's dead, that cancels the debt? It's not as if he had a wife and kids or anything."

"Ask your DA sponsor, dude."

I had never been crazy about Gary. He'd just confirmed my low opinion. Still, he'd opened up a whole new area of speculation. Could Tim have been stealing from his employer? Selling stuff out the back door? Maybe not while he was clean and sober. But when you're getting high, you'll do anything for the money to score. Maybe Gary wasn't his only customer. Maybe somebody else thought a blow to the head was a good way to cancel an inconvenient debt.

By the day before New Year's Eve, I hadn't found the murderer. And neither had the police. They had come by a couple of times to go over exactly what I'd done, seen, and touched between the front door of Manny's and the puddle around Tim's head. But I could account for all of it. By now, they knew that Tim had been in AA. They'd probably found the Big Book on his night table and program phone numbers in his address book. But I'd never given him my number. And they didn't have probable cause to search my apartment. So I played dumb and shook my head politely when they asked me if I went to AA too.

"Now what?" I asked Jimmy and Barbara. I picked a strand of tinsel off the tree and ran it through my fingers. "I've been to tons of meetings, and nobody's raised their hand and said, 'Hi, I'm Bob, I'm an alcoholic. I killed the guy in the hardware store, and I want to turn it over.'"

"Tomorrow is Amateur Night," Jimmy said. He peered at me over the row of lights Barbara had run across the top of his computer monitor.

"So?" I had been only seven days sober and pretty fogged out last New Year's Eve, but I knew that's what sober alcoholics called it: the one night a year when all the civilians went out and got what they naively thought was drunk.

"There'll be a marathon only a few blocks from Manny's."

He didn't mean a race for runners, but round-the-clock AA meetings to help us get through the holidays clean and sober. I'd gone with Jimmy on Christmas Eve. We'd stayed for a couple of hour-long meetings. It hadn't been boring. Recovering alcoholics telling holiday war stories can be very, very funny. Then I'd gone to sleep on Barbara and Jimmy's couch with the Christmas lights, all present and accounted for, glowing softly, the tinsel shimmering, and the smell of pine in my nostrils. In the morning, there'd been stockings—Barbara had insisted—and presents under the tree. And between one thing and another, I hadn't missed the booze.

"Did you get any clues at the Christmas marathon?" Barbara asked.

"No," I said, "but I was kind of distracted."

"Of course you were," she said. "You were dealing with the holiday and having found Tim dead only a couple of days before, and it was the first anniversary of your Christmas hitting bottom in detox on the Bowery."

Barbara never leaves anything to the imagination. But I could see the love in her eyes, so I responded with a token snort and left it at that.

"It has to be someone with anywhere between ninety days and one year sobriety," Jimmy said. "More than that, and I don't think they'd have gotten entangled with him either financially or emotionally."

"Suzanne did," Barbara said. "But she's a total codependent. Can I come with you guys to the AA marathon? I *do* have boundaries, but it is New Year's Eve, and I hate to get left out."

Understatement.

The meeting was packed. The holiday season was tough on the clean and sober. There was an AA joke about the "threefold disease" being Thanksgiving, Christmas, and New Year's. But everyone in this room tonight had made it through without picking up. As people shared, the word "gratitude" came up a lot. It didn't even embarrass me much any more.

Since the meetings would run all night, even people who usually didn't raise their hands got a chance to share. We heard from guys with forty years' sobriety and newbies who had crawled in after celebrating Christmas with a binge and blackout, like me last year. In the back, people milled around chugging coffee and scarfing down Christmas cookies. I grabbed a styrofoam cup of java and leaned against the wall alongside the rows of folding chairs, where I could see as many faces as possible.

"Tomorrow," one guy said, "the civilians will all be making New Year's resolutions—and breaking them within a week or two."

Everybody laughed.

"I don't make resolutions any more," he said. "I live one day at a time, and it works for me."

A pillar blocked my view of the woman who spoke next. I was wondering if one more cup of coffee would make me hyper, so I didn't hear her name. But I tuned back in when she said, "I made my ninety days right after Thanksgiving." I started to work my way around to where I could see her as she went on about how things happen the way they're meant to happen. "Sometimes life doesn't come out the way you expect," she said, "but maybe it's for the best."

I saw the white-on-black hair before I saw her face. It was Cruella. For the best, huh? For her, maybe, but not for Tim. She must have been the other girlfriend. She'd met him behind the store *before* she came around the front to use me as her alibi. Once I told the cops, they'd find someone who'd seen her. They might even find the murder weapon. They sell a lot of stuff at Zabar's. But not blunt instruments.

Elizabeth Zelvin is a New York City psychotherapist whose mystery series includes *Death Will Get You Sober*, *Death Will Help You Leave Him*, and, coming in 2012, *Death Will Extend Your Vacation*. Three of Liz's short stories, including "Death Will Trim Your Tree," have been nominated for the Agatha Award. Liz's work has appeared in *Ellery Queen's Mystery Magazine* and various anthologies and e-zines. Her author website is www.elizabethzelvin.com. Liz blogs on Poe's Deadly Daughters.

DEATH PLAYS SANTA CLAUS

Johnston McCulley

Deep disgust formed a picture in the face of Detective-lieutenant Mike O'Hara as he sat before his desk in the Homicide Squad's room at Police Headquarters. It was nine by the clock on Christmas Eve.

O'Hara had anticipated a Christmas Eve at home with his wife and their two young children, for it was his regular time off duty. He had intended donning a Santa Claus costume and giving the kids the time of their young lives. A Christmas tree had been prepared, and a closet was filled with presents.

But lots had been drawn to decide which members of the Squad would spend Christmas Eve on duty and which would serve through Christmas Day, and O'Hara had drawn a Christmas Eve position.

So had Detective Sergeant Ed Rassman, who was busy now with the radio in a corner of the room, and bringing in Christmas music. In deference to O'Hara's fit of gloom, he kept the radio turned low. "So it's Christmas Eve," O'Hara growled. "When a man should be at home, if he's got kids. The only homicides we ever have on Christmas Eve are simple killings, the result of fights which are the result of too much Christmas firewater. There's never any question about 'em. No mysteries to solve. The patrolmen on the beats could handle 'em and make a report. Right?"

"Right!" Rassman agreed. "But you never can tell. And by workin' tonight, Mike, we get tomorrow off. We can eat Christmas dinner with our folks."

The telephone bell on O'Hara's desk gave three quick jangles, the alert signal. O'Hara's face grew stern, and he reached for the phone. Those three jerky rings meant business.

"O'Hara at this end!" the lieutenant barked into the mouthpiece.

"Maybe you'd better take that call, lieutenant," the telephone desk sergeant answered. "Sounds important."

"Switch 'em on."

The desk sergeant made the switchboard connection.

"Homicide Squad!" O'Hara barked. "Lieutenant O'Hara speaking."

A cultured, well-modulated masculine voice came to him over the wire.

"This is Dr. Morgan Stampf. I am at the residence of Cecil Fargall on Empire Boulevard. I regret to report that Mr. Fargall passed away a few minutes ago under circumstances that appear suspicious to me. Though I have been his personal physician for several years, I thought it best to notify the police and have an investigation made."

"Quite right, sir!" O'Hara replied. "We'll be right there." He cradled the phone and got out of his chair. "Punch the button, Ed," he ordered Rassman.

"We roll?" Rassman asked.

* * * *

O'Hara nodded assent as he reached for his hat and overcoat. Rassman pressed a button and started things moving. The Homicide Squad was going out!

The speedy sedan with daring chauffeur would be waiting for them when they hurried into the basement garage of Headquarters. The police photographer and the fingerprint expert would follow in a car always ready and carrying their equipment, and two minor Squad men would be with them. "Doc" Layne, the medical examiner on duty, would be notified promptly and chase them to the address.

With its siren wailing a warning to traffic, the sedan rushed and skidded through the streets, with red lights burning. It cut across a corner of the busy retail business district where throngs were making the usual last-minute purchases.

It turned into broad Empire Boulevard and sped along that toward an old residential part of the city where imposing mansions sat far back from the street in groves of trees, and expressed the grandeur of an earlier era.

About an inch of snow was on the ground, and fine snow was drifting through the air. Perfect Christmas Eve weather, O'Hara thought.

"And I should be home playing Santa Claus for my two kids," he growled at Rassman.

"If this turns out to be a twister case—" Rassman began.

To the sergeant, a "twister" case was one involving a mystery to be solved and calling for clever work on the part of the Squad, instead of routine stuff.

"Don't even think that!" O'Hara barked at him, as the police chauffeur, who was listening, grinned into the rear vision mirror. "A twister, with us opening it up, means we'd have to stay with it until the end. Then where'd our Christmas Day at home be? If it's a twister case, we've got to crack it wide open before morning, even if we have to beat the truth out of somebody. I'm going to spend Christmas at home! Let's hope this Cecil Fargall died of a heart attack caused by indigestion."

"I know, Mike, but there's small chance of that," Rassman warned. "Dr. Morgan Stampf is one wise medic, I've heard. He wouldn't have called us for an ordinary heart attack."

"Stampf is a fashionable society doctor," O'Hara explained. "I've met him a few times. He reminds me of a human icicle. But some doctors and surgeons get like that, seeing so much misery and pain. They harden themselves against it, same as we do."

"This Cecil Fargall has a lot of moola, huh?"

"According to common report, he has money stacked up in about a dozen banks," O'Hara replied. "He's about seventy. The family has been here since the town was only a wide place in the trail. Almost died out now. He has only one relative as far as I know—a niece named Penelope. Everybody calls her Penny. Sensible girl of about twenty-three."

Behind their sedan, a siren wailed and indicated that the second Squad car was on their heels. O'Hara relaxed in the seat, lit a cigarette and took a few puffs. The sedan was making good speed on the wide boulevard which traffic seemed to have deserted at that hour.

Finally, the car turned into a driveway and ran up to the front of a huge, old-fashioned mansion and stopped. The second car was there by the time O'Hara and Rassman got out of the first. As O'Hara and the others started up the steps to the front porch, a third car whizzed up and skidded to a stop, and Doc Layne got out of it and hurried to them.

O'Hara called a couple of men to him.

"When this gets out, the news hawks will flock here," he said. "I don't want reporters messing around until I know what's what. You two stand guard and keep 'em out. I'll tell 'em everything later."

O'Hara went up to the front door with the others of the Homicide Squad behind him, but before he could ring, the door was opened by a tall, distinguished-appearing man in evening attire.

"I am Dr. Morgan Stampf," he announced. "Thank you for being so prompt. Please come in, and I'll give you the scant details, so you can get at your work."

Dr. Stampf ushered O'Hara and the others into an elegantly furnished anteroom and waved them toward chairs. He looked what O'Hara had called him—a human icicle.

"This is a tragic occurrence," Dr. Stampf said, when they were seated. "I have been Cecil Fargall's personal physician for years. He was a splendid cultured gentleman."

"I know all that, Dr. Stampf," O'Hara cut in. "Just tell us what's happened here, and please make it as short as possible. It's Christmas Eve, and we're short-handed."

"Very well. It was Mr. Fargall's custom to have a sort of private family party on Christmas Eve. He always had a tree with presents heaped beneath it, and his old houseman, Fred Denshaw, always put on a costume and false face and acted as Santa Claus. His guests this evening were only threes—his niece and ward, Miss Penelope Fargall; Mr. Bob Blodger, her present romantic attachment; and myself."

"You've been here all evening?" O'Hara asked.

* * * *

Dr. Stamp shook his head. "Oh, no!" he said. "I had a call to make on a patient, and telephoned that I'd be in a little late to partake of Christmas cheer, and for them to go ahead with their Santa Claus show and not wait for me. I arrived only a few minutes before I called you."

"Where are the others?" O'Hara asked.

"In the living room. Mr. Fargall died in the library, where he had the Christmas tree. I left the body there and asked Miss Fargall and Mr. Blodger to retire to the living room and remain there."

"Just what happened?"

"When I came to the house and rang, the door was opened by Bob Blodger. He said Santa Claus had just done his stuff—Santa being Fred Denshaw, the old houseman—and had gone to prepare the buffet lunch. In addition to Denshaw, there are only two servants, a cook and maid. Mr. Fargall felt that, in war time, he should get along with a small staff."

"After you came in?" O'Hara hinted.

"I removed my hat and overcoat and started for the library with Bob Blodger, saying I'd be glad to have a drink and toast myself before the fireplace. As we went along the hall, we heard Miss Fargall scream, and ran to her at once. Her uncle had collapsed and dropped upon the floor.

"I asked Blodger to aid me, and we put him upon a couch. I expected the usual heart attack. Mr. Fargall was past seventy and has had repeated attacks of acute indigestion."

"But it wasn't an ordinary heart attack?" O'Hara asked.

"In my judgment, no. Your medical examiner—Doctor Layne, here—can make his own investigation. I think he will detect at once a scent of bitter almonds."

"Prussic acid?" Doc Layne snapped.

Dr. Stampf nodded his head in assent.

They went into the library. Layne went to the couch and made an immediate examination. O'Hara looked around the room, while Rassman began his usual prowling. The photographer and fingerprint men stood aside, waiting to be called to do their work if they were needed.

There was the Christmas tree in a corner. Wrappings from packages were scattered around the room. Opened and unopened boxes of presents were on the tables and chairs. A portable bar had been set up in one corner, and beside it was a table covered with luncheon foods.

Doc Layne concluded his examination.

"Prussic acid, hydrocyanic, I'd say," he reported to O'Hara. "Every symptom. And no indication it was taken through the mouth."

"He didn't drink the stuff, you mean?" O'Hara asked.

Doc Layne shook his head negatively.

"How'd he get it, then?"

"I'll continue my examination," Layne said, giving O'Hara a level look.

"All right, Doc. Rassman, come with me. Dr. Stampf, we'll join the others, please. You other boys stay with Layne."

They went to the big living room. Penny Fargall and Bob Blodger were sitting on a divan. The girl was sobbing softly, and Blodger had an arm around her, trying to comfort her.

"Tell me exactly what happened," O'Hara instructed the girl.

"We had been having a happy time," she replied. "Dr. Stampf phoned and said he'd be delayed, so my uncle told Denshaw to get into his costume and play Santa Claus."

"Usual sort of costume?" O'Hara asked.

"The same one Denshaw has used for years. Red flannel trimmed with white, and he always wore a Santa Claus mask and heavy fur gloves. He came in and got the presents from beneath the tree and handed them to us and bowed, as always before. He left Dr. Stampf's gifts in a little pile under the tree. Then Uncle Cecil remarked about the buffet supper, which was a hint for Denshaw to retire, take off the costume, and make hot coffee. Uncle had told the cook and maid they could have the evening off. He always did that on Christmas Eve."

"What happened after the houseman left?" O'Hara asked.

"Uncle was laughing at a funny little toy I had bought him as a gift. Suddenly he dropped it, tried to get out of the chair and to his feet. A horrible expression came into his face, and he dropped to the floor."

"Who was with him at the time?"

"I was alone with him," Penny said, "The door bell had rung, and we guessed Dr. Stampf had arrived, and Bob hurried to let him in, knowing

Denshaw was busy in the kitchen. I screamed when Uncle fell, and they came running."

"All that correct, Blodger?" O'Hara asked.

"Yes, sir."

O'Hara eyed him. Bob Blodger was about twenty-eight, the son of a good family. He had won a reputation in football in his college days. He had been in the Marines, had seen some hard fighting and had been invalided home. O'Hara knew young Blodger was working now for a bond company, though his family had plenty of money and he really did not have to work.

* * * *

That Bob Blodger and Penny Fargall were in love with each other, there could be no doubt. The way they looked at each other, the way they acted told that. But O'Hara, who read the newspapers religiously, even to the want ads and society news, for professional reasons, had not noticed a report of an actual engagement.

Doc Layne came to the door and called O'Hara, and he excused himself and went to talk to the medical examiner.

"He got it in his right hand," Layne reported. "Must have been a hypo needle. There's a puncture, and burn."

"You mean somebody gave it to him?"

"We searched around, and didn't find any needle. Searched his clothing and all over the room."

"How long did it take the stuff to work, Doc?"

"Hard to say. It'd depend on the strength of the solution, the condition of the victim, and all that. It was a few minutes after nine when we got the call. I'd say he died about that time.

Can't be sure, but it's close enough."

"Somebody must have jabbed him," O'Hara mused. "Far as we know now, Dr. Stampf wasn't here. According to all stories, he rang the door bell a moment before Fargall dropped. That leaves Penny Fargall and young Blodger—and the houseman. Umm! I've got an idea."

He hurried back to the living room and sat down, a picture of poise. He spoke in a voice which did not betray excitement.

"Miss Fargall, did anything unusual happen while the presents were being distributed? Did your uncle act normally?"

"Yes," she replied. "He was joking and laughing. He was always like a boy on Christmas Eve. It was one redeeming trait—" She stopped abruptly.

"Redeeming trait? Am I to gather that you didn't exactly like your uncle?"

"He was both my uncle and guardian," she replied. "He and a bank were to handle my fortune until I was twenty-five, which will be in seven months. We—we didn't see alike about some things."

"Romantic affairs, for instance?' O'Hara asked.

"Mr. Fargall didn't want Penny to marry me," Bob Blodger cut in. "Penny and I really love each other. I have plenty of money, and so has my family, though not as much as Mr. Fargall, of course."

"What was his objection to you, Blodger?" O'Hara wanted to know. "I happen to know your fine family, and if you could support her, and she was in love with you, why should there be an objection?"

"My uncle was a tyrant," Penny Fargall broke in this time. "He was a man who wanted to order the lives of all around him. I never actually quarreled with him, but I did demand that he let me marry Bob. The other day, I threatened to marry Bob anyhow, without uncle's consent."

"Any idea why he didn't want you to marry Blodger?"

"He said he wanted me to marry an older man, an established man who had attained prominence. Such a man, he held, should always marry a young woman of good family and estate, so she could preside like a queen over his household, and give him strong, healthy children to carry on the line. That sort of thing was a mania with him."

"I see."

O'Hara got up and paced around the room for a moment, while the others watched. Doc Layne was standing in the doorway, and Dr. Stampf was sitting off to one side saying nothing. O'Hara stopped pacing and faced them.

"Mr. Fargall was murdered!" he snapped.

"Murdered?" Penny cried, as she gripped Bob Blodger's arm. "But—he just collapsed. Nobody touched him!"

"You said he was laughing and joking while the presents were being distributed. Think, now! Did anything at all unusual happen?"

"It may not amount to much—" Blodger began.

"I'll decide that," O'Hara snapped at him. "What was it?"

"Well, when Santa Claus handed him one of the packages—the very last, if I'm not mistaken— Mr. Fargall cried 'Ouch!' and shook his right hand. An instant later, he said a pin in the ribbon around the package had stuck him."

"Santa Claus handed him the package?"

"Yes, sir. Mr. Fargall unwrapped it, and Santa Claus—that is Den-shaw, left to get rid of his costume and make coffee. A little later, the door bell rang, and Penny asked me to answer it because Denshaw was busy. I let in Dr. Stampf, as you know."

"Where is Denshaw, the houseman, now?" Hara asked. "I think I'll have a little talk with him."

"Probably in the kitchen," Penny replied. Straight back to the cross hall, then to the right. Denshaw's living room is just off the kitchen, too."

"Get him, Ed!" O'Hara snapped at Rassman.

* * * *

As Rassman hurried away, O'Hara looked at the others again.

"As I said," he told them, "Mr. Fargall was murdered. Prussic acid killed him. It was injected in the right hand. When he said a pin had stuck him, he got the poison."

"Then Denshaw did it!" Blodger cried. "But why should he?"

O'Hara signaled for him to be silent, and faced the girl again. "Miss Fargall, how long have you lived here?" he asked.

"My mother, who was my last surviving relative except Uncle Cecil, died when I was ten. Uncle Cecil brought me here. Almost immediately, I was sent away to school, and that kept up until schooling was over. Then I had a debut, and since that have lived on here, with frequent trips abroad—before the war."

"How long has Fred Denshaw been houseman here?"

"He was here for some years before I came. He really was butler, when Uncle Cecil had a big house staff. He's been a sort of general handy man since Uncle cut down the staff because of the war. He thought it was the patriotic thing to do. My uncle had his faults, but he was a real patriotic American. I'll say that for him."

"Did he ever have any trouble with Denshaw?" O'Hara asked.

"I can answer that," Penny replied. "I've heard them several times recently when they seemed to be quarreling, and it surprised me that Uncle Cecil, so proud and arrogant, would tolerate it. I expected him to discharge Denshaw, but he didn't."

"Know what they were quarreling about?"

"No, sir. I didn't hear actual words, just their angry voices. And once I saw Denshaw come from the library, and his eyes were blazing and his fists were clenched."

Rassman came to the door, and called, and O'Hara hurried out to him. Rassman called to Doc Layne, too.

"I found the houseman, Denshaw," Rassman whispered. "He's on the floor in his own room— dead."

"Put the photographer in front of the library door," O'Hara snapped. "Put the fingerprint man on guard at this door. Call in one of the men outside—Carlson will do—and tell him to stand by here in the hall. Quick!"

Rassman hurried down the hall toward the door, barking orders.

"So we've got a twister, maybe," O'Hara said to Doc Layne.

The men were stationed quickly, then Rassman took O'Hara and Doc down the hall, through the enormous kitchen and to the houseman's room.

Denshaw was stretched on the floor, face upward. On the floor beside him was a tumbled Santa Claus costume, as if he had just cast it off. Doc Layne made a swift examination.

"Same stuff," he reported. "Puncture and burn in the left hand."

Layne went on with his examination while O'Hara and Rassman searched the room.

"So Fargall and this man had been quarrelin' about somethin'," Rassman summed up. "He jabs Fargall and kills him, then comes back to his own room and jabs himself."

"With what?" O'Hara said, "We haven't found a needle."

"This man got a heavy shot most instantly," Layne reported

"Would he have had time to needle?"

"I'd say not. He probably dropped a second after he was jabbed. Somebody could have held him, jabbed, waited until the stuff did its work and then dropped him on the floor."

O'Hara looked at Rassman. "Ed, let's assume that Denshaw decided to kill his employer and then commit suicide. If so, why the trickery? Why didn't he just kill Fargall with a gun or some other weapon and then make away with himself? Why the jab in the hand while playing Santa Claus? And housemen, as a rule, don't go packing prussic acid and hypo needles. Prussic isn't easy to get."

"I've guessed it, Mike—somebody else killed them both," Rassman decided. "Tried to make it look like Denshaw had killed Fargall and then himself. It'd look good, specially since Fargall and Denshaw had been quarrelin' about somethin'."

"So it seems, Mike," O'Hara picked up the discarded Santa Claus costume. It was of ordinary red flannel, trimmed in white, and the mask had been tossed down near it. O'Hara sniffed at the costume, then held it for Rassman to sniff.

"Moth balls," Rassman said.

"Right! And why not? They've been using this costume each Christmas Eve, and packing it away meanwhile."

O'Hara went over to Denshaw's body, knelt beside it, bent forward and sniffed and sniffed. He motioned for Rassman to do the same.

"No moth ball smell," Rassman said.

"Right again," O'Hara declared. "Which means that poor Denshaw didn't have on that Santa Claus costume tonight. Somebody killed him in here as he was preparing to put the costume on. That somebody played Santa Claus in Denshaw's place—and killed Fargall."

"So it's a twister," Rassman said.

"And we're goin' to crack it quick," O'Hara declared. "I'm not going to spend Christmas Day away from my family working on a case. Get out your flashlight and come with me."

* * * *

They went out the kitchen door and flashed their lights. There was an inch or more snow on the ground, and tracks were in the snow. They led around the side of to the driveway. The tracks were all alike. Somebody had come around the house and entered, then had gone back the same way.

"Let's get inside," O'Hara said. "Things are commencing to shape up. We'll get some facts, now, maybe. Keep your mouth shut about things."

They went back to the living room. Penny Fargall was sitting on the divan beside Bob Blodger again. Dr. Morgan Stampf was still in his chair, puffing languidly at a cigarette.

"The houseman, Denshaw, is dead," O'Hara announced bluntly. "In the same manner. The first reaction was that he killed Mr. Fargall because of their quarrel, and then committed suicide. But certain things now lead us to believe that somebody else killed them both."

"Killed them both?" Dr. Stampf cried. "Who could have done it? How—and why?"

"There is no indication of any stranger being in the house tonight, though such a thing is possible," O'Hara told them, standing beside Dr. Stampf's chair. "So…well, look at yourselves. Who had the opportunity? Miss Fargall did. Mr. Blodger did. Denshaw did, but he was a victim himself so is out of it."

"How dare you suggest such a thing?" Blodger began indignantly.

"Tut, tut!" O'Hara interrupted, shaking a finger at him. "To me, everybody is guilty until proved innocent. By the way, do any of you happen to know who benefits by Mr. Fargall's will?"

"I can tell you something of that," Dr. Stampf replied. "Mr. Fargall made a new will about a year ago, and consulted me regarding one part of it. And he happened to tell me what he intended doing with the estate."

"What?"

"Large amounts for various charities, of course. A fortune for Penny, his only surviving relative. Denshaw was down for ten thousand dollars for long and faithful service."

"And you—?" O'Hara questioned.

"Mr. Fargall's wife died of cancer. He spoke to me some years ago about leaving an amount to be used as a special fund for the study of cancer. I was to use the money to found a clinic and build a sanitarium, of which I was to be the supervising director. A splendid idea!"

"I agree with you," O'Hara said. "Have you had any recent disagreements with Mr. Fargall?"

"I? Only because he disregarded my instructions about his diet. He had grown subject to fits of irascibility and was rather difficult at times, as Penny can tell you."

"Disagree about anything else?"

Dr. Morgan Stampf hesitated a moment, puffed his cigarette, took it from his mouth.

"It must come out, I suppose," he replied. "Mr. Fargall had an idea—and he was a man always fixed in his ideas—that I could make myself famous as director of the cancer clinic. I suggested he found it at once and not wait until after his death and settlement of his estate. He disagreed with me on that. And there was another matter."

"What was it?" O'Hara asked.

"Well—he had ideas about family. He wanted his fortune to remain in the family to a degree, same as many men do. He wanted his niece to be connected in some manner with whatever his money accomplished. That is why he did not want her to marry Mr. Blodger. In fact, he desired a marriage between Penny and myself."

"What?" Penny and Blodger cried together.

Dr. Stampf smiled slightly. "Yes, Penny, I was the man he meant when he said he wanted you married to an older man with an established reputation. I have never married, you know. I told him the idea was ridiculous, and he grew angry. Not that any man in his right mind would refuse such a bride as you, my dear"—he bowed to Penny—"but my heart interest is elsewhere. I had a college sweetheart. We quarreled and she married another man. Two years ago, she became a widow. We have met and renewed our attachment."

"I understand," O'Hara broke in. "Let's get back on the beam. You and Fargall fussed about it?"

"To such an extent that he told me, recently, that if I didn't agree to a marriage with Penny he would change his will and name another physician to head the clinic."

"Well, let's check on everything," O'Hara said. "You told me, Dr. Stampf, that you were late for the party here because you had to call on a patient."

"Yes. Henry Zeller, who lives in the Royal Arms apartment house a block down the street. He's rather old and getting almost helpless. Has a nurse continually."

"Did he have a bad attack tonight?"

"Oh, nothing like that!" Dr. Stampf replied. "The nurse wanted to get off to go to a Christmas Eve party. So I called and let her go, then I sat with Mr. Zeller and gave him a sedative that would put him to sleep for hours, so the nurse wouldn't have to hurry back. When he dozed off and I was sure he was all right, I hurried here."

"Remember what time you got here?"

"A little before nine."

"When did you go to visit Zeller?"

"About eight or a little before. The nurse possibly can verify the time."

* * * *

O'Hara gave Rassman a direct look, and the detective sergeant slipped into the hall quickly. The Squad man, Carlson, appeared to take his place.

"Dr. Stampf, in fairness to you, I'm having your story checked," O'Hara told him. "If you people will excuse me for a few minutes, I'll attend to matters and then come back."

Doc Layne had made arrangements for the removal of the bodies. The police photographer had flashed bulbs and exposed films. The fingerprints man had searched everywhere for prints. Reporters had got word of Fargall's death and were waiting outside the front door, held there by O'Hara's guard.

O'Hara hurried back to the living room, got from Penny the name of her uncle's attorney, and went to the library to telephone him and apprise him of Fargall's death. Then he went out and faced the reporters.

"Bear with me a little longer, boys, and I'll give you the whole thing," he said. "It'll be a clean-up of the case, I hope. Mr. Fargall was murdered, and so was his old houseman, Fred Denshaw. That's all for now."

He got away from them, slammed the door shut in their faces, and went back along the hall, his head bent, thinking.

In the living room, he sat down on the end of a couch, lit a cigarette and glanced at the others.

"Miss Fargall, and you, Blodger, think carefully now before you answer. When did you see Denshaw last?"

"If he wasn't the Santa Claus, it was just a little before Santa Claus came to the library," Penny replied. "Uncle told him it was time for Santa Claus to appear. Denshaw was putting food on the buffet table."

"This Santa Claus—did he resemble Denshaw?"

"Well, we supposed he was Denshaw," Penny said. "Seemed the same size."

"How about his voice?"

"He never spoke. Uncle never allowed that. Said it broke the illusion to have Santa Claus speak. He just gave us the presents and bowed."

"Notice his hands?"

"He was wearing big fur gloves," Bob Blodger put in.

"And very handy when it came to concealing a stubby hypo needle," O'Hara remarked. "Just before your uncle collapsed, Miss Fargall, did you touch him?"

"No. I was sitting on the corner. Bob was beside me. Uncle was in the big easy chair beside the reading desk."

"You touch him, Blodger, or shake hands with him?" O'Hara asked.

"No, sir. Are you intimating I killed him? And I wasn't out of the library, so I couldn't have killed Denshaw."

"Very cleverly put," O'Hara

O'Hara turned to Dr. Stampf. "Since this tragedy has occurred, I suppose hasn't been changed, and you'll have the chance to go ahead with the sanitarium."

"I presume so," Stampf replied. "It will be a monument to Mr. Fargall."

"How long ago was it you would not marry Miss Fargall, and he threatened to change the will and name another doctor?"

"Three days ago, I believe."

O'Hara got up and killed time pacing around the room. He was waiting for Rassman, who had gone to the Zeller apartment a block away. And finally Rassman returned and beckoned him, and O'Hara went into the hall. He listened to what Rassman had to say, then went back into the living room with Rassman beside him.

Rassman whispered to the squad man, Carlson, as he entered, and Carlson drifted across the room and unobtrusively took up his position. O'Hara took the center of the floor.

"I think we have this thing solved," O'Hara said. "One of you now in this room killed both Mr. Fargall and Fred Denshaw."

Penny and Bob Blodger and gave gasps of horror. Stampf brought out his cigarette case, carefully selected a cigarette, lit it with an expensive lighter, and returned lighter and case to his pockets. He fumbled for an instant in his waistcoat pocket, then settled back to smoke and listen.

"By the way, Dr. Stampf, you didn't see Denshaw this evening?" O'Hara asked.

"I didn't."

"Nor see the Santa Claus, whoever played the part?"

"I did not."

"When did you see the costume last?"

"Why, last Christmas Eve. I was a guest here at the usual party, and Denshaw played Santa Claus. I'll always remember it, because Denshaw got nervous and knocked over a table and smashed a vase, and was apologizing all over the place."

"I remember that, too," said Penny.

"Dr. Stampf, you travel in fashionable society," O'Hara said, "and I presume you wear evening clothes a great deal?"

"Almost every evening," Stampf replied, smiling slightly. He also had a look of slight bewilderment in his face.

"You don't have to put up your evening clothes in moth balls then," O'Hara said, smiling also.

* * * *

Lieutenant O'Hara puffed at his cigarette a few times, then extinguished it carefully in an ash tray and straightened.

"Well, I think we can consider this case closed, which will give me a chance to spend Christmas at home with my family," he said. "Dr. Stampf, you went to Zeller's apartment a little before eight, as you said. Sergeant Rassman checked on that. The nurse had returned when Rassman was over at the apartment a few minutes ago. She says you came and she left immediately at about a quarter of eight."

"That's correct," Stampf replied. "I talked with Zeller for a time, and finally gave him a sedative, then came here."

"Isn't it true, Doctor, that you gave him a sedative at once? He became unconscious immediately, and gave you an opportunity to leave, and Zeller couldn't tell afterward what time you had left. His apartment on the second floor is served with a private automatic elevator, and nobody saw you leave. You hurried back here, entered house and accosted Denshaw in his room as he was preparing to put on the Santa Claus costume."

"I beg your pardon!" Dr. Stampf expressed indignation.

"Wait until I am done," O'Hara requested. "You held Denshaw, who was not a strong man, jabbed him with a needle and killed him. You put on the costume and hurried to the library and played Santa Claus. You killed Mr. Fargall. Then you went back to Denshaw's room, took off the costume, hurried out of the house and around to the front door and rang the bell, getting here about the time Mr. Fargall dropped dead."

"Are you daring to intimate—"

"I'm not intimating. I'm accusing you, and arresting you, for the murders of Mr. Fargall and Fred Denshaw. And knowing that the undertakers might discover the cause of death, you couldn't certify to a natural death from a heart attack, so you called the police. You probably thought Miss Fargall or Mr. Blodger would be suspected and blamed. You believed your alibi perfect."

"Why should I—have killed those two men?"

"To get the fat job of handling a fortune for a clinic and sanitarium, make yourself an international reputation possibly, and have plenty of money to marry your old college sweetheart. You knew Fargall would change his will."

"Preposterous!"

"Oh, let's end it!" O'Hara snapped. "The Santa Claus costume reeked with moth balls. Denshaw's clothes did not, so he didn't have the costume on over them. But your evening clothes, which you use continually and which are never packed away in moth balls, do. You put on that costume and played Santa Claus tonight and killed Fargall… Watch him, Carlson!"

O'Hara barked the last words at his Squad man. Dr. Stampf had lifted his left hand and taken the cigarette from his mouth. Then his right hand went up swiftly and slipped something between his lips. His teeth crunched a capsule.

"This will make three of us," Stampf said.

"You guessed it right, Lieutenant O'Hara."

His head jerked up, he gasped, his eyes rolled, and he would have toppled from the chair if Carlson had not held the body back.

"I didn't even have time to tell him how he left his tracks plain in the snow," O'Hara said.

––––––––––––

Johnston McCulley is best known as the creator of Zorro, although he wrote more than fifty novels, numerous short stories, and screenplays for both television and movies. He also appears in this book with "Thubway Tham's Chrithtmath."

A STAKE OF HOLLY

Lillian Stewart Carl

Jacob Marley had been dead as a doornail, to begin with, and soon Ebenezer Scrooge would no longer be debating just why a doornail, rather than a coffin nail, was considered a fatal bit of ironmongery.

Tim Cratchit bent over his benefactor's bed—it was his deathbed, but Tim was not yet ready to admit to that awful fact—Tim bent over Scrooge's wasted features and said, "You sent for me, sir?"

Scrooge's eyes fluttered open, and took a long moment to focus, as though they were already inspecting the new world to which they were bound. Then they lit with a pleasure that plumped the deep furrows in his face and tinged its ashen color with pink. "Tim, my lad. Always a good lad, aren't you?"

"Thanks to you, sir." The young man pulled a chair, lately abandoned by the nurse, closer to the bed and sat down. "Your generosity to my family these nineteen years . . ."

Laboriously Scrooge waved his hand in the air and let it fall back to the counterpane. It made a thump no louder than that of thistledown. "What right have I to demand thanks for going about my business as a steward of mankind and fulfilling my responsibility to my neighbor?"

"Still," Tim insisted, "I owe you not only my health and my education, but my position with Lord Ector."

"No, no, no, pass your gratitude on to someone else. Teach your children.... But I assume you will be blessed with offspring, even though you as yet have no prospects?"

Tim ducked his handsome features shyly. "I shall find a wife, never you fear, Mr. Scrooge. I don't spend all my time cataloguing Ector's collections."

"No, you spend your spare hours scribbling stories."

"Only the occasional tale for *The London Illustrated News* and the like."

"And fine tales they are, Tim. Take care, though, not to neglect the finer sentiments." The old man wheezed a moment, then coughed. "I was once engaged to be married, Tim."

Tim, having heard this story many times before, nodded patiently.

"Belle Fezziwig, she was, daughter of my old employer. I let her slip through my fingers, for I preferred the touch of gold to that of a human hand."

"Such was the curse of Midas," murmured Tim.

The apron-swathed nurse clattered about the room, building up the fire and making mysterious motions with vials, spoons, and porringers. "Don't be tiring him out now, young sir. He needs his rest, he does."

"Bah," muttered Scrooge. "Before long I'll have rest aplenty. We all come to the grave in the end, as the Ghost, the Spirit of Christmas Yet to Come, reminded me. I can only hope that my efforts these last years have shortened the heavy chain I once dragged behind me and ensured that my death will be remarked upon with grief, not indifference, and never pleasure."

Tim had heard that story as well. Indeed, he remembered his own part in it as vividly as any occurrence of his childhood. Scrooge claimed to have been visited one icy Christmas Eve first by the ghost of his old partner, Marley, and then by three mysterious spirits, who had thawed his cold heart and softened his flinty disposition. Tim would have thought the story merely a fancy on the old man's part, save that Scrooge was the least fanciful man in the city of London. Save that Scrooge had manifestly changed his ways that Christmas, to the benefit of all.

"You sent for me, sir?" Tim repeated, sensing that his patron had matters burdening his sensibilities far and beyond the usual courtesies and reminiscences.

"Yes, so I did. Tim, I'd like for you to do something for me."

"With pleasure, sir."

"The three spirits, the Ghost of Christmas Past with its white dress and the jet of light springing from its head, the Ghost of Christmas Present, a jolly giant, the Ghost of Christmas Yet to Come, shrouded in a black hood. Were they dreams, thrown up not from a feverish but from a frozen mind? Or were they truly visions from another dimension of this familiar world?"

Scrooge's talon-like hand seized upon Tim's, with its ink-stained forefinger. "The ghost of my old partner Marley told me this: that if a man's spirit does not walk abroad among his fellow men in life, then it must do so after death. And, conversely, that a spirit working kindly in this little sphere of earth will find its mortal life too short for its vast means of usefulness."

"There are the spirits paying penance," said Tim, elucidating the old man's words, "and those whose generosity of temper persists beyond the grave."

"Marley was one of the former. He told me this himself. But what of the other three ghosts? What events in their mortal lives sent them to me? Soon I too, shall be a spirit among spirits. I would like to seek out those who came to me, and thank them most humbly for their efforts. I must know, Tim, who they were in life."

Tim had barely begun to digest this strange request when he felt a presence at his back, the bulk of the nurse looming over him like a great warship under full sail bearing down upon a dinghy. "Begging your pardon, sir . . ."

"Yes, Mrs. Gump?"

"If you're wanting to contact the spiritual world, there's none better at it than Mrs. Minnow in Bedford Square."

"A medium?" Tim asked. "I know that even Her Majesty has employed spiritualists, endeavoring to speak with her late consort, Prince Albert, but still...."

Scrooge's hand tightened upon his, grasping the young man's warm flesh as it had once grasped at gold coins, but to much greater effect. "Tim, I know not if this Mrs. Minnow could be of help to you, and through you to me, but if you please . . ."

"Yes," said Tim, setting aside his qualms as unworthy of both mentor and student. "Yes, of course. I shall do everything in my power to answer your questions, Mr. Scrooge."

"Bless you, my boy." Releasing Tim's hand, the old man settled back onto his pillow. The blush drained from his cheeks, leaving them the color of cold gruel. Still he smiled gently, even affectionately, up at his bedcurtains.

Tim took his leave, and walked out into a swirl of snowflakes with less spring in his step than steely determination in his soul.

* * * *

Mrs. Minnow's parlor was all respectability. Not one hint of either charnel house or circus detracted from the sprigged wallpaper, the ponderous rosewood furniture, the circular table draped with a paisley-pattern shawl. The lady herself resembled a doll clothed in taffeta. When she told Tim to join those seated at the table, he did, even though he would have had more confidence in the spiritualist if either her apartments or her person had offered evidence of things, if not unseen, at least unsuspected.

With a sly silken rustle, Mrs. Minnow turned the flame in the oil lamp down to the smallest of flickers. "Let us all join hands," she instructed, putting her words into effect by taking Tim's right hand in her own soft grasp. He felt as though he were holding a mite of warm bread dough.

He allowed the bewhiskered gentleman on his left to clasp his other hand, and strained his eyes through the wintry gloom, but could see only shadows and implications, grey writ upon grey.

Another crinkle of fabric, and Mrs. Minnow began to murmur softly in what might or might not have been the Queen's English. She could as well have been summoning a waiter as summoning spirits, Tim thought....

A sudden swish in the air above the table, and a spatter of ice-cold water droplets, sent a ripple of surprise around its periphery. Like the gentleman on his left, Tim jerked in surprise. Mrs. Minnow did not.

The odor of pine boughs freshly cut in a snowy field came to Tim's nose. A masculine voice reached his ears, although it seemed to issue from the female shape to his right. "There is someone here who remembers a Christmas Eve long ago."

After a long pause, Tim found his voice. "Ah—yes."

"I see a lad," said the voice, "a small boy with a crutch, sitting before a fireplace."

Now how did Mrs. Minnow know of this? For a moment Tim entertained the thought that Scrooge and his nurse and Mrs. Minnow herself were conspiring in an elaborate joke at his own expense. But if so, why?

In for a penny, in for a pound, he told himself, and directed the—the spirit guide—to speak of Scrooge's past, not his own. "I was that boy. That I survived, nay prospered, and have achieved hale manhood I owe to a benefactor. It is on his behalf that I come here today. He is searching for the identity of three, er, friends who once did him the greatest of good turns."

Another silence. Then the voice, tentative now, as though pondering, said, "Fezziwig. Arthur Fezziwig."

"I beg your pardon?"

"Of Fezziwig's Chandlery, supplier of goods to His Majesty's Navy during the French wars."

Tim knew quite well the name of Scrooge's former employer, Belle's father. Again and again had the old man spoken of the Christmas parties held in Fezziwig's warehouse, of how much joy he and his fellow apprentice Dick Wilkins had found there, of how Belle had refused to dance with anyone but young Ebenezer Scrooge—difficult as it was to conceive of a man so withered by age ever being flush with youth. What Tim did not know was whether Mrs. Minnow or her spirit guide meant to name Scrooge's employer as one of his ghosts.

"If Arthur Fezziwig is one of my benefactor's friends," Tim asked, "then who are the other two?"

"Fezziwig's Chandlery," said the voice. "Christmas Eve. A pudding soaked in brandy and set ablaze. A sprig of holly. The gleam of gold."

Tim leaned forward and the spongy hand in his drew him back. Mrs. Minnow's own feminine voice said, "You have had your answer, sir."

"But...." Tim began, and then stopped, sensible of the other ears ranged about the table.

A wobbly note of music sounded near the ceiling of the room, not the last trumpet, certainly, but one that was near to expiring. Again the male voice spoke from Mrs. Minnow's lips. "There is someone here who has recently lost a beloved brother."

The gentleman with the luxuriant whiskers stirred and spoke. "Yes, yes. Dreadful accident it was, the poor soul burned to a cinder in his rooms."

"Spiritous liquors," intoned the ghostly voice. "Fumes and fire."

Resisting the urge to inquire just which liquors were consumed by spirits, Tim retired into his own thoughts. If Scrooge's partner Marley could return from the grave to assist him, then why not Arthur Fezziwig? That, at least, Tim could credit. But a pudding garnished with holly, and the gleam of gold—if those were clues, they were maddeningly slender ones.

Fezziwig's Chandlery, though. There was a place, a time, and a person. While Tim very much doubted he had any answers as yet, he now had more specific questions.

* * * *

The gleam of sunlight on the new-fallen snow made even the dirty, dingy streets of London shine as brightly as the streets of heaven. Each windowpane seemed to Tim to be gilded like the illuminated manuscripts in Lord Ector's library. Soon it would be Christmas yet again.

Passing beneath the weathered old signboard reading *Scrooge and Cratchit*, he opened the door to the counting-house offices. There was his father, sitting at his desk, a ledger book open before him. Tim remembered how thin and careworn the man had once been, for many years supporting his family on fifteen bob a week, until at last Scrooge had his change of heart, raised his salary, and in time made him a full partner in the firm.

Now it was his hair that was thin, above a face lined with age, not care. Still, Tim could not remember a time when Bob Cratchit had not displayed a cheerful and confident disposition.

"It does my heart good to see you, Tim," said the old man, greeting his son with a clap on his shoulder. "Why, but for Mr. Scrooge I might not have you to see, and for that I am grateful not only at Christmas Eve, but on every day of the year. How fares our benefactor?"

"Not well. I fear his days have grown short."

Bob's face contracted to a pinpoint of sorrow and resignation mingled. "I wish there were some service we could render him, here at the end."

"There is," said Tim, and acquainted his father with Scrooge's request, and with the step he had already taken to fulfill it.

Bob tossed Tim's tale from thought to thought, then said gravely, "I remember when Scrooge saw Christmas merely as the one day of the year he could turn no profit. It was that same fateful Christmas Eve that I heard him say, 'If I could work my will, every idiot who goes about with Merry Christmas on his lips should be boiled with his own pudding and buried with a stake of holly through his heart.'"

"He tempted fate, then," said Tim, "and summoned the spirits with his own words."

"And yet, just what spirits were they? A fine question, an apt question. Surely, to have had such a profound impact on Scrooge's disposition, these ghosts were indeed friends and acquaintances, as you suggest."

"No, as Mrs. Minnow and her spirit guide suggest." Tim looked about the offices, shabby still. His gaze settled upon the ledgers mounting higher and higher up a tall shelf, until the topmost row of books made a veritable Himalayan peak of dust and cobwebs. "What happened to Arthur Fezziwig, Father? His business failed, didn't it?

"Yes. With the defeat of Napoleon and the ending of the French wars the demand for his goods dropped away, and new means of production superseded the old ones to which he clung, as we all cling to that which is familiar. Fezziwig died impoverished in wealth but not in spirit, or so I heard."

"Aha," said Tim.

"Scrooge, I believe, considered his employer's fate to be a cautionary tale, and so made his fortune not by selling goods susceptible to spoilage and changes in taste, but by dealing in properties and making loans. Always he felt the shadow of insolvency looming over him, even though he had funds enough to buy and sell a business like Fezziwig's Chandlery ten times over."

"Could it be, then, that Scrooge's engagement to Belle Fezziwig was broken off because her father had been unable to bequeath her a dowry?"

"I believe so, although I doubt if even Scrooge at his most avaricious would have stated that so bluntly."

"Did Belle ever marry?"

"Oh yes. After his miraculous transformation—and if ghosts or spirits were instrumental in that transformation, then it must truly have been miraculous . . ."

Tim smiled his agreement.

"…Scrooge asked me to seek her out, to discover if she needed his assistance. But it was too late." Bob sat down in his chair, frowning slightly and drumming his fingertips upon his ledger. "What was her husband's name? Oh yes, James Redlaw. He called in here one night, a full seven years before Scrooge's metamorphosis, seeking to borrow against his property and thereby pay his debts. But that was the night Jacob Marley lay at the point of death. Redlaw revealed a greater delicacy of feeling than Scrooge himself by going away without transacting his business."

"So Belle's husband also found himself a broken man?"

"Not only in finance, but in health—he died the next year, I'm told. In losing her father and then her husband, Mrs. Redlaw was obliged to support herself and her daughter on very little income. I can only suppose, then, that she despaired of this world and all too soon was taken up into the next." Bob shook his head sadly.

"When you went searching for her, you discovered that she was dead."

"Yes, and under most unfortunate and mysterious circumstances, although I don't know the full story. When I acquainted Scrooge with this fact, he said something about having seen her in his vision, well and happy with her family, and so he hoped that she was, indeed, in that bourne from which no traveler ever returns."

"Well then," said Tim, properly saddened by the circumstances, and yet, at the same time, wondering if his clue had disintegrated in his hands like the ashes of a Yule log on Boxing Day. "What of Belle's daughter?"

"I believe she went into service, as a governess in the house of Sir Charles Pumphrey, the financier."

Another man of business, Tim thought. The gleam of gold did indeed illuminate his quest, although what the blazing pudding illuminated, he had not the least idea.

Still, perhaps he had made some progress. If Arthur Fezziwig had been one of Scrooge's spirits, then perhaps his unfortunate daughter Belle had also been. "I shall pay a visit to the Pumphrey household," Tim told his father.

"Very good. And may I suggest you also call on your brother Peter? The lawyer with whom he has partnered himself has worked for many years with properties, deeds, and wills—although I hope to heaven they are not chaining themselves behind him, as they did to poor Mr. Marley. There you may well learn more about the Fezziwigs and the Redlaws than I can tell you."

"Then so I shall." With a firm grasp of his father's hand—strange, how that hand was growing so increasingly frail—Tim settled his hat upon his head and his feet upon the icy pavement.

* * * *

At the sound of feminine footsteps, Tim turned away from the black marble chimneypiece and its clock enclosed by a glass dome, as though time, like a jewel displayed in a shopkeeper's window, were a valuable commodity allotted only to those who could afford it instead of meted out to all humanity, to use or abuse at will.

"Do I have the honor of addressing Miss Redlaw?" Tim asked the elegant woman who entered the parlor, the white square of his card seeming tarnished against the alabaster of her hand.

"I was once Miss Redlaw," she answered. "Now I am Mrs. Pumphrey. You are fortunate, Mr. Cratchit, that the servant who answered your knock has been in our employ long enough to know my former identity."

So the governess was now mistress of the house, Tim told himself. Had she married the Pumphrey's only son, and so restored herself to the position in life to which she had been born? Such an event seemed likely—her face and form, even in mature years, held just such a blushing beauty as he had always envisioned in Belle Fezziwig's. But that was one question he saw little chance of asking.

He sank onto the chair that Mrs. Pumphrey indicated. When she had spread her voluminous skirts across a horsehair sofa—which movement released a scent of spring lilac into the air—he identified himself, detailed his family's relationship to Ebenezer Scrooge, sketched out Scrooge's story of the three ghosts, and recited the results of his researches so far.

Save for a slight creasing of her brow, Mrs. Pumphrey's delicate features did not move for several ticks of the mantelpiece clock. Perhaps, Tim thought, she would condemn him for his effrontery in asking questions about her family. Perhaps she would order the servant who had seen him here to show him hence.

At last her pink lips parted. "I commend you for visiting Mrs. Minnow. She has afforded me invaluable assistance by contacting the spirit of my grandfather Fezziwig, who is as hearty on the astral plane as he was here on Earth."

Tim made sure Mrs. Pumphrey did not notice the quick relaxation of his posture, and the sigh of relief that escaped his throat.

"As for my mother and father—well, as you perhaps already know, there is a tragic story. How it cheers me to know that they, too, are well and happy in the great beyond!"

"And perhaps Mr. Fezziwig and Mrs. Redlaw," Tim hinted in Scrooge's words, "after working kindly in this little sphere of earth, find their mortal life too short for their vast means of usefulness."

"Yes," she said, coloring prettily, "I do believe so. You see, Mr. Cratchit, my mother regretted breaking her engagement to Mr. Scrooge, because, she said, if she had been his wife she could perhaps have modified his miserly ways. And yet if she had been Mrs. Scrooge, she would never have been Mrs. Redlaw."

"It is a paradox," said Tim.

"But that was my mother, always thinking of others even when her—when our—position became dire. After my father passed over, Mother and I were reduced to the income from one rental property, a public house, and the interest from several India bonds. Still, though, there were others less fortunate then we, and Mother made sure that what we little we had, we shared."

Tim, having told himself that the ladies' income had no doubt been greater than fifteen bob a week, now congratulated himself for not stating this aloud.

"We took lodgings in a house owned by Dick Wilkins. Is that name familiar to you?"

"Why yes," Tim said, sitting up straighter. "Was he not one of Mr. Fezziwig's apprentices and a boyhood friend of Mr. Scrooge's?"

The lady nodded, setting her curls to dancing. "That he was. Grandfather Fezziwig helped Mr. Wilkins establish a weaving mill, dyeworks, and clothing manufactory, which first supplied uniforms to our troops fighting the Corsican, Bonaparte, and then went on to provide ready-made clothes to all classes of folk. While Grandfather's business failed, Mr. Wilkins's prospered. As an old family friend, my mother was quite pleased when he offered her lodgings in his house."

"He rented out rooms?"

"Yes," Mrs. Pumphrey said, a slight edge entering her voice. "By this time he owned many properties, and lived with his wife Theodora—a foreign person she was, with the exotic beauty of a gypsy—in a house that had once been a lovely villa, but which he had subdivided into many small flats, the better to turn a profit, I believe."

The gleam of gold, Tim repeated to himself, but said nothing.

The edge in Mrs. Pumphrey's voice was taking on the sharpness of that serpent's tooth mentioned in Scripture as belonging to a thankless child. And yet neither she nor her mother, Tim thought, was the person of whom she was thinking. "Mr. Wilkins persuaded my mother to sell him her properties and bonds, in return for which he guaranteed her an annuity for life. The bargain was fair, she felt. What she did not realize—what none of us mercifully, realize—is how soon one's life can end."

"What happened?" asked Tim, dreading her answer.

"My mother was found burned to a cinder, in her bed one Christmas morning."

Tim searched for some appropriate response, and found only a simple, "I am so very sorry."

Mrs. Pumphrey looked down into her lap, where her fair hands—white as the garment of the first ghost—were tearing Tim's card into shreds. "Mr. and Mrs. Wilkins put it about that my mother, in her despair, had turned to drink, for such spontaneous burnings do happen to those besotted with alcohol."

With spiritous liquors, thought Tim, realizing suddenly that Mrs. Minnow had been speaking not only to the gentleman with the whiskers but to himself. He should, no doubt, have kept an open mind and paid closer attention.

"My dear mother, though, while having her moments of despair, was still inclined to the positive outlook of the Fezziwig disposition, and took only the occasional glass of sherry." The lady lay the shreds of the card upon a marble-topped table and folded her hands. "Yes, Mother suffered from a cold that Christmas Eve. Mrs. Wilkins provided a counterpane from her own storage chest for Mother's bed, and smelling salts to clear the congestion in her throat that had rendered her speechless. But Mother took no drink, not one drop beyond the brandy soaking her portion of plum pudding."

"Was there an inquiry made?"

"The police made a brief inquiry, but brushed the matter aside, wishing to spare my feelings, they said, and those of the Wilkins family."

"But you suspect the Wilkins of taking some action to bring about your mother's death?"

"Indeed, while manifestly Mr. and Mrs. Wilkins profited by my mother's death, there are no means by which they could have accomplished it. I myself saw my mother alive, if not well, when I carried her pudding into her room on Christmas Eve, and I myself was breakfasting with the Wilkins' on Christmas morning when the maidservant came rushing in with her terrible intelligence."

Tim eyed the lady's bowed head with its trembling curls. So Belle had indeed died in unfortunate and mysterious circumstances, as his father had heard. Now he understood, with ghastly certainty, why it was that Scrooge's first ghost, the Ghost of Christmas Past, had appeared illuminated by a flame.

Collecting herself with a little shudder, Mrs. Pumphrey turned a wan smile upon her guest. "You may well ask, Mr. Cratchit, whether I have ever inquired of my mother, through Mrs. Minnow's spirit guide, exactly how she came to die."

Yes, Tim might well have asked that, had he not been reluctant to disturb the lady's sensibilities even further.

"To that, I can provide no answer, for my mother has spoken only of flames shooting suddenly up, and of merciful oblivion. I have more than once chided myself for not staying with her that evening, and yet there were guests downstairs and she gestured, smiling, for me to join them, and then, still smiling, reached for her bedside taper to light her plum pudding and make her own solitary celebration."

Tim sat in silent horror at the scene that rose before his eyes.

Clearing her throat, Mrs. Pumphrey went stoutly on, "I take great comfort in my mother's present happy circumstances, no matter how difficult was her transition to them. And in her name my husband and I have provided for many charities."

The parlor door opened, admitting a young woman so fair, so charming, that her mother with all her comeliness seemed reduced to a crone before Tim's eyes. He stared, then remembered his manners and leaped to his feet.

Mrs Pumphrey's eye glittered perhaps from unshed tears, or perhaps from maternal calculation. "Mr. Cratchit, may I present my daughter Annabelle."

"Miss Pumphrey." Making his most accomplished obeisance, Tim wondered if—Annabelle, what a lovely name—if she heard the sudden twang of Cupid's bow just as surely as he did. And yet how could he dare hope that such a lovely, nay such a stupendously beautiful, young lady could look with favor upon him?

She curtsied, the color rising past her exquisitely formed lips into her cheeks. A rose would surely have hung its head in shame at a comparison. "Mr. Cratchit," she said, in a voice resembling the song of a lark, "I trust you'll forgive me for listening outside the door. I am most impressed by the compassion of your quest, and would assist you in any way I can in its fulfillment."

Tim would have forgiven her for plunging a dagger into his heart. "Perhaps," he said through his teeth, quelling a stammer, "you will permit me to call upon you again, so that I may share with you my discoveries...." What discoveries he made, he told himself. If he knew she was waiting to hear them, he would make them, no doubt about it.

"How kind of you," Annabelle said.

Her mother rose. "And now, Mr. Cratchit, I'm sure you will want to continue making your inquiries."

Tim found himself floating down the front steps of the house in a trance—odd, how icy winter had suddenly turned balmy as spring.... Unbidden, his feet made their way toward the law offices of William Janders, Esquire.

* * * *

Peter Cratchit regarded his younger brother's air of general discombobulation and laughed. "Who is she, then?"

Tim found he was, after all, capable of stringing words together and telling the tale yet again, this time appending its most recent chapter. Peter's expression went from laughter to bemusement to astonishment. At last he emitted a long whistle. "So you think old Fezziwig and Belle are two of Scrooge's ghosts, eh?"

"I suspect Belle of being the Ghost of Christmas Past with its crown of flame," Tim replied. "I suspect her father, Fezziwig, of being the Ghost of Christmas Present, for by all accounts he was a hearty soul who loved to celebrate the holiday."

"And the Ghost of Christmas Yet to Come?" asked Peter. "Who was, if I'm remembering the old man's tale aright, a much more sinister figure, hooded in black."

"That is where you come in, brother, you and your esteemed senior partner Mr. Janders. Can we trace these properties that Belle—Mrs. Redlaw—made over to Dick Wilkins, only to die so conveniently soon thereafter?"

"Why yes." Peter conducted Tim into the next chamber, the book-lined office of William Janders, Esquire, himself.

The man's thick gray eyebrows, like caterpillars, lofted up his brow as though they would crawl onto the sleek hairless dome of his head and there set up housekeeping. "Well then," he said, upon being familiarized with the facts of the matter, "there's no need to delve into the record-books. I remember the case quite well. It all happened when I was but a clerk writing law in these very offices, younger and more junior than you are now, Peter."

"Pray tell me what you know," Tim asked politely, envisioning making his successful report not only to Scrooge but to the delectable Miss Pumphrey.

"The circumstances of Mrs. Redlaw's death were peculiar, quite peculiar. Spontaneous combustion is a well-known effect of excess drink, but, being a lady of fine breeding, she was hardly given to imbibing. Still, nothing could be proved."

That was as Mrs. Pumphrey had said, thought Tim.

"What is exceedingly interesting," Janders went on, "is that the next year Dick Wilkins was brought up on charges of murder."

Peter and Tim exchanged a significant glance.

"The circumstances were similar, save that this time the dead woman was a spinster. Again, though, she was of good family and modest property, which she had made over to her landlord, Wilkins. Her death was very obviously caused by poison. Poison in the plum pudding."

"Murder is vile enough," Tim exclaimed, "but to use an instrument of celebration in the commission of a murder!"

"Was Wilkins convicted of the crime?" asked Peter.

Janders nodded affirmatively. "That he was. And yet it was not he who prepared and served the pudding, and who then nursed the ailing woman until she died. There was some talk of charging his wife as well, but since wives are weak and subject to their husband's will, she was never tried. Not that Mrs. Wilkins struck me as being weak-willed, no, on the contrary."

Peter swallowed a chuckle, but not at this tale of murder most foul, Tim thought. Their mother was the strongest woman he knew, and Peter's own wife ruled their household firmly but fairly. There was something in the set of Miss Pumphrey's chin, Tim added silently, that told him she, too, was a woman to be reckoned with. As, in a very different way, no doubt, was Mrs. Wilkins.

"Dick Wilkins was hanged," Janders continued, "and without his guiding hand his business failed. I daresay he was guilty of abetting the murder, even initiating it. So justice was done. But as for the death of Mrs. Redlaw...."

"No charges could be brought because no one could prove that a murder had been done," said Peter.

"I am at as great a loss in the matter as you are." Janders took up his pen and dipped it in the fine brass inkwell that sat upon his desk. "Now Peter, Tim, you will excuse me...."

"Just one more question, please, sir," said Tim. "Do you remember Mrs. Wilkins' Christian name? Was she an Englishwoman?"

Janders considered a moment, tapping his nose with his pen. "Theodora, her name was. Yes, she was as English as you or me, but I do believe her father was a native of Greece. She was quite lovely, very young, with jet-black tresses and flashing eyes."

"Thank you."

Peter took Tim by the collar and steered him through the doorway and into the outer office. There he said, "There's a proper tragedy for you. Poor Belle! Scrooge will not be pleased to hear of her fate."

"No. And yet...." Tim's brows knit tightly. "Do you suppose that the visit of her and her father's ghosts to Scrooge had more than one purpose, not only to show him the error of his ways but to reveal the truth of her death? Her murder?"

"But how could the truth be revealed?"

"I wonder," Tim said, as his thoughts moved reluctantly from Annabelle Pumphrey's lovely face to the open page of a book in Lord Ector's library. *Christmas Eve. A pudding soaked in brandy and set ablaze....*

He took his leave of Peter and went back out into the cold afternoon air, this time directing his steps toward Ector House.

* * * *

Lord Ector reminded Tim of an eagle, with his arched nose and small dark eyes always alert, whether to the movement of a mouse in the grass or to a ripple among England's allies in the east, no matter.

Now he turned from positioning yet another marble bust of some ancient worthy upon a pedestal in his library and answered Tim's question. "Yes, when I served as a diplomat in Turkey I did hear stories of the *tunica molesta*, the fiery cloak that brought the hero Herakles to his death."

"If I remember the story," said Tim, holding a stepstool so that his lordship might safely regain terra firma, "the burning cloth clung to him and could not be removed, nor could the flames be doused by water, so that he burned to a cinder."

"Indeed."

"But surely this story is only legend."

"Not at all," returned Ector. "You have heard of the Greek fire employed by the ancients—a mixture of quicklime, sulfur, naphtha, and saltpeter, that would cling to, say, an enemy's ship and only burn the fiercer when wetted."

Tim nodded, even as he tried not to let his imagination dwell too long on images of flowing, clinging, unquenchable flames. "And this chemical process could be applied to cloth?"

"Cloth is manufactured using the same ingredients: dyes and pigments can be made from sulphur and petroleum and fixed with a mordant of quicklime. Tar is used as a waterproofing agent. If such materials were ready to hand, one with knowledge of the ancient formula could impregnate a cloth with petroleum, sulphur and lime. If it were stored away from the air . . ."

"In a chest," Tim murmured.

"...it might well ignite at a very low temperature and continue to burn even when wet."

"And if the cloth were a counterpane say, covering a woman incapable of crying out for assistance—ah, what a diabolical plan!"

Ector would not have regarded Tim so quizzically had he started to speak in tongues. "A diabolical plan? Do you mean to say someone has committed murder using this infernal Greek recipe?"

"Yes, yes—the key to the murder is that it took place on Christmas Eve, when either a flaming pudding or the candle used to light it set the counterpane ablaze. The scheme would certainly turn upon Belle being alone in her room at the moment of conflagration.... Ah yes. The guests downstairs would have insured that she was." Tim dashed his right fist into his left hand. "They even thought to provide smelling salts, to cover the odor of the chemicals in the cloth, which had, I'm sure, been manufactured in their own establishment. A clever scheme, but the circumstances did not favor its execution twice, and so did he—they, the souls of avarice—attempt a variation that worked less successfully."

"My dear fellow," said Ector, laying a restraining hand upon Tim's arm, "either you have quite lost your wits, or you have some wonderful tale to tell me—and no doubt, in time, to tell your readers."

"Yes, my lord, I shall most certainly tell all. And yet the tale is not finished, not quite yet."

* * * *

Between his father's ledger books and his brother's legal documents, it took Tim only a day to trace Theodora Wilkins to a poor lodging house.

The old woman admitted him to her room, then seated herself beside a small fire, no more than a few coals piled upon a dirty hearth—the remains of another victim? Tim asked himself caustically.

Her beauty had long ago been sacrificed to age. Now her hair was sparse and drab, and she was as wizened as though she had gnawed nothing but the bones of avarice these long years. Reaching for the container of grog that was warming in the ashes, she drank deeply. The reek of the cheap liquor seared Tim's nose. He wondered whether she had used expensive brandy to soak Belle's pudding, and whether she had ever wished she had drunk it instead.

"Have a care," he told her. "You have heard of what happens to those who drink too freely, and then expose themselves to fire."

"Bah," she said. Her voice was like the scrape of bare branches across a windowpane.

A basket beside her chair overflowed with scraps of cloth and packets of thread and needles, leading Tim to deduce that she eked out a meager living stitching and mending. "You have always worked with cloth," he said. "Did you once make a counterpane for a woman named Belle Redlaw, who lodged with you and your—late husband?"

"What is it to you?"

"I am a friend of Mrs. Redlaw's friends and family. Her death was mysterious. I'd like to know the truth of how it came to happen."

"She drank herself to death," Mrs. Wilkins said, and began to cough as rackingly as though she expelled smoke from her lungs.

Tim asked himself why he had come here. Did he hope to hear a confession? What if he did? What difference could it make, now? He felt sure that he stood looking at a murderess, and yet it was not his place to judge, either in this life or in the hereafter. For her crimes against humanity, Theodora Wilkins was now suffering the sharp bite of loneliness and poverty. He could do nothing else to her.

He could, however, do something for her. Had not Belle's ghost, and her father's, and yes, Dick Wilkins' dark ghost as well, carried a message of pity and compassion from the next world into this?

From his pocket Tim produced a gold coin. He held it in his hand a moment, warming it, then laid it down upon the mantelpiece. The beldame's rheumy eyes flicked upwards, so that he could almost see the gleam of gold reflected in them. "Merry Christmas," he said, and left the chill, acrid air of the room for the frosty air of the city street.

The vapor of his breath hung in the air before him like a ghost. The windows of even the meanest shop and lowliest hovel glowed with a rosy, anticipatory light. Tomorrow would be Christmas Eve. He would join his brothers and sisters, by blood and by marriage, and they would raise a glass to Scrooge, the founder of the feast. And yes, they would eat plum pudding ablaze in brandy, with a sprig of holly adorning its round and savory top.

* * * *

The bells of Christmas morning were pealing, setting the bedcurtains to shivering delightfully, like children first sighting their Christmas presents. And indeed, Scrooge had almost returned to a childlike state, opening his mouth trustingly as Mrs. Gump spooned gruel into it.

The nurse's gaze met Tim's. *Not much longer*, it said.

Behind him stood his father, and Scrooge's nephew and his wife, all kitted out in their Sunday best, for it was, after all, Christmas Day.

Scrooge tried to wave his hand and succeeded only in twitching his finger. Mrs. Gump, though, understood his meaning. Wiping his face with a corner of her apron, she vacated her chair.

Tim stepped closer to the bed. "I have the answer to your question, Mr. Scrooge. I know who your ghosts were. Who they are."

The old man's pale face seemed infinitesimally to brighten. His eyes turned in their sockets to where Tim stood. "Tim," he whispered. "Always a good lad, Tiny Tim."

Tim forbore to comment on his present height, but simply folded it onto the chair. He took Scrooge's hand between his own, gently, for it was as thin as a bird's wing. Slowly the old man's cold flesh began to warm. "The Ghost of Christmas Past," Tim told him, "of your past, is Belle Fezziwig. Belle Redlaw, as she was when she died. She is the spirit of former joys and former regrets."

"Ah," said Scrooge, summoning a blissful smile. "Belle."

"The Ghost of Christmas Present is Arthur Fezziwig, her father, the robust spirit of both gratitude and reproof. The spirit of every Christmas that has past and is yet to come."

"Fine old fellow, Fezziwig." Scrooge sighed, his smile abating only briefly.

"The Ghost of Christmas Yet to Come is your old friend Dick Wilkins. He was consumed by greed, sadly, and died with the black hood of the condemned criminal upon his head. Perhaps, though, by helping you his spirit was redeemed."

Scrooge's lips tightened to a narrow slit. "Poor old Dick. If only he had been visited by three spirits, as I was so fortunate to have been."

Tim nodded. "I have this very afternoon been invited to call upon Miss Annabelle Pumphrey, Belle's granddaughter, in whom Belle's beauty and compassion live on. I intend to take your advice, sir, and not neglect the finer sentiments."

"Good. We were not meant to be alone in this world, Tim." His hand twitched feebly.

Behind Tim's back Mrs. Gump was chatting with Scrooge's niece, a woman of sprightly disposition and great interest in the doings of mankind: "I heard it on my way here this morning, madam. The poor woman went at her pudding so greedy she ate the sprig of holly stuck in its top and choked to death upon it."

Tim glanced round. Of all the women in the city of London, surely....

"Her name was Wilkins too, so I hear. Dead as a doornail, the undertaker said, as sure as though someone had driven a stake through her heart."

"Not now," said Scrooge's niece, quelling the nurse's gossip.

Too late. Tim looked down at his strong young hands cradling Scrooge's blue-veined and fragile one. Had those same hands, then, brought justice at last to Theodora Wilkins, however unwittingly? Had she died—no. Even though she had died unredeemed, her spirit would now be walking abroad amongst her fellow human beings. Perhaps she would find peace at last, as her husband had done. As their victim had done.

Scrooge's eyes widened, beholding another vision. "I am light as a feather, I am as giddy as an angel, I am as merry as a schoolboy." His voice cracked and then steadied. "I hear old Fezziwig now: Clear away, Dick. Clear away Ebenezer. It's Christmas, a time to celebrate…. Why, Belle, you wish to dance with me? Gladly, my dear. Gladly."

Tim felt the others gathering close. Their hands, too, reached out for Scrooge's. He smiled, brilliantly. "God bless us, every…." And he sank back upon the pillow, giving up his own ghost.

Tears started in Tim's eyes. Carefully he laid Scrooge's hand down upon the clean, white counterpane, and leaned his head back against his father's chest. Perhaps Scrooge would also find his mortal life too short to spread the compassion he had learned—and learned very well—nineteen years ago today.

"He would not think it sad to die upon Christmas Day," Bob said softly, pressing his son's shoulder. "Not Ebenezer Scrooge."

"No," said Tim. And in his heart he repeated the words that his own childish mouth had once uttered, as fine an epitaph as any man could wish: God bless us, every one.

Lillian Stewart Carl writes multiple stories and multiple novels in multiple genres. All of them strike at least a glancing blow at history and myth. Her most recent novels are the Jean Fairbairn/Alasdair Cameron mysteries: America's exile and Scotland's finest on the trail of all-too-living legends. Her work is available in a variety of print and electronic editions. Her website is www.lillianstewartcarl.com

A REVERSIBLE SANTA CLAUS

Meredith Nicholson

I

Mr. William B. Aikins, *alias* "Softy" Hubbard, *alias* Billy The Hopper, paused for breath behind a hedge that bordered a quiet lane and peered out into the highway at a roadster whose tail light advertised its presence to his felonious gaze. It was Christmas Eve, and after a day of unseasonable warmth a slow, drizzling rain was whimsically changing to snow.

The Hopper was blowing from two hours' hard travel over rough country. He had stumbled through woodlands, flattened himself in fence corners to avoid the eyes of curious motorists speeding homeward or flying about distributing Christmas gifts, and he was now bent upon committing himself to an inter-urban trolley line that would afford comfortable transportation for the remainder of his journey. Twenty miles, he estimated, still lay between him and his domicile.

The rain had penetrated his clothing and vigorous exercise had not greatly diminished the chill in his blood. His heart knocked violently against his ribs and he was dismayed by his shortness of wind. The Hopper was not so young as in the days when his agility and genius for effecting a quick "get-away" had earned for him his sobriquet. The last time his Bertillon measurements were checked (he was subjected to this humiliating experience in Omaha during the Ak-Sar-Ben carnival three years earlier) official note was taken of the fact that The Hopper's hair, long carried in the records as black, was rapidly whitening.

At forty-eight a crook—even so resourceful and versatile a member of the fraternity as The Hopper—begins to mistrust himself. For the greater part of his life, when not in durance vile, The Hopper had been in hiding, and the state or condition of being a fugitive, hunted by keen-eyed agents of justice, is not, from all accounts, an enviable one. His latest experience of involuntary servitude had been under the auspices of the State of Oregon, for a trifling indiscretion in the way of safe-blowing. Having served his sentence, he skillfully effaced himself by a year's siesta on a pine-apple plantation in Hawaii. The island climate was not wholly pleasing to The Hopper, and when pine-apples palled he took passage from Honolulu as a stoker, reached San Francisco (not greatly chastened in spirit), and by a series of characteristic hops, skips, and jumps across the continent landed in Maine by way of the Canadian provinces. The Hopper needed money. He was not without a certain crude philosophy, and it had been his dream to acquire by some brilliant *coup* a sufficient fortune upon which to retire and live as a decent, law-abiding citizen for the remainder of his days. This ambition, or at least the means to its fulfillment, can hardly be defended as praiseworthy, but The Hopper was a singular character and we must take him as we find him. Many prison chaplains and jail visitors bearing tracts had striven with little success to implant moral ideals in the mind and soul of The Hopper, but he was still to be catalogued among the impenitent; and as he moved southward through the Commonwealth of Maine he was so oppressed by his poverty, as contrasted with the world's abundance, that he lifted forty thousand dollars in a neat bundle from an express car which Providence had sidetracked, apparently for his personal enrichment, on the upper waters of the Penobscot. Whereupon he began perforce playing his old game of artful dodging, exercising his best powers as a hopper and skipper. Forty thousand dollars is no inconsiderable sum of money, and the success of this master stroke of his career was not to be jeopardized by careless moves. By craftily hiding in the big woods and making himself agreeable to isolated lumberjacks who rarely saw newspapers, he arrived in due course on Manhattan Island, where with shrewd judgment he avoided the haunts of his kind while planning a future commensurate with his new dignity as a capitalist.

He spent a year as a diligent and faithful employee of a garage which served a fashionable quarter of the metropolis; then, animated by a worthy desire to continue to lead an honest life, he purchased a chicken farm fifteen miles as the crow flies from Center Church, New Haven, and boldly opened a bank account in that academic center in his newly adopted name of Charles S. Stevens, of Happy Hill Farm. Feeling the need of companionship, he married a lady somewhat his junior, a shoplifter of the second class, whom he had known before the vigilance of the metropolitan police necessitated his removal to the Far West. Mrs. Stevens's inferior talents as a petty larcenist had led her into many difficulties, and she gratefully availed herself of The Hopper's offer of his heart and hand.

They had added to their establishment a retired yegg who had lost an eye by the premature popping of the "soup" (i.e., nitro-glycerin) poured into the crevices of a country post-office in Missouri. In offering shelter to Mr. James Whitesides, *alias* "Humpy" Thompson, The Hopper's motives had not been wholly unselfish, as Humpy had been entrusted with the herding of poultry in several penitentiaries and was familiar with the most advanced scientific thought on chicken culture.

The roadster was headed toward his home and The Hopper contemplated it in the deepening dusk with greedy eyes. His labors in the New York garage had familiarized him with automobiles, and while he was not ignorant of the pains and penalties inflicted upon lawless persons who appropriate motors illegally, he was the victim of an irresistible temptation to jump into the machine thus left in the highway, drive as near home as he dared, and then abandon it. The owner of the roadster was presumably eating his evening meal in peace in the snug little cottage behind the shrubbery, and The Hopper was aware of no sound reason why he should not seize the vehicle and further widen the distance between himself and a suspicious-looking gentleman he had observed on the New Haven local.

The Hopper's conscience was not altogether at ease, as he had, that afternoon, possessed himself of a bill-book that was protruding from the breast-pocket of a dignified citizen whose strap he had shared in a crowded subway train. Having foresworn crime as a means of livelihood, The Hopper was chagrined that he had suffered himself to be beguiled into stealing by the mere propinquity of a piece of red leather. He was angry at the world as well as himself. People should not go about with bill-books sticking out of their pockets; it was unfair and unjust to those weak members of the human race who yield readily to temptation.

He had agreed with Mary when she married him and the chicken farm that they would respect the Ten Commandments and all statutory laws, State and Federal, and he was painfully conscious that when he confessed his sin she would deal severely with him. Even Humpy, now enjoying a peace that he had rarely known outside the walls of prison, even Humpy would be bitter. The thought that he was again among the hunted would depress Mary and Humpy, and he knew that their harshness would be intensified because of his violation of the unwritten law of the underworld in resorting to purse-lifting, an infringement upon a branch of felony despicable and greatly inferior in dignity to safe-blowing.

These reflections spurred The Hopper to action, for the sooner he reached home the more quickly he could explain his protracted stay in New York (to which metropolis he had repaired in the hope of making a better price for eggs with the commission merchants who handled his products), submit himself to Mary's chastisement, and promise to sin no more. By returning on Christmas Eve, of all times, again a fugitive, he knew that he would merit the unsparing condemnation that Mary and Humpy would visit upon him. It was possible, it was even quite likely, that the short, stocky gentleman he had seen on the New Haven local was not a "bull"—not really a detective who had observed the little transaction in the subway; but the very uncertainty annoyed The Hopper. In his happy and profitable year at Happy Hill Farm he had learned to prize his personal comfort, and he was humiliated to find that he had been frightened into leaving the train at Bansford to continue his journey afoot, and merely because a man had looked at him a little queerly.

Any Christmas spirit that had taken root in The Hopper's soul had been disturbed, not to say seriously threatened with extinction, by the untoward occurrences of the afternoon.

II

The Hopper waited for a limousine to pass and then crawled out of his hiding-place, jumped into the roadster, and was at once in motion. He glanced back, fearing that the owner might have heard his departure, and then, satisfied of his immediate security, negotiated a difficult turn in the road and settled himself with a feeling of relief to careful but expeditious flight. It was at this moment, when he had urged the car to its highest speed, that a noise startled him—an amazing little chirrupy sound which corresponded to none of the familiar forewarnings of engine trouble. With his eyes to the front he listened for a repetition of the sound. It rose again—it was like a perplexing cheep and chirrup, changing to a chortle of glee.

"Goo-goo! Goo-goo-goo!"

The car was skimming a dark stretch of road and a superstitious awe fell upon The Hopper. Murder, he gratefully remembered, had never been among his crimes, though he had once winged a too-inquisitive policeman in Kansas City. He glanced over his shoulder, but saw no pursuing ghost in the snowy highway; then, looking down apprehensively, he detected on the seat beside him what appeared to be an animate bundle, and, prompted by a louder "goo-goo," he put out his hand. His fingers touched something warm and soft and were promptly seized and held by Something.

The Hopper snatched his hand free of the tentacles of the unknown and shook it violently. The nature of the Something troubled him. He renewed his experiments, steering with his left hand and exposing the right to what now seemed to be the grasp of two very small mittened hands.

"Goo-goo! Goody; teep wunnin'!"

"A kid!" The Hopper gasped.

That he had eloped with a child was the blackest of the day's calamities. He experienced a strange sinking feeling in the stomach. In moments of apprehension a crook's thoughts run naturally into periods of penal servitude, and the punishment for kidnaping, The Hopper recalled, was severe. He stopped the car and inspected his unwelcome fellow passenger by the light of matches. Two big blue eyes stared at him from a hood and two mittens were poked into his face. Two small feet, wrapped tightly in a blanket, kicked at him energetically.

"Detup! Mate um skedaddle!"

Obedient to this command The Hopper made the car skedaddle, but superstitious dread settled upon him more heavily. He was satisfied now that from the moment he transferred the strap-hanger's bill-book to his own pocket he had been hoodooed. Only a jinx of the most malevolent type could have prompted his hurried exit from a train to dodge an imaginary "bull." Only the blackest of evil spirits could be responsible for this involuntary kidnaping!

"Mate um wun! Mate um 'ippity stip!"

The mittened hands reached for the wheel at this juncture and an unlooked-for "jippity skip" precipitated the young passenger into The Hopper's lap.

This mishap was attended with the jolliest baby laughter. Gently but with much firmness The Hopper restored the youngster to an upright position and supported him until sure he was able to sustain himself.

"Ye better set still, little feller," he admonished.

The little feller seemed in no wise astonished to find himself abroad with a perfect stranger and his courage and good cheer were not lost upon The Hopper. He wanted to be severe, to vent his rage for the day's calamities upon the only human being within range, but in spite of himself he felt no animosity toward the friendly little bundle of humanity beside him. Still, he had stolen a baby and it was incumbent upon him to free himself at once of the appalling burden; but a baby is not so easily disposed of. He could not, without seriously imperiling his liberty, return to the cottage. It was the rule of house-breakers, he recalled, to avoid babies. He had heard it said by burglars of wide experience and unquestioned wisdom that babies were the most dangerous of all burglar alarms. All things considered, kidnaping and automobile theft were not a happy combination with which to appear before a criminal court. The Hopper was vexed because the child did not cry; if he had shown a bad disposition The Hopper might have abandoned him; but the youngster was the cheeriest and most agreeable of traveling companions. Indeed, The Hopper's spirits rose under his continued "goo-gooing" and chirruping.

"Nice little Shaver!" he said, patting the child's knees.

Little Shaver was so pleased by this friendly demonstration that he threw up his arms in an effort to embrace The Hopper.

"Bil-lee," he gurgled delightedly.

The Hopper was so astonished at being addressed in his own lawful name by a strange baby that he barely averted a collision with a passing motor truck. It was unbelievable that the baby really knew his name, but perhaps it was a good omen that he had hit upon it. The Hopper's resentment against the dark fate that seemed to pursue him vanished. Even though he had stolen a baby, it was a merry, brave little baby who didn't mind at all being run away with! He dismissed the thought of planting the little shaver at a door, ringing the bell and running away; this was no way to treat a friendly child that had done him no injury, and The Hopper highly resolved to do the square thing by the youngster even at personal inconvenience and risk.

The snow was now falling in generous Christmasy flakes, and the high speed the car had again attained was evidently deeply gratifying to the young person, whose reckless tumbling about made it necessary for The Hopper to keep a hand on him.

"Steady, little un; steady!" The Hopper kept mumbling.

His wits were busy trying to devise some means of getting rid of the youngster without exposing himself to the danger of arrest. By this time some one was undoubtedly busily engaged in searching for both baby and car; the police far and near would be notified, and would be on the lookout for a smart roadster containing a stolen child.

"Merry Christmas!" a boy shouted from a farm gate.

"M'y Kwismus!" piped Shaver.

The Hopper decided to run the machine home and there ponder the disposition of his blithe companion with the care the unusual circumstances demanded.

"'Urry up; me's goin' 'ome to me's gwanpa's kwismus t'ee!"

"Right ye be, little un; right ye be!" affirmed The Hopper.

The youngster was evidently blessed with a sanguine and confiding nature. His reference to his grandfather's Christmas tree impinged sharply upon The Hopper's conscience. Christmas had never figured very prominently in his scheme of life. About the only Christmases that he recalled with any pleasure were those that he had spent in prison, and those were marked only by Christmas dinners varying with the generosity of a series of wardens.

But Shaver was entitled to all the joys of Christmas, and The Hopper had no desire to deprive him of them.

"Keep a-larfin', Shaver, keep a-larfin'," said the Hopper. "Ole Hop ain't a-goin' to hurt ye!"

The Hopper, feeling his way cautiously round the fringes of New Haven, arrived presently at Happy Hill Farm, where he ran the car in among the chicken sheds behind the cottage and carefully extinguished the lights.

"Now, Shaver, out ye come!"

Whereupon Shaver obediently jumped into his arms.

<h1 style="text-align:center">III</h1>

The Hopper knocked twice at the back door, waited an instant, and knocked again. As he completed the signal the door was opened guardedly. A man and woman surveyed him in hostile silence as he pushed past them, kicked the door shut, and deposited the blinking child on the kitchen table. Humpy, the one-eyed, jumped to the windows and jammed the green shades close into the frames. The woman scowlingly waited for the head of the house to explain himself, and this, with the perversity of one who knows the dramatic value of suspense, he was in no haste to do.

"Well," Mary questioned sharply. "What ye got there, Bill?"

The Hopper was regarding Shaver with a grin of benevolent satisfaction. The youngster had seized a bottle of catsup and was making heroic efforts to raise it to his mouth, and the Hopper was intensely tickled by Shaver's efforts to swallow the bottle. Mrs. Stevens, *alias* Weeping Mary, was not amused, and her husband's enjoyment of the child's antics irritated her.

"Come out with ut, Bill!" she commanded, seizing the bottle. "What ye been doin'?"

Shaver's big blue eyes expressed surprise and displeasure at being deprived of his plaything, but he recovered quickly and reached for a plate with which he began thumping the table.

"Out with ut, Hop!" snapped Humpy nervously. "Nothin' wuz said about kidnapin', an' I don't stand for ut!"

"When I heard the machine comin' in the yard I knowed somethin' was wrong an' I guess it couldn't be no worse," added Mary, beginning to cry. "You hadn't no right to do ut, Bill. Hookin' a buzz-buzz an' a kid an' when we wuz playin' the white card! You ought t' 'a' told me, Bill, what ye went to town fer, an' it bein' Christmas, an' all."

That he should have chosen for his fall the Christmas season of all times was reprehensible, a fact which Mary and Humpy impressed upon him in the strongest terms. The Hopper was fully aware of the inopportuneness of his transgressions, but not to the point of encouraging his wife to abuse him.

As he clumsily tried to unfasten Shaver's hood, Mary pushed him aside and with shaking fingers removed the child's wraps. Shaver's cheeks were rosy from his drive through the cold; he was a plump, healthy little shaver and The Hopper viewed him with intense pride. Mary held the hood and coat to the light and inspected them with a sophisticated eye. They were of excellent quality and workmanship, and she shook her head and sighed deeply as she placed them carefully on a chair.

"It ain't on the square, Hop," protested Humpy, whose lone eye expressed the most poignant sorrow at The Hopper's derelictions. Humpy was tall and lean, with a thin, many-lined face. He was an ill-favored person at best, and his habit of turning his head constantly as though to compel his single eye to perform double service gave one an impression of restless watchfulness.

"Cute little Shaver, ain't 'e? Give Shaver somethin' to eat, Mary. I guess milk'll be the right ticket considerin' th' size of 'im. How ole you make 'im? Not more'n three, I reckon?"

"Two. He ain't more'n two, that kid."

"A nice little feller; you're a cute un, ain't ye, Shaver?"

Shaver nodded his head solemnly. Having wearied of playing with the plate he gravely inspected the trio; found something amusing in Humpy's bizarre countenance and laughed merrily. Finding no response to his friendly overtures he appealed to Mary.

"Me wants me's paw-widge," he announced.

"Porridge," interpreted Humpy with the air of one whose superior breeding makes him the proper arbiter of the speech of children of high social station. Whereupon Shaver appreciatively poked his forefinger into Humpy's surviving optic.

"I'll see what I got," muttered Mary. "What ye used t' eatin' for supper, honey?"

The "honey" was a concession, and The Hopper, who was giving Shaver his watch to play with, bent a commendatory glance upon his spouse.

"Go on an' tell us what ye done," said Mary, doggedly busying herself about the stove.

The Hopper drew a chair to the table to be within reach of Shaver and related succinctly his day's adventures.

"A dip!" moaned Mary as he described the seizure of the purse in the subway.

"You hadn't no right to do ut, Hop!" bleated Humpy, who had tipped his chair against the wall and was sucking a cold pipe. And then, professional curiosity overmastering his shocked conscience, he added: "What'd she measure, Hop?"

The Hopper grinned.

"Flubbed! Nothin' but papers," he confessed ruefully.

Mary and Humpy expressed their indignation and contempt in un-equivocal terms, which they repeated after he told of the suspected "bull" whose presence on the local had so alarmed him. A frank description of his flight and of his seizure of the roadster only added to their bitterness.

Humpy rose and paced the floor with the quick, short stride of men habituated to narrow spaces. The Hopper watched the telltale step so disagreeably reminiscent of evil times and shrugged his shoulders impatiently.

"Set down, Hump; ye make me nervous. I got thinkin' to do."

"Ye'd better be quick about doin' ut!" Humpy snorted with an oath.

"Cut the cussin'!" The Hopper admonished sharply. Since his retirement to private life he had sought diligently to free his speech of profanity and thieves' slang, as not only unbecoming in a respectable chicken farmer, but likely to arouse suspicions as to his origin and previous condition of servitude. "Can't ye see Shaver ain't use to ut? Shaver's a little gent; he's a reg'ler little juke; that's wot Shaver is."

"The more 'way up he is the worse fer us," whimpered Humpy. "It's kidnapin', that's wot ut is!"

"That's wot it *ain't*," declared The Hopper, averting a calamity to his watch, which Shaver was swinging by its chain. "He was took by accident I tell ye! I'm goin' to take Shaver back to his ma—ain't I, Shaver?"

"Take 'im back!" echoed Mary.

Humpy crumpled up in his chair at this new evidence of The Hopper's insanity.

"I'm goin' to make a Chris'mas present o' Shaver to his ma," reaffirmed The Hopper, pinching the nearer ruddy cheek of the merry, contented guest.

Shaver kicked The Hopper in the stomach and emitted a chortle expressive of unshakable confidence in The Hopper's ability to restore him to his lawful owners. This confidence was not, however, manifested toward Mary, who had prepared with care the only cereal her pantry afforded, and now approached Shaver, bowl and spoon in hand. Shaver, taken by surprise, inspected his supper with disdain and spurned it with a vigor that sent the spoon rattling across the floor.

"Me wants me's paw-widge bowl! Me wants me's *own* paw-widge bowl!" he screamed.

Mary expostulated; Humpy offered advice as to the best manner of dealing with the refractory Shaver, who gave further expression to his resentment by throwing The Hopper's watch with violence against the wall. That the table-service of The Hopper's establishment was not to

Shaver's liking was manifested in repeated rejections of the plain white bowl in which Mary offered the porridge. He demanded his very own porridge bowl with the increasing vehemence of one who is willing to starve rather than accept so palpable a substitute. He threw himself back on the table and lay there kicking and crying. Other needs now occurred to Shaver: he wanted his papa; he wanted his mamma; he wanted to go to his gwan'pa's. He clamored for Santa Claus and numerous Christmas trees which, it seemed, had been promised him at the houses of his kinsfolk. It was amazing and bewildering that the heart of one so young could desire so many things that were not immediately attainable. He had begun to suspect that he was among strangers who were not of his way of life, and this was fraught with the gravest danger.

"They'll hear 'im hollerin' in China," wailed the pessimistic Humpy, running about the room and examining the fastenings of doors and windows. "Folks goin' along the road'll hear 'im, an' it's terms fer the whole bunch!"

The Hopper began pacing the floor with Shaver, while Humpy and Mary denounced the child for unreasonableness and lack of discipline, not overlooking the stupidity and criminal carelessness of The Hopper in projecting so lawless a youngster into their domestic circle.

"Twenty years, that's wot ut is!" mourned Humpy.

"Ye kin get the chair fer kidnapin'," Mary added dolefully. "Ye gotta get 'im out o' here, Bill."

Pleasant predictions of a long prison term with capital punishment as the happy alternative failed to disturb The Hopper. To their surprise and somewhat to their shame he won the Shaver to a tractable humor. There was nothing in The Hopper's known past to justify any expectation that he could quiet a crying baby, and yet Shaver with a child's unerring instinct realized that The Hopper meant to be kind. He patted The Hopper's face with one fat little paw, chokingly declaring that he was hungry.

"'Course Shaver's hungry; an' Shaver's goin' to eat nice porridge Aunt Mary made fer 'im. Shaver's goin' to have 'is own porridge bowl to-morry—yes, sir-ee, oo is, little Shaver!"

Restored to the table, Shaver opened his mouth in obedience to The Hopper's patient pleading and swallowed a spoonful of the mush, Humpy holding the bowl out of sight in tactful deference to the child's delicate æsthetic sensibilities. A tumbler of milk was sipped with grateful gasps.

The Hopper grinned, proud of his success, while Mary and Humpy viewed his efforts with somewhat grudging admiration, and waited patiently until The Hopper took the wholly surfeited Shaver in his arms and began pacing the floor, humming softly. In normal circumstances The Hopper was not musical, and Humpy and Mary exchanged looks which, when interpreted, pointed to nothing less than a belief that the owner of Happy Hill Farm was bereft of his senses. There was some question as to whether Shaver should be undressed. Mary discouraged the idea and Humpy took a like view.

"Ye gotta chuck 'im quick; that's what ye gotta do," said Mary hoarsely. "We don't want 'im sleepin' here."

Whereupon The Hopper demonstrated his entire independence by carrying the Shaver to Humpy's bed and partially undressing him. While this was in progress, Shaver suddenly opened his eyes wide and raising one foot until it approximated the perpendicular, reached for it with his chubby hands.

"Sant' Claus comin'; m'y Kwismus!"

"Jes' listen to Shaver!" chuckled The Hopper. "'Course Santy is co-min', an' we're goin' to hang up Shaver's stockin', ain't we, Shaver?"

He pinned both stockings to the foot-board of Humpy's bed. By the time this was accomplished under the hostile eyes of Mary and Humpy, Shaver slept the sleep of the innocent.

IV

They watched the child in silence for a few minutes and then Mary detached a gold locket from his neck and bore it to the kitchen for examination.

"Ye gotta move quick, Hop," Humpy urged. "The white card's what we wuz all goin' to play. We wuz fixed nice here, an' things goin' easy; an' the yard full o' br'ilers. I don't want to do no more time. I'm an ole man, Hop."

"Cut ut!" ordered The Hopper, taking the locket from Mary and weighing it critically in his hand. They bent over him as he scrutinized the face on which was inscribed:—

Roger Livingston Talbot
June 13, 1913

"Lemme see; he's two an' a harf. Ye purty nigh guessed 'im right, Mary."

The sight of the gold trinket, the probability that the Shaver belonged to a family of wealth, proved disturbing to Humpy's late protestations of virtue.

"They'd be a heap o' kale in ut, Hop. His folks is rich, I reckon. Ef we wuzn't playin' the white card—"

Ignoring this shocking evidence of Humpy's moral instability, The Hopper became lost in reverie, meditatively drawing at his pipe.

"We ain't never goin' to quit playin' ut square," he announced, to Mary's manifest relief. "I hadn't ought t' 'a' done th' dippin'. It were a mistake. My ole head wuzn't workin' right er I wouldn't 'a' slipped. But ye needn't jump on me no more."

"Wot ye goin' to do with that kid? Ye tell me that!" demanded Mary, unwilling too readily to accept The Hopper's repentance at face value.

"I'm goin' to take 'im to 'is folks, that's wot I'm goin' to do with 'im," announced The Hopper.

"Yer crazy—yer plum' crazy!" cried Humpy, slapping his knees excitedly. "Ye kin take 'im to an orphant asylum an' tell um ye found 'im in that machine ye lifted. And mebbe ye'll git by with ut an' mebbe ye won't, but ye gotta keep me out of ut!"

"I found the machine in th' road, right here by th' house; an' th' kid was in ut all by hisself. An' bein' humin an' respectible I brought 'im in to keep 'im from freezin' t' death," said The Hopper, as though repeating lines he was committing to memory. "They ain't nobody can say as I didn't. Ef I git pinched, that's my spiel to th' cops. It ain't kidnapin'; it's life-savin', that's wot ut is! I'm a-goin' back an' have a look at that place where I got 'im. Kind o' queer they left the kid out there in the buzz-wagon; *mighty* queer, now's I think of ut. Little house back from the road; lots o' trees an' bushes in front. Didn't seem to be no lights. He keeps talkin' about Chris'mas at his grandpa's. Folks must 'a' been goin' to take th' kid somewheres fer Chris'mas. I guess it'll throw a skeer into 'em to find him up an' gone."

"They's rich, an' all the big bulls'll be lookin' fer 'im; ye'd better 'phone the New Haven cops ye've picked 'im up. Then they'll come out, an' yer spiel about findin' 'im'll sound easy an' sensible like."

The Hopper, puffing his pipe philosophically, paid no heed to Humpy's suggestion even when supported warmly by Mary.

"I gotta find some way o' puttin' th' kid back without seein' no cops. I'll jes' take a sneak back an' have a look at th' place," said The Hopper. "I ain't goin' to turn Shaver over to no cops. Ye can't take no chances with 'em. They don't know nothin' about us bein' here, but they ain't fools, an' I ain't goin' to give none o' 'em a squint at me!"

He defended his plan against a joint attack by Mary and Humpy, who saw in it only further proof of his tottering reason. He was obliged to tell them in harsh terms to be quiet, and he added to their rage by the deliberation with which he made his preparations to leave.

He opened the door of a clock and drew out a revolver which he examined carefully and thrust into his pocket. Mary groaned; Humpy beat the air in impotent despair. The Hopper possessed himself also of a jimmy and an electric lamp. The latter he flashed upon the face of the sleeping Shaver, who turned restlessly for a moment and then lay still again. He smoothed the coverlet over the tiny form, while Mary and Humpy huddled in the doorway. Mary wept; Humpy was awed into silence by his old friend's perversity. For years he had admired The Hopper's cleverness, his genius for extricating himself from difficulties; he was deeply shaken to think that one who had stood so high in one of the most exacting of professions should have fallen so low. As The Hopper imperturbably buttoned his coat and walked toward the door, Humpy set his back against it in a last attempt to save his friend from his own foolhardiness.

"Ef anybody turns up here an' asks for th' kid, ye kin tell 'em wot I said. We finds 'im in th' road right here by the farm when we're doin' th' night chores an' takes 'im in t' keep 'im from freezin'. Ye'll have th' machine an' kid here to show 'em. An' as fer me, I'm off lookin' fer his folks."

Mary buried her face in her apron and wept despairingly. The Hopper, noting for the first time that Humpy was guarding the door, roughly pushed him aside and stood for a moment with his hand on the knob.

"They's things wot is," he remarked with a last attempt to justify his course, "an' things wot ain't. I reckon I'll take a peek at that place an' see wot's th' best way t' shake th' kid. Ye can't jes' run up to a house in a machine with his folks all settin' round cryin' an' cops askin' questions. Ye got to do some plannin' an' thinkin'. I'm goin' t' clean ut all up before daylight, an' ye needn't worry none about ut. Hop ain't worryin'; jes' leave ut t' Hop!"

There was no alternative but to leave it to Hop, and they stood mute as he went out and softly closed the door.

V

The snow had ceased and the stars shone brightly on a white world as The Hopper made his way by various trolley lines to the house from which he had snatched Shaver. On a New Haven car he debated the prospects of more snow with a policeman who seemed oblivious to the fact that a child had been stolen—shamelessly carried off by a man with a long police record. Merry Christmas passed from lip to lip as if all creation were attuned to the note of love and peace, and crime were an undreamed of thing.

For two years The Hopper had led an exemplary life and he was keenly alive now to the joy of adventure. His lapses of the day were unfortunate; he thought of them with regret and misgivings, but he was zestful for whatever the unknown held in store for him. Abroad again with a pistol in his pocket, he was a lawless being, but with the difference that he was intent now upon making restitution, though in such manner as would give him something akin to the old thrill that he experienced when he enjoyed the reputation of being one of the most skillful yeggs in the country. The successful thief is of necessity an imaginative person; he must be able to visualize the unseen and to deal with a thousand hidden contingencies. At best the chances are against him; with all his ingenuity the broad, heavy hand of the law is likely at any moment to close upon him from some unexpected quarter. The Hopper knew this, and knew, too, that in yielding to the exhilaration of the hour he was likely to come to grief. Justice has a long memory, and if he again made himself the object of police scrutiny that little forty-thousand dollar affair in Maine might still be fixed upon him.

When he reached the house from whose gate he had removed the roadster with Shaver attached, he studied it with the eye of an experienced strategist. No gleam anywhere published the presence of frantic parents bewailing the loss of a baby. The cottage lay snugly behind its barrier of elms and shrubbery as though its young heir had not vanished into the void. The Hopper was a deliberating being and he gave careful weight to these circumstances as he crept round the walk, in which the snow lay undisturbed, and investigated the rear of the premises. The lattice door of the summer kitchen opened readily, and, after satisfying himself that no one was stirring in the lower part of the house, he pried up the sash of a window and stepped in. The larder was well stocked, as though in preparation for a Christmas feast, and he passed on to the dining-room, whose appointments spoke for good taste and a degree of prosperity in the householder.

Cautious flashes of his lamp disclosed on the table a hamper, in which were packed a silver cup, plate, and bowl which at once awoke the Hopper's interest. Here indubitably was proof that this was the home of Shaver, now sleeping sweetly in Humpy's bed, and this was the porridge bowl for which Shaver's soul had yearned. If Shaver did not belong to the house, he had at least been a visitor there, and it struck The Hopper as a reasonable assumption that Shaver had been deposited in the roadster while his lawful guardians returned to the cottage for the hamper preparatory to an excursion of some sort. But The Hopper groped in the dark for an explanation of the calmness with which the householders accepted the loss of the child. It was not in human nature for the parents of a youngster so handsome and in every way so delightful as Shaver to permit him to be stolen from under their very noses without making an outcry. The Hopper examined the silver pieces and found them engraved with the name borne by the locket. He crept through a living-room and came to a Christmas tree—the smallest of Christmas trees. Beside it lay a number of packages designed clearly for none other than young Roger Livingston Talbot.

Housebreaking is a very different business from the forcible entry of country post-offices, and The Hopper was nervous. This particular house seemed utterly deserted. He stole upstairs and found doors open and a disorder indicative of the occupants' hasty departure. His attention was arrested by a small room finished in white, with a white enameled bed, and other furniture to match. A generous litter of toys was the last proof needed to establish the house as Shaver's true domicile. Indeed, there was every indication that Shaver was the central figure of this home of whose charm and atmosphere The Hopper was vaguely sensible. A frieze of dancing children and watercolor sketches of Shaver's head, dabbed here and there in the most unlooked-for places, hinted at an artistic household. This impression was strengthened when The Hopper, bewildered and baffled, returned to the lower floor and found a studio opening off the living room. The Hopper had never visited a studio before, and satisfied now that he was the sole occupant of the house, he passed about shooting his light upon unfinished canvases, pausing finally before an easel supporting a portrait of Shaver—newly finished, he discovered, by poking his finger into the wet paint. Something fell to the floor and he picked up a large sheet of drawing paper on which this message was written in charcoal:—

Six-thirty.

Dear Sweetheart:—

This is a fine trick you have played on me, you dear girl! I've been expecting you back all afternoon. At six I decided that you were going to spend the night with your infuriated parent and thought I'd try my luck with mine! I put Billie into the roadster and, leaving him there, ran over to the Flemings's to say Merry Christmas and tell 'em we were off for the night. They kept me just a minute to look at those new Jap prints Jim's so crazy about, and while I was gone you came along and skipped with Billie and the car! I suppose this means that you've been making headway with your dad and want to try the effect of Billie's blandishments. Good luck! But you might have stopped long enough to tell me about it! How fine it would be if everything could be straightened out for Christmas! Do you remember the first time I kissed you—it was on Christmas Eve four years ago at the Billings's dance! I'm just trolleying out to father's to see what an evening session will do. I'll be back early in the morning.

Love always,

ROGER.

Billie was undoubtedly Shaver's nickname. This delighted The Hopper. That they should possess the same name appeared to create a strong bond of comradeship. The writer of the note was presumably the child's father and the "Dear Sweetheart" the youngster's mother. The Hopper was not reassured by these disclosures. The return of Shaver to his parents was far from being the pleasant little Christmas Eve adventure he had imagined. He had only the lowest opinion of a father who would, on a winter evening, carelessly leave his baby in a motor-car while he looked at pictures, and who, finding both motor and baby gone, would take it for granted that the baby's mother had run off with them. But these people were artists, and artists, The Hopper had heard, were a queer breed, sadly lacking in common sense. He tore the note into strips which he stuffed into his pocket.

Depressed by the impenetrable wall of mystery along which he was groping, he returned to the living-room, raised one of the windows and unbolted the front door to make sure of an exit in case these strange, foolish Talbots should unexpectedly return. The shades were up and he shielded his light carefully with his cap as he passed rapidly about the room. It began to look very much as though Shaver would spend Christmas at Happy Hill Farm—a possibility that had not figured in The Hopper's calculations.

Flashing his lamp for a last survey a letter propped against a lamp on the table arrested his eye. He dropped to the floor and crawled into a corner where he turned his light upon the note and read, not without difficulty, the following:—

Seven o'clock.

Dear Roger:—

I've just got back from father's where I spent the last three hours talking over our troubles. I didn't tell you I was going, knowing you would think it foolish, but it seemed best, dear, and I hope you'll forgive me. And now I find that you've gone off with Billie, and I'm guessing that you've gone to your father's to see what you can do. I'm taking the trolley into New Haven to ask Mamie Palmer about that cook she thought we might get, and if possible I'll bring the girl home with me. Don't trouble about me, as I'll be perfectly safe, and, as you know, I rather enjoy prowling around at night. You'll certainly get back before I do, but if I'm not here don't be alarmed.

We are so happy in each other, dear, and if only we could get our foolish fathers to stop hating each other, how beautiful everything would be! And we could all have such a merry, merry Christmas!

MURIEL.

The Hopper's acquaintance with the epistolary art was the slightest, but even to a mind unfamiliar with this branch of literature it was plain that Shaver's parents were involved in some difficulty that was attributable, not to any lessening of affection between them, but to a row of some sort between their respective fathers. Muriel, running into the house to write her note, had failed to see Roger's letter in the studio, and this was very fortunate for The Hopper; but Muriel might return at any moment, and it would add nothing to the plausibility of the story he meant to tell if he were found in the house.

VI

Anxious and dejected at the increasing difficulties that confronted him, he was moving toward the door when a light, buoyant step sounded on the veranda. In a moment the living-room lights were switched on from the entry and a woman called out sharply:—

"Stop right where you are or I'll shoot!"

The authoritative voice of the speaker, the quickness with which she had grasped the situation and leveled her revolver, brought The Hopper to an abrupt halt in the middle of the room, where he fell with a discordant crash across the keyboard of a grand piano. He turned, cowering, to confront a tall, young woman in a long ulster who advanced toward him slowly, but with every mark of determination upon her face. The Hopper stared beyond the gun, held in a very steady hand, into a pair of fearless dark eyes. In all his experiences he had never been cornered by a woman, and he stood gaping at his captor in astonishment. She was a very pretty young woman, with cheeks that still had the curve of youth, but with a chin that spoke for much firmness of character. A fur toque perched a little to one side gave her a boyish air.

This undoubtedly was Shaver's mother who had caught him prowling in her house, and all The Hopper's plans for explaining her son's disappearance and returning him in a manner to win praise and gratitude went glimmering. There was nothing in the appearance of this Muriel to encourage a hope that she was either embarrassed or alarmed by his presence. He had been captured many times, but the trick had never been turned by any one so cool as this young woman. She seemed to be pondering with the greatest calmness what disposition she should make of him. In the intentness of her thought the revolver wavered for an instant, and The Hopper, without taking his eyes from her, made a cat-like spring that brought him to the window he had raised against just such an emergency.

"None of that!" she cried, walking slowly toward him without lowering the pistol. "If you attempt to jump from that window I'll shoot! But it's cold in here and you may lower it."

The Hopper, weighing the chances, decided that the odds were heavily against escape, and lowered the window.

"Now," said Muriel, "step into that corner and keep your hands up where I can watch them."

The Hopper obeyed her instructions strictly. There was a telephone on the table near her and he expected her to summon help; but to his surprise she calmly seated herself, resting her right elbow on the arm of the chair, her head slightly tilted to one side, as she inspected him with greater attention along the blueblack barrel of her automatic. Unless he made a dash for liberty this extraordinary woman would, at her leisure, turn him over to the police as a housebreaker and his peaceful life as a chicken farmer would be at an end. Her prolonged silence troubled The Hopper. He had not been more nervous when waiting for the report of the juries which at times had passed upon his conduct, or for judges to fix his term of imprisonment.

"Yes'm," he muttered, with a view to ending a silence that had become intolerable.

Her eyes danced to the accompaniment of her thoughts, but in no way did she betray the slightest perturbation.

"I ain't done nothin'; hones' to God, I ain't!" he protested brokenly.

"I saw you through the window when you entered this room and I was watching while you read that note," said his captor. "I thought it funny that you should do that instead of packing up the silver. Do you mind telling me just why you read that note?"

"Well, miss, I jes' thought it kind o' funny there wuzn't nobody round an' the letter was layin' there all open, an' I didn't see no harm in lookin'."

"It was awfully clever of you to crawl into the corner so nobody could see your light from the windows," she said with a tinge of admiration. "I suppose you thought you might find out how long the people of the house were likely to be gone and how much time you could spend here. Was that it?"

"I reckon ut wuz some thin' like that," he agreed.

This was received with the noncommittal "Um" of a person whose thoughts are elsewhere. Then, as though she were eliciting from an artist or man of letters a frank opinion as to his own ideas of his attainments and professional standing, she asked, with a meditative air that puzzled him as much as her question:—

"Just how good a burglar are you? Can you do a job neatly and safely?"

The Hopper, staggered by her inquiry and overcome by modesty, shrugged his shoulders and twisted about uncomfortably.

"I reckon as how you've pinched me I ain't much good," he replied, and was rewarded with a smile followed by a light little laugh. He was beginning to feel pleased that she manifested no fear of him. In fact, he had decided that Shaver's mother was the most remarkable woman he had ever encountered, and by all odds the handsomest. He began to take heart. Perhaps after all he might hit upon some way of restoring Shaver to his proper place in the house of Talbot without making himself liable to a long term for kidnaping.

"If you're really a successful burglar—one who doesn't just poke abound in empty houses as you were doing here, but clever and brave enough to break into houses where people are living and steal things without making a mess of it; and if you can play fair about it—then I think—I think—maybe—we can come to terms!"

"Yes'm!" faltered The Hopper, beginning to wonder if Mary and Humpy had been right in saying that he had lost his mind. He was so astonished that his arms wavered, but she was instantly on her feet and the little automatic was again on a level with his eyes.

"Excuse me, miss, I didn't mean to drop 'em. I weren't goin' to do nothin'. Hones' I wuzn't!" he pleaded with real contrition. "It jes' seemed kind o' funny what ye said."

He grinned sheepishly. If she knew that her Billie, *alias* Shaver, was not with her husband at his father's house, she would not be dallying in this fashion. And if the young father, who painted pictures, and left notes in his studio in a blind faith that his wife would find them,—if that trusting soul knew that Billie was asleep in a house all of whose inmates had done penance behind prison bars, he would very quickly become a man of action. The Hopper had never heard of such careless parenthood! These people were children! His heart warmed to them in pity and admiration, as it had to little Billie.

"I forgot to ask you whether you are armed," she remarked, with just as much composure as though she were asking him whether he took two lumps of sugar in his tea; and then she added, "I suppose I ought to have asked you that in the first place."

"I gotta gun in my coat—right side," he confessed. "An' that's all I got," he added, batting his eyes under the spell of her bewildering smile.

With her left hand she cautiously extracted his revolver and backed away with it to the table.

"If you'd lied to me I should have killed you; do you understand?"

"Yes'm," murmured The Hopper meekly.

She had spoken as though homicide were a common incident of her life, but a gleam of humor in the eyes she was watching vigilantly abated her severity.

"You may sit down—there, please!"

She pointed to a much bepillowed davenport and The Hopper sank down on it, still with his hands up. To his deepening mystification she backed to the windows and lowered the shades, and this done she sat down with the table between them, remarking,—

"You may put your hands down now, Mr. ——?"

He hesitated, decided that it was unwise to give any of his names; and respecting his scruples she said with great magnanimity:—

"Of course you wouldn't want to tell me your name, so don't trouble about that."

She sat, wholly tranquil, her arms upon the table, both hands caressing the small automatic, while his own revolver, of different pattern and larger caliber, lay close by. His status was now established as that of a gentleman making a social call upon a lady who, in the pleasantest manner imaginable and yet with undeniable resoluteness, kept a deadly weapon pointed in the general direction of his person.

A clock on the mantel struck eleven with a low, silvery note. Muriel waited for the last stroke and then spoke crisply and directly.

"We were speaking of that letter I left lying here on the table. You didn't understand it, of course; you couldn't—not really. So I will explain it to you. My husband and I married against our fathers' wishes; both of them were opposed to it."

She waited for this to sink into his perturbed consciousness. The Hopper frowned and leaned forward to express his sympathetic interest in this confidential disclosure.

"My father," she resumed, "is just as stupid as my father-in-law and they have both continued to make us just as uncomfortable as possible. The cause of the trouble is ridiculous. There's nothing against my husband or me, you understand; it's simply a bitter jealousy between the two men due to the fact that they are rival collectors."

The Hopper stared blankly. The only collectors with whom he had enjoyed any acquaintance were persons who presented bills for payment.

"They are collectors," Muriel hastened to explain, "of ceramics—precious porcelains and that sort of thing."

"Yes'm," assented The Hopper, who hadn't the faintest notion of what she meant.

"For years, whenever there have been important sales of these things, which men fight for and are willing to die for—whenever there has been something specially fine in the market, my father-in-law—he's Mr. Talbot—and Mr. Wilton—he's my father—have bid for them. There are auctions, you know, and people come from all over the world looking for a chance to buy the rarest pieces. They've explored China and Japan hunting for prizes and they are experts—men of rare taste and judgment—what you call connoisseurs."

The Hopper nodded gravely at the unfamiliar word, convinced that not only were Muriel and her husband quite insane, but that they had inherited the infirmity.

"The trouble has been," Muriel continued, "that Mr. Talbot and my father both like the same kind of thing; and when one has got something the other wanted, of course it has added to the ill-feeling. This has been going on for years and recently they have grown more bitter. When Roger and I ran off and got married, that didn't help matters any; but just within a few days something has happened to make things much worse than ever."

The Hopper's complete absorption in this novel recital was so manifest that she put down the revolver with which she had been idling and folded her hands.

"Thank ye, miss," mumbled The Hopper.

"Only last week," Muriel continued, "my father-in-law bought one of those pottery treasures—a plum-blossom vase made in China hundreds of years ago and very, very valuable. It belonged to a Philadelphia collector who died not long ago and Mr. Talbot bought it from the executor of the estate, who happened to be an old friend of his. Father was very angry, for he had been led to believe that this vase was going to be offered at auction and he'd have a chance to bid on it. And just before that father had got hold of a jar—a perfectly wonderful piece of red Lang-Yao—that collectors everywhere have coveted for years. This made Mr. Talbot furious at father. My husband is at his father's now trying to make him see the folly of all this, and I visited *my* father to-day to try to persuade him to stop being so foolish. You see I wanted us all to be happy for Christmas! Of course, Christmas ought to be a time of gladness for everybody. Even people in your—er—profession must feel that Christmas is one day in the year when all hard feelings should be forgotten and everybody should try to make others happy."

"I guess yer right, miss. Ut sure seems foolish fer folks t' git mad about jugs like you says. Wuz they empty, miss?"

"Empty!" repeated Muriel wonderingly, not understanding at once that her visitor was unaware that the "jugs" men fought over were valued as art treasures and not for their possible contents. Then she laughed merrily, as only the mother of Shaver could laugh.

"Oh! Of course they're *empty!* That does seem to make it sillier, doesn't it? But they're like famous pictures, you know, or any beautiful work of art that only happens occasionally. Perhaps it seems odd to you that men can be so crazy about such things, but I suppose sometimes you have wanted things very, very much, and—oh!"

She paused, plainly confused by her tactlessness in suggesting to a member of his profession the extremities to which one may be led by covetousness.

"Yes, miss," he remarked hastily; and he rubbed his nose with the back of his hand, and grinned indulgently as he realized the cause of her embarrassment. It crossed his mind that she might be playing a trick of some kind; that her story, which seemed to him wholly fantastic and not at all like a chronicle of the acts of veritable human beings, was merely a device for detaining him until help arrived. But he dismissed this immediately as unworthy of one so pleasing, so beautiful, so perfectly qualified to be the mother of Shaver!

"Well, just before luncheon, without telling my husband where I was going, I ran away to papa's, hoping to persuade him to end this silly feud. I spent the afternoon there and he was very unreasonable. He feels that Mr. Talbot wasn't fair about that Philadelphia purchase, and I gave it up and came home. I got here a little after dark and found my husband had taken Billie—that's our little boy—and gone. I knew, of course, that he had gone to *his* father's hoping to bring him round, for both our fathers are simply crazy about Billie. But you see I never go to Mr. Talbot's and my husband never goes—Dear me!" she broke off suddenly. "I suppose I ought to telephone and see if Billie is all right."

The Hopper, greatly alarmed, thrust his head forward as she pondered this. If she telephoned to her father-in-law's to ask about Billie, the jig would be up! He drew his hand across his face and fell back with relief as she went on, a little absently:—

"Mr. Talbot hates telephoning, and it might be that my husband is just getting him to the point of making concessions, and I shouldn't want to interrupt. It's so late now that of course Roger and Billie will spend the night there. And Billie and Christmas ought to be a combination that would soften the hardest heart! You ought to see—you just ought to see Billie! He's the cunningest, dearest baby in the world!"

The Hopper sat pigeon-toed, beset by countless conflicting emotions. His ingenuity was taxed to its utmost by the demands of this complex situation. But for his returning suspicion that Muriel was leading up to something; that she was detaining him for some purpose not yet apparent, he would have told her of her husband's note and confessed that the adored Billie was at that moment enjoying the reluctant hospitality of Happy Hill Farm. He resolved to continue his policy of silence as to the young heir's whereabouts until Muriel had shown her hand. She had not wholly abandoned the thought of telephoning to her father-in-law's, he found, from her next remark.

"You think it's all right, don't you? It's strange Roger didn't leave me a note of some kind. Our cook left a week ago and there was no one here when he left."

"I reckon as how yer kid's all right, miss," he answered consolingly.

Her voluble confidences had enthralled him, and her reference of this matter to his judgment was enormously flattering. On the rough edges of society where he had spent most of his life, fellow craftsmen had frequently solicited his advice, chiefly as to the disposition of their ill-gotten gains or regarding safe harbors of refuge, but to be taken into counsel by the only gentlewoman he had ever met roused his self-respect, touched a chivalry that never before had been wakened in The Hopper's soul. She was so like a child in her guilelessness, and so brave amid her perplexities!

"Oh, I know Roger will take beautiful care of Billie. And now," she smiled radiantly, "you're probably wondering what I've been driving at all this time. Maybe"—she added softly—"maybe it's providential, your turning up here in this way!"

She uttered this happily, with a little note of triumph and another of her smiles that seemed to illuminate the universe. The Hopper had been called many names in his varied career, but never before had he been invested with the attributes of an agent of Providence.

"They's things wot is an' they's things wot ain't, miss; I reckon I ain't as bad as some. I mean to be on the square, miss."

"I believe that," she said. "I've always heard there's honor among thieves, and"—she lowered her voice to a whisper—"it's possible I might become one myself!"

The Hopper's eyes opened wide and he crossed and uncrossed his legs nervously in his agitation.

"If—if"—she began slowly, bending forward with a grave, earnest look in her eyes and clasping her fingers tightly—"if we could only get hold of father's Lang-Yao jar and that plum-blossom vase Mr. Talbot has—if we could only do that!"

The Hopper swallowed hard. This fearless, pretty young woman was calmly suggesting that he commit two felonies, little knowing that his score for the day already aggregated three—purse-snatching, the theft of an automobile from her own door, and what might very readily be construed as the kidnaping of her own child!

"I don't know, miss," he said feebly, calculating that the sum total of even minimum penalties for the five crimes would outrun his natural life and consume an eternity of reincarnations.

"Of course it wouldn't be stealing in the ordinary sense," she explained. "What I want you to do is to play the part of what we will call a reversible Santa Claus, who takes things away from stupid people who don't enjoy them anyhow. And maybe if they lost these things they'd behave themselves. I could explain afterward that it was all my fault, and of course I wouldn't let any harm come to *you*. I'd be responsible, and of course I'd see you safely out of it; you would have to rely on me for that. I'm trusting *you* and you'd have to trust *me!*"

"Oh, I'd trust ye, miss! An' ef I was to get pinched I wouldn't never squeal on ye. We don't never blab on a pal, miss!"

He was afraid she might resent being called a "pal," but his use of the term apparently pleased her.

"We understand each other, then. It really won't be very difficult, for papa's place is over on the Sound and Mr. Talbot's is right next to it, so you wouldn't have far to go."

Her utter failure to comprehend the enormity of the thing she was proposing affected him queerly. Even among hardened criminals in the underworld such undertakings are suggested cautiously; but Muriel was ordering a burglary as though it were a pound of butter or a dozen eggs!

"Father keeps his most valuable glazes in a safe in the pantry," she resumed after a moment's reflection, "but I can give you the combination. That will make it a lot easier."

The Hopper assented, with a pontifical nod, to this sanguine view of the matter.

"Mr. Talbot keeps his finest pieces in a cabinet built into the book-shelves in his library. It's on the left side as you stand in the drawing-room door, and you look for the works of Thomas Carlyle. There's a dozen or so volumes of Carlyle, only they're not books,—not really,—but just the backs of books painted on the steel of a safe. And if you press a spring in the upper right-hand corner of the shelf just over these books the whole section swings out. I suppose you've seen that sort of hiding-place for valuables?"

"Well, not exactly, miss. But havin' a tip helps, an' ef there ain't no soup to pour—"

"Soup?" inquired Muriel, wrinkling her pretty brows.

"That's the juice we pour into the cracks of a safe to blow out the lid with," The Hopper elucidated. "Ut's a lot handier ef you've got the combination. Ut usually ain't jes' layin' around."

"I should hope not!" exclaimed Muriel.

She took a sheet of paper from the leathern stationery rack and fell to scribbling, while he furtively eyed the window and again put from him the thought of flight.

"There! That's the combination of papa's safe." She turned her wrist and glanced at her watch. "It's half-past eleven and you can catch a trolley in ten minutes that will take you right past papa's house. The butler's an old man who forgets to lock the windows half the time, and there's one in the conservatory with a broken catch. I noticed it to-day when I was thinking about stealing the jar myself!"

They were established on so firm a basis of mutual confidence that when he rose and walked to the table she didn't lift her eyes from the paper on which she was drawing a diagram of her father's house. He stood watching her nimble fingers, fascinated by the boldness of her plan for restoring amity between Shaver's grandfathers, and filled with admiration for her resourcefulness.

He asked a few questions as to exits and entrances and fixed in his mind a very accurate picture of the home of her father. She then proceeded to enlighten him as to the ways and means of entering the home of her father-in-law, which she sketched with equal facility.

"There's a French window—a narrow glass door—on the veranda. I think you might get in *there!*" She made a jab with the pencil. "Of course I should hate awfully to have you get caught! But you must have had a lot of experience, and with all the help I'm giving you—!"

A sudden lifting of her head gave him the full benefit of her eyes and he averted his gaze reverently.

"There's always a chance o' bein' nabbed, miss," he suggested with feeling.

Shaver's mother wielded the same hypnotic power, highly intensified, that he had felt in Shaver. He knew that he was going to attempt what she asked; that he was committed to the project of robbing two houses merely to please a pretty young woman who invited his coöperation at the point of a revolver!

"Papa's always a sound sleeper," she was saying. "When I was a little girl a burglar went all through our house and carried off his clothes and he never knew it until the next morning. But you'll have to be careful at Mr. Talbot's, for he suffers horribly from insomnia."

"They got any o' them fancy burglar alarms?" asked The Hopper as he concluded his examination of her sketches.

"Oh, I forgot to tell you about that!" she cried contritely. "There's nothing of the kind at Mr. Talbot's, but at papa's there's a switch in the living-room, right back of a bust—a white marble thing on a pedestal. You turn it off *there*. Half the time papa forgets to switch it on before he goes to bed. And another thing—be careful about stumbling over that bearskin rug in the hall. People are always sticking their feet into its jaws."

"I'll look out for ut, miss."

Burglar alarms and the jaws of wild beasts were not inviting hazards. The programme she outlined so light-heartedly was full of complexities. It was almost pathetic that any one could so cheerfully and irresponsibly suggest the perpetration of a crime. The terms she used in describing the loot he was to filch were much stranger to him than Chinese, but it was fairly clear that at the Talbot house he was to steal a blue-and-white thing and at the Wilton's a red one. The form and size of these articles she illustrated with graceful gestures.

"If I thought you were likely to make a mistake I'd—I'd go with you!" she declared.

"Oh, no, miss; ye couldn't do that! I guess I can do ut fer ye. Ut's jes' a *leetle* ticklish. I reckon ef yer pa wuz to nab me ut'd go hard with me."

"I wouldn't let him be hard on you," she replied earnestly. "And now I haven't said anything about a—a—about what we will call a *reward* for bringing me these porcelains. I shall expect to pay you; I couldn't think of taking up your time, you know, for nothing!"

"Lor', miss, I couldn't take nothin' at all fer doin' ut! Ye see ut wuz sort of accidental our meetin', and besides, I ain't no housebreaker—not, as ye may say, reg'ler. I'll be glad to do ut fer ye, miss, an' ye can rely on me doin' my best fer ye. Ye've treated me right, miss, an' I ain't a-goin' t' fergit ut!"

The Hopper spoke with feeling. Shaver's mother had, albeit at the pistol point, confided her most intimate domestic affairs to him. He realized, without finding just these words for it, that she had in effect decorated him with the symbol of her order of knighthood and he had every honorable—or dishonorable!—intention of proving himself worthy of her confidence.

"If ye please, miss," he said, pointing toward his confiscated revolver.

"Certainly; you may take it. But of course you won't kill anybody?"

"No, miss; only I'm sort o' lonesome without ut when I'm on a job."

"And you do understand," she said, following him to the door and noting in the distance the headlight of an approaching trolley, "that I'm only doing this in the hope that good may come of it. It isn't really criminal, you know; if you succeed, it may mean the happiest Christmas of my life!"

"Yes, miss. I won't come back till mornin', but don't you worry none. We gotta play safe, miss, an' ef I land th' jugs I'll find cover till I kin deliver 'em safe."

"Thank you; oh, thank you ever so much! And good luck!"

She put out her hand; he held it gingerly for a moment in his rough fingers and ran for the car.

VII

The Hopper, in his rôle of the Reversible Santa Claus, dropped off the car at the crossing Muriel had carefully described, waited for the car to vanish, and warily entered the Wilton estate through a gate set in the stone wall. The clouds of the early evening had passed and the stars marched through the heavens resplendently, proclaiming peace on earth and good-will toward men. They were almost oppressively brilliant, seen through the clear, cold atmosphere, and as The Hopper slipped from one big tree to another on his tangential course to the house, he fortified his courage by muttering, "They's things wot is an' things wot ain't!"—finding much comfort and stimulus in the phrase.

Arriving at the conservatory in due course, he found that Muriel's averments as to the vulnerability of that corner of her father's house were correct in every particular. He entered with ease, sniffed the warm, moist air, and, leaving the door slightly ajar, sought the pantry, lowered the shades, and, helping himself to a candle from a silver candelabrum, readily found the safe hidden away in one of the cupboards. He was surprised to find himself more nervous with the combination in his hand than on memorable occasions in the old days when he had broken into country postoffices and assaulted safes by force. In his haste he twice failed to give the proper turns, but the third time the knob caught, and in a moment the door swung open disclosing shelves filled with vases, bottles, bowls, and plates in bewildering variety. A chest of silver appealed to him distractingly as a much more tangible asset than the pottery, and he dizzily contemplated a jewel-case containing a diamond necklace with a pearl pendant. The moment was a critical one in The Hopper's eventful career. This dazzling prize was his for the taking, and he knew the operator of a fence in Chicago who would dispose of the necklace and make him a fair return. But visions of Muriel, the beautiful, the confiding, and of her little Shaver asleep on Humpy's bed, rose before him. He steeled his heart against temptation, drew his candle along the shelf and scrutinized the glazes. There could be no mistaking the red Lang-Yao whose brilliant tints kindled in the candle-glow. He lifted it tenderly, verifying the various points of Muriel's description, set it down on the floor and locked the safe.

He was retracing his steps toward the conservatory and had reached the main hall when the creaking of the stairsteps brought him up with a start. Some one was descending, slowly and cautiously. For a second time and with grateful appreciation of Muriel's forethought, he carefully avoided the ferocious jaws of the bear, noiselessly continued on to the conservatory, crept through the door, closed it, and then, crouching on the steps, awaited developments. The caution exercised by the person descending the stairway was not that of a householder who has been roused from slumber by a disquieting noise. The Hopper was keenly interested in this fact.

With his face against the glass he watched the actions of a tall, elderly man with a short, grayish beard, who wore a golf-cap pulled low on his head—points noted by The Hopper in the flashes of an electric lamp with which the gentleman was guiding himself. His face was clearly the original of a photograph The Hopper had seen on the table at Muriel's cottage—Mr. Wilton, Muriel's father, The Hopper surmised; but just why the owner of the establishment should be prowling about in this fashion taxed his speculative powers to the utmost. Warned by steps on the cement floor of the conservatory, he left the door in haste and flattened himself against the wall of the house some distance away and again awaited developments.

Wilton's figure was a blur in the star-light as he stepped out into the walk and started furtively across the grounds. His conduct greatly displeased The Hopper, as likely to interfere with the further carrying out of Muriel's instructions. The Lang-Yao jar was much too large to go into his pocket and not big enough to fit snugly under his arm, and as the walk was slippery he was beset by the fear that he might fall and smash this absurd thing that had caused so bitter an enmity between Shaver's grandfathers. The soft snow on the lawn gave him a surer footing and he crept after Wilton, who was carefully pursuing his way toward a house whose gables were faintly limned against the sky. This, according to Muriel's diagram, was the Talbot place. The Hopper greatly mistrusted conditions he didn't understand, and he was at a loss to account for Wilton's strange actions.

He lost sight of him for several minutes, then the faint click of a latch marked the prowler's proximity to a hedge that separated the two estates. The Hopper crept forward, found a gate through which Wilton had entered his neighbor's property, and stole after him. Wilton had been swallowed up by the deep shadow of the house, but The Hopper was aware, from an occasional scraping of feet, that he was still moving forward. He crawled over the snow until he reached a large tree whose boughs, sharply limned against the stars, brushed the eaves of the house.

The Hopper was aroused, tremendously aroused, by the unaccountable actions of Muriel's father. It flashed upon him that Wilton, in his deep hatred of his rival collector, was about to set fire to Talbot's house, and incendiarism was a crime which The Hopper, with all his moral obliquity, greatly abhorred.

Several minutes passed, a period of anxious waiting, and then a sound reached him which, to his keen professional sense, seemed singularly like the forcing of a window. The Hopper knew just how much pressure is necessary to the successful snapping back of a window catch, and Wilton had done the trick neatly and with a minimum amount of noise. The window thus assaulted was not, he now determined, the French window suggested by Muriel, but one opening on a terrace which ran along the front of the house. The Hopper heard the sash moving slowly in the frame. He reached the steps, deposited the jar in a pile of snow, and was soon peering into a room where Wilton's presence was advertised by the fitful flashing of his lamp in a far corner.

"He's beat me to ut!" muttered The Hopper, realizing that Muriel's father was indeed on burglary bent, his obvious purpose being to purloin, extract, and remove from its secret hiding-place the coveted plum-blossom vase. Muriel, in her longing for a Christmas of peace and happiness, had not reckoned with her father's passionate desire to possess the porcelain treasure—a desire which could hardly fail to cause scandal, if it did not land him behind prison bars.

This had not been in the programme, and The Hopper weighed judicially his further duty in the matter. Often as he had been the chief actor in daring robberies, he had never before enjoyed the high privilege of watching a rival's labors with complete detachment. Wilton must have known of the concealed cupboard whose panel fraudulently represented the works of Thomas Carlyle, the intent spectator reflected, just as Muriel had known, for though he used his lamp sparingly Wilton had found his way to it without difficulty.

The Hopper had no intention of permitting this monstrous larceny to be committed in contravention of his own rights in the premises, and he was considering the best method of wresting the vase from the hands of the insolent Wilton when events began to multiply with startling rapidity.

The panel swung open and the thief's lamp flashed upon shelves of pottery.

At that moment a shout rose from somewhere in the house, and the library lights were thrown on, revealing Wilton before the shelves and their precious contents. A short, stout gentleman with a gleaming bald pate, clad in pajamas, dashed across the room, and with a yell of rage flung himself upon the intruder with a violence that bore them both to the floor.

"Roger! Roger!" bawled the smaller man, as he struggled with his adversary, who wriggled from under and rolled over upon Talbot, whose arms were clasped tightly about his neck. This embrace seemed likely to continue for some time, so tenaciously had the little man gripped his neighbor. The fat legs of the infuriated householder pawed the air as he hugged Wilton, who was now trying to free his head and gain a position of greater dignity. Occasionally, as opportunity offered, the little man yelled vociferously, and from remote recesses of the house came answering cries demanding information as to the nature and whereabouts of the disturbance.

The contestants addressed themselves vigorously to a spirited rough-and-tumble fight. Talbot, who was the more easily observed by reason of his shining pate and the pink stripes of his pajamas, appeared to be revolving about the person of his neighbor. Wilton, though taller, lacked the rotund Talbot's liveliness of attack.

An authoritative voice, which The Hopper attributed to Shaver's father, anxiously demanding what was the matter, terminated The Hopper's enjoyment of the struggle. Enough was the matter to satisfy The Hopper that a prolonged stay in the neighborhood might be highly detrimental to his future liberty. The combatants had rolled a considerable distance away from the shelves and were near a door leading into a room beyond. A young man in a bath-wrapper dashed upon the scene, and in his precipitate arrival upon the battle-field fell sprawling across the prone figures. The Hopper, suddenly inspired to deeds of prowess, crawled through the window, sprang past the three men, seized the blue-and-white vase which Wilton had separated from the rest of Talbot's treasures, and then with one hop gained the window. As he turned for a last look, a pistol cracked and he landed upon the terrace amid a shower of glass from a shattered pane.

A woman of unmistakable Celtic origin screamed murder from a third-story window. The thought of murder was disagreeable to The Hopper. Shaver's father had missed him by only the matter of a foot or two, and as he had no intention of offering himself again as a target he stood not upon the order of his going.

He effected a running pick-up of the Lang-Yao, and with this art treasure under one arm and the plum-blossom vase under the other, he sprinted for the highway, stumbling over shrubbery, bumping into a stone bench that all but caused disaster, and finally reached the road on which he continued his flight toward New Haven, followed by cries in many keys and a fusillade of pistol shots.

Arriving presently at a hamlet, where he paused for breath in the rear of a country store, he found a basket and a quantity of paper in which he carefully packed his loot. Over the top he spread some faded lettuce leaves and discarded carnations which communicated something of a blithe holiday air to his encumbrance. Elsewhere he found a bicycle under a shed, and while cycling over a snowy road in the dark, hampered by a basket containing pottery representative of the highest genius of the Orient, was not without its difficulties and dangers, The Hopper made rapid progress.

Halfway through New Haven he approached two policemen and slowed down to allay suspicion.

"Merry Chris'mas!" he called as he passed them and increased his weight upon the pedals.

The officers of the law, cheered as by a greeting from Santa Claus himself, responded with an equally hearty Merry Christmas.

VIII

At three o'clock The Hopper reached Happy Hill Farm, knocked as before at the kitchen door, and was admitted by Humpy.

"Wot ye got now?" snarled the reformed yeggman.

"He's gone and done ut ag'in!" wailed Mary, as she spied the basket.

"I sure done ut, all right," admitted The Hopper good-naturedly, as he set the basket on the table where a few hours earlier he had deposited Shaver. "How's the kid?"

Grudging assurances that Shaver was asleep and hostile glances directed at the mysterious basket did not disturb his equanimity.

Humpy was thwarted in an attempt to pry into the contents of the basket by a tart reprimand from The Hopper, who with maddening deliberation drew forth the two glazes, found that they had come through the night's vicissitudes unscathed, and held them at arm's length, turning them about in leisurely fashion as though lost in admiration of their loveliness. Then he lighted his pipe, seated himself in Mary's rocker, and told his story.

It was no easy matter to communicate to his irritable and contumelious auditors the sense of Muriel's charm, or the reasonableness of her request that he commit burglary merely to assist her in settling a family row. Mary could not understand it; Humpy paced the room nervously, shaking his head and muttering. It was their judgment, stated with much frankness, that if he had been a fool in the first place to steal the child, his character was now blackened beyond any hope by his later crimes. Mary wept copiously; Humpy most annoyingly kept counting upon his fingers as he reckoned the "time" that was in store for all of them.

"I guess I got into ut an' I guess I'll git out," remarked The Hopper serenely. He was disposed to treat them with high condescension, as incapable of appreciating the lofty philosophy of life by which he was sustained. Meanwhile, he gloated over the loot of the night.

"Them things is wurt' mints; they's more valible than di'mon's, them things is! Only eddicated folks knows about 'em. They's fer emp'rors and kings t' set up in their palaces, an' men goes nutty jes' hankerin' fer 'em. The pigtails made 'em thousand o' years back, an' th' secret died with 'em. They ain't never goin' to be no more jugs like them settin' right there. An' them two ole sports give up their business jes' t' chase things like them. They's some folks goes loony about chickens, an' hosses, an' fancy dogs, but this here kind o' collectin' 's only fer millionaires. They's more difficult t' pick than a lucky race-hoss. They's barrels o' that stuff in them houses, that looked jes' as good as them there, but nowheres as valible."

An informal lecture on Chinese ceramics before daylight on Christmas morning was not to the liking of the anxious and nerve-torn Mary and Humpy. They brought The Hopper down from his lofty heights to practical questions touching his plans, for the disposal of Shaver in the first instance, and the ceramics in the second. The Hopper was singularly unmoved by their forebodings.

"I guess th' lady got me to do ut!" he retorted finally. "Ef I do time fer ut I reckon's how she's in fer ut, too! An' I seen her pap breakin' into a house an' I guess I'd be a state's witness fer that! I reckon they ain't goin' t' put nothin' over on Hop! I guess they won't peep much about kidnapin' with th' kid safe an' us pickin' 'im up out o' th' road an' shelterin' 'im. Them folks is goin' to be awful nice to Hop fer all he done fer 'em." And then, finding that they were impressed by his defense, thus elaborated, he magnanimously referred to the bill-book which had started him on his downward course.

"That were a mistake; I grant ye ut were a mistake o' jedgment. I'm goin' to keep to th' white card. But ut's kind o' funny about that poke— queerest thing that ever happened."

He drew out the book and eyed the name on the flap. Humpy tried to grab it, but The Hopper, frustrating the attempt, read his colleague a sharp lesson in good manners. He restored it to his pocket and glanced at the clock.

"We gotta do somethin' about Shaver's stockin's. Ut ain't fair fer a kid to wake up an' think Santy missed 'im. Ye got some candy, Mary; we kin put candy into 'em; that's reg'ler."

Humpy brought in Shaver's stockings and they were stuffed with the candy and popcorn Mary had provided to adorn their Christmas feast. Humpy inventoried his belongings, but could think of nothing but a revolver that seemed a suitable gift for Shaver. This Mary scornfully rejected as improper for one so young. Whereupon Humpy produced a Mexican silver dollar, a treasured pocket-piece preserved through many tribulations, and dropped it reverently into one of the stockings. Two brass buttons of unknown history, a mouth-organ Mary had bought for a neighbor boy who assisted at times in the poultry yard, and a silver spectacle case of uncertain antecedents were added.

"We ought t' 'a' colored eggs fer 'im!" said The Hopper with sudden inspiration, after the stockings had been restored to Shaver's bed. "Some yaller an' pink eggs would 'a' been the right ticket."

Mary scoffed at the idea. Eggs wasn't proper fer Christmas; eggs was fer Easter. Humpy added the weight of his personal experience of Christian holidays to this statement. While a trusty in the Missouri penitentiary with the chicken yard in his keeping, he remembered distinctly that eggs were in demand for purposes of decoration by the warden's children sometime in the spring; mebbe it was Easter, mebbe it was Decoration Day; Humpy was not sure of anything except that it wasn't Christmas.

The Hopper was meek under correction. It having been settled that colored eggs would not be appropriate for Christmas he yielded to their demand that he show some enthusiasm for disposing of his ill-gotten treasures before the police arrived to take the matter out of his hands.

"I guess that Muriel'll be glad to see me," he remarked. "I guess me and her understands each other. They's things wot is an' things wot ain't; an' I guess Hop ain't goin' to spend no Chris'mas in jail. It's the white card an' poultry an' eggs fer us; an' we're goin' t' put in a couple more incubators right away. I'm thinkin' some o' rentin' that acre across th' brook back yonder an' raisin' turkeys. They's mints in turks, ef ye kin keep 'em from gettin' their feet wet an' dyin' o' pneumonia, which wipes out thousands o' them birds. I reckon ye might make some coffee, Mary."

The Christmas dawn found them at the table, where they were renewing a pledge to play "the white card" when a cry from Shaver brought them to their feet.

Shaver was highly pleased with his Christmas stockings, but his pleasure was nothing to that of The Hopper, Mary, and Humpy, as they stood about the bed and watched him. Mary and Humpy were so relieved by The Hopper's promises to lead a better life that they were now disposed to treat their guest with the most distinguished consideration. Humpy, absenting himself to perform his morning tasks in the poultry-houses, returned bringing a basket containing six newly hatched chicks. These cheeped and ran over Shaver's fat legs and performed exactly as though they knew they were a part of his Christmas entertainment. Humpy, proud of having thought of the chicks, demanded the privilege of serving Shaver's breakfast. Shaver ate his porridge without a murmur, so happy was he over his new playthings.

Mary bathed and dressed him with care. As the candy had stuck to the stockings in spots, it was decided after a family conference that Shaver would have to wear them wrong side out as there was no time to be wasted in washing them. By eight o'clock The Hopper announced that it was time for Shaver to go home. Shaver expressed alarm at the thought of leaving his chicks; whereupon Humpy conferred two of them upon him in the best imitation of baby talk that he could muster.

"Me's tate um to me's gwanpas," said Shaver; "chickee for me's two gwanpas,"—a remark which caused The Hopper to shake for a moment with mirth as he recalled his last view of Shaver's "gwanpas" in a death grip upon the floor of "Gwanpa" Talbot's house.

IX

When The Hopper rolled away from Happy Hill Farm in the stolen machine, accompanied by one stolen child and forty thousand dollars' worth of stolen pottery, Mary wept, whether because of the parting with Shaver, or because she feared that The Hopper would never return, was not clear.

Humpy, too, showed signs of tears, but concealed his weakness by performing a grotesque dance, dancing grotesquely by the side of the car, much to Shaver's joy—a joy enhanced just as the car reached the gate, where, as a farewell attention, Humpy fell down and rolled over and over in the snow.

The Hopper's wits were alert as he bore Shaver homeward. By this time it was likely that the confiding young Talbots had conferred over the telephone and knew that their offspring had disappeared. Doubtless the New Haven police had been notified, and he chose his route with discretion to avoid unpleasant encounters. Shaver, his spirits keyed to holiday pitch, babbled ceaselessly, and The Hopper, highly elated, babbled back at him.

They arrived presently at the rear of the young Talbots' premises, and The Hopper, with Shaver trotting at his side, advanced cautiously upon the house bearing the two baskets, one containing Shaver's chicks, the other the precious porcelains. In his survey of the landscape he noted with trepidation the presence of two big limousines in the highway in front of the cottage and decided that if possible he must see Muriel alone and make his report to her.

The moment he entered the kitchen he heard the clash of voices in angry dispute in the living-room. Even Shaver was startled by the violence of the conversation in progress within, and clutched tightly a fold of The Hopper's trousers.

"I tell you it's John Wilton who has stolen Billie!" a man cried tempestuously. "Anybody who would enter a neighbor's house in the dead of night and try to rob him—rob him, yes, and *murder* him in the most brutal fashion—would not scruple to steal his own grandchild!"

"Me's gwanpa," whispered Shaver, gripping The Hopper's hand, "an' 'im's mad."

That Mr. Talbot was very angry indeed was established beyond cavil. However, Mr. Wilton was apparently quite capable of taking care of himself in the dispute.

"You talk about my stealing when you robbed me of my Lang-Yao— bribed my servants to plunder my safe! I want you to understand once for all, Roger Talbot, that if that jar isn't returned within one hour,—within one hour, sir,—I shall turn you over to the police!"

"Liar!" bellowed Talbot, who possessed a voice of great resonance. "You can't mitigate your foul crime by charging me with another! I never saw your jar; I never wanted it! I wouldn't have the thing on my place!"

Muriel's voice, full of tears, was lifted in expostulation.

"How can you talk of your silly vases when Billie's lost! Billie's been stolen—and you two men can think of nothing but pot-ter-ree!"

Shaver lifted a startled face to The Hopper.

"Mamma's cwyin'; gwanpa's hurted mamma!"

The strategic moment had arrived when Shaver must be thrust forward as an interruption to the exchange of disagreeable epithets by his grandfathers.

"You trot right in there t' yer ma, Shaver. Ole Hop ain't goin' t' let 'em hurt ye!"

He led the child through the dining room to the living-room door and pushed him gently on the scene of strife. Talbot, senior, was pacing the floor with angry strides, declaiming upon his wrongs,—indeed, his theme might have been the misery of the whole human race from the vigor of his lamentations. His son was keeping step with him, vainly attempting to persuade him to sit down. Wilton, with a patch over his right eye, was trying to disengage himself from his daughter's arms with the obvious intention of doing violence to his neighbor.

"I'm sure papa never meant to hurt you; it was all a dreadful mistake," she moaned.

"He had an accomplice," Talbot thundered, "and while he was trying to kill me there in my own house the plum-blossom vase was carried off; and if Roger hadn't pushed him out of the window after his hireling—I'd—I'd—"

A shriek from Muriel happily prevented the completion of a sentence that gave every promise of intensifying the prevailing hard feeling.

"Look!" Muriel cried. "It's Billie come back! Oh, Billie!"

She sprang toward the door and clasped the frightened child to her heart. The three men gathered round them, staring dully. The Hopper from behind the door waited for Muriel's joy over Billie's return to communicate itself to his father and the two grandfathers.

"Me's dot two chick-ees for Kwismus," announced Billie, wriggling in his mother's arms.

Muriel, having satisfied herself that Billie was intact,—that he even bore the marks of maternal care,—was in the act of transferring him to his bewildered father, when, turning a tear-stained face toward the door, she saw The Hopper awkwardly twisting the derby which he had donned as proper for a morning call of ceremony. She walked toward him with quick, eager step.

"You—you came back!" she faltered, stifling a sob.

"Yes'm," responded The Hopper, rubbing his hand across his nose. His appearance roused Billie's father to a sense of his parental responsibility.

"You brought the boy back! You are the kidnaper!"

"Roger," cried Muriel protestingly, "don't speak like that! I'm sure this gentleman can explain how he came to bring Billie."

The quickness with which she regained her composure, the ease with which she adjusted herself to the unforeseen situation, pleased The Hopper greatly. He had not misjudged Muriel; she was an admirable ally, an ideal confederate. She gave him a quick little nod, as much as to say, "Go on, sir; we understand each other perfectly,"—though, of course, she did not understand, nor was she enlightened until some time later, as to just how The Hopper became possessed of Billie.

Billie's father declared his purpose to invoke the law upon his son's kidnapers no matter where they might be found.

"I reckon as mebbe ut wuz a kidnapin' an' I reckon as mebbe ut wuzn't," The Hopper began unhurriedly. "I live over Shell Road way; poultry and eggs is my line; Happy Hill Farm. Stevens's the name— Charles S. Stevens. An' I found Shaver—'scuse me, but ut seemed sort o' nat'ral name fer 'im?—I found 'im a settin' up in th' machine over there by my place, chipper's ye please. I takes 'im into my house an' Mary'—that's th' missus—she gives 'im supper and puts 'im t' sleep. An' we thinks mebbe somebody'd come along askin' fer 'im. An' then this mornin' I calls th' New Haven police, an' they tole me about you folks, an' me and Shaver comes right over."

This was entirely plausible and his hearers, The Hopper noted with relief, accepted it at face value.

"How dear of you!" cried Muriel. "Won't you have this chair, Mr. Stevens!"

"Most remarkable!" exclaimed Wilton. "Some scoundrelly tramp picked up the car and finding there was a baby inside left it at the road-side like the brute he was!"

Billie had addressed himself promptly to the Christmas tree, to his very own Christmas tree that was laden with gifts that had been assembled by the family for his delectation. Efforts of Grandfather Wilton to extract from the child some account of the man who had run away with him were unavailing. Billie was busy, very busy, indeed. After much patient effort he stopped sorting the animals in a bright new Noah's Ark to point his finger at The Hopper and remark:—

"'Ims nice mans; 'ims let Bil-lee play wif 'ims watch!"

As Billie had broken the watch his acknowledgment of The Hopper's courtesy in letting him play with it brought a grin to The Hopper's face.

Now that Billie had been returned and his absence satisfactorily accounted for, the two connoisseurs showed signs of renewing their quarrel. Responsive to a demand from Billie, The Hopper got down on the floor to assist in the proper mating of Noah's animals. Billie's father was scrutinizing him fixedly and The Hopper wondered whether Muriel's handsome young husband had recognized him as the person who had vanished through the window of the Talbot home bearing the plum-blossom vase. The thought was disquieting; but feigning deep interest in the Ark he listened attentively to a violent tirade upon which the senior Talbot was launched.

"My God!" he cried bitterly, planting himself before Wilton in a belligerent attitude, "every infernal thing that can happen to a man happened to me yesterday. It wasn't enough that you robbed me and tried to murder me—yes, you did, sir!—but when I was in the city I was robbed in the subway by a pickpocket. A thief took my bill-book containing invaluable data I had just received from my agent in China giving me a clue to porcelains, sir, such as you never dreamed of! Some more of your work—Don't you contradict me! You don't contradict me! Roger, he doesn't contradict me!"

Wilton, choking with indignation at this new onslaught, was unable to contradict him.

Pained by the situation, The Hopper rose from the floor and coughed timidly.

"Shaver, go fetch yer chickies. Bring yer chickies in an' put 'em on th' boat."

Billie obediently trotted off toward the kitchen and The Hopper turned his back upon the Christmas tree, drew out the pocket-book and faced the company.

"I beg yer pardon, gents, but mebbe this is th' book yer fightin' about. Kind o' funny like! I picked ut up on th' local yistiddy afternoon. I wuz goin' t' turn ut int' th' agint, but I clean fergot ut. I guess them papers may be valible. I never touched none of 'em."

Talbot snatched the bill-book and hastily examined the contents. His brow relaxed and he was grumbling something about a reward when Billie reappeared, laboriously dragging two baskets.

"Bil-lee's dot chick-*ees*! Bil-lee's dot pitty dishes. Bil-lee make dishes go 'ippity!"

Before he could make the two jars go 'ippity, The Hopper leaped across the room and seized the basket. He tore off the towel with which he had carefully covered the stolen pottery and disclosed the contents for inspection.

"'scuse me, gents; no crowdin'," he warned as the connoisseurs sprang toward him. He placed the porcelains carefully on the floor under the Christmas tree. "Now ye kin listen t' me, gents. I reckon I'm goin' t' have somethin' t' say about this here crockery. I stole 'em—I stole 'em fer th' lady there, she thinkin' ef ye didn't have 'em no more ye'd stop rowin' about 'em. Ye kin call th' bulls an' turn me over ef ye likes; but I ain't goin' t' have ye fussin' an' causin' th' lady trouble no more. I ain't goin' to stand fer ut!"

"Robber!" shouted Talbot. "You entered my house at the instance of this man; it was you—"

"I never saw the gent before," declared The Hopper hotly. "I ain't never had no thin' to do with neither o' ye."

"He's telling the truth!" protested Muriel, laughing hysterically. "I did it—I got him to take them!"

The two collectors were not interested in explanations; they were hungrily eyeing their property. Wilton attempted to pass The Hopper and reach the Christmas tree under whose protecting boughs the two vases were looking their loveliest.

"Stand back," commanded The Hopper, "an' stop callin' names! I guess ef I'm yanked fer this I ain't th' only one that's goin' t' do time fer house breakin'.'"

This statement, made with considerable vigor, had a sobering effect upon Wilton, but Talbot began dancing round the tree looking for a chance to pounce upon the porcelains.

"Ef ye don't set down—the whole caboodle o' ye—I'll smash 'em—I'll smash 'em both! I'll bust 'em—sure as shootin'!" shouted The Hopper.

They cowered before him; Muriel wept softly; Billie played with his chickies, disdainful of the world's woe. The Hopper, holding the two angry men at bay, was enjoying his command of the situation.

"You gents ain't got no business to be fussin' an' causin' yer childern trouble. An' ye ain't goin' to have these pretty jugs to fuss about no more. I'm goin' t' give 'em away; I'm goin' to make a Chris'mas present of 'em to Shaver. They're goin' to be little Shaver's right here, all orderly an' peace'ble, or I'll tromp on 'em! Looky here, Shaver, wot Santy Claus brought ye!"

"Nice dood Sant' Claus!" cried Billie, diving under the davenport in quest of the wandering chicks.

Silence held the grown-ups. The Hopper stood patiently by the Christmas tree, awaiting the result of his diplomacy.

Then suddenly Wilton laughed—a loud laugh expressive of relief. He turned to Talbot and put out his hand.

"It looks as though Muriel and her friend here had cornered us! The idea of pooling our trophies and giving them as a Christmas present to Billie appeals to me strongly. And, besides we've got to prepare somebody to love these things after we're gone. We can work together and train Billie to be the greatest collector in America!"

"Please, father," urged Roger as Talbot frowned and shook his head impatiently.

Billie, struck with the happy thought of hanging one of his chickies on the Christmas tree, caused them all to laugh at this moment. It was difficult to refuse to be generous on Christmas morning in the presence of the happy child!

"Well," said Talbot, a reluctant smile crossing his face, "I guess it's all in the family anyway."

The Hopper, feeling that his work as the Reversible Santa Claus was finished, was rapidly retreating through the dining-room when Muriel and Roger ran after him.

"We're going to take you home," cried Muriel, beaming.

"Yer car's at the back gate, all right-side-up," said The Hopper, "but I kin go on the trolley."

"Indeed you won't! Roger will take you home. Oh, don't be alarmed! My husband knows everything about our conspiracy. And we want you to come back this afternoon. You know I owe you an apology for think- ing—for thinking you were—you were—a—"

"They's things wot is an' things wot ain't, miss. Circumstantial evi- dence sends lots o' men to th' chair. Ut's a heap more happy like," The Hopper continued in his best philosophical vein, "t' play th' white card, helpin' widders an' orfants an' settlin' fusses. When ye ast me t' steal them jugs I hadn't th' heart t' refuse ye, miss. I wuz scared to tell ye I had yer baby an' ye seemed so sort o' trustin' like. An' ut bein' Chris'mus an' all."

When he steadfastly refused to promise to return, Muriel announced that they would visit The Hopper late in the afternoon and bring Billie along to express their thanks more formally.

"I'll be glad to see ye," replied The Hopper, though a little doubt- fully and shame-facedly. "But ye mustn't git me into no more house- breakin' scrapes," he added with a grin. "It's mighty dangerous, miss, fer amachures, like me an' yer pa!"

X

Mary was not wholly pleased at the prospect of visitors, but she fell to work with Humpy to put the house in order. At five o'clock not one, but three automobiles drove into the yard, filling Humpy with alarm lest at last The Hopper's sins had overtaken him, and they were all about to be hauled away to spend the rest of their lives in prison. It was not the police, but the young Talbots, with Billie and his grandfathers, on their way to a family celebration at the house of an aunt of Muriel's.

The grandfathers were restored to perfect amity, and were deeply cu- rious now about The Hopper, whom the peace-loving Muriel had cajoled into robbing their houses.

"And you're only an honest chicken farmer, after all!" exclaimed Talbot, senior, when they were all sitting in a semicircle about the fire- place in Mary's parlor. "I hoped you were really a burglar; I always wanted to know a burglar."

Humpy had chopped down a small fir that had adorned the front yard and had set it up as a Christmas tree—an attention that was not lost upon Billie. The Hopper had brought some mechanical toys from town, and Humpy essayed the agreeable task of teaching the youngster how to operate them. Mary produced coffee and pound cake for the guests; The Hopper assumed the rôle of lord of the manor with a benevolent air that was intended as much to impress Mary and Humpy as the guests.

"Of course," said Mr. Wilton, whose appearance was the least bit comical by reason of his bandaged head,—"of course it was very foolish for a man of your sterling character to allow a young woman like my daughter to bully you into robbing houses for her. Why, when Roger fired at you as you were jumping out of the window, he didn't miss you more than a foot! It would have been ghastly for all of us if he had killed you!"

"Well, o' course it all begun from my goin' into th' little house lookin' fer Shaver's folks," replied The Hopper.

"But you haven't told us how you came to find our house," said Roger, suggesting a perfectly natural line of inquiries that caused Humpy to become deeply preoccupied with a pump he was operating in a basin of water for Billie's benefit.

"Well, ut jes' looked like a house that Shaver would belong to, cute an' comfortable like," said The Hopper; "I jes' suspicioned it wuz th' place as I wuz passin' along."

"I don't think we'd better begin trying to establish alibis," remarked Muriel, very gently, "for we might get into terrible scrapes. Why, if Mr. Stevens hadn't been so splendid about *everything* and wasn't just the kindest man in the world, he could make it very ugly for me."

"I shudder to think of what he might do to me," said Wilton, glancing guardedly at his neighbor.

"The main thing," said Talbot,—"the main thing is that Mr. Stevens has done for us all what nobody else could ever have done. He's made us see how foolish it is to quarrel about mere baubles. He's settled all our troubles for us, and for my part I'll say his solution is entirely satisfactory."

"Quite right," ejaculated Wilton. "If I ever have any delicate business negotiations that are beyond my powers I'm going to engage Mr. Stevens to handle them."

"My business's hens an' eggs," said The Hopper modestly; "an' we're doin' purty well."

When they rose to go (a move that evoked strident protests from Billie, who was enjoying himself hugely with Humpy) they were all in the jolliest humor.

"We must be neighborly," said Muriel, shaking hands with Mary, who was at the point of tears so great was her emotion at the success of The Hopper's party. "And we're going to buy all our chickens and eggs from you. We never have any luck raising our own."

Whereupon The Hopper imperturbably pressed upon each of the visitors a neat card stating his name (his latest and let us hope his last!) with the proper rural route designation of Happy Hill Farm.

The Hopper carried Billie out to his Grandfather Wilton's car, while Humpy walked beside him bearing the gifts from the Happy Hill Farm Christmas tree. From the door Mary watched them depart amid a chorus of merry Christmases, out of which Billie's little pipe rang cheerily.

When The Hopper and Humpy returned to the house, they abandoned the parlor for the greater coziness of the kitchen and there took account of the events of the momentous twenty-four hours.

"Them's what I call nice folks," said Humpy. "They jes' put us on an' wore us like we wuz a pair o' ole slippers."

"They wuzn't uppish—not to speak of," Mary agreed. "I guess that girl's got more gumption than any of 'em. She's got 'em straightened up now and I guess she'll take care they don't cut up no more monkey-shines about that Chinese stuff. Her husban' seemed sort o' gentle like."

"Artists is that way," volunteered The Hopper, as though from deep experience of art and life. "I jes' been thinkin' that knowin' folks like that an' findin' 'em humin, makin' mistakes like th' rest of us, kind o' makes ut seem easier fer us all t' play th' game straight. Ut's goin' to be th' white card fer me—jes' chickens an' eggs, an' here's hopin' the bulls don't ever find out we're settled here."

Humpy, having gone into the parlor to tend the fire, returned with two envelopes he had found on the mantel. There was a check for a thousand dollars in each, one from Wilton, the other from Talbot, with "Merry Christmas" written across the visiting-cards of those gentlemen. The Hopper permitted Mary and Humpy to examine them and then laid them on the kitchen table, while he deliberated. His meditations were so prolonged that they grew nervous.

"I reckon they could spare ut, after all ye done fer 'em, Hop," remarked Humpy.

"They's millionaires, an' money ain't nothin' to 'em," said The Hopper.

"We can buy a motor-truck," suggested Mary, "to haul our stuff to town; an' mebbe we can build a new shed to keep ut in."

The Hopper set the catsup bottle on the checks and rubbed his cheek, squinting at the ceiling in the manner of one who means to be careful of his speech.

"They's things wot is an' things wot ain't," he began. "We ain't none o' us ever got nowheres bein' crooked. I been figurin' that I still got about twenty thousan' o' that bunch o' green I pulled out o' that express car, planted in places where 'taint doin' nobody no good. I guess ef I do ut careful I kin send ut back to the company, a little at a time, an' they'd never know where ut come from."

Mary wept; Humpy stared, his mouth open, his one eye rolling queerly.

"I guess we kin put a little chunk away every year," The Hopper went on. "We'd be comfortabler doin' ut. We could square up ef we lived long enough, which we don't need t' worry about, that bein' the Lord's business. You an' me's cracked a good many safes, Hump, but we never made no money at ut, takin' out th' time we done."

"He's got religion; that's wot he's got!" moaned Humpy, as though this marked the ultimate tragedy of The Hopper's life.

"Mebbe ut's religion an' mebbe ut's jes' sense," pursued The Hopper, unshaken by Humpy's charge. "They wuz a chaplin in th' Minnesoty pen as used t' say ef we're all square with our own selves ut's goin' to be all right with God. I guess I got a good deal o' squarin' t' do, but I'm goin' t' begin ut. An' all these things happenin' along o' Chris'mus, an' little Shaver an' his ma bein' so friendly like, an' her gittin' me t' help straighten out them ole gents, an' doin' all I done an' not gettin' pinched seems more 'n jes' luck; it's providential's wot ut is!"

This, uttered in a challenging tone, evoked a sob from Humpy, who announced that he "felt like" he was going to die.

"It's th' Chris'mus time, I reckon," said Mary, watching The Hopper deposit the two checks in the clock. "It's the only decent Chris'mus I ever knowed!"

BELIEVING IN SANTA

Ron Goulart

As it turned out, he didn't get a chance to murder anybody. He did make an impressive comeback, revitalizing his faltering career and saying goodbye to most of his financial worries. But in spite of all that, there are times when Oscar Sayler feels sad about not having been able to knock off his former wife.

Twenty-five years ago Oscar had been loved by millions of children. Well, actually, they adored his dummy, Screwy Santa, but they tolerated Oscar. For several seasons his early morning kid show was the most popular in the country, outpulling Captain Kangaroo and all the other competition. Multitudes of kids, and their parents, doted on Oscar's comic version of Santa Claus and tried to live by the show's perennial closing line—"Gang, try to act like it was Christmas every day!"

For the past decade or more, though, Oscar hadn't been doing all that well. In early December of last year, when he got the fateful phone call from the New York talent agency, he was scraping by on the $25,000 a year he earned from the one commercial voice job he'd been able to come up with lately. Oscar lived alone in a one-bedroom condo in a never-finished complex in New Beckford, Connecticut. He was fifty-five—well, fifty-seven actually—and he didn't look all that awful.

Since he'd given up drinking, his face was no longer especially puffy and it had lost that lobsterish tinge. His hair, which was nearly all his own, still had a nice luster to it. There was, really, no reason why he couldn't appear on television again.

When the agent called him at a few minutes after four P.M. on a bleak, chill Monday afternoon, Oscar was flat on his back in his small tan living room. He'd vowed to complete two dozen situps every day.

He crawled over to the phone on the coffee table. "Hello?"

"Is your son there?"

Oscar pulled himself up onto the sofa arm, resting the phone on his knees. "Don't have a son. My daughter, however, is the noted television actress Tish Sale, who stars in the *Intensive Care* soap opera, and hasn't set foot across dear old Dad's threshold for three, possibly four—"

"Spare me," requested the youthful, nasal voice. "You must be Oscar Sayler then. You sounded so old that I mistook you for your father."

"Nope, my dad sounded like this—'How about a little nip after dinner, my boy?' Must more throaty and with a quaver. Who the hell are you, by the way?"

"Vince Mxyzptlk. I'm with Mimi Warnicker & Associates, the crackerjack talent agency."

"Oops." Oscar sat on a cushion and straightened up. "That's a powerful outfit."

"You bet your ass it is," agreed the young agent. "You're not represented at the moment, are you?"

"No, because I find I can get all the acting jobs I want without—"

"C'mon, Oscar, old buddy, you ain't exactly rolling in work right now," cut in Vince disdainfully. "In fact, your only gig is doing the voice of the infected toe in those godawful Dr. Frankel's Foot Balm radio spots." He made a scornful noise.

"I do a very convincing itching toe, Vince. Fact is, there's talk of—"

"Listen, I can get you tons of work. Talk shows, commercials, lectures, TV parts, eventually some plum movie work. But first you—"

"How exactly are—"

"But first you have got to win your way back into the hearts and minds of the public."

"Just how do I accomplish that, Vince?"

"You just have to sit there with that lamebrained dummy on your knee."

"Screwy Santa? Hell, nobody's been interested in him for years."

"Let me do the talking for a bit, okay? Here's why's under way," continued the agent. *Have a Good Day, USA!*, which has just become the top morning talk and news show, is planning a six-minute nostalgia segment for this Friday. The theme is 'Whatever happened to our favorite kids' shows?' Something they calculate'll have a tremendous appeal for the Boomers and Busters who make up their pea-brained audience. So far they've signed that old differ who used to be Captain Buckeroo and—"

"Kangaroo."

"Oscar, are you more interested in heckling me than in making an impressive comeback? Would you prefer to go on living in squalor in that rural crackerbox, to voice tripe for Dr. Frankel throughout the few remaining years of your shabby life?"

"Okay, but his name is Captain Kangaroo, not—"

"Attend to me, Oscar. I assured Liz, who's putting this segment together, that I'd dig you up, wipe off the cobwebs, and have you there bright and early Friday. Can you drag yourself into Manhattan and meet me at the Consolidated Broadcasting headquarters building on Fifty-third no later than six A.M.?"

"Sure, that's no problem."

"Most importantly, can you bring that dimwitted dummy?"

Without more than a fraction of a second of hesitation Oscar answered, "Of course, yeah, absolutely." It didn't seem the right time to tell Mxyzptlk that his former wife, who currently loathed him and had ousted him eleven long years ago from the mansion they once shared, had retained custody of the only existing Screwy Santa dummy in the world. "We'll both see you on Friday, Vince."

* * * *

It commenced snowing at dusk, a paltry, low-budget snow that didn't look as though it was up to blanketing the condo-complex grounds and masking its raw ugliness.

Glancing at his wristwatch once more, Oscar punched out his daughter's New York City number.

After four rings there came a twanging noise. "Merry Christmas," said Tish in her sexiest voice. "I'm not able to come to the phone right now, but if you'll leave your name and number, I'll get back to you real soon."

Oscar had been working all afternoon on the voice was going to use. A mixture of paternal warmth and serious illness. "Patricia, my dear," he began, getting the quaver just about perfect, "this is your dad. Something quite serious has come up and I'd like very much to speak to you, my only child, in the hope that—"

"Holy Jesus," observed his daughter, coming onto the line. "What was that old television show you used to tell me about when I was little? Where they gave the contestants the gong for a rotten perf—"

"*The Amateur Hour.* Now, kid, I need—"

"Consider yourself gonged, Pop."

"Okay, all right, I overdid it a mite," he admitted. "Yet I do have a serious problem."

"My time is sort of limited, Dad. I'm getting ready for a date. You should've phoned me earlier."

"I assumed you were taping *Intensive Care.*"

She sighed. "Didn't you tell me you watched my soap faithfully?"

"I do, kid. It's on my must-see list every day."

"I've been in a coma for two weeks. So I don't have to show up at—"

"Sorry to hear that. Anything serious?"

"Near-fatal car crash. We killed that asshole, Walt Truett, thank God."

"But you'll survive?"

"Sure, with only a touch of amnesia."

Oscar asked, "When are you due to come out of your stupor?"

"Next Thursday."

"I'll start watching, I swear," he promised his daughter. "Now, as to the purpose of this call."

"It's Mom, isn't it?"

"Well, not exactly, kid." He filled her in about the offer from the talent agency and the upcoming appearance on *Have a Good Day, USA!* "This will revive my career."

"You think so? A couple of early morning minutes with a pack of over-the-hill doofers?"

"It's a shot. The only snag is—well, kid, they insist that I bring Screwy along."

"Obviously. You guys are a team."

"And your dear mother has custody of him."

Tish said, "She's not going to loan him to you."

"She might, if you were to—"

"Nope, she won't. A few months ago, when I noticed him up on a shelf in the mud room, I suggested that—"

"She keeps the most beloved dummy in America in the mud room?"

"In a shoe box," she answered. "And, Dad, Screwy Santa hasn't been beloved for a couple of decades now."

"I know, neither have I," he said ruefully. "But, damn it, he helped pay for that mansion."

"Her romantic novels are paying for things now. Did you notice that *Kiss Me, My Pirate* was number two on the *Times*—"

"I extract the books section from the Sunday paper with surgical gloves nad toss it immediately into the trash unopened. To make certain I never see so much as a mention of that slop she cranks out or, worse, a publicity photo of her mottled countenance."

"Let's get back to the point. I suggested to her back then that she return Screwy Santa to you."

"And?"

"You don't want to hear what she said," his daughter assured him. "It had, among other things, to do with Hell freezing over. But can't you dig up another dummy by Friday?"

"Impossible, that's the only one extant. We lost the backup copy during that ill-fated nostalgia tour through the Midwest years ago."

"Couldn't you carve another, since you built the others?"

"Kid, I may've fudged the truth a bit when I used to recount Screwy's history to you," he said. "In reality, the dummies were built by a prop man at the old WWAG-TV studios. And he, alas, is long in his grave."

"This is very disillusioning," Tish complained. "One of the few things I still admired about you, Dad, was your woodcarving ability."

"Listen, couldn't you call Mitzi and tell her that I'm expiring, that I want to be reunited with my dummy for one last time before I go on to glory?"

"She'd burst out laughing if I told her you were about to kick off, Dad. And probably dance a little jig."

"Okay, suppose we make a business deal with her? Offer the old shrew, say, fifteen percent of the take."

"What take? *Have a Good Day, USA!* pays scale. I know, I did one last year to plug my abortion on *Intensive Care.*"

"You looked terrific on that broadcast."

"You didn't even see it."

"Didn't I?"

"No, and you admitted as much at the time."

"Well, back to my immediate problem."

"Why don't you use one of the old Screwy Santa dolls? They look a lot like the dummy."

"Except that they don't have movable mouths."

"It'd be better than nothing. I can loan you mine," she offered. "It's stuffed away in a closet."

"No, kid, I really have to have the real dummy."

"Afraid there's nothing I can do. I mean, if I so much as mention that you need Screwy Santa, Mom's liable to take an axe to him."

"Well, thanks anyway for listening to an old man's woes and—"

"Here comes the gong again," his daughter said. "Anyhow, I have to go put on some clothes. Bye."

After hanging up, he stayed on the sofa and brooded. After about ten minutes he said aloud, "I'll have to outwit Mitzi."

* * * *

The snow improved the next morning, giving a Christmas-card gloss to the usually dismal view from his small living room window.

At ten A.M. he put the first phase of his latest plan into operation. He phone his former wife's mansion over in Westport.

"Residence of Mitzi Sunsett Sayler," answered a crisp female voice.

"Yes, how are you?" inquired Oscar in a drawling, slightly British accent. "Ogden Brokenshire here."

"Yes?"

"Ogden Brokenshire of the Broadcasting Hall of Fame. Have I the honor of addressing the esteemed novelist Mitzi Sunsett Sayler herself?"

"Of course not, Mr. Brokenshire. I'm Clarissa Dempster, Mrs. Sayler's secretary."

"I see, my dear. Well, perhaps I can explain my mission to you, child, and you can explain the situation to your employer."

"That depends on—"

"We would like to enshrine Screwy Santa."

"Enshrine whom?"

"The ingenious dummy that Mrs. Sayler's one-time husband used in the days when he brought joy and gladness to the hearts of—"

"Oh, that thing," said the secretary. "My parents, wisely, never allowed me to watch that dreadful show when I was a child."

"Nonetheless, dear child, our board has voted, unanimously I might add, to place Screwy Santa on permanent display in the museum."

"Hold on a moment. I'll speak to Mrs. Sayler." The secretary went away.

In less than two minutes Mitzi started talking. "Who is this?"

"Good morning, I'm Ogden Brokenshire. As I was explaining to your able secretary, my dear Mrs. Sayler, I'm an executive with the Broadcasting Hall of—"

"You haven't improved at all, you no-talent cheesehead."

"I beg your pardon, madam?"

"Oscar, love, you never could do a believable Brit."

"I don't happen to be British, dear lady. The fact that I was educated in Boston sometimes gives people that impression."

"Forget it, Oscar," advised his erstwhile wife. "I don't know why you want to get your clammy hands on that wooden dornick, but you'll never have him. And, dear heart, if you ever try to communicate with me again—in whatever wretched voice—I'll sic the law on you." She, rather gently, hung up on him.

"Looks like," decided Oscar, "I'm going to need a new plan."

* * * *

He kept working on plans for nearly an hour, pacing his small living room, muttering, pausing now and then to gaze out at the falling snow.

Then the phone rang.

"Yeah?"

"We have hit a slight snag," announced Vince Mxyzptlk.

"Don't they want me?"

"Sure they want you, old buddy. Hell, they're prowling the lofty corridors at Consolidated crying out for you," said the youthful agent. "In fact, they can't wait until Friday."

"What do you mean—do they want me to do a separate segment on my own?"

"Not exactly. But Liz, *and* her boss, are very anxious to see you tomorrow."

Frowning, Oscar nodded. "An audition, huh?"

"Sort of, yeah," admitted the agent. "It has nothing, really, to do with you. But when one of their scouts unearthed the clunk who used to be Mr. Slimjim on that *Mr. Slimjim & Baby Gumdrop* turkey, he turned out to weigh three hundred pounds now and posses not a single tooth. So, as you can understand, Oscar, they want to see and hear all these wonderful stars of yesteryear in advance."

"Tomorrow?"

"At three P.M. Is that a problem for you?"

"Not exactly, but I—"

"I'm getting a lot of interest in you. Once you do well on Friday, the jobs will start rolling in."

"I understand, it's only—"

"I needn't remind you, Oscar, that a lot of talents in your present position would kill for this opportunity."

"You're absolutely right," he agreed. "See you tomorrow."

* * * *

He had a great new plan worked out by three that afternoon. But he had to wait until after dark to get going on it.

Dressed in dark clothes, Oscar slipped quietly out of his apartment and into the lean-to that passed for a garage. As usual, none of the roads in the sparsely inhabited complex had been plowed. The snow was soft, though, and not too high, and Oscar was able to drive down to the plowed lanes and byways of New Beckford without any serious delays.

He drove over to nearby Westport and parked in the lot behind Borneo's. There were only a few spaces left and he could see that the restaurant-bar was packed with people. The food and drink at Borneo's was just passable, but it sat only a half mile over the hill from Mitzi's mansion.

As he was crossing the lot a fire engine went hooting by, heading downhill.

Borneo himself was behind the bar. "Evening, Oscar."

He managed to elbow his way up to a narrow spot at the ebony bar. "The usual."

Borneo scratched at his stomach through the fabric of his bright tropical shirt. "Refresh my memory."

"Club soda, alas."

"Coming up."

Outside in the snowy night another fire engine went roaring by, followed by what sounded like a couple of police cars.

Oscar hoped all this activity wouldn't foul up his plan. So far everything was going well. People were seeing him, he was establishing an alibi. In another ten or fifteen minutes he'd go back to the john. Then he'd slip out the side door.

Once in the open, he'd make his way down to the mansion. Being careful, of course, that no one noticed him sneaking off.

Mitzi, being a skinflint, and in spite of her great wealth, had never bothered to put in a new alarm system. The original setup was still in place, and he know how to disarm that.

Okay, once he got inside, after making certain that she was alone, he'd...well, he'd use the length of pipe he dug up in the garage this afternoon.

Once Mitzi was dead and done for, he'd gather up enough jewels and valuables to make it look like the usual burglary. Then he'd rescue Screwy Santa from the mud room and get the hell away.

Back here at the parking lot he'd stash the loot in his car, slip unobtrusively back into the place, and tell Borneo he'd had a sudden touch of stomach flu and had to stay back in the bathroom a few minutes.

It wasn't exactly foolproof, but it ought to work. He'd own Screwy again and Mitzi would be gone from his life.

He chuckled at the thought. Yeah, the idea of killing her off had come to him this afternoon and he'd taken to it immediately.

Tish might be a little suspicious about how he came by the dummy. He'd tell her something along the lines that he'd found the heirs of the old defunct prop man at the last minute and, gosh, they had a spare Screwy Santa. He'd always been a gifted liar and conning his daughter wouldn't be all that difficult.

"Don't worry about that now," he told himself.

"How's that?" inquired Borneo, setting a glass of sparkling water down in front of him.

"Nothing, I was just—"

"That must be some fire." Borneo paused to listen as yet another truck went howling by out in the night.

Oscar sipped the club soda, drumming the fingers of his free hand on the dark bar top. He'd make his move in about five minutes.

The phone behind the bar rang and Borneo caught it up. "Borneo's. Huh? Channel eight? Okay." Hanging up, he switched channels on the large television set mounted above the mirror.

And there was Mitzi, glowering out of the screen. Wearing a fuzzy bathrobe and not enough makeup, she was being interviewed by a slim black newswoman and gesturing at the mansion that was blazing behind her up across the wide night lawn.

"Good God," muttered Oscar.

"That's just downhill from us," observed Borneo.

"Yeah, I know."

The entire sprawling house was going up in flames.

"What exactly happened, Mrs. Sayler?" the reporter asked her.

"It was that goddamn cheesehead."

"Which cheesehead would that be?"

"Screwy Santa, that abominable dummy."

"I'm not certain that I quite under—"

"Aw, you're too damn young. Everybody is these days. I always knew that dornick would do me in eventually."

"You mean this was arson?"

"I mean, dear heart, that I decided to cremate that loathsome lump of wood. I took him and his shoebox, carried them into the living room, and tossed him into the fireplace."

Oscar pressed both hands to his chest. "There goes my comeback."

Mitzi continued. "Then...I don't know. His stupid beard seemed to explode...flames came shooting out of the fireplace. They hit the drapes and those caught fire...then the damn furniture started to go." She shook her head angrily. "Now the whole shebang is ablaze." Looking directly into the camera, she added, "If you're out there watching, Oscar . . ." She gave him the finger.

Borneo raised his shaggy eyebrows high. "Hey, is she talking to you, Oscar?"

"I'm not in the mood for conversation just now." Abandoning his club soda, he walked out into the night.

* * * *

His daughter phone a few minutes shy of midnight. "I didn't want you to worry."

"I'm way beyond worry, kid."

"When I caught the report about Mom's mansion on the news, I figured you'd assume that Screwy Santa was gone."

"Certainly I assumed that. There was Mitzi, fatter than every, hollering for all the world to hear that my poor hapless creation was the cause of the whole blinking conflagration."

"It was a ringer, Dad."

"Eh?"

"I dropped by to visit Mom this afternoon and when she went away to yell at Clarissa, I substituted my old Screwy Santa doll for your dummy," explained Tish. "In a way, I may be responsible for that dreadful fire. The doll's a lot more flammable than—"

"No, there was some parent flap at the time, but we proved beyond a doubt that the dolls were perfectly safe if—"

"I have your dummy here in my apartment."

"You've really got Screwy?"

"Yes, he's sitting on my bed right this minute," she assured her father. "It's lucky I went out there when I did and saved him before Mom got going on her plan to destroy the little guy. Why did you go and telephone her and make it crystal clear that you were in desperate need of him? That was dippy, since it inspired her to destroy him."

"I didn't call her as myself. But somehow she penetrated my—"

"That's because, trust me, you do a terrible British voice. When do you need him?"

"Tomorrow."

"I thought you weren't doing the show until Friday."

"Well, and keep this to yourself, kid, there's a possibility they'll devote a separate seg all to me."

"That would be great."

"So can I pick him up tomorrow?"

"Sure, come by around one and I'll take you to lunch."

"Can't make lunch, because I have some people to see while I'm in the Apple. But I'll pop in, give you a paternal hug, and grab Screwy Santa," he said. "Thanks. You're a perfect daughter."

"Perfect for you, I guess. Bye."

Everything worked out well for Oscar. He did, in fact, do a segment of his own, which ran nearly four minutes, on *Have a Good Day, USA!*. And Vince Mxyzptlk was able to get him an impressive batch of other jobs. At the moment there's also the possibility of a new kid show for Oscar and Screwy Santa on cable.

Oscar was able to leave his forlorn condo for a three-bedroom colonial in Brimstone, Connecticut last month.

While he was packing, he came across the length of pipe he'd intended to use on Mitzi. He slapped it across the palm of his hand a few times, and, sighing, tossed it into a carton.

Ron Goulart has been a freelance writer for several decades now. He sold his first short story while a sophomore at UC, Berkeley. He worked for 13 years writing humorous copy for ad agencies in San Francisco and Hollywood. He said goodbye to all that in 1968 and has been a freelance ever since. He has written nearly 200 books. Seventy some science fiction books, about fifty mysteries. It's been estimated that he's sold over 700 stories and articles. He's been nominated twice for the Edgar from MWA, once for the Nebula from SFWA. His short stories have appeared in over sixty five mystery and science fiction anthologies. Not including this one. He has written a dozen nonfiction books, mostly about comic books, comic strips and pulps. Within the next few months, his two novels about the Victorian occult detective, Harry Challenge will be reissued as e-books by Wildside Press. Three of his other SF novels, including *Skyrocket Steele*, are due in audio-book editions. His brand new website will also appear shortly.